NICK ALEXANDER

Better Than Easy

C000157079

BIGfib

Nick Alexander

Nick Alexander was born in Margate, and has lived and worked in the UK, the USA and France. When he isn't writing, he is the editor of the gay literature site www.BIGfib.com.

Better Than Easy, is Nick's fourth novel. The other titles in the series, *Fifty Reasons to Say Goodbye, Sottopassaggio, Good Thing - Bad Thing,* and *Sleight Of Hand* are also available, as are the standalone novels *The Case Of The Missing Boyfriend,* and *13:55 Eastern Standard Time.*

Nick currently lives in the southern French Alps with two mogs, a couple of goldfish and a complete set of Pedro Almodovar films. For more information, to contact the author, or to order extra copies please visit his website on: www.nick-alexander.com

Legal Notice

Better Than Easy - ISBN: 978-2952489973

Cover image © Nejron Photo/Shutterstock.com

Text and cover design by Nick Alexander, Copyright © 2009,2010, 2012

Acknowledgements

Thanks to Richard Labonte and to Rosemary, Allan and Giovanni for their help with the final manuscript. Thanks to Apple computer for making such wonderful reliable work tools, and to BIGfib Books for making this book a reality.

Do not pray for easy lives.
Pray to be stronger men!
Do not pray for tasks equal to your powers.
Pray for power equal to your tasks.

– Phillips Brooks

Combining

Sleep evades me. The wind is hurling itself, invisible battalions crashing against the shutters. I imagine that the subsonic thuds are the lines they show on weather maps, smashing to smithereens, cartoon style, on the walls of the building, hopelessly, pointlessly.

Tom sleeps through it all, dreaming it would seem – his mouth is working constantly, his tongue clicks occasionally against the roof of his mouth.

I can feel the warmth of his body or maybe something more than just warmth – *his aura?* – jumping across the gap where our thighs nearly meet. From the waist up our bodies curve away into separateness.

Another subsonic wave collides with the bedroom window. I can feel the air inside the room move too. There must be a gap somewhere.

I roll onto my side and study Tom's features; he looks beautiful. He's no slouch when awake, but asleep he looks younger – peaceful, neutral somehow.

I know he's still asleep precisely because our bodies *aren't* touching. When awake Tom always positions himself so that there is at least one point of contact – unless we're at war. In winter he hugs me like a koala, hot and comforting against the cold extremities of the bed, while in summer it can be just a heel, or a shin; the simple contact of a finger, a toe, his dick... but whatever the season, there's always a spot where our bodies meet. And then sleep takes him and he rolls away.

I sigh and smile at the contented look on his face and wonder if he is truly happy. He's so hard to read when awake – he gives so little away. And then I roll onto my back and wonder what the day will bring.

I think of a song by Holcombe Waller – my current musical obsession. *"Hey oh, hey oh, hey oh; who controls your emotions?"*

For Tom will wake up soon and the nature of the day will begin to crystallise, like some complex mathematical result of putting his star sign or biorhythms, or whatever controls our emotions, together with mine. Or maybe the day already exists somewhere over the horizon, and we just have to sit and watch as the weather of the day – sunshine or storms, cold shoulders or popcorn – slides invisibly into place.

A few drops of rain lash against the window revealing at least one aspect of what's in store. I move myself an inch to the right so that our legs are touching. It feels so good, that soft human warmth, magical – mystical almost. Tom replies with an "Umh," sound and then with stunningly crisp diction, does his sleep-talking thing – answering, I reckon, a dream telephone.

"Hello? Yes?" he says. "One moment. I'll put you through."

As I start to smirk he raises his knees and breaks wind – a vibrating two-second whoopee-cushion number.

"Jesus!" I snigger. *"Tom!"*

Tom clears his throat. "Uh?" he says, maybe to me, maybe to his dream caller.

I study his face and see the smoothness slip away, see the brow wrinkle, see him change from angel (OK... *farting* angel) to human being as something slips into and possesses his body. Ego maybe? His face takes on a recognisable configuration: bleary, slightly irritated. "You woke me," he says.

"You farted," I reply.

"I was asleep," he says, groaning and rolling away. As he turns he pushes a foot out backwards to find my leg – all is not lost.

I yawn and stretch luxuriantly, then curl towards his back and think that no matter what the day brings – rain and storms or sunshine and laughter – fifteen hours from now we will be back in this bed, cuddled together in animal comfort, for the simple reason that we have decided that, from now on, this is how it is going to be.

***

We duck, laughing, into Monoprix. It's raining hard now, and still too windy for umbrellas – water is trickling down my back.

Tom runs his fingers up through his normally spiky hair. "Wow!" he says. "You never warned me about the joys of the Mediterranean climate."

I shrug and shiver. "It's November – at least when it rains it rains... And it never lasts more than a couple of days." I pick up a shopping basket.

"So," Tom says pushing through the turnstile. "Where's the frozen stuff?"

"You're gonna be disappointed," I say, pointing the way. Monoprix is like a New York supermarket, sandwiched into the available, ancient space, aisles not big enough for a full-width trolley. The frozen food section is about three square meters.

I follow him – intrigued and determined not to say anything, just to see what he buys. I'm thinking about this strange mutant entity that is coupledom: not Tom, nor I, but a pick and mix of both. It's surprising and intriguing to watch the boundaries fade, the compromises form, as this third entity that is *us* appears.

In French law, legal associations or companies are called a *Personne Morale* – those thus joined together create a new legal "person," with the same legal and moral requirements as an individual, and it strikes me that coupledom is similar. There is Mark and there is Tom, and there is a third person called *us*. A third person that likes this but not that, that hangs out with him but not her... And right now we're in the process of deciding every aspect of who this new being will be.

We've been together a while now, of course. But when we lived apart, though there were moments when we formed an *us*, ultimately we still had very individual identities, habits: the books I read, the TV Tom watches, the friends Tom sees, the shopping that goes into each refrigerator – in my case, vegetables, cheese, butter, in Tom's, frozen pizzas and oven chips. Now we're living together we're slowly whittling away at the individualities to get to a common core. It's not less... for every friend I stop seeing because Tom doesn't seem to like them much, I usually gain one from his side, and for every meal I stop cooking, something else replaces it. But it is different. And that process of negotiating common ground isn't dull, and it's not entirely without pain.

Tom drops two frozen pizzas into the basket, and says, as an afterthought, "Two of these? I love these spinach ones."

I used to make pizza – with flour and yeast and mozzarella cheese. Frozen pizza somehow feels naughty, hedonistic even. "Sure!" I say, grinning and following Tom on through the store.

He grabs a bag of washed salad leaves and despite myself I intervene. "Can we just get a lettuce?" I ask. I'm sure someone, somewhere in the world truly doesn't have the time or energy to rinse a lettuce leaf, but that person isn't me.

Tom hesitates then drops the bag. "Sure," he says, then, looking perplexed, as if this is maybe a challenge, a trick question he thinks he might get wrong, he adds, "You choose."

As we leave the store with our hybrid shopping – Tom's pizzas, my lettuce, Tom's Molten Centre Chocolate Pudding (!), my eggs and flour, Tom says, "So... A film?"

I frown. "A film?"

Tom smiles. "Yeah," he says. "Shall we go see what's on in English?" He nods in the direction of the cinema, not two hundred yards away across Place Garibaldi.

I smile and nod. "Sure," I say. "Why not?"

"Not much else to do on a rainy Saturday afternoon," Tom says, pulling his collar up and heading off.

Not much indeed – it's a great idea, and strangely, one that would never cross my mind, for no reason I can think of except that it isn't something I *do* on a Saturday afternoon.

"Will the frozen stuff be OK?" I ask, trotting to catch up.

"We'll just eat it when we get back," he says.

So, it's a pizza and cinema kind of a Saturday then. I feel like I'm living someone else's life. I push my lip out and nod approvingly. It feels just fine.

"Tom," I say, back at the flat. "Do you *have* to?" After our special Saturday, I'm feeling quite in love with Tom. I would have liked the feeling to last a little longer.

"Have to *what*, babe?" he asks.

We've been in for seconds. The shopping is still defrosting in the carrier bags beside him on the big red sofa. "Do you have to skin up?" I ask trying to keep the petulant tone from my voice.

Tom shrugs and clicks the remote, switching on the TV. "Have you come over all evangelical on me?" he asks, licking the edge of the paper and expertly sealing the joint.

I force a smile and move to the arm of the sofa. I ruffle his hair. "It's not that. It's just that once you start smoking, well, that's it. Nothing else happens," I say.

Tom lights the end of the joint and shrugs. "We've been out," he says. "We've seen a film, we've bought dinner, what else do you want to do?" He clicks the remote, swapping from one Saturday game show to another; only this one is a little louder.

I was thinking of a snooze and a shag actually. I've nothing against dope, though it doesn't seem to do it for *me* – if anything it makes me paranoid and depressed. But if you can't join in, if you're sitting on the outside, it just makes other people so *boring*. I'm not evangelical at all – it's just, well, give me an evening with someone doing coke or speed any day. And Tom, once he starts smoking, really *won't* do anything else. The joint equals *Game Over*. No cooking, no cleaning, no going out – that I can cope with. But it also means permanent trash TV dominating the living room, no visible awareness of my existence, no meaningful discussion, and above all, no sex. Despite the myth, dope does *not* make Tom horny. I try to think how to reply, but the moment has passed. Tom is already lost in the TV, blowing smoke rings into the air, and settling back into the couch, struggling half-heartedly to kick off his trainers.

"You smoke a lot these days," I say.

Tom replies without pulling his eyes from the TV. "I always did," he says. "It's just you weren't there to see it. It's what I do. It's how I relax." He proffers the joint over his shoulder at me.

"Nah," I say. "I think I'll go out for a walk along the seafront. The weather's changed. The rain's stopped. I'll check at Jenny's on the way out – see if she's up for it."

"Why?" he asks. "We just got in."

I shrug. "Dunno really," I say. "It's just what I do."

***

Sunday morning and who could ask for more? I writhe and stretch, basking in the warmth of the bed, the sound of the rain hammering down anew mixes with Tom's saxophone practice wafting from the office. Strips of dim light pushing through the shutters pattern the ceiling.

The sax inevitably makes me think of Steve – it always happens

13

and it always makes me feel a little guilty, as if thinking about Steve is being unfaithful to Tom in some way. I sigh and stretch again and tell myself that it's OK to think about him. It was of course, Steve's *Selmer* that Tom is playing.

I wonder how good his playing was. He was a professional; it's what he did for a living, so he must have been good. I listen for a while. For once Tom is playing a complete tune – a Sade song I recognise – dodgy taste but tuneful. I wonder, in a vague, parallel universe kind of way, what would have happened if Steve hadn't died. Would he have been next door instead? I smile and wonder if *he* farted in his sleep. Would we have even got to this stage or was it just another of those illusory love affairs? Silly to be wasting thinking time over it if that's the case. Silly to be wasting time thinking about a dead man anyway.

"He's dead!" I think, jerking myself out of the reverie. *"Get over it!"*

Tom's playing pauses for a second as he coughs with gusto, then picks up where he left off. "Your Love Is King" – yep, that's the song. A bit dated, but as Tom pointed out, he's been half-heartedly trying to learn it since it first came out.

I think about other relationships I've had and how some of them were better in some ways, some of them worse in others, but then I decide it's ultimately pointless – like browsing Ikea catalogues or reading beauty magazines; it can only make you feel dissatisfied with what you've got – a solid relationship with farting, burping, underpant-discarding, pot-smoking Tom. Far better to focus on the positives of here and now.

I throw back the quilt, suddenly optimistic and ready for the day. I stand and pull on my jogging trousers and head through to the office. Tom pauses his playing as I open the door, lowers the sax and grins at me. He looks hopelessly cute in a dishevelled kind of way. "Did I wake you?" he asks.

I bat a hand at the thick smog hanging in the air and grin to show I don't really mean it. "Nah," I say. "It's lovely. Can't think of a nicer way to wake up."

Tom grins again and raises the instrument to his lips again, then pauses and says, "Oh, there are croissants and coffee in the kitchen."

I blink at him slowly and nod. "Thanks," I say.

As I pour the coffee I think about the fact that this gorgeous feeling – Sunday morning with someone playing the sax in another room – was a sort of recurring dream of my perfect relationship. It all started years ago when a busker woke me up in exactly that way one Sunday morning by playing beneath my window. He had been cute, and I remember having thought, *"Imagine waking up to that every Sunday."* And I wonder at the power of life to order coincidences, meetings, chance; to replace actors with fresh personnel when required – seemingly whatever it takes to make sure the future manifests exactly as imagined.

Dogs, Rhubarb And Pantaloons

For a moment, above the noise of the vacuum cleaner, Tom isn't aware of my presence, and I'm able to observe him. He's wearing just his boxer shorts and a t-shirt, plus thick woolly socks, and he has a rolled cigarette – or more probably a joint – hanging from his mouth. He's frowning with concentration as he tries to get the supposedly marvellous, but in reality useless, Dyson to suck up the dust in the corners.

I close the front door loudly and he looks up and grins, then, in reaction to the rising smoke, closes one eye and winks madly. The ensemble is so funny I can't help but laugh.

Tom smiles back and kicks the OFF button on the cleaner. "I take it the smile means that it went well," he says as the machine whirs to a halt.

I nod and pull my jacket off. "Piss easy," I say. "France may be a bureaucratic nightmare, but there's nothing so easy as signing on for unemployment benefit."

Tom nods and pouts thoughtfully. "I guess they've had a lot of practice at getting *that* one right," he says.

I pull a folded sheet of paper from my back pocket. "I didn't actually need to go there at all you know. You can do it by Internet now, or even over the phone."

Tom raises an eyebrow. "Isn't that making it a bit too easy? I take it you have to go to some kind of Job Centre so they can at least *pretend* to try to find you a job?"

I shake my head. "Apparently they *may* call me in – in three months' time."

"Cool," Tom says. "And what about the dole cheque? How do you get that?"

"Paid direct into my account," I tell him. "Seventy percent of my salary."

Tom gasps. "Seventy percent? Jesus! I wish *I* could get that."

"For eighteen months..." I add.

"Eighteen months! I don't suppose anyone really looks for a job for eighteen months then do they?"

I wink at him. "Not me anyway," I say.

"So you're on holiday," Tom says. "Officially." He proffers the joint.

I wrinkle my nose. "It makes me feel a bit guilty, but then I just think how much tax I have paid over the years..."

"Oh go on!" he says, still waving the joint. "You're free. It's the end of one thing, the beginning of another. Have a smoke!"

I shrug and take the joint. "I guess so," I say. "I wasn't planning doing anything else today."

"There's nothing else *to* do is there? Not until we get the keys to the gîte."

"Actually, I think there's plenty to do," I tell him. "We need to get some kind of marketing plan sorted, a website and stuff..."

Tom nods. "Yeah, I already started actually. Only, I need some decent photos of the place. Hers are all crap."

"And budgets," I say. "I want to work out how we're gonna make a living at it. But I need some figures from Chantal – profit margins and stuff. I think we need to go up there, have lunch, maybe even stay a weekend – pump her for as much information as we can. Because once it's ours I get the feeling she'll be out of there and never want to look back."

"I can't wait to get started on the place though," Tom says. "I was wondering – do you think we can grow rhubarb up there?"

I frown at Tom and snort in amusement.

"What?" he asks.

I half-shrug. "I just don't think growing rhubarb is gonna be very high on the urgent list of things to do," I say.

Tom scowls like a child. "So what's going to be on the *Fuehrer's* list of things to do?"

I unplug the lead from the Dyson, hand it to him and then stroke his back. "Hey," I say. "You can grow rhubarb, of course you can. I just mean, what with all the redecorating and marketing we need to be doing... Well, that's the stuff *I'm* worried about. We need to make sure the place makes money."

Tom scratches his chin and slumps on the sofa. "Yeah, we *so* need to redecorate," he says. "I was thinking it would be nice to do something quirky," he says. "Like themed rooms, you know bright colours and stuff."

I nod. "Yeah, I thought so too, pick up some bits of funky second-hand furniture..."

"I love rhubarb though," Tom says, instinctively reaching for his smoking box and taking out the ingredients for his next joint. "I've got this craving for rhubarb crumble. Maybe I'm pregnant."

I slip beside him on the sofa and contain a sigh. His brain works differently to mine, drifting laterally from one subject to another. Mine is much more linear, logical. If I'm talking about decorating I'm not going to drift onto rhubarb. "And a dog," Tom says. "Can we have a dog?"

"A *dog?!*" I exclaim. "Where did *that* come from?"

Tom shrugs. "It's just a sort of recurring dream," he says. "A daydream more I suppose. I always imagined one day I'd have a husband and a vegetable plot and rhubarb growing and a big country dog."

I nod at Paloma on the chair opposite; she's cutely cleaning her forehead by licking her paw. "I'm not sure what madam will have to say about it," I say, thinking about Tom's use of the word husband. It's not a word he uses generally – I like it.

"It's a *country* dog," Tom says. "It will live outside in a kennel. And I can take it for walks on those footpaths along the ridges.

I nod and smile at the image. I get it. These things *are* linked for Tom. Just as Sunday mornings are somehow linked to croissants and saxophone for me, gîtes, dogs and rhubarb are part of *his* dream. I shrug. "I guess," I say. "A dog and rhubarb. Why not? We could call the dog Rhubarb and kill two birds with one stone."

Tom runs his lighter along the edge of the lump of dope. "Wasn't that a cartoon dog? Rhubarb and Custard or something."

I wrinkle my nose. "I don't think Rhubarb was a *dog...*" I shrug. I think for a moment. "No, I can't remember. Where do you get this stuff from anyway?" I ask pointing at the dope. "I mean, I hope you didn't bring it back from Brighton?"

Tom tuts. "Don't be crazy! I wouldn't go through customs with it. No, Jenny gets it off that bloke she's seeing."

"Jenny?" I repeat. "And what do you mean that *bloke she's seeing?* I don't know anything about a bloke!"

Tom sprinkles the dope and glances up at me. "You didn't know? About Rick?"

"Rick?" I say. "This guy has a *name?*" It's a dumb comment – of *course* he has a name. But I'm shocked, and a little outraged that Tom is on first name terms with a guy Jenny is seeing. Jenny is *my* closest friend after all, and I didn't even know that Rick existed.

Tom shrugs. "She hasn't been seeing him long," he says. "A couple of weeks tops."

"What's he like?" I ask wondering if he's one of the guys I've crossed on the stairs. "And he's what? A drug dealer?"

Tom shakes his head and runs his tongue along the edge of the paper. "I haven't seen him," he says. "He sounds nice though. And no, he's not a dealer at all. He's a doctor I think."

"Jenny is dating a drug dealing doctor," I say. "And I didn't know."

Tom shrugs. "The disadvantage of being at work. And he's *not* a dealer. Don't say that. You'll upset her. *And* him! He just had some – for you know, personal use, and she asked him for it and then gave it to me. Said it makes her too lazy."

I shake my head. "I just can't believe that I didn't know this," I say. "How can I not know this? Why didn't *you* tell me?"

Tom shrugs. "It didn't come up I suppose. Hey, you know the redecorating thing," he adds, his voice suddenly velvety.

I give him a puzzled smirk. "*Yeah?*" I say. I'm guessing he's going to tell me he doesn't like decorating.

"Well, I had an idea what we could do with the cellar," he says, wiggling an eyebrow.

I roll my eyes. "I was wondering when that would come," I say.

Tom winks at me. "So you thought of it too," he says, lighting and then passing me the joint.

I take a hit. My head spins instantly. "Wow, this one's strong," I say. "This one's gonna make me *really* lazy. Yeah, I knew you'd want a dungeon down there."

Tom wiggles his head sideways. "There's no reason why we can't is there?"

I roll my eyes. "Again Tom, nice idea, but not that high on the list of priorities."

"Oh go on!" he laughs. "We could make it a *gay* hotel. Charge extra for the dungeon key... like those places in Amsterdam," he says, "with whips and chains in every room."

I laugh and shake my head. "You dirty birdie," I say.

"Nice idea though," Tom says.

I nod and grin. The dope is working and it all suddenly seems not only a very funny idea but also a very good idea. Except... "You crazy guy," I say. "We're not going to be *in* Amsterdam though, are we?"

Tom frowns.

"They have hotels like that in Amsterdam because it's a city of clubs and bars and cruising zones," I say. "Loads of guys want to go there anyway. Up in the Alps I think you're much more likely to get hearty Christian heterosexual hill-walking types in those green convertible short/long trouser things."

Tom sighs. "I guess," he says sadly.

"What are they called anyway?" I ask, dragging on the joint again and then passing it to Tom. "Those zippy short/trouser things?"

Tom shrugs and looks mock-despondent. "Pantaloons?" he says.

"Pantaloons?" I repeat, and we both collapse into laughter.

"Anyway, they usually have good muscled walking legs," I say when I manage to stop sniggering. *"Pantaloons* indeed."

Tom flashes the whites of his eyes at me. "I love a chunky calf," he says. "A chunky calf protruding from the bottom of a pantaloon."

I nod. "I know you do," I say. "Only they're *so* not called pantaloons."

Tom reaches out and rubs my own, not-so chunky calf. "Fancy a siesta?" he says.

I open my mouth to say, "Yes," but the phone starts to ring. With a little difficulty I stand and cross the room. "Allo?" I say. I frown at the officious voice on the other end, then I cover the mouthpiece and roll my eyes at Tom. "It's about the gîte," I tell him. "Just hold that thought, OK?"

Dreams On Hold

The phone call takes forever. The information I am given is irritating and confusing and particularly hard to decipher through my dope smoke screen. By the time I hang up, Tom has given up and wandered off, so I sit and frown and sigh repeatedly until he returns, two carrier bags of food hanging from his wrists.

"What kind of a country *is* this?" he asks, pushing his way in. "I mean the French think they're so civilised – some guy on telly said it was *the* most civilised country in the world the other day – anyway, I think that's what he said." *"Le pays le plus civilisé du monde,"* he mocks pompously. "But they've never even heard of rhubarb crumble. Can you imagine that? You see, we *do* need to plant rhubarb. Urgently! Anyway, I found lemon meringue pie – I suppose that'll have to do..." He looks at me and pauses as he notices my expression. "What was that about then?" he asks, nodding sideways towards the phone and pulling a frozen lemon meringue pie in a box from the Picard bag.

"That," I say rolling my eyes, "was bad news."

"About the gîte?"

I nod sadly. "About the gîte."

"She's *not* pulling out?" he asks, suddenly serious, frozen in the doorway, the pie still half in, half out of the bag. "She can't now, can she?"

"Not quite," I say. "But you know Chantal's missing husband."

Tom shrugs. "I never saw him."

I shake my head. "None of us did – it seems he's *really* missing."

"Missing?"

"Yeah, like missing-person missing," I explain. "He walked out on her eighteen months ago and never came back."

"What, like, popped out for a packet of cigarettes?" Tom asks. "Or a lemon meringue pie?"

I shrug. "Something like that. Only trouble is, because they were married, the place automatically belongs to both of them. So he needs to be present to sign the sale."

Tom's mouth drops. "And what? Chantal didn't know this when she signed the papers?"

I shake my head and interrupt. "She says not. I mean, that wasn't her – it was the lawyer, but no, he said she inherited the gîte, so she just thought it was hers."

"So what, until this bloke turns up we can't buy the place?"

I shrug. "Unless they declare him dead," I say. "I think *missing presumed dead* is the term."

Tom nods and then looks at the pie box again, frowning as he reads the French defrosting instructions. "Shit," he says. "It takes ages. You have to leave it to defrost. So how long is *that* gonna take?"

I shrug. "I dunno, doesn't it say on the box?"

Tom shakes his head and turns, a bemused expression on his face. "Not the pie! For him to be declared dead!"

I frown, and then slip into a smirk.

"What?" Tom says.

I shrug. "I forgot to ask," I say, biting my tongue and crossing my eyes in a caricature of stupidity.

Tom grins at me in disbelief. "You *are* joking, right? I mean, it's the only really important bit of information in there."

I shrug. "I'm stoned," I say, starting to snigger. "Sorry."

Tom turns his palms skywards and looks at the ceiling and shakes his head, then turns to the kitchen. "I can't wait that long," he says, as he disappears. "There's only one thing for it."

"Yeah?" I shout, standing to follow him.

"We'll have to eat it frozen," he replies.

All About Tom

My beloved Kawasaki purrs and rolls beautifully from one bend to the next. The air is crisp and clear, the sky a deep shade of blue after the rain. Despite thick, gleaming bike leathers and somewhat less sexy Damart underwear, the cold is starting to reach my thighs and I'm still only a third of the way up. I wonder just how cold it is going to be up there.

Despite the ride, the air, the sky, the sun, I'm feeling blurry and irritable. As I pass through tiny abandoned villages I wonder how much of my mood is due to the dope hangover, and how much is caused by circumstance – the holdup on the sale and Tom's refusal to come with me (his own reaction to the hangover being a day in bed.)

As I leave the 202 and head up towards Guillaumes, little patches of snow start to appear at the roadside and my visor starts to mist up as the temperature plummets. The cold really starts to penetrate my leathers now, but it's a good feeling – bracing and somehow real, invigorating. I pass a group of cars parked for no apparent reason in the middle of nowhere, then a police car and another, and I vaguely wonder what that's all about.

In Guillaumes there seem to be far more people milling about than usual, but I don't really pay any attention – I put it down to some kind of village fête and continue on up towards Chatauneuf d'Entraunes, the hilltop village where the gîte is located. The snowfall here has been heavy, and though the road has been cleared, I start to wonder if it's actually possible to get to the top on a motorbike. Cars may slip and slide in the snow, but two hundred kilos of motorbike (two-eighty if you include the rider) on two motorbike tyres – well, if I meet snow on the road then there's really no way. I wonder about the state of my front tyre and suddenly can't remember when I last checked the tread. It can't be far from illegal.

The scenery is incredible and eventually it manages to pierce my dope bubble. The pines, deepest green, are heavily laden with brilliant white, icing-sugar snow. It looks more and more like a Swiss postcard the higher I ride.

As I take the final turn towards Chateauneuf d'Entraunes the snow starts to encroach upon the road – there has clearly been far less traffic on this stretch. I pass another policeman sitting in his car on the bend and almost stop to ask what's up, but really I am just too lazy to pull the brake lever.

I keep the bike in one of the narrow tracks left by car tyres and slow to walking pace. The bike slithers a little from time to time, but nothing so bad that it doesn't seem like fun.

The gîte, when I finally arrive, looks stunning – far more beautiful than my memories. The roof is blanketed with ten inches of snow, rising and falling as it hugs the contours of the roof tiles. Everything – the deep grey stone walls, the plastic table and chairs, even the wheelbarrow – looks different and beautiful topped with this fresh glittering whiteness. But the blue, weather-beaten shutters are closed; there is no trail to the front door. The place has been closed for a while.

I park the bike and slip and slide my way – my bike boots don't seem to have much tread left either – round the back of the building and up into the tiny village square, but here too, apart from a couple of single sets of footprints, the place shows no sign of life. I'm not going to be able to speak to Chantal today.

As I head back through the snow-dampened silence, it strikes me for the first time how *difficult* it is going to be to fill this place in winter; to get paying guests up here at all, in fact to get anyone, *even friends*, to visit. And I realise that if the seller has closed the place up awaiting the sale, it's probable that there aren't any paying guests in winter anyway – and further, that if she isn't here to take bookings then we are no longer buying a going concern but a clean slate with an empty diary. It's going to be harder than I ever imagined to make ends meet.

I clean the snow from a chair and sit in the sun for a while enjoying the view, which is undeniably stunning and definitely the thing to concentrate on in any marketing we do. I imagine life here, with Tom walking his big dog along the ridge, or tending his rhubarb. I imagine us play fighting over who has to get up to do breakfast for the early-starting hill-walkers. After half an hour my stomach starts to rumble – I had hoped to have lunch here – so I start the bike and crawl back down the hill. The heavy bike on the snow feels much scarier heading back down – lethal in fact – but I make it to the main road without a mishap. The nail of realisation about just how tough winter can be up here is driven in a little further. The bike will be unusable a lot of the time; even in a car it could be hard to get in and out. We're going to be pretty isolated, pretty cold and money will be tight too. But in the end, as long as I imagine Tom in the picture doing it all with me, as long as I imagine us shovelling snow together or building huge log fires, then it seems fine, brilliant in fact. And I realise that my own dreams really don't have much to do with the gîte at all. Of course its fun, it's an adventure, it's a change, but the more I analyse things, it's really all just about Tom. And I wonder if that isn't a good definition of being in love.

Mental Infidelity

As I round the final bend of the track and the main road comes into view, I jolt with the surprise of seeing someone – a policeman – in the middle of the junction. He has blocked the end of the road with red tape stretched between his wing mirror and a signpost. Beside me a French *pompier* is sitting in his red fire-truck-come-ambulance thing; a small group of people are standing at the roadside.

My first thought, because that is what is on my mind, is that it has something to do with Chantal's missing husband, and then I discount this and presume there's been an accident. A few feet before the policeman, I slither to a halt.

"La route est fermée," he says raising his hand. – *"The road is closed."*

"Fermée?" I repeat.

"Yes," he tells me. "For the rally."

I shake my head. "Rally? But I have to get out," I say, adding a *Monsieur* at the end hoping this will help.

"Not until six," he replies. "If you're lucky."

I know there's no point arguing with French policemen about anything, *ever*, but the *pompier* in his truck and one of the rally organisers are looking our way, so hoping to gain their support I carry on meekly. "But I have to go to work; I didn't know there was a rally. What can I do?"

"Where are you trying to get to?" the policeman asks.

"Nice," I reply. "I work in Nice."

"Well you won't be able to get there until after six," he says.

"Where *can* I get to?" I ask.

"From here?" he says. "Today?" He pauses dramatically, then shakes his head and says, "Nulle part." – *"Nowhere."* There is no trace of humour in his voice.

I shake my head and a *Jesus!* slips out despite myself. "Look, the rally hasn't started yet has it?" I plead, glancing at a steward in an attempt at including him. "Can't I just slip out before it starts?"

The policeman sighs unhappily. "Are you sure you want to argue with me?" he asks, one eyebrow raised. He glances at my front tyre, which means of course that he has won.

I shake my head. "Non, Monsieur," I say.

With difficulty I turn the bike around. It would be easier if the policeman moved back a foot, but he stands there like a rock, so I have to do the manoeuvre – which on the sloping, snowy hill is hard enough – whilst also trying not to run over his foot. I park it next to the *pompier's* van a few yards back up the hill.

"Il ne vous laisse pas passer?" he says from his window. – *"He's not letting you through?"*

I shake my head. "Not till six he says."

"If you're lucky," he laughs. "The last one I went to, we were there till midnight – a car crashed in the tunnel."

"Minuit!" I exclaim, then in English I mutter, "Brilliant... Fucking brilliant."

Thinking, "What the fuck am I going to do till midnight?" I remove my crash helmet.

"So! English!" he says enthusiastically, shooting me broad grin. I reply with a frown. It's not the usual reaction of a Frenchman.

As if he has picked up on my surprise, he says, "I'm learning." He flashes another smile at me and beckons. "Climb aboard," he says. "You'll freeze out there."

The kid in me squeals and I break into a smile. I get to sit in the cabin of a red-fire truck!

I cross to the passenger side, pull the heavy door open and climb up, thinking about the number of times I have drooled over the fit guys in the front of these trucks, never quite sure if I want to *be* one of them or just sleep with them.

I turn to see what this *pompier* looks like. He fits the mould exactly. He's fit and muscular, big brown eyes, bristle sprouting on his chin, jet-black hair, tanned, thick swirls of fur down his arms. "Ricardo," he says, holding out a hand.

French pompiers! The ultimate fantasy: they spend half the day doing daring deeds to save people's lives, the other half working out. Their red-striped navy-blue outfits are about as sexy as a uniform can get, their boots have something S&M-ish about them... I swallow and shake his hand. "Mark," I say.

His palm is warm, the handshake, confidant and friendly. "You are very cold!" he says, starting the engine and turning on the heater. "Your hands like ice."

"It's OK," I say. "You get used to it."

"So, you're English," he says again. "I'm having lessons. For a very long time."

A friend once told me that voice is fifty percent of seduction, and this voice is proof: deep – a good octave below mine, smooth and velvety. His tempo is slow and rolling, open and inviting, the accent intriguing. He grins cheekily at me and I then I notice that he's ever so slightly cross-eyed, and that really does it. I groan inside. Weird, I know, but I have always had a thing for people with cross-eyes – it just spells fragility, sex, and physical attraction. God knows why! I notice that my heart is beating faster than usual. I swallow again.

He crosses his legs and turns as far towards me as the cramped cabin will allow. His boots are *very* shiny. "Alors?" he prompts. – *"So?"*

I realise that I haven't spoken for a while and that my heart is actually pounding and my dick is stirring. Lucky I have such thick motorcycle gear on otherwise he'd see by now. I cross my own legs away from him and swallow hard and open my mouth, but I can't really think of anything to say. "Yes," I murmur. I clear my throat. "English," I say, a little too loudly.

"Nice boots," Ricardo says. "And I like your... *Alpine Star* – what do you call this? *Combinaison?*"

"Erm, bike leathers," I say. "Or one-piece. You need it in this weather."

Ricardo nods. "I used to have a bike too," he says. "I had all the same thing... these boots and an Alpine Star coat like yours."

I nod.

"But I never use it, my girlfriend didn't like... so I sell it."

I nod, registering the word *girlfriend* and trying not to let any disappointment show.

"So what are you doing up *here?*" he asks.

"Oh, I went to visit a gîte," I say.

"A *gîte?*" he says.

"It's like a small hotel, or a big bed and breakfast. I'm buying it with my... partner." I point up the hill. "Up there." I kick myself for saying *partner* – but I'm enjoying the heterosexual chumminess; I don't want any barriers going up, and ironically, considering their status as the ultimate gay fantasy, French fireman are renowned for being macho, *and* homophobic.

Ricardo nods. "Yes, but up there?" he asks doubtfully. "It's very isolated."

I nod. "Yeah," I say nodding and goggling my eyes to show just how much that isolation is starting to play on my mind. "And you?" I ask. "What are you doing here?"

Ricardo laughs and switches to French. "Getting bored mostly," he tells me.

"Why are you here? In case of accidents?" I ask.

He nods. "Just in case. It's a legal requirement. But nothing ever happens, so I listen to the radio, I chat to people, I practice my English..." He adds an amiable wink at the end. "I like your leathers," he says again. "They're very nice. I miss my bike."

I frown at him. Some deep down instinct tells me that he's hitting on me. And then, all available evidence tells me that he really *isn't*. *"Do straight men have leather fetishes?"* I wonder.

He sighs and looks out of the windscreen. His radio crackles indecipherably.

"They're starting," he says, reaching for the door handle. "Shall we go watch?"

I shrug. "Why not?"

As we walk down the hill, I lose my footing in the snow and Ricardo grabs my elbow and steadies me. I smile at him in thanks and he winks, making me blush. At the roadside we join the policeman and the steward and three other people who have appeared on the opposite side of the road, I'm not sure where from.

"I like these races better," Ricardo says, peering down the hill towards Guillaumes. "The vintage ones."

I nod. "Oh, it's old cars? Classic cars?" I say. "Cool!" The air is cold. I can see my breath rising, but the sun is warm and heats the front of my bike gear like a solar panel. "Are you French?" I ask.

Ricardo tips his head sideways. "Why?" he asks.

I shrug. "The name, I guess... Sounds kind of Italian. And something about your accent."

He smiles broadly. He has one of the widest smiles I have ever seen. "I'm Colombian," he says. "Well, French-Colombian."

"Like Ingrid Betancourt, that hostage woman?" I ask, attempting to demonstrate at least one grain of knowledge about Colombia.

"Huh!" Ricardo grunts. "Don't get me started on her! The bitch. Let them kill her!"

I bite my lip. "Oh," I say, frowning. It's not the humanistic approach one expects from a professional lifesaver. "She's still a hostage though... I mean, surely whether you like her or not, you have to feel sorry for her?"

"There are thousands of hostages, and yet they still talk about her – only her. There are *thousands* of better people to worry about – good people, not corrupt politicians..." he sighs, visibly interrupting his rant. "Sorry, it just drives me insane, the whole world talking about one woman, the whole world ignore the rest of Colombia's problems. But anyway, yes. Not quite French. The accent never goes away huh?"

I frown. "It's not quite the accent, more the intonation. I wouldn't criticise anyone's accent!" I laugh. "Not with mine! I've been here years, and I still open my mouth to say, *"Un demi bière s'il vous plait,"* and everyone knows I'm English.

Ricardo laughs. "That will be because it's *Une demie,* because it's a beer – feminine. You English never get the masculine and feminine right."

I nod and laugh. "You're right," I say. "I don't think we have the necessary circuits to remember whether beer is a boy or a girl. At least, I don't."

"Nor does Jane Birkin," he says. "Her whole life in France and she still says, *un* chanson. You know, she's a singer. She could remember that this one word is feminine – the word for *song*, right?" He touches my elbow and turns to face down the hill again. "They come!" he says.

"They're coming!" I correct, unable to resist pointing out that every language has its challenges.

Five cars slither and screech around the bend right before our eyes. The last one splatters us with mud. I blink and rub my eyes.

It strikes me that the policeman, or whoever is supposed to decide these things, is letting us stand too close – much too close. Still blinking through my watery vision, I take a step back. Ricardo stays where he is and shoots me a smile and a nod, which somehow manages to communicate, *"You're fine, don't worry; but I understand why you are moving away."*

Only five cars go by and with the exception of the fifth one – the mud-hurling Karmann Ghia – they don't strike me as very impressive. The first two were Simcas – the same car my aunty had! The third was a Hillman Imp and the fourth a Ford Escort. Do such cars count as vintage? Am I that old now that the most banal cars of my childhood are now classics?

The other spectators seem impressed though, and they clap and cheer as the cars go by. When it becomes apparent that the pause is going to be prolonged, Ricardo steps back and frowns at me. "You OK?" he asks.

I shake my head. "I've got some dirt or something in my eye," I say. Tears are streaming now and the pain in my left eye is quite shocking.

Ricardo grabs my elbows and turns me towards the sun. He tips my head back and peers into my eye. Despite the pain and the tears, I'm hyper-aware of his face mere inches from mine, of his lips within striking distance, his stubbly chin a lick away. He even somehow places a thigh behind me and presses it against my arse as he steadies me. It's weird that the presence feels so sexual. "Je le vois," he says. – *"I see it."*

He pulls a clean tissue from his pocket, twists the end, and expertly swipes the grit from my eye. "Voila!" he says, proudly showing me the black speck on the tissue.

I rub the tears away and sniff. My nose is running too for some reason. "Gosh, thanks!" I say. "It doesn't look like much, but that really hurt!"

The radio in the van bursts into life and Ricardo runs a reassuring hand casually down my back, stopping just as it touches the top of my arse and then excuses himself and turns and starts to jog up the hill. Behind me I hear the policeman's and then the steward's radios chirrup simultaneously and I guess that there's a reason there are no more cars.

When I hear Ricardo's truck start, I step forward to ask the policeman – now removing the red tape – what's going on. "Is that it?" I ask.

He shakes his head. "Accident," he tells me. "Just after Guillaumes. The road's blocked."

The red van slides past and Ricardo hangs a hairy arm from the window and tells me the same thing, "Accident – I have to go check. Maybe see you later."

He gives a little wave and then accelerates down the hill in a plume of overpowering diesel fumes.

When the policeman starts to pull the tape back across the road, the steward intervenes. "You might as well let him go," he tells him, pointing at me. "There won't be anyone through for a while."

The policeman freezes, I'm sure considering which of the two options will give him the most pleasure: never seeing me again, or using his power to keep me here. I wonder myself whether I actually want him to let me go, or if I'd rather wait, even till midnight, stuck here with the fabulous fireman.

The policeman sighs, looks at the bike, then back down the road, and then tosses the words, "Go then, and be quick," over his shoulder at me.

I hesitate for a second - the van is now out of sight.

"Can I go south?" I ask. "I might be able to fit through the blockage with the bike..."

The cop shakes his head and points north. "That way, and be quick. Now or never."

"OK, OK," I say, already running for the bike. "Thanks."

I slither back down the hill, and with a final glance south, I head on up into the Alps. As I ride, I wonder how long it will be before I can loop back towards Nice. And I wonder what the sexy fireman is doing right now, if he'll be at all disappointed to see that I have gone.

I come across a road to Valberg which is high and is going to be cold, but at least it's in the right direction, so I turn the bars, shift down a gear and head upwards, bracing myself for the cold to come. To avoid thinking about the cold, which is already piercing, I think about the gorgeous Ricardo and wonder what his girlfriend looks like. I wonder if Ricardo was at the wreckage of my own car crash not a hundred kilometres away and briefly fantasise that maybe he saved my life, but then I'm forced to discount the idea as unlikely. And then I have a thought which shocks me so much that I manage to think about the thought *and* the fact of it shocking me at the same time: that if I ever got the chance to sleep with someone as stunningly seductive as Ricardo that I wouldn't be able to resist; that, Tom or no Tom, I don't think I would even *try* to resist. And I realise that despite the fact that I'm in love with Tom (or does this mean that I'm not?) there *are* men out there that are *so* beautiful, *so* masculine, who give off such a smooth, confident, friendly, sexy vibe, that given the choice I would dump Tom in a second. The thought strikes me as so dark, so dank, so disappointing, so *shameful* that I don't even know where to put it. So I push it away, and decide to think about the cold instead. And boy is it cold.

All About Who?

It's five p.m. by the time I get back, and I'm so cold that the only way I can think of to get some heat back into my bones is to have a hot bath. Tom is watching TV – another French game show – but simultaneously working on his laptop, which placates me. He says he's, "Mucking around with the website for the gîte," and doesn't comment that I'm late and so I don't mention the rally. As I lower myself into the hot bath, though, I wonder why this is, and decide that if not mentioning the rally seems like omission, mentioning the rally but not mentioning Ricardo would seem like a lie.

But once I'm warm and dressed, I return to the lounge and sit next to Tom so that our thighs touch. It would be the first thing I ever purposely failed to tell him and so I decide against it. "I met a really nice *pompier* today," I say. "There was a rally and I was stuck and I spent a while chatting to him. Straight but dead sexy."

Tom murmurs an, "Uhuh," but continues looking at the TV.

I stare at him and wait for a reaction, and then when none comes, I laugh at the anti-climax. Honesty is the easy option after all.

"What are you laughing at?" he asks.

I shrug. "Nothing," I say. "Just being silly... How's the web site going?"

Tom shrugs and glances at the screen. "I need new photos," he says. "Did you take any?"

"Shit," I mutter. "I forgot. I took the camera as well."

"Oh Mark!" Tom whines.

"I'm sorry," I say. "I was kind of distracted – what with the snow and the fact that the place was all closed up, and the rally. To be honest, it looked a bit cold and desolate. I'm not sure it would be that good for sales anyway."

"You still could have taken a *couple,*" Tom says, glancing at the TV, then at the laptop, and then finally at me.

"Well, if I had remembered, I *would* have," I say. "You could have come and taken some yourself," I point out.

"I can't do everything," Tom counters. "I can't do that and this." He flourishes a hand before the screen.

I sigh and realise that we're at one of those crossroads – pointless conflict or not pointless conflict – I choose the high road. "Yeah, well, never mind, eh?" I say, running a hand across his back. "We can go up together another day and take some photos. Maybe even stay a night if she opens the place up."

Tom clicks and adds a drop-shadow to the *Le Gîte* logo he's working on on-screen. "Not bad huh?" he says.

I nod. "Yeah, it's good," I agree. "Looks like a TV thing, you know, *Chaos at the Castle* or something."

Tom smiles. "Yeah," he says. "I bet it will be too. You and me trying to run a gîte."

"You must come and see the place though Tom," I insist. "While there's snow. It's a bit bleak. It makes you realise just how isolated the place really is."

Tom pauses, saves his work-in-progress and then looks sideways at me, his brow wrinkled. "So what are you saying? Are you having doubts?"

I shake my head. "No, not at all," I say. "I just think, well, *you* need to see it – to be prepared."

Tom stares into my eyes, seemingly deep in thought. For a moment I think he's going to say something important. But then he just shrugs and turns back to the TV. "If the holdup on the sale goes on much longer, I'll probably go back to the UK anyway," he says lightly.

"You got stuff to do?" I ask.

Tom shakes his head but still doesn't look at me. His sudden interest in the TV strikes me as suspicious. "No, not really," he says. "But I might as well get some temp work, get some money coming in. And I kind of miss the nightlife."

I remove my hand and sit back on the sofa, a separate being again. "I thought you meant just for, you know, a visit," I say. "For a few *days*. How long are you thinking of going for?"

Tom shrugs. "How long is a piece of string?" he says.

"Tom!" I say, plaintively.

"How long will the gîte thing take?" he says. "How long a mission will I get offered? It all depends, doesn't it? How should I know?"

I cough and stand, and start to move towards the kitchen, and then I pause and turn back. "Tom," I say, chewing the side of my mouth. "Can we turn the TV off for a minute?"

He glances up at me. "Why?" he says.

"We have to talk."

He reaches for the remote and somewhat theatrically clicks off the TV. "What's up?" he asks, his tone vaguely mocking.

I move back to the sofa and sit sideways, half facing him. "I'm a bit surprised," I say. "I mean, that you're thinking about going back already. We haven't discussed this *at all.*"

Tom shakes his head and sighs. "I knew you were going to have an argument with me today," he says. "It's been brewing all day."

I frown. "I haven't *been* here all day," I protest. But I wonder all the same if it's true, if he isn't somehow right. It *could* be my hangover making me play up, but then it's hard to tell. When your perception gets skewered by drugs you're always the last to know.

"Whatever," Tom says, before continuing in a calmer tone of voice. "What I mean is, we can *argue* about this, or ... *not.* But I can't really see any point in me staying here if there's no gîte project happening, can you?"

"I'm not sure really," I say, trying to work out my thoughts, and trying to keep an eye on them for wanton negativity at the same time. "I mean, I suppose I just thought that this was *where we lived* now."

Tom frowns at me so I continue, "I thought the gîte was about us being together, not the other way around. I didn't realise we were together just so we could do the gîte."

Tom tuts, and turns towards me and takes my hand. "Hey," he says. "Don't make this about *us.* I just think it's a good idea for me to go and earn some money," he says. "You can see the sense in that, surely?"

I nod. "Yeah," I say vaguely. "I mean, I know that makes sense; I know there's a certain logic to it..."

"So?" Tom asks.

"Well, I don't know," I say. "I mean, I understand the need for change, but if you need more nightlife, well, that's fixable *here.* This is *where we live.* Or it's supposed to be. And we're not exactly broke, not with my dole and your..."

"Well, this is *where we live* because we're buying a gîte," Tom says.

I nod. "So what happens if it falls through then?"

"What, the whole thing? Completely?"

"Yeah," I say. "What happens if, say, Chantal *can't* sell us the gîte? If the whole project crashes and burns."

Tom shrugs. "We look for another property?" He says this in a tone of voice that implies that the answer is obvious.

I nod. "OK, but *who* does? Will *you* be here to do that?"

Tom shakes his head. "Hell Mark, I don't know. I suppose you could look and then we could make the final choice together."

I nod.

"I don't really see what the prob..."

"The problem *is*..." I interrupt quietly, still working it out, "that unless there's a gîte, we aren't together."

Tom frowns, first nods, and then shakes his head. "And?" he says.

"So you're being here wouldn't seem to be about me really, or *us*, but about the gîte."

Tom laughs sourly.

"What?" I ask genuinely confused.

"Why does everything have to be about *you?*" He shakes his head apparently in dismay.

I sigh. I grind my teeth a little, and then when I'm sure I can keep my tone neutral, I say earnestly, "So what's the gîte thing about? For you?"

Tom shakes his head. "I don't kn..." he protests.

"No, go on," I interrupt. "In a nutshell, why do you want to do this?" "Maybe we should have asked these questions before," I think.

Tom shakes his head and pouts. "I don't know. Life change?"

I nod. "OK, life change."

"Yeah, changing my life. You know that. We talked about it – around when my dad died."

"OK, but living here with me, that's a life change isn't it?"

Tom shrugs. "Kind of. But I could be with *you* anywhere. I don't mean that to sound... What I mean is that the reason I'm *here* is because we're buying a gîte. *Here.* And if that goes, then the reason goes. I don't see what's so wrong with that."

"So it *isn't* about being with me?" I say, wincing at the statement.

"Well, no," he says. "Why does it have to be about *you?*"

I nod. "So let me get this right."

"Mark..." Tom whines.

"Your decision to live here or stay in the UK wasn't about us being together."

"Not primarily, no," Tom says.

"So it's about... What?" I say.

Tom shrugs.

"Well, it would have to be about ... *you?*" I say.

Tom shakes his head. "You see," he says, clicking the TV back on. "I told you. You're impossible today."

"End of intermission?" I ask.

"End of intermission," Tom replies.

"Fuck you too," I think. What I actually *say* is, "OK. Enjoy the game show. It looks like a really good one." It somehow means the same thing.

Sixty-Forty Split

Jenny hands me a mug of tea and sits opposite at the tiny kitchen table. She's wearing a huge Arran jumper that makes her look like some clinical over-eater from a TV documentary. I wrinkle my nose and she looks down at herself.

"The jumper?" she asks.

I nod. "It makes you look huge!" I laugh.

"I know. Mum made it. Isn't it the worst? I never wear it outdoors. It's very warm though, very good for keeping the heating bill down. I've *lost* weight actually."

I nod. "It shows in your face, but the jumper kind of hides everything else." I raise my chin towards the sofa where Sarah is sleeping. "A bit early for her isn't it?"

Jenny glances over and sighs. "She's got a cold. She's been dozing all day. Poor little thing." She sips her tea. "So come on then," she says. "Tell aunty Jenny all about it."

I roll my eyes. "Actually, I want *your* news," I say. "I can't believe I haven't seen you for so long."

"Five weeks," she says, running her fingers through her hair. "I saw you the morning I left for England. I *was* away for two weeks, so..."

I nod. "Yes, I expect that's it. I just kind of lost the habit of popping upstairs."

"I've been busy too," she says. "I've been out more than usual."

"Been having a lot of doctor's appointments?" I snigger.

"Tom *told* you!" she says, flashing the whites of her eyes at me.

I nod. "I was a bit surprised to be learning the intimate details of your life from Tom," I say. "But, well, I can hardly complain; if I can't be bothered to come up two flights of steps... Anyway, tell me."

"Well..." she says, licking her lips, flicking her hair back and clearly relishing the story. "He's a doctor, he's very, very cute, he speaks wonderful English – thank God – he's good in bed..."

"Thank God he's *good in bed?*" I ask, grinning.

"No, the English... well, yeah, both. Anyway, he's the slowest man

43

to, you know, *come,* that I've ever met."

I frown. "And for you girls that's a *good thing*, right?"

She nods. "Sure is!" she says.

I pull a face and shrug. "More than ten minutes of foreplay and I'm bored," I say.

Jenny laughs and flicks her hair back again. "Men!" she says. "Tom said the exact same thing. You're all the same!"

"Except Doctor Sex," I say.

Jenny blushes and flicks her hair yet again. "Except Doctor Sex."

"So Jenny has a boyfriend," I say. I suddenly realise I'm supposed to be noticing something here. "What *exactly* has happened to your hair?" I ask.

Jenny bounces the edges of her new haircut against her knuckles, shampoo-ad style and frowns at me. "What's wrong with it?" she asks.

I shake my head. "Nothing," I say. "It looks great. It's just... well, you suddenly look like you fell out of a Garnier advert or something, that's all."

Jenny smirks, blushes slightly, and twists her head as if to demonstrate just how swirly the new hair is. "I kind of forgot about my appearance for a while back there – when I had Sarah, I think. Anyway, I walked into this really posh salon a few weeks ago and said, 'Fix this.' I think it's called coming back to life after having a baby."

I push my lips out and nod appreciatively. "I think it's called cruising your doctor actually," I say. "Anyway, they sure fixed it. It makes you look heaps younger."

"Thanks. I'm not sure how long it will last though. It seems you have to keep going back there if you want it to carry on looking this way."

"The first hit's free," I laugh.

"Exactly," Jenny says. "Only it wasn't. Far from it."

"So how did you meet him anyway? He's not *your* doctor is he?"

Jenny smirks. "He was, for one visit – for thrush of all things. Very romantic! And then he phoned me and asked me on a date – well, it wasn't really a date. We talked for ages and I told him I was having trouble meeting people here and so he asked me out for a drink... and then, well, you know how it goes."

I grimace. "Thrush?" I say. "Gross. So he saw the goods beforehand so to speak?"

Jenny blushes and shrugs coyly.

"Is that allowed anyway?" I ask. "Shagging patients? *Patients with thrush!*"

Jenny laughs. "Well no! That's why I had to find a new doctor. He was very professional about it. We didn't shag to start with."

"Not until the thrush had gone," I say.

"Well... no," Jenny says. "I changed doctors, and the cream worked and... Actually I think the new one is a lesbian. She's all plaid shirts and stretch pants."

"Maybe she'll ask you out as well."

Jenny laughs. "Heaven forbid," she says. "She's about eighty."

"So is it love?" I ask her. "Or just a good time?"

Jenny clears her throat and looks thoughtful. "I'm not sure really," she says, ignoring or missing my Rose Royce reference. "I mean, he's quite unusual, he's a bit, you know, metro-sexual, and he has lovely clothes, always very clean and tidy. It makes a change after all that beer and football and shell-suits with Nick."

"He sounds gay!" I laugh.

Jenny squashes her lips together. "I knew you'd say that, but no, he's very masculine. Not every straight man is a caveman you know. No, he's good looking and fun and great company and good in bed..."

I laugh. "So you *are* in love with him!"

"I'm not that sure I understand the love thing anymore. I mean, I loved Nick, really I did, and he used to give me a black eye every other weekend. So..." She sighs. "I think maybe I don't trust my judgement anymore," she says. "And anyway it's just temporary. I think. Maybe I have commitment issues... anyway, we'll see. Plus, I keep waiting to find out what's wrong with him, you know?"

I laugh. "Yeah, I know that one," I say.

"Anyway, it's just good to have sex to be honest," she says. "And good sex at that. I was worried that my vagina was gonna heal over."

I pull a face. *"Jenny!"* I protest.

"Oooh, never use the V word with a gay man," she says mockingly. "We have to listen to all *your* gruesome details! At any rate, it's good at the moment, so I'm just trying to enjoy it while it lasts."

"Well, I'm intrigued," I say. "I'd like to see him."

Jenny nods and squints. "Yeah, I'd like a second opinion really. I mean he's very sweet, but... Oh, I don't know. I'll arrange a dinner or something so you can meet him and judge for yourself. If it lasts that long."

I frown at her. "You don't sound very convinced."

Jenny shrugs and laughs. "Anyway," she says. "What's up with you and Tom? I mean, I'm assuming that if you've finally remembered my existence it's because you two have had a row."

"That's *so* unfair!" I protest.

"But you have?" she asks.

I shake my head. "It's so not true that I only come and see you when..."

"Tom *told* me," Jenny interjects. "I saw him at the *boulangerie* this morning and asked how things were, and he pulled a face. And now here you are. That's all."

I frown at this news. "This morning, we hadn't *had* a row," I say. "Anyway, it's not really a row."

"But?"

"OK. Ready?"

Jenny nods and settles into her chair. "Ready," she says.

So I tell Jenny about Tom and the gîte. I try not to exaggerate his words, nor to make myself sound better by deforming my own. I'm honestly searching for understanding, not just an ally.

"So you see," I finish. "It just worries me – it seems important to me – that our motives are so different. For me it's about Tom – I don't really give a damn about the gîte. And Tom..."

"Tom doesn't really give a damn about *you*," Jenny says.

I roll my eyes. "I *so* didn't say that," I say.

Jenny nods, seriously. "I know," she says. "I'm just pushing things to extremes to think about them more clearly."

"It's like that Dante character," I say. "You remember?"

Jenny nods. "The serial killer psychopath mafia guy?"

I nod. "Yeah. That'll be the one. Well, *that* was all about Tom's mid-life crisis and his need for change too. He was far more in love with the farm, with the idea of a new life, than he was with anything Dante had to offer."

Jenny nods. "I see what you mean."

"Dante was like a complete package deal," I say. "I'm not sure I *want* to be Tom's life change package."

Jenny frowns, then smiles. "Why not?"

I shrug. "Why not what?"

"Well, if he's the man you love, if it's *all about* him like you say it is, then why *not* be the life change package he needs?"

I laugh. "Yeah, I suppose you have a point."

"And of course it doesn't mean he doesn't *love* you," Jenny says. "It's like Nick. You know he was, well, pretty loaded really. And I used to sit and think – it's a terrible thing to say – but I used to sit and try to work out what I liked about him. And part of it, quite a big part really, was the nice house and the holidays and the car. And sometimes I think that if he'd been some poor skivvy builder I never would have ended up with him."

I grimace. "Ouch," I say.

"But that doesn't mean I didn't love him," Jenny says. "And it doesn't mean I was only with him for the money. It's just that you, you know, have a relationship with the whole thing, the whole package. And that includes love and sex, and how easy they are to get on with, but also lifestyle, holidays and house, and blah-dy-blah. What I mean is... no, I'm not quite sure *what* I mean."

She pulls a face and frowns, then smiles and looks at me intently. "Yes I do! What I mean, is that you'd have to have a computer for a brain to be able to separate each bit out, to isolate each part of your overall contentment, or lack of..."

I nod. "Yeah, I kind of see what you mean," I say. "So, say Tom's motivation is sixty-percent the gîte and forty-percent me and mine is the other way around – does it really matter?"

Jenny shrugs. "Well yeah," she says. "Not if you're happy with it. That's what I would say."

I nod and smile. "Wise words," I say.

"It's like people with, you know, toy boys or sugar daddies. People get so self-righteous about it all." She shakes her head and then sips her tea. "But I always think, what does it matter? As long as everyone's happy. People leave all the time because of shit lifestyle, because the husband never gets up from in front of the telly, because there's always too much debt; shit like that breaks up relationships every day. If you can't get the things you need in a relationship, then you fuck off. So what's so wrong with enjoying being with someone because they *do* give you the things you need? Including, in some cases, *money*."

"I suppose so," I say, doubtfully.

"And just because one person supplies money and the other one doesn't, well that doesn't mean that there isn't any love or respect," Jenny says. "That's my point. Surely the whole basis of love *is* the desire to give the person you love whatever they need, whether that be sex, or security, or hard cash?"

"Or a new-life-in-a-box," I say.

Jenny nods. "Exactly!" she says, clapping her hands. "Well, in a gîte. So it's settled."

I grin at her. "You are very wise," I say. "When you try."

Jenny laughs, picks up her mug and peers inside. "Only for other people though," she says. "Not so good at my own shit. More tea vicar?"

I hand her my mug. "More tea!" I say.

Jenny's right of course, and my anger slips away, and suddenly I'm left wondering quite why I was angry in the first place. But then, as she makes the tea one last thought does cross my mind – that if sixty percent of Tom's equation *is* the gîte, then what happens if it *doesn't* work out? Then and only then will we find out if the forty percent that remains is enough to keep us together. And that *doesn't* strike me as an entirely irrational worry.

Uh Oh!

When I get back downstairs to our flat, Tom is being chirpy. He doesn't really do *sorry*, not even sorry-lite, the, *I'm sorry you're upset,* kind of sorry that placates without accepting any personal responsibility. But he does a great, *let's-change-the-subject-and-pretend-it-never-happened* act, and when he makes that effort – for it clearly costs him quite a lot to do so – I do my best to take it as an apology and let whatever is happening go.

"Hey, if we found the husband, would that mean we could buy the place?" he asks me excitedly as I step back into the flat.

I shake my head, a little stunned by his energy levels. "Sorry?" I say. "If we found a husband *what?*"

"Chantal's husband, Jean. If we found him, would that mean we could buy the gîte, or would it make it more complicated?"

I push my lips out and give a Gallic shrug. "No idea. It's not likely though is it? I mean, if the police haven't found him. Anyway, he could be dead."

"Well," Tom says. "I was looking on the net for places to promote the place. And I found a hill-walking forum that mentions *Chateauneuf d'Entraunes*, and there was a post by him. By *Jean.Ancey@wanadoo.fr.*"

"Yeah?"

Tom wrinkles his nose. "It's from 2004, so it's before he disappeared. I don't suppose the email works anymore anyway."

"If it does, it'll be Chantal picking it up," I say.

"Exactly, but anyway, that got me thinking so I Googled him. There are only three others on the web that I could see – Ancey seems quite rare. There's a politician, so that won't be him, and there's a BMW dealer in Los Angeles and a satellite dish installer in Italy."

"The BMW dealer doesn't sound likely," I say. "But I suppose he could have run off with some Italian floozy to install satellite dishes."

"Well, I emailed them both anyway," he says. "I sent fake business enquiries, asking them how long they have been established; I joined that hill-walking thing too. Seemed like a good idea."

"You? Hill-walking?" I laugh.

Tom winks at me. "You'd be surprised what I'm capable of," he says.

At the exact moment he says this, his computer makes an *Uh Oh,* sound. It would be cute were it not the *you have a message* signal from the Recon chat sites. Leathermen.com, bikermen.com, bondagemen.com... I've checked them all out at one time or another, sometimes through boredom, sometimes through desperation. I know the little, *Uh Oh,* sound only too well.

"What's that?" I ask.

Tom frowns and peers at the screen. "I'm working on the website," he says vaguely.

"The *Uh Oh* noise," I say. "It's Recon."

"Oh that," Tom says, casually. "Yeah, I was just, erm, chatting to someone."

I nod. "Yeah?" I say. "Anyone I know?" I'm trying not to sound like a desperate housewife here. I think I'm failing.

"Nah, I don't think so," Tom says, forcing a disinterested tone of voice.

I frown and swallow, trying to decide whether to pursue the issue. "Who then?" I eventually ask.

"Someone *I* know," Tom replies pedantically.

"OK," I say, moving to his side on the sofa. "You had better show me."

Tom swallows, glances sideways at me and apparently realising that there's no escape, sighs and switches to the web browser.

"Hot butt!" the most recent message says. *"When can I fill your hole?"*

I raise an eyebrow and look at Tom. "Nice," I say. *"Sophisticated."*

"I sent him one of the dirty photos you took," Tom says, apparently deciding to brazen it out.

I nod. We spent the previous weekend playing around with the digital camera. I didn't think the end result was destined to be sent to all and sundry. "Oh good!" I say sarcastically.

"Huh," Tom says. "I knew it, and now you're jealous, and you're going to be in a huff all evening."

I frown at him. I haven't even started to react yet. I haven't even the first inkling of how I might feel about this.

"I was gonna tell him," Tom says. "I was just about to tell him that I'm married and that no-one fills my hole without my husband's approval."

I nod, perplexed. "And that's supposed to what? *Reassure* me?"

Tom sighs deeply and with a theatrical flick of the wrist, closes the chat window with *hungry-tool-brighton*, and says, "If you're determined to make this into a drama, go ahead."

I stand. I'm still feeling pretty much nothing. Not anger yet, though I can sense it coming. No real jealousy, though it's probably not far off either. No, for the moment, I just feel numb. It seems to me that Tom is being provocative, and yet somehow blaming me for reacting. I need to walk away – to be on my own to think out a reasonable attitude to this new data without Tom prodding and poking, manipulating my reactions. I don't want to react blindly to the provocation. Otherwise, my onboard computer says, it could *really* be a biggy.

"My fault," I say, as I put on my coat. "Sorry. Of course."

"Oh don't go out in a *huff*," Tom says. "It's not what you think. I was just..."

"I DON'T..." I interrupt him; my voice comes out in a shout, so I pause, calm it, and then continue, "I don't want to talk about it with you right now." I manage to close the front door quietly behind me.

As I walk down to and then along the seafront, still wet from the rain, I turn the problem over in my mind, probing it from different angles.

Intelligent thoughts don't come easily, and the best process I find seems to be to think about how other people I know would react to *their* partners sending naked pictures out over the net and discussing the filling of holes. Most of my straight friends would be outraged, offended, jealous, and more than anything disappointed in something I reckon most of them would find a bit pathetic – a bit distasteful.

Most of my gay friends would say, I think, that it was harmless fun – mere text porn with a stranger in a moment of boredom. Unless it was happening to them of course, in which case it would be cause for drama if not actual divorce.

I slip and slide down to the edge of the Med and start to throw pebbles into the smooth, undulating sea – the lights from the prom' are reflecting on the waxy surface.

After what seems like a few minutes but, my rumbling stomach tells me, is more like an hour, I start to walk home. I'm still not quite sure what I'm going to say, but it seems I need to ask Tom if this is fantasy browsing, or something else. And I need to work out whether Tom is still the stable adult with whom I thought I was building a relationship; or whether he has revealed himself to be – *God knows...* an adolescent sex junky, always trolling the net for something new, something better? A short term affair, only in it for the adventure of opening a gîte? I'm feeling angry too of course, but mainly it's his attempt at pinning the blame for the "huff" on me that runkles the most. That really seems unfair.

The Pot And The Kettle

By the time I get up on Wednesday, Tom has long gone. Wednesday is his morning at the swimming pool, but today he has headed out more efficiently than usual. I can't blame him – nothing was resolved yesterday. I don't think either of us had the energy to face round two, or three, or whichever round it would have been, so we both respected the tacit desire to make it to bed without a fist fight by saying not one word that wasn't essential to each other.

This morning, when I open up the laptop, mug of coffee in hand, Tom's Recon page is still onscreen, and I think for a moment that he's rubbing my nose in it – until that is, I read the text in the middle of the screen: *Your recon profile has been deleted. We're sorry to see you go.* That's clear enough for me and close enough to an apology and as I shower, I start to feel that if the Recon thing isn't of any consequence – as Tom is clearly trying to demonstrate – then the bad vibes are probably at least *partly* my fault. Maybe I overreacted a bit – it has been known!

It's a sunny day – icy cold in the shade, but with a clear blue sky – and as I wander through the old town towards the *Nice Etoile* shopping centre I rack my brain for something I can buy for Tom's coming birthday. It's hard to think about shopping for gifts; though my anger has faded, I'm still not feeling particularly loving. But it has to be done; failure to get a birthday gift, would, as the advert says, turn a drama into a crisis, or a crisis into a drama, or whichever is supposed to be worse.

Workmen are out pulling down the barriers around the road works for the new tramway and the town is starting to look human again. On top of this it must be one of the rare weekends in the Nice tourist calendar when there are no carnivals, no bank holidays over the border, and no conferences: the streets are deserted, and it feels unusual and almost luxurious to be able to wander so easily though the streets.

After an hour or so of browsing, I find a very cool parka affair for

Tom. I think that it's the perfect thing for him to wear as he walks his dog along the ridges around the gîte, and the symbolism of saying, *"Yes, we're still going to do this,"* and *"Yes, you can have your dog,"* strikes me as perfect.

I head back with the huge carrier bag, through the Cours Saleya flower-stands and on to where they are hosing down the closing vegetable market. The sun is so wonderfully warm that I hesitate in front of a big pavement café, the most gay-friendly of them all – La Civette – hoping for a table to come free, but it's lunchtime and everyone is eating leisurely, so I give up and decide to have my coffee at home. Just as I turn to leave, I notice a flashy Italian looking guy in sunglasses waving my way. I check right, left and behind, but, no; he's definitely waving at me.

As I reach his table he takes off his shades. I swallow hard. "Hello!" I say with a grin. "I didn't recognise you, what with the suit and the sunglasses."

He grins at me. "Can't wear the uniform all the time," he says. "Shame huh? It would be so much easier. Please, have a seat."

I look around the terrace and then shrug. "You sure you don't mind?" I say. "It is very full today."

Ricardo grins and gives me an open handed gesture. "Please," he says. "I have to go soon anyway."

I grab a spare chair from a nearby table and join him, stuffing the bag under my seat.

He's finishing off an omelette and salad. "Sorry," he says, wiping bread around the plate. "I hope you don't mind."

"No," I say, shaking my head. I cast around for a waiter, but they are all studiously avoiding eye contact in the way that only French waiters know how. As I scan from left to right, I steal a glance at Ricardo – the sequel.

His suit is dark brown with a turquoise pin stripe – it hangs beautifully, settling in silky folds. He's wearing a deep pink shirt also with turquoise stripes – open necked – and shiny pointy city-shoes. The overall effect is elegant and fashionable and maybe just a bit over the top. He looks like he should be hosting a chat show or something.

I feel a pang of jealousy at his ability to dress like that and pull it off. You need exotic looks to get away with something like that, I decide. He smiles at me broadly. It's that incredible face-cracking grin again, a smile so deep that I can feel it in the back of my head.

I bare my teeth and make a mock-scratching gesture. "Lettuce," I say with a wink, unable to quite believe how different he looks out of uniform.

Ricardo pulls a funny face and scratches the green from his front tooth. "Thanks," he says. "You look different too," he adds, as if he can hear my thoughts.

I feel myself blushing, I'm not quite sure why. "That sun's hot!" I say, vaguely, looking away, pretending to look for a waiter again. Then I add, brazenly, surprising myself, "Yeah, well, I can't wear bike gear all the time either. Shame huh?"

Ricardo shrugs one shoulder and smirks at me. "You look fine," he says, half closing his eyes.

I restrain a frown, and then turn and wave to a waiter as a welcome distraction. "Oh!" I say. *"S'il vous plaît?"* But the waiter ignores me with studied expertise. "They're incredible here," I say, turning back to Ricardo. But he's standing, pulling a banknote from his wallet and pushing it under the ashtray.

"I'm sorry," he says, shrugging. "I really *do* have to go." He glances at his watch. "I have a..." he cocks his head, *"rendezvous?"*

I nod. "A meeting."

He winks at me and nods and smiles again. "Yes, a meeting. At two."

"Oh, I..." I say, looking up at him and taking his outstretched hand.

He shakes my hand solidly and then keeps hold as he says, "Maybe another time. I'm usually here on Wednesdays. As long as it's sunny."

I nod and say, "Sure," and I start to wonder about the overly long handshake. I notice my heart speeding up again. "I'll keep watch... I mean, a look out... an eye open for you," I say in a confused manner.

Ricardo smiles and releases me, then says with another wink, "I'll keep a look out for you too." And with this he spins and walks away.

I shake my head and finger the ashtray and Ricardo's banknote. I move round to take his seat – it's facing the sun. It's still warm from his arse. I swallow hard and blow a little air between my lips and think, *"What the hell was that?"*

"Autres choses?" the waiter asks, apparently unaware of the change of occupant at Ricardo's table.

"Oui, un café," I tell him, "s'il vous plait." And he grabs the plate, dumps the knife, fork and napkin on it and sweeps away leaving me to sit and think about Ricardo's body language.

The problem, I realise, is that I don't know what his gestures, the long handshake, the eye contact, the face-cracking smile, might mean to a straight guy, to a straight *Colombian* guy – I'm trying to interpret them through my own built-in dictionary, but it doesn't work, because my own vocabulary of male-to-male contact is all about sex and attraction. But straight men presumably do actually meet people they like sometimes, and occasionally they must decide to make an effort to befriend them, and so maybe Ricardo's winks and smiles are just innocent signals within a language – a foreign language – of heterosexual male bonding?

I realise, I think for the first time in my life, just how vague my grasp of that language, those rites, actually is.

"Maybe I can learn with Ricardo," I think. "Maybe he can be my new, straight friend. I could catch him here, next Wednesday, and we could talk about motorbikes... Maybe we can go on bike rides together. He said his girlfriend isn't keen."

But my dick is stirring at the image in my mind – of Ricardo on the back of my bike – and it forces me to take in the truth of the situation. *"Who am I kidding?"* I think. The answer clearly is – *not even myself.*

And with the realisation that my heart is pounding and that, beneath the table, my dick is distinctly heavier than normal; that I'm blushing and fantasising about a guy I don't know at all, a fireman from *God-knows where*, I start to feel guilty, and so I think of Tom and his gift beneath the chair, and realise that it is a case of the pot calling the kettle black; that his cyber-crimes, put into perspective by my own thought-crimes, really aren't so bad after all.

By the time I get home the Parka strikes me as an insignificant gift. It's probably something to do with my guilt.

Tom is still out, so I check my email and as I sit and stare at the screen, a loving feeling comes over me, and I want, urgently, desperately, to forget it all, to find a gesture magnificent enough to wipe out the recent grumpiness: the arguments about why Tom is living here, his internet chatting, my own unclear thoughts about Ricardo and fidelity.

I want everything back to normal, and I want it that way in time for Tom's birthday. "That's what you have to do," I tell myself. "When things get rough and irritable, when the desire to stray comes on, there are only two choices: walk away and give up, or fight to put the flame back in. And I'm damned if I'm walking away this time."

A flashing advert for weekend breaks on the screen gives me an idea. If Tom needs more fun than he has been getting, then what could be better for his coming birthday than a weekend away? What could be better than for us to forget our stupid arguments and rekindle that loving feeling? Wonderful, wonderful Internet: it takes me less than twenty minutes to find two cheap flights and a dodgy hotel, and by the time Tom walks in the door, the surprise is all fixed.

A Perfect Day

It's the day of the trip, and Tom is proving more difficult to wake up than expected. I smile at his sleeping form and shake my head and place the breakfast tray on the blue metal cabinet beside the bed.

I slither onto the bed beside him and nuzzle his warm neck. "Tom," I say quietly. "I've got a birthday surprise for you, but it involves getting *up!* You *really* have to get up." As I say this Tom pulls a pillow over his head and groans, so I shout, "NOW!" and pummel the bed either side of him until he bounces.

It's not until Tom – still in a daze – has stepped out of the shower into the clothes I have waiting, picked up his ready-packed rucksack, and is being pushed towards the front door, that intrigue starts to penetrate his morning-head. "Where are we going?" he asks. "And why the hell are we going there at seven thirty?"

I wink at him, run a hand down his back, and give him a gentle push forward. "If we don't get a move on," I say, checking my watch, "you'll never find out."

He pauses to look at a package discreetly left by Jenny on the sideboard. "What's that? A gift?" he asks.

"It's from Jenny," I say, "DVDs – English Classic Cinema. You can open it when we get back." It's brutal and a little dismissive of the gift, but there really isn't time for anything else.

On the airport shuttle, Tom grins at me for the first time of the day. "I know where we're going," he declares, then repeats himself in a child's sing-song voice, *"I know where we're going."*

The bus lurches out of the depot, and I grin back. "Don't get overexcited," I say. "It's *not* San Francisco."

Tom shakes his head slowly and beams at me. "I know it isn't," he says confidently.

At Nice airport we check the screens for the departure gate; I will have to give Tom his boarding pass at security, but I'm holding out as long as I can. He scans the screen alongside me, still with a cocky grin that says he has me sussed.

"So, I would say," he says, matter-of-factly, "that it's zone A; somewhere around... gate... twelve... Right?"

I scan the screen for our flight and then shake my head at him. "Nope," I say. "Wrong!"

And then I scan the list to see where Tom thinks we're going – KLM2163 – 8:55 am – Zone A, Gate 12 – Amsterdam.

I swallow hard. "Shit Tom, no," I say. "I told you not to get too excited." I pull his printed boarding pass from my bag.

"No?" he says, starting to unfold the sheet.

I study his reactions. Poor Tom, bless him – the shadow that crosses his face, the twitch downwards of the mouth, the swallowing of the forty percent of his excitement that has turned out to be unnecessary, lasts mere milliseconds. He covers it all up with every ounce of willpower he can muster. But I see it all the same, and I kick myself for not thinking of bloody Amsterdam myself.

Then, mind over body, he slides back into the broadest of grins and hikes his bag onto his shoulder. "Paris!" he exclaims. "Paris is great! Brilliant!"

***

After an uneventful orange-themed low-cost flight, and two rubber-themed high-cost sandwiches, a couple of efficient French trains and a five minute walk, we find ourselves outside the grotty Hotel des Trois Fréres, freed of our bags – left in the lobby.

And we spend a perfect Paris day. It's *the* perfect Paris day. It's the same day that millions of other couples have done before us. It's the same day *Emilie Poulain* did onscreen, seemingly over and over again.

Paris is eternal, the adverts say, and of course they're right – Paris is a stunningly preserved, beautifully maintained jewel of a city. But as we wander along the Seine, our breath rising before us on this icy but thankfully sunny day; as we peer up at the Eiffel tower or drink cups of coffee served by overbearing white-shirted waiters and wander past the boating pond in the Tuileries, it does strike me that the eternal nature of Paris is a double-edged sword. The city may be better preserved than any other European city, the architecture may be a historical diamond in Europe's crown; but if you have ever been to

Paris before – no matter when in the last sixty years – then the sense of déjà vu in every visual, culinary or cultural experience is simply overpowering. And as we wander along, enjoying it immensely, I can't help but think that, like any permanent exhibition, Paris is a city you only ever need to visit once. I'm hoping Tom doesn't feel the same way.

We have fun of course, in the understated gay district – le Marais – eyeing up the cute French boys. And boy *are* they cute. We peer in at the outrageously priced clothes shops, and wander, wide-eyed around Rob Leatherstore – more S&M museum than clothing shop – before treating ourselves, giggling like adolescents, to a set of rubber balls on a string. They're red, washable and hygienic and range from gob-stopper size to terrifying-tennis-ball. By the time we spill onto the street, good humouredly arguing about who gets to inflict the balls on whom, we both have half-baked stiffies.

The cheap room, when we finally get to check-in, is architecturally gorgeous with big bay windows and three-meter ceilings. But of course this is Paris, a city where you truly get what you pay for – or a little less – and so in every other way it is abysmal: we haven't paid enough for anything else.

The carpet is threadbare, the paint is peeling, the shower is down the hall, and the bed sags in the middle. But neither of us cares in the slightest; in fact, if anything, it all just adds to the fun of the trip. *"Thank God Tom isn't a chic-queen,"* I think, as we dump our stuff and run, laughing, back down the stairs ready for our night on the town.

The rap is that it's impossible to get a good, reasonably priced meal in Paris, so we're thoroughly chuffed when Tom's touristy first pick turns out to be a good one. The Café Beaubourg with its soaring columns and trendy décor, with its windows overlooking the steel plumbing of the Pompidou Centre, looks, to my eye, far too chic to be promising; but the second we step inside and are greeted by a grinning waitress (yes, *grinning*, in *Paris*), I think we might have struck lucky after all.

The food – we both choose grilled jumbo prawns – is speedy and excellent, and the Croatian waitress returns to smile and chatter at us throughout the meal, telling us amongst other things that her brother is gay, *"too."* This causes Tom, once she has gone, to whisper, "Jesus! Is it stamped across our foreheads or something?" We toast to Tom's birthday, eat a sickening heap of profiteroles, and then, stuffed and happy, head on for the next leg of our Parisian adventure.

The first gay bar we find in the Marais is the Quetzal. I remember it vaguely from some distant visit to Paris, and am again stunned at how unchanging France is. American and English cultures are so dominated by novelty and fashion; France manages to just chug along as the rest of the world repeatedly implodes and reinvents itself. However, once inside the Quetzal the idea of change starts to seem quite appealing. Though the barman is smiley and welcoming, there are only five guys in the bar, and none of them look particularly happy, well or wise.

Tom flashes the whites of his eyes at me, takes a gulp of his beer and grabs a free sheet from beside the door. "I think we might be needing some alternative addresses," he declares. "This *really* isn't Amsterdam."

We drink our beers quickly, and – for some reason feeling a little naughty – shuffle out the door.

"How low energy was *that?*" Tom says outside.

I turn the map around as I try to find my bearings. "Must be something they put in the beer," I mutter. "Anyway let's hope it's better in the next place."

As we near the Cox, there are so many people on the pavement that I wonder for a moment if they aren't having some kind of private function, but as we push through the fifty smokers outside, and squeeze intimately past another hundred leathered bodies *inside*, it transpires that, tonight, the Cox is simply, *the* place to be.

"Wow," Tom says. *"How* many cute men?"

And they are, without a doubt, the prettiest bunch of leathery, bearded men I have ever seen. "Tell me about it," I say.

"Wow! I'd do just about *any* of them," Tom says, making me frown in mock outrage. As we reach the bar, I tap him on the shoulder and say, "Check out the bar-staff."

There are three men working the bar: two identical Tweedle Dee / Tweedle Dum boys with tattoos and beards and a third steroid-pumped hair-bear with pierced nips, leather jeans and a Sam Browne belt. They are all taking themselves very seriously and pouting so much they look like post face-lift Cher, which strikes me as a terrible waste of so much work at the gym. With some difficulty, I order two pints from Tweedle Dum. He's so terribly caught up in his own aura that he's unable to lean towards me far enough to actually hear me, so I'm forced to transmit the message in mime. Once he seemingly has understood – and it's hard to know really because he neither smiles nor speaks, but sweeps instead, dramatically away – I hand Tom a twenty Euro note before pushing through to the toilets, wondering exactly *why* this bar is so popular, and the other with the friendly service, so empty. Maybe Parisians thrive on rudeness?

The urinals are so close together it seems impossible to use the third stall, so I wait until two are free and occupy the farthest. But the second I start to piss, a guy – another man-mountain in chaps-over-jeans and a Lucky Strike motorcycle jacket – squashes in beside me. I move as far sideways as I can, but I can still see that, a) he isn't pissing, and, b) he's looking at *me* pissing. Maybe he's searching for inspiration.

As I squeeze my way out past his butt – and the size of the place is such that it really *is* a squeeze – he distinctly says, in an angular foreign accent, "Very nice."

Back in the bar, Tom has lined up two pints each. "It's only happy hour for another ten minutes," he tells me, "So I thought I might as well."

I grin and take a huge gulp of beer. "You did good," I say.

In the corner of the bar a DJ is playing some very danceable electro and I watch him groove to the mix for a while, but when he looks up at me and I smile and nod approval, he does the same pouty thing as the muscle barman.

"What's with the Parisian pout?" I ask Tom.

He frowns at me.

"Mr Muscle," I nod at the barman, "and the DJ – they both have the same pout."

Tom glances at one and then the other. The DJ rewards us by sucking in his cheeks and pursing his lips even further.

Tom laughs. "Oh give them a break," he says. "Even I look like that sometimes." He swivels back to face me, and mimics the DJ.

"You do?" I say.

"Yeah," he says. "When I'm constipated."

I snigger and have to spit my beer back in the glass. Some of it goes up my nose. "They look more like they're trying to keep something *in* to me," I laugh.

Tom winks at me. "Maybe they are," he says. "That *Rob* shop is just around the corner. Maybe they are all trying to keep those balls in."

"I like it here though," I say, checking out the other faces in the crowd, most of which are smiling and animated.

"Yeah, it's a *great* place," Tom says enthusiastically. "It feels like Brighton after work."

I nod and grin. "Cuter boys though," I say. "The French did so well in the genetic lottery. It makes me sick."

Someone squeezes behind me. Space is tight – this I know – but this particular squeezing past still feels more intimate than necessary. The guy's hands distinctly grasp my hips as he pushes by, causing me to wrinkle my brow in amused concern. As he moves on through the crowd and into view, I see that it's my neighbour in the motorbike jacket – the guy from the toilets. Now that he's more than an inch away I'm able to check him out, and I realise that he's pretty hot. His arse is pert, his chaps are supple and shiny and his jacket is open revealing a muscular looking, lightly furred chest. And above all he's smiling – at me. *But why?*

At the beginning of the second pint, Tom notices him too. "Don't look now," he laughs, "but two thirds of the way around the bar, beefy blond guy, red and black bike jacket."

"Yeah?"

"He's been cruising me for ages," he declares happily.

I open my mouth to say, *"Me* actually," but remembering that it's Tom's birthday, I say nothing and simply smile.

"What *is* it about being in a couple?" Tom asks. "I mean, when I'm single, guys like that never look at me."

I nod. "Yeah," I say, glancing over at Lucky Strike – who winks very obviously at me. "I know what you mean."

When happy hour ends, the crowd, including Lucky Strike, disperse and the ambiance becomes relatively chilled. Most of the people who remain seem to be couples. When Tom comes back from the toilets, he grins broadly and kisses me – a surprise. He's not generally one for public displays of affection.

"What's that for?" I ask slipping a hand into the rear pocket of his jeans.

"Oh nothing in particular," he says. "For my birthday present maybe; it's really good to be somewhere else for a change."

I smile at him and pinch his arse through the fabric. "Yeah," I say. "I thought the change would do us good."

Tom nods towards the door. "Talking of which..." he says. "Shall we?"

The Bear's Den is a small neighbourhood bar, with standing room for maybe twenty people and a few chairs outside under an awning. On reflection, there's probably only standing room for *ten*. The big muscles of Cox are replaced here by beer bellies. *Big* beer bellies. Tom's wrinkled nose tells me what he thinks about the place, but because the bearded barman – who is as huge as his customers – serves us immediately, we order two halves and retreat to the farthest corner of the room to watch.

"It's a *local* bar for *local* people," Tom sniggers, and it's true, people are looking at us as if we just climbed out of a rocket.

"I don't think we're *big* enough," I whisper.

Tom sips his beer. "Not obese, you mean?" he murmurs.

"Tom!" I say.

"Well, call a spade a spade," he says

I drop my mouth in horror. "You can't say that either!" I laugh. "That's worse."

"Tom frowns at me. "Why?" he asks, genuinely confused.

"It's racist."

"Oh!" Tom giggles, covering his mouth. "I always thought it was to do with, you know, spades and shovels. Anyway, you know what I mean," he continues in a whisper. "All this eroticising fat – it just strikes me as an excuse for laziness really."

I frown at him and scan the bar once again. It's true that most of the guys here probably *would* be diagnosed as clinically obese. But then, these days, so would most of the straight men in Birmingham. "I find it a bit of a relief," I say. "A break from all the Stallone lookalikes."

"Don't tell me you'd rather look at *these* guys?" Tom says.

I gesture for him to *keep it down*. I know no one can hear us, but the conversation is making me nervous. If nothing else, our hushed tones are drawing attention to ourselves. A grey haired guy with a *humungous* belly crammed into a paw-print t-shirt and khaki, military combat-pants is definitely looking our way.

I smile at him but he just frowns and looks away. "Let's drink up," I say to Tom. "We can carry on this conversation outside. I feel like I've invaded someone else's patch. I don't think the bears are that friendly."

"So you think they're cute?" Tom asks as we negotiate our way to the next venue.

"Who?"

"The fatties?"

"No," I say. "Not at all. But I like that they exist. I respect their right to eroticise something other than the Jean-Claude Van Damme model that we're all somehow supposed to look like."

"Humph," Tom says. "You're just pretending to be politically correct. But you don't find that kind of lard appealing any more than I do."

I nod half-heartedly and grab his elbow and steer him across the street. Our breath is rising in the cold night air. "You're right, I don't – though actually, big muscle guys don't really do it for me either. But I really *do* like that they exist. I'm being honest."

"I don't get it," Tom says, then, "Fuck, it's cold, isn't it?"

"Yeah," I say. "It is. You know how women these days have all these body-image problems because every woman the media idealises spends her evenings vomiting? Well, the fact that bears exist somehow reveals that the other model – the gym-bunny one – is just *one* model; it opens a route to feeling happy about who you are, no matter what you look like."

"If you say so," Tom says, squeezing between two cars and joining the pavement.

"It just means that it's OK to not spend all your time trying to look like Schwarzy," I say. I pause and nod at the door to Wolf. "Looks like the next stop," I say.

"Well, we know what the bears are like," Tom says. "Time to throw ourselves to the wolves."

Wolf is a much bigger space than the other bars, and interestingly the men – lone, predatory, hungry looking – do meet a whole range of wolfy adjectives.

I grab a couple of stools and wait for Tom to return with drinks and think about the whole body-image thing, and it strikes me that we set impossible targets for ourselves – we're all supposed to be well-read intellectuals but with the bodies of nineteenth century foundry-workers and the incomes of eighties city traders. And there just aren't enough hours in a life to do them all.

As the moon rises, the wolves gather, inexorably filling the room with rapacious, leather clad testosterone. Though the sexual tension is exciting, the solitary nature of the guys around us depresses me a little. No one seems to be having much fun, and Parisian pouts abound. But Tom is enjoying himself – he grins like a kid in a sweetshop as he compares this guy to that guy. My jealousy is peeping through a crack in the door, but for the moment I have it under control. When I can't wait any longer, I thread my way through the crowd to the rear of the bar. But as I start to descend the stairwell, and as the light behind me starts to fade, I realise that I have mistaken the backroom for the toilets.

When I get back, Tom is looking puzzled. "People keep wandering off and then coming back," he says. "I think there's another bar."

I grin and nod. "Yeah, I found it," I say. "There's a backroom downstairs."

Tom's face lights up. "A Parisian backroom," he says sexily. "And?"

I shrug. "I *didn't* go down."

Tom is already gulping down his beer. "Come on," he says, wiping his lips and standing.

I frown. "I'm not really..."

But Tom has grabbed my hand and is already pushing off through the crowd. "Oh come on!" he says. "You can't miss the opportunity to see a Parisian backroom."

The blue lighting downstairs is low. At some intersections the light is *so* low you have to feel your way around the corner. When my hand touches an arm tucked in a recess, I shriek.

"Try to shriek in manly way," Tom whispers, laughter in his voice. "I know it's hard, but..."

"Yeah, well," I say. "Body parts on the right – beware."

Tom pushes on my shoulders and we advance a few feet. "God!" he whispers in my ear. "He had his dick out. I touched his dick."

"Nice," I say.

At the end of the series of rooms my eyes start to adjust to the lack of photons and I start to make out... yes, that's it, two guys... making out. A short one with his jeans around his ankles, and a tall skinny guy in a leather shirt.

"Um," Tom says quietly, sliding behind me and nuzzling my ear. "Live porn. I love these places... there's something, I don't know, something almost tribal about it."

"Yeah," I say thoughtfully. The atmosphere is electric with sex. No doubt thanks to the beer; my moral censor is keeping schtum.

"For someone who didn't want to come," Tom sniggers, sliding a hand down my jeans. "You sure feel like someone who... wants to come."

I snort.

Tom slides a hand under my sweatshirt and fumbles for my nipple, and then with the other he twists my head around and forces his tongue into my mouth. "Kiss me," he murmurs.

The kiss and the sensation of his hand sliding across my chest makes me melt and under the influence of beer and whatever chemical is released in the brain during arousal, I forget pretty much where I am – the whole thing just feels irresistibly erotic.

Tom releases my nipple and starts fumbling with my belt. "No!" I say. I think I sound fairly convincing.

"Let me do..." Tom says, carrying on regardless, "what I want to do."

"But..."

"Shhh," he says, sliding his fingers around my dick. "It's my birthday, remember?"

It feels great, but when he forces my jeans lower and my dick springs out, I become hyper aware of the fact that we're kind of in public here.

"No one's here," Tom says, anticipating my protests. "Except those two – and they're much too busy."

I glance over at the couple opposite. The shorter of the two now turned around, and the other guy is starting to fuck him.

Tom kisses me again, and his tongue in my mouth, his hand on my dick, his fingers on my nipple, it all conspires to produce a rush of adrenalin. My eyes flicker half open, my dick pulsates. "Oh God that's good," I exclaim.

"I want to fuck you," Tom says.

"Jees Tom," I say, "Not *here!* Can't we..."

"Here," he interrupts.

Tom rarely wants to be the active partner, and he rarely acts this dominant. And the terrible truth is that I like it. I like it so much that I don't fight it. Instead, I pull a condom from my jacket pocket and hand it to him. I feel small and held, and dominated. And it feels surprisingly good. And so, for the first time in my life, I fuck in public. It's not very public, I tell myself. There are only a couple of guys lurking in the shadows, and the couple opposite are now way too busy – thrusting and groaning – to notice us. But something about the taboo of the whole thing makes it – terrifyingly – by far the best fuck I have ever had.

As Tom starts to pump into me, I close my eyes and shudder, a little at the cold, but mainly with ecstatic arousal. Tom nuzzles my neck and pulls me tight with his arm. "Oh God," he says.

A movement to the right catches the corner of my eye, but I forcibly remind myself that we're in Paris, that we don't know anyone. Tom fumbles for the other nipple and then spits in his hand and starts to rub my dick. Just for a second, he freezes. It's almost imperceptible, but it's enough to make me open my eyes.

The Lucky Strike Viking is standing less than two feet away with his jacket open and his dick hanging out. He grins at me and says, simply, "Can I?"

I open my mouth to say, "No," but Tom covers it with a hand and replies for me. "Yes," he says. And I let him. I feel owned. I feel liberated of responsibility.

Lucky Strike steps forward and slides two hands under my sweatshirt, and starts to play with my nipples. Tom removes his and slides it around my waist again, pulling me closer. I swallow and think that this is crazy; that I should stop it.

But having two men playing with my body – Tom inside me, his arms around me pulling me tight, his tongue slithering between my ear and my mouth, and the magnificent Viking fiddling with my nips, is almost too much to bear. My body starts to tremble.

Lucky Strike – his hands still on my nipples – sinks to his knees, and he slips his mouth around my dick. I flinch, but Tom says, "No. Let him."

I wonder vaguely if it's safe and tense up, and then as the mystery man starts to deep throat me, I close my eyes and shudder and give in.

Tom starts to thrust harder and *Lucky* continues to slide my dick down his throat. *"So deep throat does exist,"* I think. I always somehow thought it was a myth; or something only porn stars or people born without gag-reflexes could do.

The sex washes over me, and the result is drug-like. My eyelids flutter half open: I feel used and abused and at the same time dominating, as if the whole world is here for my pleasure, just to satisfy me. And because Tom is seemingly masterminding it all, pushing it forward for his own birthday pleasure, I feel lifted of the moral responsibility for whatever happens next. And though there is a vague shadow lurking in the corner of my mind, ever watchful and already promising to criticise all of this as slutty and unbelievable, the experience is so sublime, so like some kind of religious revelation, or as Tom says, some tribal ritual, that I find myself powerless to do anything but submit, and so, in semi-public, in the middle of Paris, with a growing group of onlookers, I shriek and groan my way into the longest, most pumping, most Earth-shattering orgasm of my life.

Tom comes mere seconds after me, grunting loudly in my ear. Lucky releases my dick and my nipples and stands before me, grinning from ear to ear. "Nice," he says, simply, wiping his lips. Then, surprisingly, his links his hands behind Tom's back and hugs us both, resting his head on my shoulder for a while. And then he steps back and vanishes into the shadows.

"Wow," Tom sighs, buttoning up. "Now there's a birthday present."

"Yeah, well... Never let it be said that I cramp your style," I say, pulling up my own trousers, suddenly hyper aware of where I am and what I have just done, and determined to cast responsibility for it as Tom's.

We return to the bar for another drink, then I suggest we return to the Cox. I need, for some reason, to get out of here.

The Cox is still apparently being run by the placebo group of an antidepressant drug trial, but the place is now as empty as Quetzal, so we go there instead. At least we can chat to the smiling barman.

Finally, at three a.m., we head back to the hotel through the almost-deserted streets. I still can't quite work out what I feel. Maybe I'm just too drunk to work it out. There are moments when everything you believe about yourself, everything that morality teaches you to believe about everyone else, collides head on with the empirical fact of everyday life. I've avoided anything except one on one sex pretty much my whole life. But the truth is that the sex I have just had was simply mind-blowing. It wasn't lovemaking – which has its own codes and its own wonderful qualities. But in purely sexual terms, well, it's incomparable; it's on a whole different plane of experience, a plane that I just didn't know was possible without drugs.

And yet, a sickly unease has taken over my stomach. I'm pretty sure it's guilt, but guilt about which crime? Surely no one was hurt, no one was lied to... But yes, that's the feeling. All-pervasive, sickening guilt. We humans! We're such strange creatures.

It's still Tom's birthday, and he is happily tripping along beside me, so it's clearly not the moment for any philosophical debate, so I just smile back and stumble on. But I can't help but wonder – where do we go from here? I can't help but feel that something has shifted, not only in my self-image, but also in our relationship, in the power balance between us. And I can't work out yet whether that's good or bad.

Post-Mortem

I have never been much of a believer in blackouts – those supposedly alcohol-induced memory lapses. Every time in my life anyone has claimed not to remember doing something, it has always seemed to have more to do with convenience and guilt than alcohol *per se*. But this morning, as I wake up, as I notice first my pounding headache, then the desert dryness of my mouth, then finally Tom's sweaty stomach against my back, and his voice, *"Ugh, the price you pay for a wild night huh?"* I honestly *don't* remember how we got back to the hotel.

"Um," I mumble, trying to piece together rare fragments of the evening. A bar full of big guys, another full of cute guys, and now a hangover and a sick feeling in my stomach. It doesn't, somehow, quite add up.

"What time did we get back?" I ask. "I don't remember anything much. *God* my head hurts."

"Four-ish I think," Tom says. "Mine hurts too – bad beer."

"Um," I mumble. "I remember – salty. The beer was salty in the last place. Where *was* the last place?"

"Quetzal," Tom says. "But the salty beer was in... Wolf was it? The Lucky Strike bar anyway."

I cough to clear my throat. "Lucky Strike?"

Tom slides an arm around me and pulls me tight. "Yeah, you remember the Lucky Strike guy I hope? He was the kind of the highlight."

"Lucky Strike," I repeat. It means something to me but I can't say yet quite what.

"The guy's jacket – the German guy. I think he was German anyway. He was wearing a bike jacket with a Lucky Strike logo."

In my mind's eye, I see the Lucky Strike logo, and then moving out from that the jacket, the chaps, the blond haired chest, the face, the body, the lips...

"Ugh," I groan painfully, as the image of part of *my* body between those lips comes back to me. "Oh God," I groan.

Tom sniffs and coughs. "That's what you said last night," he mumbles, an amused tone in his voice. "Over and over again. I don't think I've ever seen you so excited, you were trembling all..."

"Tom," I interrupt. "Later, OK?"

Tom snorts. "Sure," he says. "Whatever."

Over breakfast in the tiny café opposite the hotel, jumpstarted into consciousness by double espressos, I silently remember everything.

"You OK?" Tom asks, his mouth full of croissant. "You seem funny."

"Hangover," I say. But it's not the whole truth.

Tom nods. "OK," he says.

"I feel funny about last night," I add – an understatement. "I couldn't remember when I woke up, and now I do, and, well, I'm not quite sure what to think about it."

Tom frowns at me and sips his coffee. "Are you angry with me? Do you think I made you do..."

"No," I interrupt. "No – I wanted to do everything I did. But the drunken me and the sober me don't always agree about what's good, what's constructive."

Tom rolls his eyes. "You worry too much," he says.

I shrug. "You're probably right."

"Anyway, constructive for what?" Tom asks.

I shrug. "For us."

"For us? It's not like we cheated on each other."

I nod slowly. "I guess not," I say. "But sober me doesn't think that random drunken sex with strangers in darkrooms is the strongest foundation for a long term relationship," I say. "Plus I just feel slutty really. Good old Christian guilt."

Tom shrugs.

"You don't think that at all then?" I ask, a little jealous of his peace of mind.

"I thought it was fun," he says. "But I guess I don't really believe in the whole constructing thing anyway so maybe it doesn't affect me so much."

I frown and sip my coffee. "What do you mean you don't *believe* in it?"

"Well... it's a hefty thing, isn't it?" he says. "All that stuff about building stability and lifelong partners – it's just about having kids really. It's like you say, a Christian thing. It doesn't seem to have much to do with *our* lives if you're honest."

I rub a hand over my forehead, which feels clammy, and then over my eyes. I stare out of the window for a while. I watch a Muslim woman in a headscarf opposite, she's begging, her face racked with a theatrical demonstration of her suffering. The weeping-moaning-whining technique – it's supposed to provoke sympathy but it makes me just want to tell her to get a grip. Eventually I turn back to face Tom, wrinkle my nose and say, "I see what you're saying, but surely we're allowed to have long term relationships too, right?"

Tom tips his head sideways. "Look, I don't have a very romantic view of things, it's probably better not to..." His voice fades out.

I finish my coffee and wave at the waiter and then point at the cup. Through a couple of circular gestures I transmit the concept of *same again* and turn back to Tom. "No go on," I say. "We never talk like this."

Tom raises one shoulder in a half shrug and sighs. "It's just, you know, if you're honest, well, the probability that we'll be together in twenty years time, it's pretty low really, isn't it? Gay men don't really do that stuff. I mean there are no kids binding us together. Even ten years is pretty good going. Even five."

I nod slowly and scratch my head. "I see," I say. I stare back out at the street. The beggar is shuffling on down the hill. I think of the words of a shrink – the first shrink I ever saw, before I came out. They were the words that had pushed me rebelliously into finally dealing with my sexuality. *"Homosexuals don't have loving relationships,"* she had said. *"They have sex; sex in bars, sex in back streets, sex in toilets."*

"It's like the Buddha said," Tom continues. "The only thing that's permanent is impermanence, and the source of all suffering is trying to hang onto things as they are. You're better off just trying to have fun. And sex is fun. And it's supposed to be."

I stare at Tom and blink slowly as I try to gather my thoughts.

"Well, he didn't say the last bit," Tom adds. "That's more my take on things."

I nod again. "Yeah," I say vaguely. My brain feels grey and glutinous; analysis of Tom's mini speech seems challenging and complex. The idea that Tom and the shrink in some way agree depresses me. And it all seems too important, too critical even, for me to do the subject justice. Trying to think about it here, now, with a hangover, this far from home, strikes me as downright dangerous. So I let it slide into the grey swamp of my hangover.

"I'll tell you what," I say, glancing at my watch. "Let's have this conversation another day. When my head isn't pounding like a steam hammer."

Tom nods and smiles weakly. "Yeah," he says, sounding relieved. "Or not at all. I don't know *what* I'm saying this morning."

I turn my watch to face him. "Twelve-twenty. Right now what we need to do is get back to the hotel and get on our way," I say.

Tom nods, smiles gently at me and reaches out for my hand. "I guess so," he says. "And hey – thanks for a great birthday."

I swallow and force a smile. "You're welcome," I say, wondering what this particular birthday will come to mean. It seems that only time will tell.

A Question Of Belief

The conversation with Tom festers deep within like an infected wound. I don't say anything, but as the days pass, as we wait for news of the gîte, I can't help but calculate the sum total of our recent conversations: that Tom is looking for work in the UK again, that Tom is staying with me, not *for* me, but for the gîte, and now seemingly, that Tom doesn't believe in long-term relationships *at all*.

Part of the problem of course – and I am aware of this – is that there's too much time to think about it. Nothing much else is happening. Chantal is as absent as her husband, and her lawyer seems to have taken a vow of silence. Jenny's never at home when I call, and this all conspires to leave Tom and me tiptoeing around each other, avoiding almost every subject worth discussing. I feel like I'm drowning in slow motion.

By Wednesday, I can't take it anymore, and so when Tom gets back from the pool, I'm waiting for him. "Hiya," he says brightly as he pushes in the door. He looks red-faced and healthy after his swim.

I watch him hang his new parka up.

"Great coat, but actually a bit hot for Nice," he says. "It'll be great for the mountains though." He frowns at me. "Something up?"

I shake my head. "Nah," I say. "Not really. But I do need to talk to you."

Tom crinkles his lips comically and crosses the room to join me. "Have I done something *bad?*"

I shake my head again and smile. "No," I say. "Not at all. But, well... you know the conversation we had in Paris? Just before we came back? Well, it has been playing on my mind. I wondered if we could talk about it – in a constructive way. I don't want to fight."

Tom settles beside me and crosses his legs defensively. "Sure," he says. "I knew that would be eating away at you, but I wasn't sure whether to bring it up."

"I..." I start, but I'm not sure what to say.

"I didn't mean... I mean, it wasn't a death sentence or anything,"

Tom says, stumbling. "For us. I just... if I think logically about relationships, any relationship, well, I suppose I don't believe that they last."

"Except for heterosexuals?" I say. Tom frowns, so I continue, "That's what you said, wasn't it? That it's a *'hetty thing.'* A *'Christian thing.'*"

Tom glances at the laptop's screen saver and then back at me. "I meant... Sorry, I'm trying to choose words carefully here." He sighs. "I meant, that the moral... *imperative*... to build a lifelong marriage – well, it's more of a Christian ideal; a Christian heterosexual ideal. I've got nothing against it *per se*... as an option – amongst many – but it hardly seems designed for us, for our lifestyle. That's all. Do you see what I'm getting at?"

I nod. "Yeah," I say. "But I find it depressing – the idea that I can't have that with you. That we can't even *aim* for it simply because we aren't straight. Because, for whatever reason – and I admit that it may be because I grew up in a mainly Christian, mainly hetero environment – but for whatever reason, it's the model I always wanted, the thing I always dreamt of."

Tom frowns thoughtfully.

"Do you see what *I* mean?" I say. "Why *can't* we choose that, just because we're gay?"

Tom sighs and says, "Can I make a cup of tea? I'm not running away or anything, I want to continue, but can I?"

I nod. "Sure," I say, happy to have some thinking time. "I'll have one too."

When he returns with the tea he hands one mug to me, then sits back next to me on the sofa and turns as far as he can to face me. "We're nearly out of milk," he says. "Sorry."

I glance at the semi-transparent contents of the cup and shake my head. "It's fine," I say.

"I was thinking," Tom says, "about what you said. But it's not really a gay thing at all. I don't think *any* relationships last these days. Straight *or* gay."

I raise an eyebrow at the statement.

"Well, look at your parents – they split up. And Jenny and Nick. And my cousin and that asshole Pete."

"*Your* parents didn't," I point out.

Tom wrinkles his nose and nods, vaguely conceding the point. "Yeah, but they should have. Actually I think they *would* have, if Mum hadn't... if she hadn't had the accident. She spent her whole life in love with my uncle, my dad's brother. He came back from Australia just before she... I think she would have left Dad if she had had the chance. So even when they do stay together for thirty years, like my parents did, well, that doesn't stop it being a sham. Most of the time they'd rather be doing something else. Most lifelong couples would *rather* split up, but they don't because of the kids."

I wrinkle my brow to show that while I accept his logic, I'm not happy with the outcome.

"Do you see what I mean?" Tom says. "I don't see staying together forever, *what*ever, as a dream at all. It always looks like a prison sentence to me."

I nod slowly. "But it's just so depressing," I say.

Tom shrugs. "It's only depressing if you think that's what you *have* to have, that that's how it *should* be. If you just give up on the idea and take each day as it comes, if you just assume that everything is transitory, then it's fine. Fun even."

I nod vaguely and reach out to stroke Tom's leg. "I *do* see what you're saying," I say. "But... I don't know. It doesn't *work* for me."

Paloma leaps onto Tom's lap and starts to turn round and around in an attempt at getting comfortable. Tom uncrosses his legs to help her. "Dizzy cat," he says.

"What you say makes sense, Tom, especially coming from where you're coming from. Your parents, my parents, Jenny, Nick... I mean, I can't fault the logic, but I don't see how you can *live* like that. How can you plan for anything, build anything? How can you do anything other than live day-to-day if it's all going to end?"

"That's the idea I think," Tom says. "To live day-to-day."

"So, what about, say, the gîte? There are things that take planning, things that take more than a day. Things you can only do with the assumption that you'll still be here tomorrow."

"It's like life," Tom says. "We all know we die at the end; we all know it's ultimately pointless, but we do it anyway."

I swallow hard and nod slowly. "Except that that isn't how I live," I say. "What you say is true, but it's not how I live. I don't think about the fact that I'm gonna die all the time; that it's all *pointless* – if I did I

79

wouldn't get out of bed in the morning. It's how humans live – we pretend we *aren't* going to die. And it may not be logical or scientific, or right even, but it can still be a better, happier way to live. And I do pretend that we'll be together forever – or at least that we'll *maybe* be together forever. Because the alternative – believing, as you do, that it's all destined to dust anyway – makes me want to just not bother, not make any effort; it makes me want to give up at the first hurdle."

Tom grits his teeth and pulls his bottom lip down into a cartoon grimace. "That bad huh?" he says.

"But beyond the..." I shrug. *"Emotional?* side of things... I think that even in practical terms, well, I think that we *make* our own destiny. Through what we choose to believe."

"We *do* all die though," Tom says. "Whether we believe it or not."

I nod. "Yeah, sure," I say. "But not all *relationships* are doomed. Some *do* last a lifetime. But practically speaking, it kind of seems to me that if you don't believe that it can, if you don't even entertain that possibility, well, then it *is* doomed."

"Doomed," Tom says in a Scottish accent. "We're all *doomed."*

I frown at him.

"Sorry," he says, pulling a guilty face.

"Don't mock me," I say.

"It's just all getting a bit dramatic," Tom says gently. "A bit metaphysical."

"I know. But it *is* metaphysical," I say. "There's a bit of me that thinks that what you choose to believe is important. And if you believe that something can happen, then maybe it can, and if you believe that it can't, then, well, it really can't."

"So if I believe in UFO's..." Tom says.

"No. But if you believe our relationship *might* last forever then it *might,"* I say. "And if you *don't*, then, well, it just won't."

Tom nods. "I just think, take it a day at a time and see what happens," he says, tipping his head sideways.

And though I'm not quite sure why, I can sense that the communication is lost for now. That there's no common ground, no meeting of the paths, and nowhere, following my or Tom's logic, for us to go here. If we push this to the end of either road there's only one conclusion. We are *doomed*. And I don't want to go there. I'm not ready for it. I still want to believe.

"Yeah," I say vaguely. I sigh. "I guess that's all anyone can do."

Tom looks relieved as if he just got released from a job interview. "On a more practical note," he says. "Shall we go and get some food in?"

I nod sadly and stand. "Yeah," I say. "Let's do that."

Surprise Guest

I can't believe you're both abandoning me," I say, taking the knives and forks from Jenny's grasp.

Tom's shouts his contribution from the next room. "You see what I have to put up with?" he whines.

Jenny smiles at me good-naturedly. "We're hardly *abandoning* you," she says.

"Abandoning," Tom wails mockingly.

"We'll both be back for New Year's Eve," Jenny continues as she searches for five identical spoons, "but it's just, well, my mum *needs* me around at Christmas." She holds out the spoons. "I *have* to go home, at least for Christmas."

I move to the other room and start to distribute the cutlery around the table. "You're such a hypocrite," Tom says, his eyes following me around the room, his lazy smile revealing that he's only half joking.

"How?" I say, glancing up at him. "Why a hypocrite?"

"Only yesterday you were complaining that France is supposed to be secular – but that the secular rules only apply to religions *other* than Catholicism.

Jenny enters the room with glasses and napkins. She puts them on the table and ruffles Sarah's hair. "How does *that* work?" she says.

"I..." I start to explain.

"Oh he was going on about how, you know, Muslim girls aren't allowed to wear headscarves to school, but crosses are still everywhere, and all the public holidays like Ascension and Easter are all still Catholic holidays – and how all the the Pope needs to do is fart and French TV covers it immediately in HD stereo."

Jenny nods and pushes her bottom lip out. "Well, that's true," she says. "They even tell you which saint's day it is at the end of the weather forecast for God's sake."

I raise an eyebrow and nod at Tom in a, *you see,* kind of way.

"Oh yeah, it's true all right, but..."

"Not what you said yesterday," I mutter.

"But..." Tom pauses pedantically, before continuing, "You can't then start having a go at me because I'm not going to be here for Jesus' birthday."

"I was talking about the French state banning Muslim stuff in the name of secularity but not... Anyway, it's not *about* Jesus' birthday."

"Well, it *is* actually," Jenny says, laughing.

"I know, but I mean, for *me* it's not about that at all. It's simply the one day a year when you're supposed to spend the day eating and drinking and cuddling up with your loved one. Christmas isn't a day you're supposed to spend on your own looking at the cat."

"Christmas," Sarah repeats.

Jenny shoots her a smile. "Yes," she says. "Christmas," then to me, "I suppose you think I'm indoctrinating her."

I frown. "Not at all. As long as you're not telling her that she was born in sin or any of that mediaeval rubbish."

Sarah frowns at the opaque turn the conversation has taken again and concentrates on her remote control puppy, which waddles straight into the wall.

"She's made a list for Father Christmas, haven't you," Jenny says.

Sarah glances up and nods wide-eyed at me.

"Maybe I should make one," I say.

"What would you put on it?" Jenny says. "I haven't got you anything yet, so..."

"A boyfriend to have Christmas dinner with," I say.

Tom lets out a theatrical groan. "That's why we're having Christmas dinner tonight," he says.

"Maybe you should go with him," Jenny says, methodically folding napkins and putting them in the wineglasses. "If it's that important to you."

"He doesn't want me to go," I say. "He hasn't suggested it once."

"And Mark doesn't really care," Tom says, moving to my side. "He's just being pissy." He nudges my side and winks at me. "Aren't you?" he adds.

I sigh and, noting that the table seems finished, I pull out a chair and sit. I don't bother arguing because a) the sparring is starting to tire me, and b) he's perfectly right – the truth is that my flat is too small for both of us, and in secret I'm looking forward to a TV-free, dope-free, yes, Tom-free break. My complaints have more to do with my own guilt about that than anything else.

"There," Jenny says, surveying the table. "That's better."

Tom stands beside her, hands on hips. "Very festive," he says. "Shall I light the candles?"

"Crackers?" Jenny inquires, looking from Tom to myself.

I shake my head.

"I left them downstairs," Tom says. "I'll go get them."

"So are you angry with Tom?" Jenny asks, once he has left. "About Christmas."

I wrinkle my nose and tip my head to one side. "A bit," I say. "More about the whole going home to work than Christmas itself. But I could do with a break too. We've been so on top of each other since I stopped work."

She nods thoughtfully and smiles blankly, revealing that her mind is really elsewhere. "Well that's OK then," she says.

"So what did you ask Father Christmas for?" I ask Sarah.

She turns her moon-face at me. She has a serious nature for a little girl, an often-blank expression and glassy eyes. She's a pretty girl but she somehow looks a bit too serious for her age – like she might be about to cry, or that deep down she might be crying already, *silently*. Of course she isn't, it's just something about her features, her lack of expression.

"A wee," she declares forcefully.

I frown and look to Jenny for translation.

Jenny shrugs. "That's what it's called. It's a computer game. It's W-I-I – Wii. But I'm not sure Father Christmas will be able to run to a Wii this year lovey. And I'm not sure he agrees that it's appropriate for a wee young thing like yourself."

Sarah looks again like she might cry but actually smiles in a mechanical kind of way that leaves the rest of her features intact. She turns back to the puppy. "A Wii," she repeats quietly – her passing shot at obstinacy.

"So are we to be blessed with the presence of Doctor Love?" I ask.

I hear Tom bound back up the stairs, and turn to take the box of Christmas crackers from his hands. But the person standing behind me isn't Tom. I'm so shocked to see who *is* there that my heart stops beating completely for a second or so. When it resumes normal function it beats double to make up for lost time.

I let my mouth drop and stare at him. My brow slowly wrinkles. *"How on Earth can he be standing here?"* I think. I actually blink, just in case this is a trick of the mind and he will mysteriously morph back into Tom. But it is still Ricardo's face that stares back at me, his expression identical to my own. I cock my head to one side and work my mouth but nothing comes out.

Jenny moves into view from my right. "Mark, Ricky, Ricky, Mark."

I swallow hard and let out a prolonged, *"Oh!"* My mouth starts to form the shape for the 'W' of "We've met," but Ricardo beats me to it. His face clicks and shifts into action forcing a blank expression and then a winning smile as if he is responding to a *meet new person* button on Sarah's remote control.

"Mark!" he says. "I'm so happy to meet you. Jenny has tell me so much about you."

"Told," Jenny corrects him, then as an aside to me she adds, "Rick is learning English."

I swallow my forming sentence, swallow again, and then take a deep breath and form an unconvincing copy of his expression. "Great! Well. Jenny *told* me almost nothing about you!" I joke acerbically. "Except that you're a... What is it you do again? A *doctor*? Is that right?"

Ricardo nods. "Yes, that's right." He turns to Jenny, kisses her on the lips and hands her a bottle of Champagne. "Here. Because it's Christmas," he says.

Petites Mensonges

Jenny looks from Rick to myself and back again, frowning as she picks up on the weird atmosphere. My brain is racing as I try to work out all of the implications of Ricardo being Rick, and Rick being Jenny's boyfriend; his pretending to be a doctor when he's really a fireman. I'm also trying to work out why we're pretending we haven't met before, and why – if my allegiance is to Tom and Jenny, as it clearly should be – I am playing along with his little game, whatever that is. I'm also trying to work out what exactly will happen if I *stop* playing along – if I say, *"Surely, we have met, haven't we?"*

Tom bounds into the room holding the absurdly sized box of Christmas crackers, and his presence, the fact that he knows Rick already, somehow complicates the dynamic even further and, overloaded with questions, my brain slides into numb submission and gives up any attempt at processing.

"Rick! Hi!" Tom says. "Good to see you again. Spivvy as ever, I see!"

Ricardo frowns. "Spivvy?"

"It just means well dressed," Jenny says, starting to ease off his coat which is glistening from the rain.

Ricardo is indeed looking spivvy – he's wearing a brown suit with a vague orange check, a striped shirt and a pink tie. The result looks like something from *The Apprentice*.

"Tom expects everyone to dress like a crusty," Jenny adds. "Just because he does."

"Hey! I used to wear suits," Tom says. "For work."

"Yes, I come from work," Ricardo says.

"Came," Jenny corrects – a little savagely it strikes me.

"So, Rick," I say. "Is that Richard or..."

"Ricardo," he confirms. "But Jenny likes Rick better."

"Actually I like Ricky best of all but he doesn't like it," she laughs. "Did you know he's Colombian?"

I nod. "Y... No," I say, struggling to work out what I'm supposed to know and what I'm not.

Ricardo nods. "Franco-Colombian," he says, then with a wink. "Like Ingrid Betancourt. You know her?"

"Anyway," Tom says. "Shall we sit? There's not really room for all this standing around."

"Please," Ricardo says, waving a hand above the dining table. "I go help Jenny with the aperitifs."

"What's up with *you?*" Tom asks me once Ricardo has swept Sarah from the floor and followed Jenny into the kitchen.

"What do you mean?" I ask, wondering if I can brazen it out, or indeed if I should.

"Do you fancy him or something?" Tom asks. "You're acting all weird."

I shake my head. "Am I?" I say. "No, it's just..."

"Huh, now I *know* you're being weird," Tom says. "You *don't* fancy him?"

I frown. "Yeah, no, I mean, he's cute. But that's not..." I glance at the door wondering if they will reappear to save me, to give me some more thinking time, but I can hear Jenny laughing and Sarah shrieking over her in a bid for Ricardo's attention.

"Well?" Tom asks.

I shrug. "He reminds me of someone," I say. "He reminds me of someone I met on a bike run so much it's uncanny."

"Are we talking about one of your many conquests?" Tom asks mockingly.

"No, I..."

Jenny clumps back into the room carrying a tray with assorted bottles of alcohol and dishes of nuts and olives. Ricardo, Sarah and the pink puppy follow behind. I glance down at Jenny's feet and notice that they are suddenly, unusually, squashed into shiny black high heels.

So what'll it be?" Jenny asks putting the tray down.

"Whisky!" I say.

"Me too!" Ricardo says flashing the whites of his eyes at me. "I need a drink after that."

"Hard day?" Tom asks.

"Shocking," Ricardo says, with meaning.

I'm so lost in my thoughts, so analytical of everything everyone says, that I don't say much myself for the first hour. Sarah sits on my lap and I use her as a cover for my strange mood.

Jenny serves prawn cocktails, declaring, "And yes I *know* it's a cliché – that's why I'm serving it."

She follows this with an excellent nut roast and trimmings. In my silence I manage to avoid putting my foot in it or lying any further, but when Tom says, "Just think! This time next year we might all be living up at the gîte!" I realise that there are multiple deceptions taking place.

Jenny half chokes on her food and then has to swill it down with some wine, more, I guess, for thinking time than anything else.

"The gîte?" asks Ricardo.

"Yeah," I explain. "Tom and I are buying a gîte up in the hills."

"I know," Ricardo replies. "You..." Here, he realises his error and swivels to face Jenny. "You told me. But I didn't know you were going to live there as well."

Jenny swallows and frowns. "I didn't... I don't think so. I mean, I don't *think* I mentioned it."

"Oh," Ricardo says. He turns to Tom. "Maybe it was Tom."

Tom frowns, then thankfully shrugs. "Maybe," he says.

"Anyway, the only reason I didn't mention it," Jenny continues, "is because, well, it's not certain yet. And even if it does happen it won't be for ages."

"We're having problems with the sale," I tell Ricardo.

He nods, sighs and swallows. "Yes, these things often are complicate," he says.

"Complicat*ed!*" Jenny says.

"Complicated," Ricardo repeats.

"To be honest, I don't think it's going to happen at all," Tom says. "I think it's just a question of when we find that out."

I turn my stare on Tom. He hasn't said *that* before. "Don't say that, Tom!" I protest.

"He's right," Ricardo says ominously. "You should be careful what you believe. Things that..." He frowns then breaks into French. *"Si on dit assez souvent qu'une chose ne se fera pas, eh bien, ça ne se fait pas."*

"If you say something won't happen enough then it won't," I translate.

"Sounds like something Dante would say," Tom says. Another

phrase which shocks me. The guilt over Dante has now finally faded enough for him to become the subject of dinner conversation it would seem.

"Dante?" Ricardo asks.

"You don't want to know," Jenny says. "Believe me."

I nod. "You really don't."

"It is this bad?" Ricardo says.

"Anyway," Jenny says with a cough. "I agree with Rick. We all know deep down what's going to happen. It's just a question of tuning in."

Ricardo shakes his head. "No, I don't say that at all. I say that what we think *changes* what happen."

"Huh, now you sound like Mark," Tom says.

Ricardo slips into one of his winning smiles and winks at me. "I think I prefer," he says.

The rest of the dinner party goes without hiccups. Tom talks about dogs and rhubarb and the gîte. I think he's trying to make amends for having expressed his doubts so clearly. Ricardo tells us about the constant rain in Bogotá, and makes us laugh by telling us about a hypochondriac woman who comes to his surgery every day. I wonder if telling us is breaching professional protocol and then I wonder if the surgery exists at all.

I sit and watch and enjoy his prettiness as one might take succour from a great work of art – it's a pleasure to look at him – but something about his double life, doctor/fireman, Rick/Ricardo, Jenny's boyfriend/what? I can't work out exactly why that shocks me, but it does.

At one point, Jenny and I find ourselves alone in the kitchen staring into a pan of custard. "Well?" she asks me quietly. "What do you think?"

I nod. "He's gorgeous," I say. "Really sexy and fun. And cute too."

She nods. "You don't think there's something... odd about him?"

I shrug. "Not really," I say. "Like what?"

"I don't know. He's too smooth. He's too... he's just *too*." She shrugs.

"Too good to be true?"

She nods. "Yeah."

I shrug again. "Maybe it's like he says. Maybe you just have to believe for it to be so."

"I guess," she says, looking at the custard. "This looks done. There's a Coldplay song that says something like that, you know, that saying things makes you believe in them. I suppose it's not quite the same... but I do think that sometimes... you know if you can just stop being cynical and throw yourself at something... Anyway..." She nods thoughtfully as the custard starts to bubble. "Shall we?"

As I follow her back through to the dining room, I notice that her arse has developed a distinct catwalky wiggle.

I watch her lean and put the custard down on the trivet. "So..." I say. "What's with the heels hon?"

Jenny blushes and flicks her hair. "They're new," she says. "I'm just breaking them in, that's all. A few minutes every day."

I glance at Tom, who raises an eyebrow and shrugs, and we both snigger and look back at Jenny. It's a terrible thing, but though I could usually catalogue exactly what every man at a party looks like, I rarely even notice what the women around me are wearing. But I notice now, and Jenny is dressed up to the proverbial nines. On top of the new clumpy heels – which though absurdly noisy in her tiny tiled apartment, it has to be said, do give a certain *je ne sais quoi* to her posture – she's wearing a black skirt and cardigan. And the top is unbuttoned to show enough cleavage to make me think she has been shopping for accessories of the lift-and-separate variety.

"Leave me alone," she mutters with a frown. She shoots a glance at Ricardo, who I realise of course, must remain blissfully unaware that Jenny generally wears jogging bottoms, slippers and a vast Arran jumper.

The meal goes perfectly until about one a.m. when something happens between Jenny and Ricardo. I'm chatting to Tom and they are in the kitchen, so I miss it entirely. Simply, all of a sudden they are back and the atmosphere has turned distinctly un-festive. Within half an hour, claiming an early start the next day, Ricardo stands to leave.

Jenny, who has been knocking back glass after glass of wine, frigidly accepts a peck. She and Tom are deep in discussion in hushed voices, not easy to do at a small dining table, and impossible to do without being rude, so I show Ricardo to the door myself.

He uses the opportunity to slip a business card into my hand.

"Appelle-moi," he murmurs. "Trop de petits mensonges. Il faut qu'on parle." – *"Call me. Too many little lies. We have to talk."*

He kisses me on both cheeks, winks again and leaves. I can't help but notice that he shook Tom's hand. I can't help but notice that I'm getting a damned erection again. I stand and look at the card for a moment, then return to the lounge. With Ricardo's departure, the cloud has already lifted.

"What was that all about?" I ask.

They both look at me blankly. "All what?" Tom says.

I frown at them. "What do you mean, *all what?*"

Jenny tuts. "It's just a lover's tiff," she says, symbolically pulling off the torture-shoes and casting them into a corner with a sigh of relief. "Anyway, let's talk about something else, can we? It is Christmas – Christmas dinner at any rate."

But it doesn't really matter to me what we talk about. With the card sitting in my pocket, I'm unable to concentrate on anything they are saying anyway. Instead I sit and wonder what *exactly* Ricardo and I have to talk about.

Badly Timed
Abandonment

Something wakes me from my dream – from my very *sexy* dream. I try to grasp it, to keep hold of it, but as another drip lands on my cheek, the same thing which woke me in the first place I now realise, the dream slips from my grasp once and for all. I slide a hand to my cheek. Another drip. I force my eyes open, and roll across the cold, damp bed and sit and peer up at the ceiling. A beige stain is spreading from the ceiling fan. Drips are gathering in three, four, five different places and falling directly on the bed.

"Oh, no!" I groan, forcing my still-sleepy legs to stand and carry me to the bathroom. I grab the first clothes I find – my jogging trousers and the t-shirt Tom was wearing yesterday, pull them hastily on and jog barefoot to the door of the flat. With a final glance down to check that my morning glory has faded to invisibility, I head up to Jenny's.

Two suitcases are propping the door open and Jenny is kneeling just beyond the threshold buttoning Sarah's coat. "Mark!" she squeals as she sees me.

"Hello," Jenny says, glancing over her shoulder. "You're just in time to see us off."

"There's a leak," I say, surprisingly breathless after the flight of stairs. "A big leak. And it's coming from your flat."

"Leak?" Sarah asks.

"It's water darling. Drips, dripping," Jenny explains, turning to face me.

"Drips, dripping," Sarah repeats seriously.

Vaguely irritated by Jenny's lack of urgency, I push past her into the flat. "It must be the... bathroom," I say, as I enter it. "Nope. The kitchen then."

Jenny meets me in the kitchen. "There's nothing dripping here," she says.

"Well it's pouring in our bedroom, and that's there," I say pointing at the floor.

"I don't think it's from here, Mark; anyway, we're just off to the airport."

I turn on her. "It *is* from here. It has to be. And no, you *can't* go. I've got Niagara Falls in the bedroom."

"Really?" Jenny says vaguely whilst checking her watch. "Is it bad?"

"Yeah," I say. "Very."

"What are you going to do?" she asks.

"What am *I* going to do?" I say.

Jenny grabs my arm and leans her head slightly to one side so she can look into my eyes. "Mark," she says earnestly. "I love you dearly. I'm most concerned about your drips dripping. But we're *going*. The flight's at twelve, my mum is already driving to the airport to pick us up. We have to *leave*."

"But you can't," I protest. As I say it, I realise that I'm feeling anxious about her leaving, especially because Tom is also leaving this evening. I wonder for a second if he hasn't already left – he's certainly not around – but I remember the flight was definitely an evening one.

"I can give you five minutes," Jenny says. "Tell me what you need. But from there you'll have to deal with it. I'm sorry."

I shake my head and gasp in frustration.

"Mark!" Jenny says.

"OK," I say wearily. "Your keys."

"They're in the door. You can hang onto them. I've got a spare in my purse."

"And the stopcock; we have to shut the water off."

"I think it's that big tap there," Jenny says pointing at the corner of the room next to the entrance. "But I never touched it, so..."

I crouch down and turn the tap off. "Yeah, that should be it," I say. "And I need the phone number of..."

"The owner, of course." She rifles through a pile of bills next to the phone and gives me the rent demand. "There," she says.

I nod. "OK," I say. "I suppose that's it. I wish you wouldn't..."

"I'm sorry. Bad timing. But we really..."

I nod. "Just go," I say, shaking my head.

"I'll call you," she says. "As soon as we get in."

"Sure," I say. "Whatever."

"I'm sorry," she says again, turning and reaching for Sarah's hand.

"Shit!" I say. "The bed." I push past them and run back down, taking the stairs two at a time.

When I reach the bedroom, Tom is standing in the doorway. "What's all this then?" he asks, also surprisingly calm.

"A water leak," I say, pushing him gently to one side and squeezing past. "Where were you?"

"From Jenny's?" he asks, then, "Swimming. At the pool."

"You could have done that here," I say.

"You need to shut her water off before she leaves," Tom says. "She's flying out today."

"It's done," I say.

Tom raises an eyebrow and looks at the ceiling. "It doesn't look like it," he says doubtfully.

"Well, no," I agree. "I expect it will take a few minutes."

As I grasp the corner of the mattress, Tom says, "You should have moved the mattress out of the way really."

"What do you think I'm *doing* Tom?" I say, my irritation shifting from the leak to him.

"Before, I mean," he says.

I strain to lift the corner of the mattress but it's too heavy. It's solid at the best of times, but waterlogged it's impossible.

"Why didn't *you* move it?"

"I wasn't here," Tom says.

"Well help me then!" I exclaim. "Stop just standing there criticising!"

"Jees!" Tom says, removing his backpack and crossing the room. "I think that's called shutting the door after the horse has bolted."

"So what, we just leave it here?" I say. "Is that your idea?"

Tom shrugs. "I thought it was yours," he mutters.

"And lift!" I instruct.

With difficulty we manoeuvre the soggy mattress against the wall, but in truth, the mattress *is* already soaked, the dripping is slowing, and it is all pretty pointless. Plus as soon as we move it we simply have to find other receptacles to catch the drips.

Tom immediately busies himself with packing, leaving me to catch the drips, mop the floor, phone Jenny's landlord, the building company, and half of the emergency plumbers in the phone-book.

When my anger – mainly from having to move *around* him – finally gets the better of me and I make a snide comment, he retorts, "What do you want *me* to do? You have everything under control anyway, Mister Efficiency."

This annoys me so much that my mood shifts from dreading his departure, to being unable even to look him in the eye.

Just after three p.m. the dripping stops completely. Tom points this out as he leaves – a little early it strikes me – for the airport. "It's stopped," he says, then adding, as if this is maybe something he predicted, or something he caused to happen, *"You see."* He pecks me on the cheek, and says, "I'll call you."

"Thanks!" I say, still trying to decode what the, *"You see,"* implies.

I sink into the sofa – which I realise is likely to be my bed as well – and watch as he pulls the front door closed behind him. I let out a sigh and glance at the clock again and wonder when the plumber will turn up. I'm feeling angry and upset, a bit over-dramatic about the whole thing I guess, and actually, I now realise, a bit tearful. I'm feeling abandoned. Abandoned for Christmas on a wet day in a wet flat, in a big wet world.

After a few minutes of self-indulgent misery I make myself snap out of my doldrums to mop the floor in the bedroom. I then head upstairs to Jenny's to try again to find the leak. I check out beneath the sinks; I follow pipes along walls into cupboards, but other than a vague damp patch beside the bath I can find no clues. I'm just standing, hands on hips, noting the strange vacant air the flat has taken on now that Jenny has gone, when her phone rings. Thinking it might be the plumber or Jenny herself I pick up. But it's Ricardo's voice that greets me, and though I'm intrigued by the whole Ricardo story, truth is, right now, here today, my life seems complicated enough.

"Jenny's not here, Ricardo," I tell him. "She's already left."

"I know," he says. "She phoned from the airport. I think, thought, you might need help with the water."

I wrinkle my nose. Quite what a water-leak in *Jenny's* place, leaking into *my* place has to do with Ricardo escapes me. Unless he and Jenny truly are an item these days, as it now dawns on me that they must be. It's the first time the idea has crossed my mind. "It's fine, thanks," I tell him. "I'm waiting for the plumber, that's all."

"I thought I could..." he starts, but hearing a noise from the stairwell, I interrupt him.

"Sorry, but I think he's here," I say. "It's the plumber. I have to go."

The plumber, who I find lumbering up the stairs with his heavy toolbox and heavier body – he's massive in breadth and height – is a grumpy brute of a man. He's wearing stained overalls and has body-hair sprouting from his collar, his cuffs and his nostrils. Initially I greet him jovially, but realising that he is a plumber of the glum school – all grimaces and air sucked through clenched teeth – I quickly give up and sink into a chair with an old newspaper. He prowls and growls, on all fours for the most part, around the flat. Thoughts of dog training make me want to giggle.

He may be grumpy, and he's certainly no looker, but he has a sixth sense when it comes to water leaks, and that, after all, is all anyone can really hope of a plumber. Muttering, "They really should have put in an inspection hatch," he smashes the tiles from the side of Jenny's bath with a sledgehammer. It makes me pretty nervous, but sure enough, crouched beside me in the rubble, he points out the sheered pipe.

He saws and files and solders for another hour, and then stands up and declares his work finished. I enter the bathroom and take in the desolation of rubble and smashed tiles.

Before I can comment, he says, "I don't do tiling, so you'll have to get someone else in for that, but at least your ceiling won't come down," and hands me a bill. It's an amazingly reasonable bill, so I let it go and write the check.

By the time I have cleaned up Jenny's rubble (the place still looks terrible), and returned downstairs, I am feeling exhausted and fed up. My own flat, filled with buckets and saucepans and mops and the propped up mattress, and without Tom, feels lonely and almost as desolate as Jenny's. I sigh deeply. I'm over-hungry but I can't be bothered to cook, so I vaguely consider going out for a pizza, but I hate eating alone in restaurants, so I sigh again. This time the sigh is interrupted by a knock on the door. I stand, still lost in my drama of weariness, and open the door to Ricardo's smiling face. He's holding two pizza boxes.

"I think you are maybe too busy to cook, so..." he says grinning broadly and jiggling the boxes from side to side.

The perfect timing plus the fact that I now remember Ricardo was in my dirty dream leaves me momentarily speechless. And then I think of a feminist joke from the eighties, and start to grin myself. "Q: What's the ideal man? A: One that shags you senseless and then morphs into a pizza."

Sex Like Chocolate

Ricardo smiles and frowns simultaneously. "Why you laugh?" he asks.

I shake my head and stand aside. "No reason, please, come in."

He places the pizza boxes on the coffee table and shoots me a quizzical glance. "It's OK?" he asks. "Maybe you are busy?"

I shake my head and smile in reassurance. "To be honest," I tell him, "it's perfect. I'm starving, too tired to cook, too lazy to go out. I don't really want to be on my own and I was just thinking how nice a pizza would be."

Ricardo laughs. "All this!" he says. "Good timing then." He undoes his tie, rolls it and puts it in his pocket, then hangs his jacket over the back of a chair. "Jenny phoned me," he says. "She felt so guilty leaving you like that, so I thought I would come and..."

"Ah! So you're here as Jenny's surrogate." Ricardo frowns at this, so I continue, "On her behalf. Never mind. Anyway, I'll get some knives and the mayo."

Ricardo frowns. "Mayonnaise? With pizza?"

I nod and grin sheepishly. "It's magical – you'll see."

The pizzas are oversized, over cheesy and generally orgasmic. As I fill my mouth with the first hot slice, Ricardo, who is rolling his shirtsleeves – revealing a glimpse of his tanned furry arms – says, "So you stop the water? It's OK now?"

I nod and fan my mouth to help the steam escape. "Yeah, the plumber came, he fixed it. He left a hell of a mess though."

Ricardo nods. "Maybe I can help you?" he says.

I shake my head. "Should be able to get Jenny's insurance to pay for it all, so..."

Ricardo nods. "Well, if you do – I'm very good at... *bricolage.*"

"DIY," I say. "For *Do It Yourself.*"

"DIY," he repeats, grinning and reaching for pizza. "I like."

"A man of many talents," I say, wondering as I say it, if I am now lapsing into cheesy flirtation. I decide I need to get a grip on myself.

Ricardo nods and grins innocently. "Many!" he laughs.

"So are you really a doctor?" I ask.

He frowns at me. "Of course!" he says.

"So are you really a *pompier?*" I ask, in exactly the same voice.

Ricardo frowns and grins. "Of course!" he says. "A part-time *pompier.* Just one weekend a month at the moment."

I laugh. "OK," I say. "I thought there was something fishy going on."

"Fishy?" Ricardo repeats.

I nod. "Strange. Never mind."

"It's for my French – how you say? – *dossier.* I think it helps for my French nationality request that I work as a *pompier.* I hope."

I frown and cock my head to one side. "But you *are* French, no?"

"Not yet," he replies, pouting and shaking his head.

"But you said..."

"Yes, I tell everyone this. I have waited five years now. If you say just Colombian to the French, they think Third World, or cocaine, or both – but nothing else. They think of you as *étranger* – a stranger?"

"A foreigner," I say. "It's the same with the English. You say you're English and they either start going on about how we burned Joan of Arc, or the fact that we're not in the Euro. They never seem to mention the Second World War for some reason."

Ricardo nods. "Yes. And they like their doctors to be not foreign. So I *say* I already have double nationality."

I nod. "Fair enough," I say. "I don't think anyone in Britain would care if you weren't French – I mean, English. Plenty of the doctors are from elsewhere."

Ricardo nods. "No. Probably not."

"And you think being a *pompier* will help?"

Ricardo raises an eyebrow. "Maybe. I hope," he says. "Everyone in France loves the *pompier.* How do you say in English?"

I shrug. "It's difficult," I explain. "We have fireman for fires, and then ambulances with medics. We don't really have the combined paramedic thing. I suppose that's it – a paramedic."

He nods. "OK," he says. "Paramedic. Though I like *fire-man* better. Anyway, everyone in France loves the fire-man."

I nod. "Yeah," I say. "Tell me about it."

Ricardo laughs. "You too?"

I nod. "Fit guys, great uniform, saving children from burning buildings, giving the kiss of life... What's not to like?"

Ricardo nods and stuffs pizza into his mouth.

"So why didn't you tell Jenny we met?" I ask. "Why pretend like that?"

He shrugs and finishes his mouthful before replying. "I don't know," he says. "I ask myself the same question."

I twist my mouth sideways, showing I'm unconvinced.

"I think because I didn't mention it before," he says. "We met two times and I never told her. So..."

I nod. "OK," I say. "But *why* didn't you tell her?"

Ricardo shrugs. "I don't know," he says. "Really. And you? You tell Tom?"

"Yeah... no... sort of," I say. As I stumblingly reply, it strikes me that if Ricardo is worrying about telling/not telling his partner that he met me, it must mean something – and it probably means the same thing it meant when I didn't, then guiltily *did* tell Tom. Otherwise, why would he care? "I mentioned it in passing," I say.

Ricardo nods and, it seems to me, looks disappointed. "OK," he says.

We eat in silence for a moment, and then he knocks the wind right out of me by saying, "Jenny tell me you were lovers."

I almost cough my pizza out. "We *dated,*" I correct, when I can speak. "A long time ago. It *didn't* work."

"Why not?" Ricardo asks.

I think of a line from *Torchsong Trilogy* and produce an approximation: "Well, she needed a big strong man. And I needed... a big strong man," I say.

Ricardo laughs. "OK," he says.

"It was my last attempt with a woman," I say. "Before I realised."

Ricardo nods again. "And now you are married with Tom."

I laugh. "Yeah, well, not married. We're together."

Ricardo smiles. "So no more Jenny."

I frown. "No! You don't think... Surely you're not worried that..."

Ricardo laughs. "No! I mean, no more girls!"

"Oh!" I grin. "Ah! No. I, erm, prefer guys."

Ricardo nods and looks serious for a moment.

"Does that shock you? Is it difficult for you?" I ask.

He pushes out his lips and shakes his head. And then he shocks me even more. "Not at all!" he says. "I have also... with men."

I pause chewing for a moment. Did he *really* just say that?

"Maybe that shock *you*," he says.

I swallow. "A bit," I say. "I mean, not... just, well, because it's *you*... because you're dating Jenny. Does she *know?*"

Ricardo shakes his head. "That I have been with men? No."

I nod. "I see," I say.

"I don't tell her about my other girlfriends either."

I frown. This is getting worse and worse. "You have *other* girlfriends?"

Ricardo laughs and waves a hand over his shoulder. "Before, I mean!"

I blow through my lips. "Oof! OK," I say. "So why didn't you tell her?"

Ricardo shrugs. "What would be the reason? So that she would worry about..." he waves a hand at the space between us, "this, now?"

I nod. "But it's kind of lying by omission."

"Noo!" Ricardo says dismissively. "Not lying. You tell everyone *everything* about yourself?"

I shrug. "I guess not," I say. "Well, pretty much maybe. So you're what? Bisexual?"

Ricardo shrugs. "I don't know. I don't worry. I'm me. I'm Ricardo."

"OK," I say. "But what do you say if someone asks you?"

He shrugs again. "They don't." He points at the final slice of pizza. "Can I?"

I nod. "It's yours. Go ahead."

"I always knew I was not, you know, one hundred percent straight. But I do feel attracted to women too. Just not all."

"I'm not attracted to *all* men," I say.

"No," Ricardo says. "And never women?"

I shake my head. "Not really," I say. "So do you have a preference, or is it just..."

"It's a complex thing," he says. "I prefer a good looking man to an ugly woman, or a good looking man to... I mean, a good looking woman... you know what I mean."

I nod. "Sure," I say. "But if they're the same – *equally* good looking. What then? You must have an overall preference, surely?"

Ricardo shrugs. "It never happen, so... I suppose I like the sex with men better. It's more direct. But I prefer relationship with woman."

I wince at his *deballage*, suddenly wondering just how much of this I want to know. Jenny after all, *is* my oldest friend. "Plus," Ricardo says, definitely pushing through the limits of what I want to hear, "a woman can't fuck you, not ever."

I clench my teeth at this truth, causing Ricardo to pull a face. "Sorry," he says. "I tell you too much. The problem with doctors. Doctors and nurses. It's all *banale* for us."

I wobble my head from side to side, Indian style, to indicate, *kind of.* "It all just sounds a bit messy really," I say.

"Messy?"

"Bordelique," I translate. "It sounds complicated."

Ricardo shrugs. "Not always. Sometimes. But life often *is* complicate. *Your* life is never *bordelique?"*

I laugh. "OK," I say. "Sure it is. Sometimes. I take your point."

"I don't have," he says soberly shrugging. "I don't have a point. Except maybe that this is who we are. This is Ricardo."

I nod and reflect on this. "Whachagonnado?" I say.

Ricardo nods. "The mayonnaise is good," he laughs. "Maybe too fattening, not necessary, but it's OK."

I grin. "This is Mark!" I say, pinching an inch. "Wachagonnado? Don't you feel like you're lying though? I mean, when you're with Jenny – if you prefer sex with a guy, isn't it – a cliché I know – but isn't it sort of living a lie?"

Ricardo shakes his head. "No lie," he says.

"But I don't lie about my sexuality to anyone," I say.

Ricardo nods. "But again, you don't tell *everyone everything* either. Everyone does not need to know every thing," he says.

"I don't think I would feel like me," I say. "If I had to pretend."

"Validation..." He sighs and slips into French. "La validation ne vient pas de l'extérieur." – *"Validation doesn't come from outside."*

"I know who Ricardo is," he says. "That's what matters."

"But you do *prefer* sex with a man," I say.

Ricardo shrugs. "I prefer chocolate to bread," he says.

"Chocolate?"

"Yes. I love chocolate. But I can't eat *only* chocolate. You can't live on chocolate."

I shrug. "I think I could!" I laugh.

Ricardo stays for another hour. He helps me tidy the bedroom and manoeuvre the mattress back onto the bed. He points out that it will dry better if the air can get to both sides. It's a good job Tom isn't here to claim that particular victory.

He actually offers to put me up at his place until it dries, but as he describes it as a studio, this seems fraught with danger. I'm tempted, obviously I am. Were I single I'd jump at the chance just to find out what's really on offer. Were he not Jenny's guy I might even jump him none the less – he's one of the cutest, most exotic guys I have ever met. But I'm not single, nor is he, and the situation – his bisexuality or his Ricexuality or whatever he chooses to call it; the fact that he's dating my best friend, that he knows Tom – well, it's all too much, so I heroically resist, or at least that's what I tell myself. It's probably half of the truth. The other half is that I'm too tired after my disastrous day to move a single muscle, and that's probably a very good thing for everyone concerned.

So once Ricardo has kissed me on both cheeks – his stubble prickling enticingly – I close the door, grab a blanket and settle on the sofa with Paloma. As I doze off to sleep I wonder if I can muster up and maybe even continue yesterday's oh-so-enjoyable dream.

The second I fall asleep, I'm re-awakened by a phone call from Tom and then another from Jenny. I sort-of-lie to both of them by not mentioning Ricardo's visit. As I doze back to sleep, I fret that Ricardo may tell Jenny, but I feel quite sure that he won't, a fact that somehow seems even more disturbing.

***

The next morning when I awaken, I feel, despite it all, thoroughly refreshed, verging on manic even. I realise that the sofa is in fact much more comfortable than the bed and wonder if the water leak and pending insurance claim aren't the perfect opportunity to buy a new one.

The rain outside has stopped and the sun is making a half-hearted attempt at reaching planet Earth, so I get dressed hurriedly and head through the old town for breakfast at La Civette.

Breakfast out is a luxury I rarely allow myself. In the strange world of perceived value there are things I can buy without even looking at the price tag (gadgets, iPods, telephones, computers...) and things that for some reason irk me beyond belief. Paying four Euros for a seventy-cent croissant to be served on a plate is one of them. But today, after two weeks of rain, eight Euros for coffee and croissant in the sun seems like a bargain. Dark clouds are still lurking to the east and west, so whichever way the weather moves it won't last long, but for now, at least, the sun is beating down, and I close my eyes and bask in the warmth.

I glance around the terrace as it fills rapidly in the sunshine. I try to convince myself that I'm just looking around, but in truth I'm hoping to spot Ricardo, and the fact of this desire to see him again makes me feel a little disappointed in myself. As my coffee arrives, I realise that I still don't know what he actually wanted to talk to me about, unless it *was* about his bisexuality, but then why would he feel the need to tell *me?* Unless my vague suspicion – or is it my hope? – that he has been cruising me from the start, is correct.

I look around the terrace again and think back to the old days, to the dating game. I met quite a few people in this bar, either by chance or prearranged over the net. They were nearly always catastrophic disappointments, the potential Mister Right turning out to be either fifty percent bigger or smaller or madder than expected; I'm glad to be out of it, and yet, in a way I miss it too. The thrill of the hunt, the excitement of first – even if usually illusory – love.

I chew croissant and sip coffee and think about Tom in Brighton and wonder what he's doing, and inevitably question if he's being faithful. Every synapse seems to conclude that he isn't, that he's probably with tool4you or whatever his name is, already getting his *holes filled*, and I wonder why it matters to me so much.

I'm hardly the first person in the world to think that fidelity is important – that's why we have a word for it. And so I end up pondering why it *is* so important to so many people. Isn't it just a case of the ego asking, demanding, that the *wonderful person that I am* suffice? That my marvellous self should be sufficient for *all* Tom's needs? For life? That would surely be absurdly arrogant of me? And then I wonder whose potential infidelity I'm trying to excuse.

The thought makes me uncomfortable, so as the market traders start to pack up their fruit and veg stalls I turn my thoughts back to Tom. I think about phoning him not so much to check up on him but... OK, to *check up on him*. I could log into his second email account, the one he thinks I don't know about. I could surf Recon to see if he's online, maybe even create a tempting profile to trap him. But in the end it strikes me that that road can only lead to deception if I'm right, or the madness of an endless hunt for proof if I'm not. It seems wiser and easier just to choose to believe, to choose to be naive. It's perhaps revealing that the two words rhyme.

A *very* Cote d'Azur woman in *vast* Christian Dior sunglasses and gold high heels installs herself at the table in front of mine, and begins a strident conversation on her iPhone. It's one of those completely pointless, *"Hi, I'm just calling to let you know that I'm calling you,"* conversations, devoid of any useful information for the called party. She might as well be saying, *"Hi, I'm just calling to let you (and everyone around me) know that I'm one of those complete losers who still thinks having a mobile phone is groovy and hip."* I watch the chrome edge catching the light as she waves it about and think about the gîte, about how our life will be up in the mountains far away from all of this.

Tom of course doesn't believe that it will happen. So what will happen to me if he's right? Will I look for another gîte? Will I move back to Brighton to be with him? Or maybe I'll just sell up, pack up and move onto somewhere new, leaving the gîte and Nice and Tom behind.

It's surprisingly appealing, which makes me worry, not for the first time, about this self destructive streak in me, always tempted to blow everything to smithereens, always tempted by a fresh start – something new, something better, something different.

***

Back in the flat, the light already fading as the bad weather moves back in, I check my email hoping for reassuring words from Tom, but of course there are none. Feeling only vaguely guilty despite my decision *not* to do so, I check Tom's secret email account to see if he's writing to anyone else, but it only contains a reply to the message he posted in the hill-walking forum. I click on the link and watch the hill-walking pages appear, first Tom's request asking if Jean is still running hill-walking weekends from his gîte, and then below it, an anonymous reply from someone called *ChampiRando*.

"Jean has moved away," ChampiRando writes. "And he hasn't visited the forum for over a year. But I hear the gîte has been sold, so maybe the new owners will be running walking tours as well - watch this space."

I log out from Tom's account, sigh and close the laptop. And then I frown and open it again and study the messages. How could *ChampiRando* know that we are buying the gîte? Unless *ChampiRando* is Chantal. But why would Chantal say he has *moved* away? I suppose that the truth isn't something she'd want to start discussing on a public forum. But then again, if it *is* Chantal, why not say, *"We're* selling up – *I'm* selling up."

I scratch the bridge of my nose and look at the message again. The message may be anonymous, but the IP address is showing: 213.186.33.5. It probably just belongs to Chantal's Internet provider, but all the same, I google an IP tracking site and type in the numbers – a trick I learnt in my last job. The trace says that the number belongs to Egyptian Internet provider EGnet. I type the same numbers into a web-browser, fully expecting the operation to fail, but very slowly a web page appears: *Egyptour – Your local guide to the treasures of Egypt.*

Now why, I wonder, would an Egyptian tour operator be reading French hill-walking forums, and how could they know anything about the sale of the gîte? I'm just picking up the phone to call Tom to discuss it when, luckily, I'm interrupted by a knock on the door. It's only once I'm standing next to the insurance assessor, watching him peer at my stained ceiling and grimace as he lays a hand on the damp mattress, that I remember I *can't* talk to Tom about it. I'm not supposed to have been fishing in his email in the first place.

Strategic Paranoia

It turns out that Jenny's insurer can send someone to repaint my ceiling, or I can do it myself. If I do, they will pay me three hundred Euros, and because a pot of paint is less than forty, and I'm time-rich and potentially soon to be money-poor, Monday lunchtime when the phone rings I'm at the top of a ladder splattering paint everywhere. I groan at the interruption and clamber down and lay the roller in the paint tray. I wipe my hands on my old jeans and grab the handset.

"Oh, hi Tom," I say. "I'm kind of busy painting the ceiling." It's not that I don't want to talk to him, it's just truly not a good time.

"Is everything OK?" Tom asks.

"Sure," I tell him. "I'm just up to my nipples in white paint."

"Humm," Tom says, causing me to frown.

"Is everything OK with *you?*" I ask.

"I suppose," he says.

I crease my brow and scrunch my nose at the handset. Whatever this is, I had better call him later to sort it out. "OK then, well, I'll call you as soon as I've finished the first coat," I say.

"I'll be out by then," he says gloomily.

"OK, then we'll talk this evening."

"OK," he says. "If I'm in."

I let out a huge sigh and resign myself to scraping dried paint off the floor and maybe even buying a new roller. "OK Tom, what's up?" I ask.

"Nothing," he says, somehow managing to make the denial sound aggressive.

I say nothing, knowing that it's the best way to prompt him to continue.

"Last time I called you were just going out," he says.

I nod. "Yeah?" I say, puzzled.

"And the time before you were just going to sleep."

I roll my eyes. "OK," I say. "Well, it's just coincidence. These things happen. Everything's fine Tom. It's just I'm... I was worried about the paint drying on the roller, but..."

"Just go then," Tom says.

"But," I continue forcefully, "I've decided it doesn't matter, so here I am. What do you want to talk about?"

"Nothing really," Tom says. "You just seem distant lately."

"Lately?" I say.

"Yeah, since I came home."

I frown at the use of the word *home*, but decide not to take issue with it right now. "Well, since you went *home*, I *am* distant Tom," I say. "I'm about a thousand miles distant. But you chose that, not me, babe." The babe is an afterthought, an attempt at avoiding all-out conflict. "It's nothing we can't handle though, is it?" I add.

Tom clears his throat. "I'm not sure," he says.

"What do you mean, 'You're *not sure?'"*

"It's just, well, if we go on this way, it could be the end of us," he says.

I pull a grimace at the sudden dramatic twist. "What are you on about? Carry on like *what?"*

"I feel like I'm single," he says. "I don't feel like I'm in a couple. You're just not there. Only I don't feel able to do the things I used to do when I was single either. It's weird. I'm bored."

I rub the bridge of my nose. "It's not weird Tom," I say. "You're *not* free to do the things you used to do when you were single because you *aren't single."*

"Yeah," he says vaguely. "Only every time I even try to talk to you you're too busy even to do that."

I run a hand across my beard and wonder if this is true in any way. It certainly doesn't feel true. It sounds to me like pure paranoia, or an attempt at engineering a dispute. "Babe," I say. "I'm on the phone with you right now. I'm..."

"But even now, you'd rather not be," he says. "Even now, you'd rather be painting the ceiling. And you *hate* painting ceilings. You told me. I mean, if something's changed then you should tell me, that's all I'm saying. Because, I need to know where I'm at so that... I need to know, that's all."

"Look Tom," I say, starting to feel riled. "It sounds to me like you want to go shag around and you're trying to pin the blame for that..."

"How can you say that?" he interrupts. "You see what you're like? I mean, where did that come from?"

"You're going on about what you used to do when you were single,"
I say. "What did you mean? Masturbation?"

"I meant going out clubbing and stuff."

I shake my head. "And what's to stop you doing that?" I say.
"Certainly not me."

"Well if I do, I might meet someone," he says. "I mean, that's why I
used to go out in the first place."

"I think you want me to authorise you having a shag, but I'm not
going to. You chose to go back. You chose to be on your own for
Christmas. You chose for me not to come with you."

"I can't believe what I'm hearing," Tom says. "I haven't even
thought of having *a shag*, as you so beautifully put it."

My mobile starts to vibrate and then chime.

"Is that your mobile?" Tom asks.

"Yeah," I say.

"Who is it?"

"I don't know," I answer pedantically. "I haven't *looked.*"

"Why?" Tom asks. "Who *might* it be?"

I shake my head. "Tom," I say. "What's got into you? Have you
taken something? Have you smoked some dodgy weed or something?
Because you're sounding really weird, really paranoid."

"Be my guest," Tom says, ignoring the question. "Answer it. It's
probably your lover."

For a second I'm speechless. I'm just about to cry foul, just about
to tell Tom that he's projecting his own guilty desires onto me, when
he beats me to the punch by making the exact same accusation.
"That's why the accusations are flying," he says. "You're projecting your
own desires onto me. It's you who wants to shag around."

I cross the room shaking my head and glance at the screen of my
mobile. "It was Ricardo," I say. "Happy now?"

"Ricardo?" Tom says.

"Rick – Jenny's boyfriend."

"Oh," he says glumly.

I sit back down and spin the mobile on the coffee table. "I just
don't know where all this has come from," I say.

"You had better phone him back," Tom says. "Say hi from me."

"Right," I say.

"OK, talk later," Tom says.

I struggle to get past my anger, to find a soothing comment to end this conversation, something that will prepare the way for the *next* call, but before I can think of anything Tom hangs up. I put the paint-stained handset back on the stand, making a mental note to clean it quickly, and shake my head. "Jesus!" I say.

I finger the mobile, wondering whether to phone Ricardo back or wait till later, when there's an heavy rap on the door. "That'll be my lover," I mutter, opening the door to reveal the *pompier* version of Ricardo, mobile in hand. *If only.*

"I call, but..." he says, somehow smiling but looking worried at the same time.

I wave the mobile at him. "I was about to phone you back," I say. "I was on the phone to Tom."

"He's OK?" he asks, still hovering on the doormat.

I nod and struggle to wipe away the slapped-arse expression I'm sure I have on my face. "Yeah, fine." I say.

"You eat already?" Ricardo asks. "Only I just finished." He makes an open palmed gesture here conveying that this is the reason he is dressed as he is, "and I think maybe you will have lunch with me."

I sigh. "I'm actually painting, Ricardo," I say, copying the gesture, to explain the paint-splashed outfit.

He grins. "I can see," he says, reaching out and touching my nose. "You have on your face. Maybe I can help you and then we have lunch."

I shrug. "No, I have loads of food in and I only have one roller, so..." I say.

"OK, maybe I make lunch and you finish the paint?" he says.

Back at the top of the ladder, as I listen to Ricardo clomping around my kitchen in his boots, and even occasionally breaking into song – in Spanish – I can't help but wonder whether his calm assured insistence is a sign of naivety or arrogance.

Personally, I'm always over-primed to take things as a sign that I'm *not* wanted, already on the verge of bowing out at the slightest hint that someone might *not* prefer my presence. And then I think about how easily, lazily generous Ricardo is. For all his good points, and though I can't think of them at this instant, I acknowledge to myself that he has many, Tom would never turn up with surprise pizzas, he would never offer to make lunch while you finish something. You can *ask* Tom to do just about anything, and if you start to do it he will watch and be ready to help, but he would never spontaneously offer, let alone insist. There's something infinitely touching about Ricardo's gestures, and, I wonder, something maybe lacking in Tom's inability to ever act in the same way.

Ricardo makes two simple salads from the contents of the refrigerator, and for some unknown reason toasts *ten* slices of bread, and then we sit to eat, he in his navy blue *pompier* outfit, me in my paint splattered clothes. He's in a good mood, smiling and jovial (is he *always* like this I wonder?), and he tells me about his morning, *"So boring, I just wait for the phone to ring, but nothing. It's a terrible thing to hope for some catastrophe,"* and I explain about the insurance deal, and why I'm painting the ceiling myself, and when we finish, as if he lives here, he clears the table, dumps the plates in the dishwasher, kisses me on both cheeks and makes for the door. "I have to go change," he says. "And then I have to go do some shopping."

I hold the door open and smile at him. "Thanks," I say. "That was a good surprise. Again!"

He nods. "Oh, yes. And tomorrow – I want to ask you what you are doing tomorrow?"

I shrug. "Tomorrow?" I repeat.

"Christmas!" he laughs, all white teeth and smile lines. *"La Réveillon!"*

"Ah shit, yeah," I say. "Christmas Eve. I forgot. I've been *trying* to forget I think."

"Jenny say you should come have dinner at home. She say, says?"

I nod. "Says," I repeat.

"She says you don't like to be alone. So you should have dinner with me."

I shrug and grin. "Well, if Jenny says," I say. "Who would *dare* defy her?"

Ricardo frowns. "You will come?"

I nod. "Sure," I say. "That would be great. I'll bring wine, and what, maybe a dessert?"

"Bring champagne," Ricardo says. "It's Christmas. Again!"

I work my way, incredibly slowly it seems, through the day. As I apply a second coat of paint, note that the stain is already seeping through, and head off to the DIY store for fresh advice, it strikes me that the three hundred euro deal maybe isn't so generous after all. I think vaguely about Christmas dinner with Ricardo, and what I should wear, and what I should take, but mainly it's the conversation with Tom that plays over and over in my mind, tying my stomach in knots as my mood swings from concern to anger and back again.

I decide to wait for him to call me once he's feeling more rational. Trying to talk before he reaches that point can, it seems, only make things worse. But at midnight, fearing that even the noxious paint fumes won't get me to sleep, I cave in and phone first his landline, and then his mobile. This only makes my sleep problems worse because he doesn't answer either.

At three a.m. and then again at six, I awaken and have to peer bleary-eyed at my email just in case it bears news, so by ten a.m. on Christmas Eve, by the time I finally get up, I feel like I have barely slept at all.

While the coffee brews, I try Tom's numbers again, but there's still no answer, so I call Jenny and ask her to intervene, mentioning the spectre of Tom's mini breakdown to justify my concern.

She seemingly relishes our little drama. "To be honest," she tells me, "I'm going out of my mind with Christmas TV and sunflower seeds. And it's not even Christmas yet. It'll be a pleasure."

"Sunflower seeds?" I say.

"Don't ask," Jenny says.

"But what..."

"*Really,*" Jenny says. "Don't ask."

We agree that if she manages to speak to him at all she'll call me back, which she fails to do, and as evening approaches, I start to realise that the last thing I feel like is a celebratory dinner with Ricardo. When I phone him however to test the idea of cancelling, he not only declares that everything is ready for the, *"best English Christmas dinner ever,"* but that he has just spoken to Jenny and that she has instructed him not to let me back-out.

Unavoidable Mistletoe

Ricardo's flat, overlooking the port, is in a typical Niçois building – the staircase is all blown light bulbs and flaky paintwork. But when he opens the door, I find myself in something that looks like an Ikea demonstrator: how to fit everything into twenty square meters – *gorgeously*.

The lounge, which has two French windows overlooking the harbour, has a parquet floor, a shaggy woollen rug and a velvety designer-sag sofa bed. The lighting is provided by six small spot-lamps highlighting tasteful paintings on the rough whitewashed walls. I smile at him and hand him my dripping brolly, which he props up in the shower.

I look around approvingly. It's all a bit too tidy – he could turn out to be a bit of a maniac which could end up being a challenge for Jenny – but it has to be said, the tiny flat is really quite beautifully arranged.

"Come!" he says, beckoning me to follow. "I cook!"

Ricardo welcomes me into his space like an old friend, pointing me towards the bar and leaving me to serve drinks while he battles in the tiny kitchen. I feel at home; I feel like an old friend, but this all leaves me feeling a little confused, because, of course, I'm neither. I serve two glasses of whisky on ice and we clink glasses and Ricardo resumes beating his Yorkshire pudding batter. "Jenny gave me," he says, nodding at the recipe. "She says it is *essential* for Christmas dinner."

I sip my whisky and watch Ricardo, and the drink works its magic and the edge fades from my mood, leaving only the relaxed at-home feeling. It crosses my mind that everything looks, in this instant, even more like a page from a brochure, all good use of space, low lighting and easy smiles. But it feels good – it feels a damned sight better than wherever my head has been for the last forty-eight hours; I can feel the muscles in my neck relaxing one by one as Ricardo babbles on.

He has made a huge effort to make me an *English* Christmas dinner, as he keeps emphasising, and I start to salivate as he finishes trimming the Brussels sprouts, and as the smell of roast potatoes begins to waft from the oven.

"This I do last, I think?" he asks, pointing the plastic jug of batter at me.

I shrug. "Sorry, I never made Yorkshire pudding," I say.

"But is *essential* Ricky," he says, apparently mocking Jenny.

I nod and smile. "Yes, it is. But I don't know how to do them."

Ricardo shrugs and nods to himself. "I think when the turkey is nearly done."

I grit my teeth. "Turkey?" I say.

Ricardo nods. "Traditional also," he declares.

I nod. "I'm a vegetarian. You know that, right?"

He nods. "Yes. I know," he says happily. "No meat. Only turkey." He glances up and catches my eye and begins to frown with realisation.

Amazingly, my principles desert me. After twenty years of vegetarianism, I just can't bring myself to tell him that vegetarians don't eat turkey. I force a grin. "Oh, that's good then," I say. "As long as there's no meat."

Ricardo smiles again, and that smile in that instant, strikes me as far more important than the poor bird's life. I wonder what has come over me. He nods towards the doorway. "Shall we go," he asks, "to the bedroom?"

I laugh and lead the way. "The *living* room," I correct him.

"Ah," he says, cheekily. "But is also the bedroom."

I cross to the French windows and stare out at the lights on the jetty.

"Cool, huh?" he says, sounding, for an instant, pure American.

I nod. "I used to live here – well, a bit further down that way." I point to the right. "It's a great view. Noisy in summer though."

"Yes," he says, moving to my side. "The... *livraison*..."

"The concrete deliveries," I say. "All that grey powder. Awful!"

"Yes," he agrees. "And so early in the morning."

We stand in silence for a minute and I become aware, first of the sound of his breathing next to me, and then of the heat of his body reaching across the gap between us and warming my arm through my shirt-sleeve. It feels peculiarly romantic, almost like a date – almost like that moment when you wonder when the first kiss will come.

"So what happen with Tom?" he asks, thankfully breaking the

116

silence.

I shrug. "I don't know. He's having a wobble I think."

"A wobble?" he repeats.

I nod and sip the whisky. "He's being strange."

Ricardo nods. "All human beings are mad. It's just whether you can find one whose madness you can live with," he says.

I laugh. "Yeah... sounds about right. But I do worry. He had a sort of breakdown about a year ago. He was on anti-depressants – Prozac. Still, I suppose lots of people are."

"Oh yes," Ricardo says. "Lots. In France, many, many."

"We had this really weird conversation," I say. "He phoned and said he didn't feel like he was in a couple, that he was missing doing the things he did when he was single."

"Sexual things?"

I shrug.

"Not so good," Ricardo says, swilling the whisky around the glass.

"No," I agree.

"He should not make you worry like this. He should just do quietly his needs."

I turn to him, a confused expression forming. "Well, it's not really how *loud* he is about them," I say. "It's the needs themselves that worry me."

Ricardo shrugs. "People do what people must do," he says. "If it's the end then it's good to tell, if it's important. But otherwise, it's better to be quiet. Better not to worry everyone. Life is too short."

I combine a small laugh and a little outrage into a short gasp. "So *you* think he should just lie to me?"

Ricardo nods seriously. "The end is the same," he says. "Only you are worried. You don't agree?"

I shake my head. "No," I say. "I think he should be faithful. I don't need to shag around, I don't see why Tom would... should, whatever."

Ricardo wobbles his head from side to side and then looks back out over the port. "You are special maybe. I think it is better. I think faithful is better, but most men – they have needs. But if they are, *comment dire...*"

"Speak French if you want," I say.

Ricardo shakes his head. "It's good for me to use English. No, if they are little needs – I don't see why to hurt your partner by telling everything."

I sigh. "I see your point," I say. "But..." I shrug and sigh again.

"You never?" Ricardo says.

"What, cheat?" I ask.

"Yes," he says. "With other people."

I shake my head.

"Never!" he says again.

I shake my head and laugh. "No, never," I say.

Ricardo nods. "You very serious boy."

I shrug. "You seem very surprised."

Ricardo tilts his head wistfully. "Even normal men..." he says.

I wince. *"Hetero* is better," I say. "Or straight."

Ricardo frowns in incomprehension.

"I'm *normal* too," I say. "Or I like to think so."

He nods. "Yes," he says. "Sorry, of course. So most, *hetero* men, even Catholic, they do things they shouldn't. Sometimes – often maybe – I think it saves a marriage. Lets people do what they must without ending everything. I suppose I think that gay men will be more – *flexible."*

I laugh. The whisky and my tiredness are hitting home and the lights on the jetty are blurring. I blink hard, then, normal vision restored, I say, laughing, "Most of them are. More *flexible*, that is."

"But not you," Ricardo says. He sounds impressed. "Not Mark."

I feel a bit prudish, so I answer, "Not yet," and then wonder if that sounded flirtatious and rephrase, "never up until now," and wonder if that didn't sound even worse.

"Pas encore..." Ricardo translates. "OK."

"And you?" I ask, trying to move the conversation away from how up-tight I apparently am. "You don't cheat on Jenny, do you?"

Ricardo stares back out at the sea. *"Pas encore,"* he says, laughter in his voice.

I nod and grin. "But if you did you wouldn't tell her anyway. Or me either."

He sighs and shuffles his feet. "It depends," he says.

"On?" A first uneasy pang about where this is going hits me. I notice that I'm feeling slightly flushed, and vaguely aroused. I wonder if the two are connected.

Ricardo sighs. "Oh I don't know," he says. "If it is a little thing, of no importance, then no."

I nod. "And where do you draw the line?"

"The line?" he asks.

"How do you decide if something is important?"

Ricardo blows through his lips. "Maybe a kiss. Maybe a kiss is not so important. And maybe feelings. Maybe if I'm drunk and something happen, but it is not important – maybe then I don't tell."

I nod. "I guess," I say, vaguely.

"But if, you know, you see someone many times – well, then, maybe you have to decide who you want to be with."

I nod. "I can see the logic," I say. "But it just..."

"And it depends who," he continues. "Say it's a friend of Jenny – say I kiss you, or Tom, or a girlfriend of her – she would be hurt. So I would not tell."

I try to swallow but my mouth is suddenly dry. I swig the last of my whisky. My dick is hardening – I'm hyper aware of his physical presence beside me – and I'm not sure if it's just the whisky or my tiredness, but the situation seems increasingly unreal. "And is that something you're likely to do?" I say. "Kiss Tom?"

Ricardo laughs lightly. "Tom? No!" he says. "But with you, it might be good."

I clear my throat and summon my final reserves – my final reserves *of reserve*. I place the glass carefully on the wooden sideboard and turn to Ricardo. I touch his arm gently and nod and smile wryly. I wrinkle my nose and nod. "This is where I should leave," I say calmly, with certainty.

He smiles at me broadly and tilts his head to one side. "I like you," he says simply, a glint in his eye.

We stare at each other for a few moments. His eyes are deep seductive wells, and it's a struggle not to let go of the rope, a struggle not to relinquish myself to the free-fall into ecstasy or oblivion or whatever is calling to me from those depths. But my mind is a cacophony of screaming alarm bells. In the stupidity stakes of life, sleeping with Jenny's boyfriend would clearly be hard to beat. "I know," I say. "And I'm flattered, but..."

Ricardo raises an eyebrow. "Just a kiss then," he says, leaning towards me.

"I don't..." I say, but it's all I can manage.

Ricardo licks his lips and shrugs one shoulder. "Just a quick kiss –
for Christmas. Oh, yes! I have this!" He produces a sprig of mistletoe
from the sideboard and lifts it above his head. "Now you *can't* refuse."

I smile and he leans in a little further, but at the last minute I turn
sideways to avoid the impact. His stubble grazes my cheek. I brazen it
out and move and kiss him on the other cheek turning the whole sorry
episode into a goodbye peck.

He sighs, straightens and looks at me with an amused, circumspect
expression. "So here," he says, theatrically, almost *camply*, pointing at
his cheek, "is OK. And here," he points at his lips, "is not?"

I nod and laugh. "Something like that," I say.

He measures the distance between his cheek and his lips with
finger and thumb and then shows me the result. "So, what, *six*
centimetres between good and evil? I must read my Bible again."

I snort, part out of amusement, part out of embarrassment. "You're
right," I say. "It's absurd, but..."

He shrugs and looks at me quizzically. "So don't be," he says with a
mini-shake of the head. "Don't be absurd."

I stand before him and freeze as his face comes closer; I can feel his
breath on my lips, the heat of his nose beside mine. And like a dam
weakened first by a tiny leak and then crumbling into a gush and
finally rupturing into a torrent, I sense my defences collapsing. When
his lips touch mine, lightly at first, I think, *"Oh God, no,"* and then
simply, *"Oh God."*

He kisses me on the lips and I don't hinder or abet; I just stand
there in that thought, *"Oh God,"* and let him. And then he slides a
hand behind my neck, pulls away and says, "I really *like* you, you know.
Since the day in the mountains." And then he moves in for a second
kiss, and this time, as he pulls me towards him, I turn my head so that
we make a better fit and it seems that at that instant, because of that
simple act of acquiescence, I am as steeped in the sin of the moment as
he is. Curiously, I think of something my auntie used to say: *"You
might as well be hung for a sheep as a lamb."* I think of Tom, pissing me
around and think, *"Fuck him!"* And perversely,*"Huh! Two can play at
that game."*

I wonder if there is a *scale* of infidelity, or is that *it; is it simply now,
done?* And if so, if I *am* to be hung for my crimes, why *not* just go the
whole hog? It's at this point that I open my jaw and let Ricardo's

tongue enter my mouth; it's at this point that I pull my stomach in so that his hand can work it's way past the waistband towards my dick.

"*Eh, oui,*" he murmurs, pulling me towards the sofa, then sitting and unbuckling my belt. As he pulls my jeans down, I catch sight of myself in the mirror. For an instant, I see myself exactly as I am: a sad, weak, human being, with no willpower, no principles – someone who would cheat on his partner with his best friend's boyfriend. And in that instant, I almost summon the willpower to stop it all – my muscles even begin to move in the right direction. But then he lies back on the sofa and wriggles his own jeans off, and I stop looking in the mirror, and look instead at his tight body, at the swirls of fur around his belly button, at his expectant, naive grin, and he's as tempting as a fireplace on a rainy day, and I simply forget about walking away. I remember instead, the thought I had the first time I saw him: that there are people who are *so* pretty, *so* seductive, *so* charming, that there's just no point *trying* to resist.

He pulls me to the sofa beside him and we press our bodies together – delicious. I unbutton my shirt and help him shuck his polo, and then we pull each other tight, desperate to maximise the skin-to-skin contact. He reaches and pushes his stiff dick down so that it sits between my thighs, and then, amazingly, nothing else happens.

We lie there together, kissing occasionally, looking into each other's eyes, smiling. I stroke his back, he strokes my hair, and each twitch of his dick solicits an identical twitch from my own and that makes us snigger, and the simple fact of that laughter on a rainy Christmas Eve feels like a gift from some open-minded, benign God.

After maybe twenty minutes, I start to doze, and my arousal fades, and I wonder confusedly why this act should count for anything at all; I wonder how our societies became so fucked-up that a cuddle became a crime?

And then the moment is broken and I'm awake and my mobile is vibrating across the coffee table and Ricardo is jumping up and saying, "*Merde, la dinde,*" and there's smoke in the room, and I'm blinking at my nudity and pressing a button and listening to Tom sing, "*We wish you a merry Christmas. We wish you a merry Christmas...*"

When he has finished, I say, as one might to a child, "Thanks Tom, that was lovely."

"You OK?" he says. "You sound weird."

"Sorry, yeah, I dozed off."

"You're at Rick's aren't you?" he says.

I clear my throat guiltily. "Yeah," I say. "He's in the kitchen. Burning the turkey. But I'm knackered. I hardly slept."

"Turkey?" Tom says.

"Don't ask."

"Anyway, I know it's only the twenty-fourth, but I wanted to say happy Christmas, and, well, sorry. For everything."

"I tried to phone you," I say, realising as I say it that Tom has actually apologised – a first!

"Yeah, I was out," he says.

"But I phoned you this morning too," I say, re-buttoning my jeans, and thinking that I'm not in the best position to be expressing outrage no matter where he was, but that this probably won't stop me.

"Yeah," he says vaguely. "Anyway, give Ricky boy a big kiss from me, and you two have a lovely evening, OK?"

"And you, Tom? What are you doing?"

"I'll call you tomorrow, OK?" he says. "Byeeee." *Click.*

"Yeah," I say, frowning and putting the already silent phone back on the table. "Bye."

I refasten my belt and button my shirt, and think that Tom is hiding something, and think that there are problems closer to home, and then wonder briefly which problem I need to think about first.

I head through to the kitchen where Ricardo, still bare-chested, is using his polo shirt to fan a smoking, turkey-shaped lump of charcoal on the windowsill.

"I burn the bird," he says despondently.

I bite my lip and smirk despite myself.

"What?" he asks. "It's not so funny."

I crack into a broad grin. "Actually, it *is*," I say. "Vegetarians don't eat turkey."

Ricardo shakes his head. "No?" he says. "And you? You *don't?*"

I shake my head slowly.

Ricardo feigns outrage. "So you do this on purpose," he says. "You seduce me and drug me to sleep and burn my dinner?"

I mimic his outrage. *"I seduced you?"*

Ricardo opens his arms and walks towards me. "OK," he says. "We seduce each other."

I take a step back and shake my head. "I think I should go," I say. "I mean, this really isn't such a good..."

"No," Ricardo says. "You burn my dinner and then leave me? I don't think so."

I laugh. "Well, is any of it even... I mean, are even the potatoes OK?" I say.

Ricardo shrugs pathetically. "Sorry," he says, opening a cupboard and peering inside. "Pot Noodle?" he says. "I have lots of Pot Noodle. And we have Champagne."

I laugh and shake my head. "Crazy guy," I say.

"It's OK?"

I laugh. "OK, Ricardo. Pot Noodle. But no funny business."

He nods. "OK," he says. "No funny business if you don't want. Just Pot Noodle and then Champagne, and then we sleep. Chicken and Mushroom or... Chinese Chow Mein, or... Tikka Masala..."

He pulls a face. "I think they all have meat or bird in them."

I shake my head. "No, it's fine," I say. "They don't have anything real in them at all. I'll go for the Tikka Masala."

"OK," Ricardo says, reaching for the kettle. "You open the Champagne."

Deserving Better

I sigh and stretch and lick my lips. My mouth is dry, I have a vague headache, and a slight backache too. And there seems to be too much light in the bedroom. I wonder if I forgot to close the shutters. Tom's heavy arm around me exacerbates my backache, so I reach above the covers and move it to my hip. Something about it, the weight, the girth, the velvety hair, makes me open one eye, and I see that this is not my bedroom, this is not my bed, this is not Tom's arm, and I deduce, then remember, that the hot body pressed to my back, the erect dick squashed against my buttocks, is not Tom's either.

I groan and start to roll away, but the arm moves back around me and pulls me in tightly. "Later," Ricardo murmurs. "There's time for all that later. Sleep."

I remain frozen for a few seconds and then as if hypnotised by his command, sleep washes over me anew, and I relax into the warmth of his grasp.

The next time I awaken, I find myself alone on the sofa bed. The sky beyond the windows is bright blue and sunlight is streaming into the room catching particles of dust in its beams. Something about the hard edges of the shadows this seaside-light produces reminds me of my brother's place in Brighton. I can hear Ricardo's voice from the kitchen and I listen for a while to be sure that he's on the phone – that there are no other voices. I quietly pull on my jeans.

He is standing naked, facing the other way, staring at the horizon, one hand holding the phone, the other, absent-mindedly stroking a buttock. The coffee machine is spluttering beside him, and there's a smell of toast.

I watch him in silence. I stare at his buttocks, appreciating the proportions of his legs, the shape of his back, the neck, the bicep showing on the arm that holds the phone. And then the toaster pops up and he spins and sees me.

"Jenny," he mouths, pointing at the phone with his free hand. I point to myself and wiggle a finger at him, but he either doesn't understand or chooses to ignore me. "Yes, he's here," he says. "I give you."

I roll my eyes, stifle a groan, and accept the handset. "Hello?" I say.

"Merry Christmas," Jenny says. *"Merry Christmas!"* Sarah repeats, shrieking in the distance.

"Merry Christmas to you too," I say.

"Shit, you sound rough," Jenny says, brightly. Her voice hurts my head.

"Yeah," I say. "Too much to drink."

"Ricky said," she tells me. "Still you two must be getting on OK if you're still there. That's nice to hear."

"Yes," I say. "I fell asleep and..."

"His place is cute," Jenny says. "Don't you think?"

I clear my throat. "Yes," I say. "Real cute."

Ricardo winks at me and I roll my eyes and shake my head to indicate that we weren't talking about him.

"Small but perfectly formed," Jenny says. "Like my Ricky."

I swallow and glance at *her* Ricky. He's scratching his balls, unselfconsciously grinning. I nearly say, *"He's not so small,"* but I catch myself. "Yes," I say. "Exactly."

"You're useless today," Jenny says, "put Ricky back on, will you? Oh, by the way, Tom never did phone me back."

"No," I say. "He phoned me on my mobile."

"Oh good. That's OK then. Byeeee!"

I wince at her piercing goodbye and hand the phone back to Ricardo who chuckles and holds the phone a foot from his ear. "Yes," he says as I fill a glass with water. "Two bottles... Champagne. Yes! *And* whisky..."

He turns back to face the window, and stealing a last glance at his buttocks, I head back to the lounge. "Yes, Pot Noodle..." I hear him say. *"Si*, Pot Noodle. Because I burn it... OK, I *burned* it."

When Ricardo returns, he's wearing a towelling dressing gown, stolen apparently, from the *Majestic* hotel. He puts the pot of coffee on the table and starts to pour two cups. "How do you feel?" he asks.

"Erm – how about guilty?" I say.

This makes him smirk. "Your head, I mean," he laughs.

"Guilty," I deadpan. "And hung-over."

He shrugs and hands me a cup. "No guilt. Nothing happen," he says, now serious as if it's important to convince me of this fact.

I wobble my head from side to side. "Not quite *nothing*," I say. But of course in a way he's right. Bill Clinton claimed that a blow-job from Monica Lewinsky wasn't sex. My own definition usually widens to include any two people in the same room having an orgasm. But Ricardo and I didn't go that far. Does that make it OK? I wonder. "I didn't think you would tell Jenny," I say.

Ricardo looks shocked. "I did not," he says, categorically.

"I mean, about me staying," I say.

He slips into a relieved smile. "Oh, yes, but it's normal. I said you stayed. You *stayed*."

"But you won't tell her... the rest," I say.

He pushes his lips out and shakes his head violently. "No," he says. "Why would I?"

"Do you love her?" I ask.

Ricardo frowns. "Why? Why do you ask me this?"

I sigh through my nose and try to retrace the thought. I was thinking about Tom I suppose, wondering if this new situation implies something about my love for him, or lack of it. Before I can answer, Ricardo continues, "You must not think me a bad guy you know – I like Jenny a lot. But the truth is, it seems that we're not such a big story."

"Oh," I say.

"But I like her a lot," he repeats. "Really. She makes me laugh so much. I always like the one who make me laugh, and Jenny is very funny girl."

"But you don't think it will last?"

Ricardo shrugs. "Everything is not up to me..." He coughs. "Anyway, I want to go back to Colombia, so..."

I pull a startled expression. "Really? I... But you said you wanted French nationality."

He nods. "Yes, I must wait for the papers. But then I go home for one or maybe two years."

I nod. "I see," I say. "Jenny doesn't know that though?"

He shakes his head. "It's complicate," he says. "I don't know when I get the papers. I have been waiting for five years. So maybe next week, or maybe in five more years."

"But you definitely want to go back?"

He nods.

"You don't like it here?"

Ricardo laughs. "Sure! Otherwise I would not stay so long. But the French are not so funny, you know? I like France, but we Colombians, we have more fun. People laugh. And drink. They party. Like the English maybe. When I was in London, it reminded me of home."

I nod. "I understand that. I miss home too sometimes."

"And my mother," he says, seriously. "She is very old now. And not so good health. So..."

I nod.

"She will die soon. I don't want her to be on her own."

I nod again, more solemnly.

"It's like you say," he says. "Life is messy."

I nod. "It is," I say. A wave of sadness washes over me. I swallow with difficulty. I'm not entirely sure who I'm feeling sorry for. The thought that just drifted into my mind – that Ricardo might not love Jenny, but that I *do* love her – triggered it. Even if my own kiss and cuddle with her boyfriend never comes to light, her relationship is ultimately doomed, and that saddens me. She deserves better.

I think of Tom saying, "We're all *doomed*," in his funny, mocking way, and it seems clear in that moment that we *are* all doomed. He and I are also *doomed*. It's not that my night with Ricardo has really changed anything, but that it seems in this instant transparently obvious that the writing has been on the wall for us – in ten foot high letters – forever. And it is this thought: that nothing good can come of any of this, not for Jenny waiting for Ricardo to leave; not for his aging mother waiting for death, not for Tom, or myself – it just seems to me that we all somehow *deserve better*. That thought, combined with the tiredness and the hangover just knocks the stuffing right out of me. A tear even starts to form in the corner of my eye. I stand clumsily. "I need to go home," I say croakily.

Ricardo stands and opens his arms, a look of deep-rooted concern on his face. "Come here," he says. "You must not... this is Christmas."

But I shake my head, force a smile and push him gently away. Christmas is over. "No," I say. "I just need to go home. I'm over-tired. *Really.*"

Waam Baam...

When I leave Ricardo's, I don't go home – I head for the beach. It's stunning outside and the late morning sun is as hot as an English summer's day. The beach is almost crowded, mainly, it would seem, with over-dressed Italian holidaymakers picnicking and snoozing off their Christmas Eve hangovers. I sit at the water's edge and throw pebbles into the sea, which, after the rains, is an artificial looking opaque azure.

I let thoughts swing and sway through my mind in the hope that I can come out the other side with some logical conclusion, but everything remains a crazy swirling mess of guilt and excitement, of missed opportunity and lucky escape.

I have imaginary conversations in my head with first Tom and then Jenny, but they all lead to argument, to hand-wringing, heart-breaking loss for everyone concerned, and I come to agree with Ricardo that the best option is indeed to lie by omission – to say, quite simply, nothing. I wonder if, had I actually had sex with Ricardo, it would still be the easiest route, or would the greater guilt have pushed me to a different path? Would the path of least resistance have been to admit to everything? And then I think sadly that in a way, whatever we do, good deeds or bad, truth-telling or lie making, all we're ever really doing is pursuing a path of least resistance. It's just a question of how conscience defines that path.

I lie back and feel the warmth of the sun on my face and despite the uncomfortable pebbles I fall asleep for a while, possibly ten minutes, maybe forty, I'm not sure. I awaken when I hear myself snore, and blink up and down the beach, wondering if anyone heard. And then I notice that I have an erection, and wonder if anyone *saw*, and then I roll onto my stomach (the pebbles are even *more* uncomfortable) and try to remember again what or more importantly, who, I have been dreaming about.

Back at the house, I see that I have missed a call – number withheld. Overseas numbers often show up as withheld so maybe it was Tom, or Jenny. I'm not sure who I would like it to have been most. Ricardo maybe.

After a cup of tea and some toast, I steel myself and phone Tom in Brighton on the work number he gave me. He answers immediately with a perky, "Happy Christmas."

"Hiya, did you just call? Because I nipped out..." I start, but Tom interrupts me.

"No, it was too early when I ... when I left for work."

Something in his voice – something about how any interrogation might lead towards my own predicament – warns me off asking him the obvious question of *where* he slept last night.

"Did you have fun with Ricky boy?" he asks.

"Yeah, it was nice," I say, convincingly it seems to me. This confirms my decision to say nothing. "I actually stopped over," I say, realising that Jenny already knows this. "I got too drunk to walk home really."

I half expect, maybe even hope, that Tom will ask me about the sleeping arrangements. I have a desire, despite everything, to tell Tom about it, so that we could laugh about my near miss with Jenny's fireman boyfriend instead of it becoming a lie between us, but he either doesn't know the size of Ricardo's flat, or doesn't care, or most likely, trusts me so implicitly, that the idea of anything happening doesn't cross his mind. It's hard to *not* tell him, and I realise that it's simply because Tom is the person *I tell things to*. And that this *not telling*, is probably the biggest sin of all. "Well, I'm glad about that," he says. "It makes me feel a bit less guilty. About not being there, I mean."

"I would rather have been with you," I say. I'm not sure if it's a lie. "But it was OK. He's a really nice guy. How's work going?"

"Huh," Tom mutters. "Money for old rope. There's nothing happening at all. I'm just sitting here waiting for non-existent foreign exchange ops. I'm just surfing the net really. Hey, I almost forgot," he says excitedly. "You have a gift waiting."

With the phone nestled against my shoulder he guides me to the top shelf of the kitchen cupboard, where, balanced on a dining chair, I recover a small package from the behind the pasta. I fish it out, and sit and rip off the kitchen foil as Tom says, "Sorry, I didn't have time to buy wrapping paper."

I'm a bit stunned by the gift: an Apple iPhone. "Jesus Tom!" I exclaim.

"Don't you like it? You can chan–"

"No!" I interrupt him. "It's *gorgeous*. I *love* these. But they're so expensive. It's *too* expensive."

"Well, you said yours is playing up, and I know your mp3 player packed up too, so I kind of thought it was perfect. You can surf the web on it too."

"It's brilliant Tom. I don't know what to say."

"It's a special unlocked one. So you can just stick your own sim card in it," he says.

"Honestly. I don't know what to say. And I feel bad because you won't get your pressie till you get back. Poor boy." In my annoyance at his going away I actually didn't buy him anything at all – a situation I will now have to remedy.

"Well, now you have a toy to play with on Christmas day," Tom says. "And I know I've got something worth looking forward to when I get back as well."

On a bad, disingenuous, self-righteous day, I could get upset over that remark, but today I just silently sigh and push it from my mind. Once we have finished chatting, studiously avoiding, it seems, any in-depth discussion of Christmas Eve on either side of the Channel, I plug the iPhone in to charge and sit and finger the packaging, which, in true Apple style, is almost as beautiful as the product. I want to box it up and open the package over and over as I did with Christmas gifts when I was a kid, but I can't do that without unplugging it, so I resist.

In the afternoon, the sky clouds over again, and I use this fact as an excuse for another siesta, but once in bed, I can't get to sleep – I realise that I'm feeling horny.

In search of release, I try to think of Tom – with my gorgeous iPhone charging in the other room it seems the least I can do – but as I play with myself, it seems impossible to maintain a picture of him in my mind's eye, and eventually, telling myself that what goes on in the privacy of my own brain can't hurt anyone, I give in and let the images jumping up and down at the periphery take over the screen: Ricardo in a suit, Ricardo in fireman's gear, Ricardo naked in front of the window – it's a triple-X blockbuster which leaves me sticky and glistening. And then once cleaned up, as I start to doze, I roll onto my side – almost squashing the cat in the process – and fall into a deep, dark, hung-over sleep.

The bushes are higher than normal, but of course, I realise, it's a maze: the kind they have in stately homes cut lovingly from privet bushes. Tom is in front and Jenny is behind me and we are wandering happily, exploring the avenues and ending up repeatedly, laughingly at dead ends. It's late afternoon, and the summer air is fragrant, the sun low, and we're all best friends, almost one single being. The event is in context: I still have the contents of the picnic – strangely (since I haven't eaten meat for twenty years) pork pies and tomatoes – digesting in my stomach.

As the sun fades, I become anxious about finding the way out, an anxiety that Tom and Jenny don't seem to share. We wander down this path and then that trying out different theories, like always turning right, or following the most beaten path, but they inevitably lead to small gravelly cul-de-sacs. Each dead-end contains a homoerotic statue.

With the twilight fading, it starts to get difficult to see, and I urge Tom and Jenny on ever more frantically, but they won't take me seriously and laugh and mock me for worrying. Their ridicule makes me as fractious as a four year old.

In the dead centre of the maze, I find a tower. It's built out of planks like a child's tree house, or the lookout tower at a border crossing. I climb the steps to get a better view, but when I reach the box it morphs into a sealed white room with a single strip-light and two opposing doors. Tom is standing in front of one, and Jenny, the other. The light starts to flicker and I realise that we are actually inside an exhibit in the Tate Britain – Martin Creed's *Light Going On And Off*. I approach Tom's door and he smiles serenely at me and shakes his head. I turn and walk to Jenny but she repeats the gesture. And then I hear a banging noise coming from the far wall, and a voice calling my name. "Mark. Are you there? Mark, are you there?"

I turn to Tom and Jenny for help, but they, and the doors, have vanished, so I cross the cube and put my ear against the wall and listen to the voice – unmistakably Ricardo's – calling from beyond.

The flickering of the strip-light hurts my eyes so I close them for a moment, but when I open them again, the cube is gone and I'm in my bedroom. I hear the knocking again, then Ricardo's voice. I stand and walk to the front door. I listen, but there is nothing, so I hide behind the door, open it an inch, and peer through the crack just in time to see Ricardo turn to walk away.

"Ricardo?" I say, wondering whether pretending to be out wasn't a better option.

He turns and frowns at me. "I need to talk," he says.

I nod vaguely. "I... was asleep," I tell him, taking in only now that this is probably reality and the white cube almost certainly the dream.

He climbs tentatively back up the step to the landing. He's wearing his uniform. "I'm sorry," he says.

"It's OK," I tell him. "Just let me get some clothes." I push the door to, and return to the bedroom. I throw myself across the bed to fish my jeans from the far side, but when I turn, Ricardo has followed me and is standing right behind, so close in fact that there is barely room for me to stand.

"Shit!" I exclaim. "Don't do that!"

"Sorry," he says, smiling weakly. "I make..."

"Yes," I say, pushing him away gently, and moving my jeans so that they hide my dick. "You made me jump."

"Jump," he repeats.

With the bed against my calves and Ricardo three inches in front of me, I'm feeling a little trapped. "Can you just... ?" I make a shooing motion towards the dining room. "Let me get some clothes on?"

Ricardo laughs and takes the jeans from my hand. I frown at him. "What are you... ?"

"No," he says, grasping them and throwing them onto the bed. "You don't need."

I shake my head and look around the room for clues – this all seems a bit unlikely. Not as unlikely as a cubic room with no doors, but unlikely all the same.

"Ricardo," I say.

"Yes?" he grins.

"What do you think you're doing?

He flashes the whites of his eyes at me. "I realised," he says. "We *have* to." As he says this he slides one hand behind my back and steps forward – I can feel the hard leather of his boots against the sides of my feet. My dick – now erect – presses against his blue nylon trousers. He grasps the back of my head and kisses me hard. And I let him. We kiss deeply for a moment, our tongues rolling around together. His left hand finds its way to my dick and he squeezes it gently, making me murmur, "Oh."

This makes him laugh and repeat, almost mockingly, "Si – *Oh!*" He releases my head – he doesn't need to hold it in place any longer, and moves his hand lower, unzipping, then pulling out his own erect dick.

And then he surprises me by giving me a gentle push back against the bed. My knees buckle and I am forced to sit, my head level with his waist. He pulls me forwards and pushes himself into my mouth. "Oh, oui!" he says as I open my jaw and let him in. "This is what I want."

I am feeling a little shocked about the porn-film direction this dream is taking: fireman rapes sleeping friend. *But then again...* He grabs my head and pushes harder down my throat, making me gag. "No," he says. "You can..." and pushes again.

I think of the guy in Paris who could, and for the first time in my life, I find that *I* can. I even reach out and pull his buttocks harder towards me.

"That's right," he says. "Oh, yes."

After maybe twenty seconds though, my gag reflex returns, so Ricardo pulls out. "Turn around," he says.

My throat hurts, which must, I figure, mean that this is really happening. I look up at him. Real or imagined, it's truly a porn video.

"Yes," he says, pulling a condom from his pocket and raising an eyebrow.

"It's too late anyway," I think, standing, and nodding gravely. *"It's done."*

"No," Ricardo says. "On the bed. Like a dog."

I think to correct him, to tell him that *doggy style* sounds less aggressive. And then I wonder if I don't actually prefer, *like a dog.*

I reach towards the nightstand for some gel, but Ricardo pulls me roughly back towards the edge of the bed and spits on my arse. It's not the safest lubricant, but there's something overwhelmingly erotic about the gesture, and by the time I have thought about it it's too late anyway because he's already pushing at the gate, murmuring, opening, wheedling his way in, and then he's pumping into me, slamming against my buttocks, and I'm yelping in pain / pleasure / guilt / ecstasy / God-knows-what. Like an animal on heat; like a dog.

Despite his reputation, he comes quickly – too quickly. He pulls out too quickly as well, making me gasp at the loss. But then he gives a new set of commands. "Turn around. Yes, bring yourself – yes, I want to see you," and as I start to wank myself off, he pinches my nipples so hard he makes me yelp again.

Staring into my eyes and nodding slowly, the *pompier* now more devil than saviour says, "Yes. You like that." He's surprisingly convincing. It hurts like buggery, but I *do* like it.

As soon as I come, he releases me, ruffles my hair as if I'm a cub scout who has just performed a good deed, kisses me on the forehead, and glancing at his watch, says, "Sorry, but I must go. See you later."

I watch him button up, turn and leave. I listen to the front door closing behind him, and I lie back on the bed, my chest still glistening and still so aroused, that frankly, I could do the whole thing again.

Wham, bam, thank you ma'am – who would have thought that Ricardo could epitomise so succinctly everything that is wrong with gay men? *And* everything we fantasise about?

As the clouds outside drift across the evening sun, making the light from the window brighten and darken like a light going on and off, my mood shifts and changes too, running from a strange unexplained elation that feels almost like the buzz of first love, through depressed moody guilt, onto self loathing for my cheap infidelity, and then back onto a fresh bout of arousal.

So I lie on my bed and stare at the ceiling, and wonder where the roulette wheel of my emotions will settle. Occasionally I glance over at the used condom on the sideboard – it really is there.

Though the next day is, in France at least, nothing other than an ordinary weekday, I use the excuse of my Englishness to celebrate Boxing Day, thus avoiding the requirement to put a fresh coat of the special stain-proof paint I have bought on the *still* stained ceiling.

The weather outside is sunny, but my emotional weather map has settled towards the lows of the previous day and I'm feeling depressed and guilty and above all, sorry for myself. It seems to me today that all of my relationships are based on my fulfilling some *need* within the other party. In Tom's case, it's all about the gîte. In Ricardo's case, it would seem, judging from his quick departure, that it was all about the need to ram his genitals somewhere. Even Jenny, it now strikes me, is only *really* present in my life because Tom and I saved her from an abusive relationship with her alcoholic ex; is only *living* here, because she too needed a fresh start, far away from her own messy past.

But of course, it's Ricardo I think about the most. His attitude, though sexy at the time, can only, when analysed, be seen as macho, insulting, and possibly even verging on homophobic. *Oh, you're a gay man? Suck this would you?*

About four, halfway through a Christmas episode of *Absolutely Fabulous* on BBC Prime – an episode I have seen many times before, an episode *everyone* has seen many times before – the phone rings, and even though I can't think of anyone I really want to talk to, because the number is hidden, I pick up. It's Jenny, and she wants, she says, to have a, "natter."

"Tell me what you think about Ricky," she says. "I've been dying to ask."

I lie and tell her that I am just heading out to meet a gay friend in crisis. "Tony?" I say. "Did you never meet him? Oh well, he lives in Paris most of the time."

When I hang up I make a mental note not to forget the salient details: Tony, Paris, crisis. Another step in the lying game.

When Ricardo calls a little later I hesitate but then pick up, half wanting to tell him to go fuck himself, half desirous, simply, *strangely*, to hear his voice again. He tells me that he wants to talk, and he sounds unusually serious, so I decide that it is a good adult thing to do – to go and face the music, to name and shame; to state clearly and concisely that this chapter, whatever he thought it was, has now ended, and that all we need to do is agree in adult fashion exactly who will say what to whom, or more precisely who *won't* say what, so that we can forget the thing ever happened and move on. I arrange to meet him in the Bar du Coin – a local pizzeria, and I warn him not to tell Jenny. She thinks, after all, that I'm busy counselling the imaginary Tony.

I'm not quite sure what I'm scared of, but I feel the need to see him in a public place on neutral territory. Maybe, it's to control my anger. Or more likely I'm scared that if I go to his place, he'll say, "Suck this," again. Maybe I'm scared I would be unable to say 'no'. Again.

The End Of The World

Approaching the restaurant, I see him standing outside kicking a stone. He's casually dressed in jeans and a navy polo, and as I reach his side, he looks up and smiles broadly. "Hi," he says, standing aside, and ushering me into the restaurant.

We're shown to a small table against the big plate-glass window, and the waitress, a biker-chick with heavy eyeliner and black fingernails hands us menus.

"So why the mystery?" he asks, "With Jenny, I mean."

I frown. "Oh, it's just – she asks me questions about you all the time. It's hard enough lying without having to explain what we talk about."

Ricardo nods, glances at the menu, then looks back at me. "Just tell her you like me," he says.

I nod vaguely and check my own menu.

"You *do* like me?" he says doubtfully.

I clear my throat. "I didn't really come here to talk about how I *like* you Ricardo. I came here to say that what happened was crazy. And we have to agree that no-one needs to know."

He frowns at me. "Oh," he says.

"I... I'm feeling a bit confused to be honest," I tell him. "I don't even know *why* that happened. And it wasn't even an accident. You came to visit me. You knew what you were doing. Why?"

"Because it's nice?" he offers.

"It's not though, is it?" I say. "It's just sex, and lies, and..."

"Videotape?" he says.

I laugh weakly. "Hopefully not. It's all just pointless though. No good can come of it."

"You think?" he says. "I see."

He sounds genuinely disappointed, so I glance up from my menu to study his face, but he's studiously reading, giving nothing away. "I thought it was..." he says vaguely, flicking his brown eyes at me, "something *good*."

"Did you?" I say, puzzled. "You left pretty quickly afterwards."

He frowns at me. "Yes. I had to go see a friend," he says. "It was arranged. And I had to change first."

I nod. "I thought maybe you were going to work," I say. "But even so, it was a quick exit."

He looks at me blankly. "Even doctors don't work on Christmas day," he says.

"As a *pompier*, I mean," I say.

He snorts lightly. "Ah, the uniform. No, that was just for you. Because you say you like."

I take this in, and turn and stare out at the street for a while. "I still don't see why you did that really," I say. "It's a crazy situation. A stupid situation. How did we get here?"

When I turn back to him he's looking at me soulfully. "I think it's nice," he says naively.

"Nice?" I repeat.

He frowns at me. "I don't understand. You seem sad. I am happy."

I give a cynical gasp. "Why? Because you're cheating on your girlfriend?"

He looks shocked. "Because I..." he says, his voice fading away.

"Oh come on Ricardo. It's hardly *Love Story* is it?"

He stares at me unmoving. His eyes look soft and glassy. "Sorry," he says. "I thought..."

"What?"

He laughs, and raises his eyebrows in the middle, arching them above the bridge of his nose. "I thought you liked me," he says. He looks genuinely hurt.

I sigh and soften my voice. "I do. But that's not really what this is about, is it? It's like you said. It's just chocolate. But it's so *dangerous* – for everything else."

He pushes his lips out and shakes his head. "Not for me, no. But..." He turns away and stares across the room. Without looking at me he says, quietly, "So, you just want to stop?"

I frown at these words. They reveal something shocking to me. That he sees us in the middle of a *process*. He doesn't see this as just a freak event that has occurred between us. I'm aghast.

He turns back to face me and raises an eyebrow. "You could? Just stop?" he says.

I stare at him. "You're serious aren't you?" I say.

He vaguely shrugs his shoulders. "Serious?"

"You want this to... to *carry on* somehow?"

He nods. "Yes," he says. "But I... *pensait. Je pensait?*"

"You thought," I prompt.

"Yes, I *thought* you... like me too."

I swallow with difficulty. "I do," I say. "Only..."

"But you could just *stop?*" he says, nodding, circumspectly as if this possibility is only slowly percolating into his brain.

We are interrupted by the waitress. After a bit of frantic menu-scanning we both order no-brainer, four-seasons pizzas, more to make her go away than anything else. The interruption gives the time required for this fresh idea to percolate into *my* mind. Ricardo is being serious here. This *wasn't* just a quickie, it wasn't just a staged porn show. He wants more. And that realisation transforms everything I have been thinking about him. And I start to wish, *not* that I had never slept with him, but that everything *else* was different.

He nods at me. "It's OK," he says. "It's just – it will be hard for me. I think I..." he shrugs. "I think it is different for you. You have what you want I suppose."

I frown. "With Tom?" I say. "But so do you."

He nods. "I never met a guy I liked before. Not in that way, this way... So..." he shrugs. "It's special for me."

We sit in silence for a few minutes. Ricardo stares out of the window. He seems to swell and redden slowly. When he looks back at me he has a forced smile on his lips and a shine in the corner of his eye. "It's OK," he says bravely. "I'm an idiot."

I reach for his hand across the table and grasp his fingers. I sigh. "I'm sorry," I say. "I don't know what's going on in your head Ricardo. You're really sweet. But this *is* crazy. You're just feeling confused. Jenny will be back soon."

He shakes his head gravely. "But I don't want," he says. "Jenny is nice. But..." There is a long pause. He shakes his head and stares at me soulfully and for the life of me I don't know what to say to the guy. Everything seems stranger by the moment, and my emotions are shifting so fast they're leaving my brain behind.

Eventually he smiles sadly at me and says, "I thought about you today."

"Don't," I say.

"You didn't?" he asks.

"No, I did," I reply. "Of course I've been thinking about you."

"So it's OK," he says.

"No, it's crazy," I say. "It's a momentary thing. And it can't go anywhere. It's a blip. A random blip on a radar screen, destined to fade away." I think as I say it that he'll have no idea what I mean.

"I think to just stop," he says. "Just..." he clicks his fingers. "I think it's too hard."

I nod. "But Jenny will be back."

He swallows. "The day after tomorrow. But let's be... let's be gentle with our heart," he says.

I'm sure that this accident of poetry has more to do with his lack of English than anything else, but the words, and the contradiction of this most complex of guys, the blokey fireman, the suited spiv, the straight boy, gay boy, porn boy, *lost* boy before me, saying, "Let's be gentle with our heart," cracks me wide open leaving my heart raw and pulsating in the middle of the table between us. And in this instant, he, or perhaps the dream of him, the fantasy that he represents, is everything I ever wanted, everything I ever hoped for. I realise in that moment, that at some point I stopped believing in true love, and started believing in pragmatism. Tom is nice, lovely even. But Tom was never *it*. Tom was never *The One*, and nor were any of the others. Except maybe Steve. For I do remember feeling this raw the first time I met Steve, sat at a table around two different pizzas in another restaurant not half a mile away. That was the last time the dream seemed within reach, and then I grew up. Because, of course, it *wasn't* possible, and I saw so clearly that that was *it*, and that it would only ever happen once.

A clearing of a throat to my left averts me to the presence of the waitress. She's holding two steaming pizzas. I realise I'm grasping Ricardo's hand, and, starting to blush, I release it. I avoid eye contact with the waitress as she places the food and our carafe of wine on the table and then slowly I raise my line of vision until I'm looking through my watery lenses into Ricardo's eyes. They are shiny with a similar emotion to my own. He smiles at me.

"Two days," he says. He sighs, and then shrugs. "It's too late anyway."

I stare at him.

"Can't we just pretend?" he says. "Can't we just enjoy two days? Is it such a sin? Like the kiss? Is two days worse than one?"

And I say, weakly, "OK."

I can't think of anything sensible to say. It feels like the end of the world. It seems like someone has announced that the end of the world, the moment when everything comes crashing down, is forty-eight hours from now.

And faced with the end of the world, there is no sensible reply to anything – anything *nice* that is – except, "OK."

Two Days

It's astonishingly easy to slip into a different life. I come to understand how sudden ruptures happen after decades of marriage. The open landscape of a new relationship – no limits, no expectations – is so easy to run to from the slowly narrowing corridor of predictable behaviour and hammered-out, ever more restrictive roles.

Ricardo stays at my flat that first night and though we don't have sex, it all feels appallingly easy, shockingly natural. We lie side by side in the new bed (at least this isn't quite the bed that Tom and I have been sleeping in) and talk until the small hours of the morning, mainly about France and the French and the contrasts with our home countries. I finally fall asleep listening to the lilting English and then the almost perfect French of Ricardo's Latino accent, rambling on and on into my dreams about, yet again, the many different kinds of rain in Bogotá.

The next morning, he's up and out before I am compos mentis, rushing off home at seven a.m. to get changed into his work attire.

During the day, I repaint the ceiling (which with the new paint, finally covers) and then the walls (which against the sparkling new ceiling have started to look distinctly dowdy.)

Driven out by the smell of paint, I return that evening to Ricardo's place, and we eat takeaway Thai food on a foldout table set against the window and the vista of the port beyond.

Ricardo is different today, gentle and thoughtful, calm and collected. He tells me about his previous experiences with men (maximum duration three nights) and his longest relationship with a tormented Argentinean painter called Adriana.

Tom and Jenny play on my mind, but when I try to mention either, Ricardo says simply what I presume to be a translation of a Colombian proverb: *Don't waste a sunny day crying about rain.*

That second night on his sofa bed, the lights of the harbour twinkling in the distance, we have slower, gentler sex; no penetration, just three hours of rubbing and stroking, exploring each others bodies.

Despite what I said to Jenny, it doesn't bore me at all.

Ricardo sleeps well, snoring often, clamped to my back like a bear, but what with thinking about the future and fighting to enjoy every second of the present – I, myself, barely sleep at all.

The next morning – the day of our personal Armageddon, Ricardo surprises me. He has somehow organised a day off work. We go back to my place – God, I'm calling it *my* place again – and I lend him a set of bike leathers. They're a bit too big around the waist, but he looks stunning. Ricardo likes what he sees as well and parades in front of the mirror, a distinct bulge at the groin. "Jenny would like, he declares, the only time he mentions her during the entire forty-eight hours.

"Jenny?" I say, surprised. "She has a leather fetish too?"

"Oh, everyone has leather fetish," he informs me.

And so it is, that with Ricardo clamped around my waist again, we bob and weave and wind our way in and out of the warm sun, in and out of the chilling shadows, back up to the place where I first ever saw him at the roadside – Chatauneuf d'Entraunes.

As I ride past the very point where we met he squeezes my waist and shouts, "You remember?" and I shout, "Yes," and spend the remainder of the climb wondering how he can continue to be so easily romantic, so impossibly optimistic in the midst of such confusion and potential destruction.

I can see from a distance that the gîte is still boarded up, all the windows dead or shuttered, but I ride all the way to the top and park in the courtyard.

"So this is it!" Ricardo declares, clambering down from the bike and pulling off his crash helmet. "That was great. I miss my bike now," he says. "Adriana hated bikes. But I should have kept it."

We wander around the grounds, picking up wind-toppled chairs and peering in dirty windows. Ricardo is unexpectedly enthusiastic about it. "You should put small table here," he declares. "Catch the evening sun. Serve expensive aperitifs. And over here, maybe a pool one day, or maybe it's too cold. Maybe an ice rink!"

But the place feels dead to me. For some reason, it feels like the past.

We walk past the dark stone hut where Tom and I had impromptu sex, and Ricardo apparently has the same idea; he winks at me and points at the dark interior, but I shake my head and pull him onwards.

The memory of that place is too sweet and the future too uncertain for me to want to redefine it with Ricardo.

We sit at the rusty table in front of the gîte and Ricardo unpacks the sandwiches from his backpack.

I stare at him, handsome and manly in bike gear. Some people look like they're in fancy dress, like this clearly isn't quite *them* – but Ricardo looks entirely at ease. He smiles at me – that smile, always so broad, always so easy – and I think about the fact that we're at the top of the hill, that it's all downhill from here.

And I think that he's probably the best looking guy I've ever slept with, and then, trying to be objective, I study his face in the crisp light. Some might look at him and see the gently pitted skin as a fault, no doubt the result of acne in his adolescence, or his barely perceptible cross-eyes. Others might look at him and see the grey hairs emerging at his temples, and imagining old age to come, wonder why he doesn't dye it. But unless I really make an effort, I don't see any of these things. I just see those eyes; I just see that smile. And I suppose that this partial blindness is a symptom of love, or at least infatuation.

"What are you looking at?" he laughs. "You make me nervous!"

I smile. "Just you. In all your glorious leather."

"Your!" he laughs. "Except the boots. And they belong to *les pompiers.*"

I nod and glance at the road, snaking and twisting down the hill, back down, bend by bend, to the oh so messy future, and wonder if we're allowed to discuss it yet.

"So?" Ricardo asks, looking around. "What do you think?"

I shrug. "About what?"

He nods at the building. "The gîte," he says. "You still want?"

"Is that why we're here?" I wonder. *"To size up possible futures?"* But surely I'm projecting here. The air may feel heavy with the scent of destiny, but if it came to it, Ricardo would never really have anything to offer me – he'd run a mile, I'm sure of it.

I shrug. "What do *you* think of the place?" I say.

Ricardo scans the vista and nods. "Beautiful," he says. "Incredible. But I would not live here."

I nod.

"Too isolated," he says. "Too far from..." he laughs. "Too far from *everything.*"

I nod again and look around. "Yeah," I say.

"Unless I was very, very in love," he says. "Maybe then..."

I clear my throat. "Yes," I agree. "I suppose that's what it comes down to. I suppose that's what it all always comes down to."

Ricardo rips off a lump of his sandwich and then speaks through breadcrumbs. "And are you? With Tom? In love?"

I shrug. "I don't know," I say. "Not now. Not anymore."

Ricardo sighs. "He's been gone for six, seven days?"

I nod. "Seven."

Ricardo shrugs. "A week. If you're still not sure," he says, "then maybe you aren't."

I nod and sigh. My stomach is starting to feel tight and my appetite for the sandwich is fading. "I thought the rules were to not talk about that."

Ricardo nods. "You're right," he says. "Eat."

I wrinkle my nose. "Later maybe."

I watch him chew and think about the reply to his question. But it's so complicated; my thoughts are such a messy swirl, it's an impossible equation. For clearly, I *do* love Tom. The simple thought of him sends a pang of angsty-guilt through my intestines. But the things I would miss about him: his presence, his humour, sex... well, Ricardo has been filling the gap, so to speak. And I haven't missed them at all.

I love Tom, of course I do. But I'm not sure that I *believe* in him. I'm not sure I have ever really convinced myself that our relationship was solid enough to last, that Tom, himself, is solid enough to ever build a future with.

And now, here I am, on the verge of falling *in love*, that stupid, hysterical, illogical state of being. And that's a totally different emotion, originating, it seems to me, in an entirely different part of the brain, outside of logic or reason or even reality. But it's so powerful that, drug-like, it's starting to smother every other emotion, every other circuit of reason. "Maybe not enough," I say, finally.

Ricardo nods. "Like Jenny for me," he says.

I nod. "Christ, Ricardo," I say. "What the hell happens now?"

Ricardo raises an eyebrow and sighs again. "I know," he says. "Difficult."

"Tonight, Ricardo. Jenny comes home, *tonight*." I glance at my watch. "In *five* hours."

Ricardo nods. "What do you think we should do?" he asks, as if we're discussing a holiday route-map.

I shake my head. "I have no idea," I say.

"You want to stop?" He flattens his hand and makes a chopping gesture. "Like... it was a dream? A bip on a radar like you said?"

I shrug. "No," I say. "That's not what I *want*. But..." I shake my head and stare out at the peaks opposite, and notice for the first time that there is still snow there, the remains from my last visit slowly fading away.

A stupid, stupid song slips in to my head: *Torn between two lovers.* It's so idiotic – I'm ashamed at the workings of my own brain.

"Jenny is... important to me," I say. "And Tom. I don't want to hurt Tom. And anyway I don't know if... it's too soon, I don't know if it's real, what's real... and... I don't know, really I don't."

Ricardo nods. "OK," he says, slapping a leathered thigh. "I think of this idea when you say about Tom. About not knowing."

I nod. "Go on," I say.

"So, you and I, we stop. Today. When we get home. Maybe one last..." he winks at me. "But then we stop. Jenny arrives tonight. Tom arrives?" he shrugs.

"Tomorrow," I say.

"OK. So we say nothing. We pretend it never happened. And in a while – in, say, ten days – I think we will know better how we feel. We will feel OK or we won't. And then we talk again."

I swallow hard and then exhale with force. "OK," I say, steeling myself. "I suppose that's a plan." The truth is that my own mind is so empty of solutions I'm happy to grasp at any rope anyone cares to throw me. "Shall we go?" I say, suddenly keen to move, now we have a plan, onto the next phase.

"You are OK with this?" Ricardo says.

I nod. "It's infinitely logical," I say.

"And your sandwich?" he asks, pushing the tin-foil package towards me.

I wrinkle my nose. "Later," I say. "When I get home. This place is giving me the creeps."

Ricardo nods, pops my sandwich and his wrapper back in the backpack and stands. "I understand," he says.

"Plus," I say. "I need to get home and get my head straight before

Jenny arrives."

Ricardo puts an arm around my shoulder and tries to pull me to his side, but I blunder away as if I haven't noticed. I'm already onto the next thing.

Of course, close bodily contact is required for the descent. Ricardo asks if he can drive, and in my strange Armageddon mood, I agree, so I end up wrapping *my* arms around *him* for the entire ride home.

Despite all the stresses and fears of the situation, I find hanging onto him hopelessly sexy, and it's as much as I can do to muffle the stupid wheedling, childish voice pleading from somewhere just behind my left ear. Like Andy from *Little Britain*, it says, "I want that one."

This Friend Of Mine

It is so soon after Ricardo leaves that I open the door to Jenny's travel-weary face that I wonder if they haven't crossed paths on the stairs.

"Hi darling," she says, kissing me on the cheek, and then rattling on, "I don't suppose you've seen Ricky? Only he said he'd drop by, and he's not here and his phone's not answering and I was wondering if maybe I'd missed him."

"No," I say numbly, the taste of him still in my mouth. "I'm sure he'll call."

"OK, well, let us get settled and then come have a drink eh?" she says.

"Wouldn't you rather be alone? I mean with Ricardo?"

Jenny screws up her face as if I'm mad. "No, I want to hear all your gossip," she says. "And anyway, as I said, I can't get through to him."

I think that I need to phone Ricardo and warn him of my presence at Jenny's, then think that if his phone's switched off that I won't be able to. "Why don't you come down to mine," I say. "If he doesn't find you upstairs he'll soon guess."

But Jenny interrupts me. "No," she says forcefully. "Sarah's completely knackered, so it's best if we do it at mine. See you about..." she pauses and glances at her watch, "let's say nine thirty. OK?"

I nod. "Nine thirty," I repeat.

Jenny turns to leave and then looks back at me. "You look really well," she says. "I haven't seen you look so healthy in ages."

I blush, half at the compliment and half at the realisation that my post-coital glow isn't purely mental. "Must be all the rest," I say.

"From work, or from Tom?" Jenny asks, a sneaky tone in her voice.

"Work of course," I say.

"Humm," Jenny says thoughtfully. "If you were a woman I'd think you were pregnant. You have that kind of homely glow about you."

I pull a face. "Thank God that's not a possibility," I say.

She winks at me and nods. "Indeed," she says. "A job for life... talking of which. Madam is waiting." And with that, she turns and trudges back upstairs.

By nine-thirty, my pregnant glow has, as far as I can see, entirely faded. I actually think I look a bit pale. I run an open hand across my chin, blow out sharply through pursed lips as if preparing for round two, and head upstairs.

I haven't been able to speak to Ricardo, and the idea of bumping into him at Jenny's *really* doesn't appeal.

But Jenny puts me at ease immediately. "Ricardo can't make it," she says. "There's a mini flu epidemic and apparently they've put him on call."

"A flu epidemic," I say. "That's probably the explanation for that pregnant glow you noticed."

Jenny puts a hand to my forehead. "Maybe – you don't feel feverish though."

I close the door behind me and watch her return to the lounge and slump back into her chair.

"Mummy?" Sarah calls from the bedroom.

Jenny rolls her eyes. "Go to sleep," she says severely.

I take a detour via the bedroom, and crouch down next to Sarah. She's tucked up in her mother's bed. Beside her a new clock radio is cycling through the colours of the rainbow. "Hello you," I say in my smoothest voice. "Did you have a good Christmas?"

Sarah nods at me seriously.

"This is nice," I say, running my hand over the dome of the clock-radio-rainbow-lamp.

"It's mine," Sarah says. "Granny gave it to me for Christmas."

I stroke her hair, but she frowns at me and pulls her head away.

"Well you're very lucky," I say standing.

"Thank you," she says. "I'd like to go to sleep now."

I restrain a frown and force a smile. "OK then, night night." I leave the door ajar, and head back to Jenny who is slouched in an armchair with a glass of wine. "Well, that certainly did the trick," I say.

"Uh?" she says.

"The second I tried to talk to her she suddenly wanted to go to sleep."

Jenny wrinkles her nose. "Don't take it personally," she says. "They're just testing boundaries at that age. Trying to see what works and what doesn't. It's not personal, or even meant. She's been doing it with me all day too. Grab yourself a glass from the kitchen will you? I swear I'm paralysed from the scalp down tonight."

I grab a glass, fill it from the wine bottle, which is almost empty, and take a seat opposite her on the sofa. "So," I say. "You seem to be downing that bottle pretty quickly."

Jenny grins and nods. "It's an antidote," she says. "We were up at five and I've been drinking coffee all day – I thought alcohol might have, sort of the opposite effect. Plus my mother's been driving me insane; she's gone microbiotic. Did I tell you that?"

"Macrobiotic?"

"Yeah, that's the one. So everything I wanted to eat or drink the entire time came with a bloody twenty minute health warning."

I grimace at her. "Ouch," I say. "Happy Christmas."

"Indeed," Jenny says, raising her glass. "A toast to being an adult," she says.

I raise my glass.

"To being an adult, and having the freedom to do whatever the fuck you want, no matter what anyone thinks," Jenny says.

I lick my lips, force a big wide grin and clink my glass against hers. "To freedom," I say.

Jenny tells me at length about Christmas in England. She tells me how bowled over Sarah was by a visit to Father Christmas in Debenhams, and she makes me laugh with a blow by blow account of the negotiations with her mother over the Christmas menu which took longer than shopping for and cooking the meal combined. "That's why I dictated your menu over the phone to Rick," she says. "You got to eat everything I couldn't. Or you were supposed to."

"Are you responsible for the turkey then?" I say. "Because you really should know by now that I don't..."

"No," Jenny interrupts. "Of course not. The turkey was for Ricky, only I don't think he understood me properly. Did you really eat Pot Noodle?"

I nod. "We did," I say. "Two each. Washed down with lashings of alcohol."

"What's he like drunk?" Jenny asks. "I've never seen him drunk. Never really wanted to – not after Nick."

I shrug and push a mental image of exactly what he was like from my mind. "Normal," I say.

"Normal," Jenny says, frowning at me. "Normal nice, or normal drunken bastard?"

"Nice," I say. "You know, a bit louder, a bit funnier. Nice."

"Nice," Jenny repeats.

I laugh and pull a face. "Nice," I say.

Jenny contorts her face into a strange expression. I'm not quite sure what it means. "That bad, eh?" she finally says.

I frown at her and shake my head slightly.

"Oh come on Mark," she says. "I know you like I made you. You don't really like him do you? Only you're too scared to say."

I push my lips out and wrinkle my brow. "Not at all," I say. "I don't know why..."

"Because you're being all weird," she says. "You're purposely not telling me anything. You think he's weird or awful or something."

I shake my head.

"Or too nice. You think there's something wrong with..."

"Hey," I laugh. "Methinks ye *projects* too much," I say.

Jenny laughs. "Maybe," she says. "But you did spend the whole night with him. That would usually leave you with more adjectives than *nice*."

The only strategy I can think of is half-truth. "Look," I say. "I wouldn't want you to get the wrong idea Jenny. I think he's *really* nice."

"But," she says.

I shrug. "No buts. Except maybe that I'm a bit jealous."

Jenny's face contorts into childlike glee – a mixture of amusement and pride. "Really!" she says. "You fancy him?"

I shrug and blush. "He's *very* pretty," I say.

Jenny's cheeks rise into big pink domes of happiness. "Huh!" she says. "That's a first."

I shrug coyly. "I wouldn't say that," I say. "Nick was pretty sexy too. In a Neanderthal kind of way."

Jenny nods at me circumspectly. "Was he?" she says. "I suppose. And Ricky is cute in what way exactly?"

"Oh, he's got this whole healer–of–the–sick thing going hasn't he."

Jenny nods. "I suppose he has," she says.

"Plus the *pompier* aspect of course!"

"Yes," Jenny says. "I thought you'd like that. So you think basically that he's mister perfect?"

I nod. "He's very nice, really," I say. "Other than that, well, you know him better than I do."

Jenny nods. "I was hoping to see him tonight," she says. "I could do with a shag. A home-coming post-Christmas shag."

"A home-*coming* says it all really," I say with a laugh, which sounds, to me at least, entirely genuine.

"And Tom?" Jenny asks. "What's happening with you two?"

"I think he's probably had lots of home-*comings*," I say, happy to shift the focus of the conversation to Tom.

Jenny looks confused. "What do you mean?" she asks.

And so, to throw up a smokescreen – to escape having to discuss her relationship with Ricardo whilst avoiding admitting the sordid truth, I tell her of my suspicions that *Tom* isn't being entirely faithful over in the UK. The evidence of course, his use of Recon, his failure to mention where he spent Christmas Eve, is vague to say the least, but as I say it, it sounds true enough.

When I have finished Jenny frowns. "Well, you've not a lot to go on," she says. "But I have to say it, even though I *hate* to say it: you're not usually wrong about these things."

I shrug lopsidedly. I think, "That's probably because I'm the expert."

"Would you dump him? I mean, if you found out it was true?" she asks.

I shrug again. "It depends on circumstances I suppose."

Jenny nods thoughtfully. "So what about you?" she asks.

"Me?" I say, trying to stifle the panic in my voice.

"Yeah, are you shagging someone else?"

I shake my head. "W... Why would... ?"

"Someone called... maybe..." she says teasing me.

I'm struggling to retain my composure here.

"I don't know... erm... *Tony* maybe?"

"Tony?" I say.

"Yes, Tony."

"Who the fuck is Tony?"

"Your friend!" Jenny says. "The one you've spent all week with."

"Oh!" I say. *"Tony!"*

I take a deep breath and recover my wits. "I forgot, you haven't actually met Tony, have you," I say.

Jenny laughs. "Oh," she says. "Not a looker then?"

I shake my head. "He's sweet. But, no. Definitely not. Anyway," I add, embroidering as I go along. "He's already got a partner. *And* a lover. I think his life's quite complicated enough. He's shagging his best friend's partner. That's what all the angst is about. Should he stay or should he go?"

Jenny nods. "That's twisted. It happened to a girlfriend of mine in England. Her best friend was shagging her husband. She lost them both in one go. And they were really close too. Awful business."

Selfish Contrition

At midnight when I get back, I close the shutters and sit in the darkened flat. Lit only by the bars of orange light from the street-lamps outside, the place looks strange and alien, yet at the same time, the difference is refreshing. It feels for some reason like it's been ages since I really *saw* the place and the unusual darkness enables me to do that. It's my flat, and I love it. And of course if the gîte works out I will have to leave it. I have barely thought about that.

The street outside is silent, and with the exception of Paloma purring – she has jumped on my lap immediately – and the humming of the fridge, the world is silent. It feels almost as if everyone on the planet, with the exception of myself, is asleep.

I'm feeling a little sick, so I sit and wait for it to pass. Initially I think the cause is Jenny's cheap wine, but slowly it dawns on me that the cause is more psychological. What I'm feeling is guilt. The sickening stomach churn of a guy who has spent the evening lying to his oldest friend. I think about this, and then about the fact that pretty soon I will no doubt be actively lying to Tom as well, even if only to make sure that the stories I have told Jenny tie up. I think about the twenty years I have known her, about all the things we have been through together from failed attempts at sex to shared traffic accidents. I remember suddenly that I am Sarah's godfather and imagine Jenny explaining to her why they suddenly stopped seeing uncle Mark all those years ago.

I notice a strange taste in my mouth, and then an unusual quantity of saliva, and finally a burst of acid reflux forces me to stand and run through to the bathroom. I kneel and wait, but nothing comes; so after a few minutes I return to the lounge. I wish I had someone to talk to about it all. A sort of gay tribal chief who would dispel wise advice. It's the kind of thing I would usually discuss with Tom or Jenny, and this makes me realise anew how truly fucked-up the whole situation is. And then I think of Isabelle, once a close friend, now living in Canada. Three a.m. in France makes, I calculate, ten p.m. in

Canada. A little shocked at how quickly we forget people once they're out of sight and living in a different time zone – I reach for the phone.

A man's voice answers, presumably her Dutch boyfriend. While I wait for him to fetch Isabelle, I think about the fact that I'm an English guy dating another English guy in France, and having an affair with a Colombian, and that I'm in the process of phoning a French friend who lives in Canada with a Dutchman and I wonder when the world got so complicated. The big global mix-up seems to have happened so suddenly, and almost entirely unnoticed.

"Salut l'étranger," Isabelle says, her voice bright as a spring morning. "Ça fait longtemps!" – *"Hi stranger. It's been ages!"* I ask her about life in Toronto and she tells me that it's, "Géniale, mais glaciale."– *"Brilliant but glacial."* She tells me excitedly about her new job as a photographer's assistant, quite a difference from her previous job as a nurse, I point out.

"I know," she says. "Tell me about it. But things are different here. No one cares about what you *are*, they just want to know what you can *do*."

And then she realises that it's three a.m. in France, and I admit that I can't sleep, so of course she asks me why, and I finally get to spill the beans. The account takes almost half an hour, and she only comments a few times to say, "Uhuh," or "Well, yes," or "No! He didn't!"

When I get to the end, she says nothing, so I wait for a moment and then prompt her, "Well?"

She clears her throat. "I think... well, to start with, I think you shouldn't have told me," she finally says.

"You could have said before," I point out.

"Yeah. But it's interesting," she says. "I wanted to hear. Only now I'm not so sure."

I sigh. "You're not going to feel some moral need to tell Tom or something are you?"

Isabelle laughs. "No!" she says. "It's just, well, I was thinking really, that the only way to deal with it is never to tell anyone. *Ever.*"

"Yeah," I say. "It's pretty bad really, isn't it?"

"So what about Ricardo, or Rick or whatever. Does he love Jenny?" she asks.

I sigh. "I don't know really," I say. "I don't think so. But he might be saying that just to..."

"To make it seem less bad. Sure." she says. "And Jenny?"

"Does she love Ricardo?"

"Yeah."

I scratch my head. "I don't think she's letting herself. I think she suspects something wrong – nothing specific – certainly nothing to do with me. But all the same."

"And what about you?"

"Me?"

"Yeah, who do *you* love?"

My chest is so tight – I'm having trouble breathing. I blow through my lips in an attempt at evacuating the stress. "I love Tom," I tell her. "I do. But it's, you know, comfortable love. It's almost like he's just a friend these days."

"And Ricardo?"

"I don't know," I tell her. "I don't think so. I think I've got that, you know, new person, obsessive thing happening. I think it's more attraction than love. New things, different things, are always so much... shinier? Do you know what I mean?"

"Of course I do," Isabelle says. "Otherwise I wouldn't have run off to Canada with Lars, would I?"

"It's a mess, though isn't it," I say.

"Yeah," Isabelle says. "It is. But of course you don't know Ricardo really do you. You haven't known him long enough."

"No," I say. "I mean, I feel like I do, but logically I suppose I don't."

"What's his biggest fault?"

I shrug even though she can't see me. "I don't know," I say.

"Yeah, so you don't know him at all. Because he sure has one somewhere."

"No," I say. "I see what you mean. Sorry about dumping all this on you, only I needed to talk to someone," I say.

"No, it's fine. Lucky it's me," she says. "Because you really shouldn't be telling people about stuff like this."

"So I should just, you know, keep it to myself, forever? That's what you think."

"Yeah. It's the only way with affairs. Never tell anyone," she says, definitely.

"I'm not sure I'm capable though," I say.

Isabelle clears her throat. "Then you shouldn't be having affairs," she says.

"I just feel so guilty, every time I lie. I feel half the time like I'm on the verge of owning up to it all," I say.

"I understand that," she says. "But your desire for contrition is entirely selfish."

"That sounded very professional," I say. "You could do this for a living."

"What, the desire for contrition being selfish? Oh I read it in a book. Toronto is self-help city. It said that most of the time, owning up to things is about wanting to demonstrate what a wonderful honest person you are, and basically, fuck the consequences."

"That's quite profound really," I say.

"Yeah. It was a good book," she says. "It's true though. I mean, it will feel good for you to tell the truth, well, for a moment it will. But then everything will come crashing down. It would destroy you and Jenny, and you and Sarah, and you and Tom maybe, though you gay boys tend to be more understanding about these things. You have to decide what's more important I suppose. Happiness or honesty."

"And Jenny and Ricardo. It would be the end of them presumably as well."

"Yeah," Isabelle says. "No one left alive. A sort of relationship neutron bomb. The only things left standing would be buildings. You need to think long and hard before you do that."

"Yeah," I say. "I can see that. So I just stop the affair and take the secret of it to the grave."

"Well, stop or don't. Whatever."

"You don't think it matters?"

"It's not that. It's more – I doubt you'll have much control over it. These things tend to have a life of their own. But whatever happens. You have to keep your mouth shut."

"Sounds like experience," I say.

"Sorry?" Isabelle says.

"Sounds like you're speaking from experience," I say. "You didn't by any chance meet Dutchy before you split up with..."

"Oh no," she interrupts. "I would *never* have an affair."

"But if you did you would never tell anyway."

"Absolutely."

"Even me?"

"Even you."

Best Friend

I'm woken at eight a.m. by the sound of Jenny's washing machine – apparently off balance – in the room above. As I slowly come to (I have only slept for three hours) I decide that it's not the sound of a washing machine, but the builders repairing her bathroom. And then, with a sick feeling, it dawns on me that the noise is no other than Jenny having sex. It's the repeated thud of her bed banging against the wall.

The feelings that this generates – arousal at the thought of Ricardo pumping into her, jealousy that it's her not me, guilt that the last place his dick visited was myself – are so diverse, so unmanageable, I simply pull a pillow over my head to shut out the noise. But it doesn't work; so I eventually get up and put the radio on, repeatedly turning it up until I can no longer hear them.

I brew coffee and make toast, but just as I sit down to eat it, I realise that I can still hear banging. Marvelling at Ricardo's tenacity, I glance at the clock, calculating that they have been shagging for at least sixty minutes. Only then do I realise that the noise has changed in tone, nature and direction.

I frown and cross the room to the door. When I open it Ricardo glances behind him, and surreptitiously slips into the room. It all looks somehow very theatrical, very *résistance*, very *Allo Allo*. I grin at the thought.

"I was knocking for ages," Ricardo says.

For some reason, probably because of the *Allo Allo* thought, I answer, *"Yees. So I 'erd."*

He frowns at me, and I snap back to reality. "What are you doing here?" I say. "I thought we agreed."

Ricardo shrugs at me, somehow self-importantly. "I wanted to see you," he says. "I was upstairs."

I nod pedantically. "Yes," I repeat. "I *heard.*"

Ricardo frowns again, and then blushes. "Oh," he says. "Sorry."

I shrug. "It's fine," I say. "Really. But you shouldn't *be* here."

He smiles and opens his arms and steps towards me. "I just wanted..." he says.

I take a step backwards. "Ricardo, are you crazy?"

He shrugs and half smiles. "What?" he says.

"What happened was mad, but this? This is *dangerous.*"

"No," he says. "Jenny is busy. She put Sarah in the bath."

My mouth drops and I shake my head and let out a gasp of disbelief.

"I just wanted," he says, stepping forward again. I notice that he looks very young today, halfway between sweet naivety and demanding child.

"This isn't right," I say. "You can't go upstairs to Jenny and then... it's just not right."

"I can't not," he says, solemnly. "I can't just walk past your door."

He's wearing a tightly cut brown suit and an open necked white shirt. I imagine his body behind the material. A mini porn movie runs through my mind involving me dropping to my knees, unzipping his trousers and fishing his dick from the silky folds, sliding my hands over his buttocks and pulling him towards me.

My dick starts to harden, and I almost start to weaken, but then he winks at me, and there's something in that wink – over confidence, maybe even arrogance – and instead I step around him and put my hand on the doorknob. "Sorry," I say. "But I *can* say 'no.' We had an agreement. You need to go."

Ricardo's smile fades entirely. He shrugs and looks a little petulant. "Sorry," he says. He rearranges his dick to disguise his bulge, and when I open the door, he peers upstairs and steps back onto the landing. "You're right," he says, then, again, "Sorry. I'm stupid."

I close the door on him and return to bed, where, after running more slowly through the porn-film, I start to doze. As I edge towards sleep, I ponder that the moment just passed was a parting of the ways, each route leading to a different future. I could have sunk to my knees, and that would lead to one place. I could have dragged him into my bed and made him late for work, and that might have led somewhere slightly different. I could have told him I never wanted to see him again and that would have been the end. And at the instant I finally sink into sleep, I think that just saying, "No," and putting an end to this craziness once and for all would be the only option which makes any sense. I wonder why I haven't already done that; and then I contemplate the fact that Isabelle may be right: maybe these things do have a life of their own. And if they do, can it be said that there is truly such a thing as freewill at all? Or am I just a bottle bobbing in the waves waiting to see which way the tide will go?

It's lunchtime when I reawaken, and the sun outside looks glorious so I shower and dress quickly before heading to the beach. On the way I stop and buy a *pan-bagnat,* the local sandwich – a Niçoise salad in a bun.

Being a weekday, the beach is much quieter, just a few office workers incongruously dressed and eating their lunch.

Two beary gay guys are sunning their hairy chests at the edge of Castel Plage, the larger guy's head resting on the rounded stomach of his boyfriend, and I feel a pang of jealousy that Tom isn't here with me. Or Ricardo. I force the image back to Tom. I'm pretty sure anyway that Ricardo would never be able to do that. Not with a guy anyway.

I cross the pebbles to where a small bowl has formed, and position myself so that I'm tilted towards the sun. I select Patti Smith – *Twelve* on my iPhone and eat my sandwich. And then feeling vaguely naughty for my laziness, I fall asleep again.

When I wake up the album has ended and I can hear a child's voice nearby.

I sit up and blink at the brightness. I pull my sunglasses down over my eyes and realise that Jenny and Sarah are sitting just in front of me. They're putting stones into a bucket.

"Sleeping Beauty wakes up," Jenny says, turning to face me.

"Bonjour," Sarah says brightly.

I blink at them. "French," I say. "She's speaking French."

Jenny nods. "Yeah. She'll be teaching me at this rate. Have a nice kip?"

I link my hands above my head and stretch. "Yeah," I say. "What are you doing here?"

Jenny shrugs. "We were walking along the beach and we found you."

I clear my throat.

"I was worried about someone nicking your iPhone to be honest."

"Yeah," I say, glancing down at it. "I had it in my hand, but then I fell asleep."

Jenny creases her brow at me. "Well," she says. "You want to at least keep it out of sight."

I yawn and stretch again. "God I'm knackered today," I tell her. "I couldn't sleep last night."

"No," Jenny says. Something sharp in her tone of voice makes me study her features for clues. "Nor me," she adds.

"Really?" I say. "Maybe the moon or something. I phoned Isabelle in Toronto. She's having a great time."

Jenny nods at me. "I know," she says.

"You spoke to her?" I ask.

Jenny shakes her head. "I mean, I heard," she says. "You were talking for hours."

I feel myself pale. "You *heard?*" I say.

Jenny nods. "That's why *I* couldn't sleep," she says.

"Erm, how *much* could you hear?" I say trying to sound relaxed.

"Oh everything," Jenny says solemnly.

I swallow hard. "I..." I say.

"Joke!" Jenny says. "No, but seriously, it *was* noisy. And it went on and on. You sounded like you were reading a book to her or something. What the hell were you talking about?"

I take a deep breath and force a neutral expression. "Oh nothing in particular. Everything. Tom, the gîte, you, Ricardo."

Jenny nods. "Well, next time, sit in the bedroom would you? Your lounge is right under my bed. It did my head in."

"You should have banged or something," I say.

"Oh I couldn't," Jenny says. "I'd think I was turning into my mother. She's always banging on walls. So she's OK? Isabelle?"

"Who's Isabelle?" Sarah asks.

"She's the lady who used to baby-sit, do you remember?"

Sarah nods thoughtfully, and says, "Yes." Then she turns conscientiously back to her task, which apparently is to fill her bucket with *white* stones.

"Mark's best friend," Jenny continues.

I frown at the remark. It sounds like a challenge, and I almost rise to it. I nearly say, "No, *you're* my *best* friend." But I don't. It's just too hypocritical.

I say instead, "Not sure about *best* friend. But she's a very *good* friend. That's for sure."

Knowing

By sundown, I am actively wishing for Tom's return. Without Ricardo the gaps left in my life by Tom's absence are becoming all too clear – I feel lonely and horny. And I *need* to see him too – it seems that only when I set eyes on him will everything become clear: the depth of my feelings for him, the future of our relationship, what to tell and what not to tell.

Of course when Tom finally does return, the world does not clarify instantly into a black and white tableau of obvious choices. He arrives tired and grumpy after a delayed flight next to an overweight woman and her screaming baby, and so he rants on about heterosexuals and children, and weight allowances for baggage but not fat or babies, and I listen and wait for something comprehensible to emerge from the muddy pit of my thoughts.

I serve him a strong drink and finish cooking the special meal I have planned – caramelised endives and flash fried scallops – and the sight of it on the table finally does the trick of shifting him out of his journey and into the here and now of arrival. "Wow!" he exclaims. "This looks posh! We need candles for this."

While I uncork the wine Tom fetches then lights candles, and so it is that we sit down for a romantic looking homecoming dinner.

Tom forks a scallop and groans through his full mouth. "God, this is gorgeous! What's the sauce?"

"Honey and balsamic vinegar," I tell him. "Actually, the recipe was on the packet the scallops came in, so..."

"Well it's orgasmic," Tom says. "God you could serve this in the gîte and everyone would think we had a cordon bleu chef." He swigs at his wine and then sighs deeply. "Sorry," he says. "I've been ranting, haven't I?"

I shrug. "It's OK," I say. "Travel is stressful."

"I swear it gets worse every time," he says. "The airports are packed. Everything's late. I'm sure the leg-room gets a bit less on every trip."

I look into his eyes for the first time in weeks, and this eye-to-eye

165

contact makes me smile and I think, *"We might be all right after all."*

Tom smiles back. "Sorry. Time to forget it," he says.

"Don't waste a sunny day crying about rain," I say, grimacing inwardly as I realise where the phrase comes from.

"Yeah," Tom says. "Exactly. Is that a French proverb?"

I shrug. "Not sure where I heard it to be honest. I think so though. *Ne pas gâcher le soleil en pensant à la pluie.*"

"Have you seen much of Jenny and Ricky boy?" Tom asks, as if tuning in to the real origin of the phrase rather than my invention.

"Not much," I say. "Well, I saw Jenny when she got back last night. She was complaining because her mum had her eating macrobiotic all over Christmas. She lost another kilo though."

Tom pushes his bottom lip out and nods, impressed. "Losing weight over Christmas. Sounds impressive."

"No fun though," I say.

"No," Tom says. "I can imagine."

"And I bumped into her briefly at the beach today as well. She seems fine. Tell me about *your* Christmas," I say. The second I say it, I realise that I have forgotten, again, to buy Tom a Christmas gift.

I think of the iPhone sitting in the other room and I think about who I have been calling with it. The guilt I feel at having been so wrapped up in my fling with Ricardo that I have forgotten to buy him anything at all is such that I actually break out in a sweat. I wonder if he will remember – if he will now ask me for the gift I promised him was waiting. I wipe my forehead.

"Are you OK?" Tom asks.

I nod and cough. "Yeah, fine," I say. "Just suddenly overheating. Hot flashes. Must be the menopause or something. So how was work?"

He frowns at me as if I'm being particularly strange, which I suppose I am, and then to my relief starts to tell me of the interminable hours in the foreign exchange office. I sit and half-listen and wonder if it's now too late to get him something without drawing attention to the fact that I have forgotten – it clearly is. Plus, after my Christmas with Ricardo, any such gesture would be laced with more hypocrisy than I think I could bear – almost certainly the reason I forgot in the first place.

There were, Tom is telling me, about ten clients a day. His uncle, who is also in foreign exchange, dropped by to chat a few times.

"It was quite weird talking to him over the counter," he says, still looking at me enquiringly. "But it made the time go better. He told me all about his love affair with Mum, which to be honest, I didn't want to hear. He feels guilty that he never told Dad about it, but at the time I convinced him not to. I just thought it would hurt everyone concerned really. I still think it's better that he never knew."

"God," I say. "Your uncle and your mum – it's a bit incestuous."

"Well," Tom says. "I know what you mean, but it's not really. People are just people, you know? She was a cute bird his brother was dating when they were in their twenties. Only, Claude fell in love with her – they both fell for each other really. And then Claude went away to Australia – so they spent a lifetime pining after each other. He really thinks he missed out on his one chance for true love. It's pretty sad actually. But the big issue for him is that he never told Dad. That he lied to him for forty years. And now, well, it's too late."

"He didn't actually lie did he? I mean he just didn't tell him."

Tom nods. "Yeah," he says. "I know what you mean, but with something that big it pretty much comes down to the same thing don't you think?"

I blink at him. Did I somehow lead the conversation here? I trace the conversation back, but no, Tom made it happen. I wonder if my guilt is somehow oozing out. Or maybe everything in the universe will now unnervingly revolve around people and their affairs. Perhaps my brain is over-reacting to something which would have had no relevance, thrown into sharp relief by the same mechanism that makes you spend weeks seeing red Minis everywhere simply because your mate bought one. I decide that that's probably the explanation.

Tom peers in at me. "Hello?" he says. "Are you sure you're OK?"

"Sorry," I say. "I was just thinking about it all," I reply. "Your mum was actually going to go off with him then? That's what you said before, right?"

Tom nods. "Yeah. Claude came back after, I don't know, maybe forty years. And they fell in love all over again. I don't know all the details even now – even Claude isn't sure what she would have done. She was trying to work it out when she came down to Italy that last summer to stay with me at Antonio's place. She was pretty weird – all sort of buttoned up and ready to explode. But I thought it was seeing

Antonio and me together. I thought it was the gay thing freaking her out."

I shake my head. "It's sad. For them, I mean. Never getting the chance. But I suppose at least your dad didn't have to find out."

Tom nods. "I know. I don't think they ever even actually – you know – slept together."

I raise an eyebrow. "Not once?"

Tom shakes his head. "No, I don't think so."

"Otherwise your uncle might have been your dad."

Tom nods. "I know," he says. "The timing's about right too. But I think they were too old fashioned then."

"There was definitely no point telling him then," I say. "I mean, if nothing even happened. What would have been the point?"

Tom shrugs. "I think it's worse in a way," he says. "I mean, it wasn't just a quick fumble behind the bike sheds – my mum spent her whole married life *in love* with her husband's brother. That's gotta be worse, surely."

I nod. "I suppose," I say. "But I mean, what's the point in worrying about it now? They're both..."

"Dead, yeah," Tom says. It's OK. No, I think lies hang heavy after a while. Maybe even heavier and heavier the longer you keep them. He feels guilty about having lied to his brother for so long. But I still think it would have been madness. It would have fucked up his relationship with Dad. I mean, they never really got on *that* well anyway – but all the same, they only really had each other after Mum died. I can't see anything good that would have come out of it, except maybe Claude could have felt better about himself."

"A selfish desire for contrition," I say.

Tom nods. "Exactly," he says. "I mean, if he had told him before, *at the time*... there might have been some point – things would have been different maybe. But not forty years later... In a way, the worst crime is the fact that he *didn't* tell him. It kind of undermined their whole relationship. But it's too late now anyway."

I sit and stare at Tom. I can't believe the conversation we're having. I'm pretty certain we're discussing *us* through metaphor, but I can't work out how it happened, unless Tom truly *is* picking up on my guilt. And what, once we process the metaphorical discussion, *is* the moral of the story anyway? That lies undermine a relationship? Or that honesty does? That bad deeds should be admitted freely and quickly? Or never?

I realise that I have been staring at my plate. I look up at Tom and see him looking serious, grave even. "Are you OK?" he asks. "You look a bit green."

I'm aware that my throat is dry and that my eyes are bulging as if the pressure of the truth waiting to come out is squeezing the water from my body. For surely, if Tom and I are to survive then we need to survive the truth, not the *absence* of truth. What basis could *that* be for a relationship?

"I... I don't... I don't know why we're discussing this," I say, vaguely. My head feels swollen and dizzy. I lick my lips and wait for the words to come. *I slept with Ricardo?* Maybe better not to name him. *I had an affair while you were away?* But then if you're going for half-truths, surely it's better to smile and stick to no-truths-at-all.

I look up at Tom. His own eyes are watering too. "I..." I say again. But the words still won't come out.

"Shit," Tom says, slowly shaking his head. "That bad, huh?"

With difficulty I swallow and nod. I bite my lip and stare at my plate again.

"Jesus Mark!" Tom says.

I nod slowly. "I know," I say. "I don't know how to say it, though. I can't seem to find the words."

Tom half sighs, half gasps. He crosses his eyes, then closes them, and drops his head to his hand.

"But how?" he says. "How did you know?"

Living In A Fairytale

Tom shakes his head sadly. "It was... look – I know it's a cliché, but it was nothing," he says. I'm sitting opposite him, my chin resting in my cupped hands. I consider saying, *"You're right. It's a cliché."*

I think I'm in shock – I feel a bit sick, a bit feverish almost. I'm not sure if I'm more shocked at Tom's accidental confession or the fact that mine was cut off at the pass. I don't know whether to feel saved or damned.

The words, *"Don't worry about it, so did I,"* manifest, ready for delivery. Surely that would be the adult, honest thing to say. But as Tom blunders on, my desire to help him out fades, and it seems more and more evident that what we have done isn't the same thing, and that we don't see it in the same way either. I get involved trying to work out which is the lesser crime.

"It was just a guy off the net," Tom says, his apologetic tone fading fast. "I met him twice. I was bored and horny. That's all it was."

I nod at him.

"I mean, it's not really a surprise is it? You knew this would happen at some point."

I frown at him.

"Didn't you?" he says.

I shrug. It seems to me more to the point that *Tom* knew this would happen – from the moment he started trawling the net, even before. It was, as they say in murder cases, premeditated.

"I don't know what you want me to say," Tom says, now sounding almost belligerent.

I haven't said a word yet. I'm not quite sure why it feels like I'm in an argument.

"Oh come on Mark!" Tom says. "Give me a break here. You know that gay relationships are complicated."

I clear my throat to speak. But then I can't sort out which of the thoughts swirling through my speech centres needs expressing first.

"Did you really think we were going to be faithful?" Tom says.

"Forever?"

"Maybe," I say.

Tom continues to stare at me, his expression – red and somehow superior – unchanged.

I wonder if I actually said, "Maybe," or if I just thought it. I clear my throat and say it again, a little over-loudly it seems, "Maybe. Once upon a time."

Tom laughs. It's a sharp, ironic little laugh – mocking even.

I shake my head. "What?" I say.

"Once upon a time," Tom says. "That's the trouble." I continue to frown at him so he expounds, "You just live in this fairytale land where people get married and live happily ever after. But life's not like that."

I nod.

"You expect everyone to be perfect all the time and then you're disappointed when they're not," he continues.

"I see," I say.

"This is pointless," Tom says. "If you're not going to say anything, this is pointless."

"OK," I say. "So when you shagged Dante, and I saved your life, and you promised you'd never let me down again..."

"Jesus Mark. How long are you gonna use that one against me for?"

"And I *believed* you," I continue. "That was a failing on *my* part?"

"Mark!" Tom says. "Get real. Think about it. No one is faithful. Everyone lets you down at some point."

"Then why say it?" I say. "Why promise anything?"

Tom shrugs. "To get you off my back I suppose," he says.

The words spear me; I physically recoil at the impact.

"What does it matter?" Tom says. "So I stuck my dick in some guy's mouth? What's the big deal? Think about it."

I wrinkle my nose and stare at him in disgust. At this very second I truly hate him. I hate him as much as I have ever hated anyone. Ever. And it's not because he's had sex with someone. It's because it *was* pointless. Tom gave away his word for something of no value whatsoever. But most of all, it's because there is more bad faith coming out of Tom's mouth than I would usually come across in a decade.

"You know what Tom?" I say. "You've been having a go at me and, I don't know... You haven't even said sorry. How do you manage that?"

"Sorry," Tom says, pulling a face and shrugging, his voice that of a bored teenager.

"You know what," I say. "Why don't you go fuck yourself... Oh, *I forgot,* you prefer to get someone *else* to do it."

Tom nods as if his worst suspicions are confirmed. He stands. "I knew it," he says, turning and leaving the room. "That's why I didn't tell you," he shouts as he opens the front door.

The front door slams so hard I wince. And then it opens again – I assume he's forgotten something and think, *"So much for the dramatic exit."* But I hear Tom say, "He's in there." And then the door slams again.

Ricardo's head appears in the doorway. "Hi," he says. "Is everything OK?"

I shake my head and force a tight smile. "Please go," I croak.

"But what happen?" he asks. "Did you tell?"

"No!" I interrupt, then straining to control my voice. "Now please just go. It's just not the right time."

Ricardo nods. He walks towards me, squeezes my shoulder. "OK," he says. "Sorry." And then he turns and leaves the room. There's a delay of maybe half a minute before the front door opens and closes again behind him.

Paloma, always terrified by expressions of anger, creeps out from under a chair. She jumps on my lap and starts to lick my hand – an apparent attempt at comforting me.

"He's a bastard Paloma," I tell her. I sit in the silence of the flat and try to work out in the great scheme of things, which is the greater crime; whose karma is the most damaged. Mine for a mini love affair with my best friend's boyfriend: an affair that happened unplanned, against my will almost, and for which I have continuously been wracked with guilt. Or Tom's quicky-behind-the-bike-sheds with a guy off the net, an act which, it would seem, doesn't even merit the use of the word *sorry.* Clearly there's no particular reason sticking one part of one's anatomy into another part of someone else's should register more than a two on the great Richter Scale of life. But then why bother? Why bother at all? And why be such a complete tosser about it afterwards?

My crimes may be on a different scale but at least they happened by chance. At least they were unavoidable. *Weren't they?*

Tom's homecoming dinner remains, half-eaten, on the plate. I can't even bring myself to carry it through to the kitchen and so it sits there, apparently a symbol of our battle of wills.

He spends the night at Jenny's – I can hear them talking until the early hours of the morning. I try pressing a glass against the wall but I still can't hear the words, only Tom's voice droning on and on. It's probably just as well. Any more anger and I would go upstairs and punch him.

***

The next morning we both spend as much time out as possible, and when our paths do cross at lunchtime we move around as if in a choreographed dance, studiously avoiding the horror of ever occupying the same space.

The weather holds, so I spend the afternoon up in the Parc du Chateau reading a brilliant but somewhat depressing novel and watching the *pompiers* doing their daily training. I wonder if Ricardo has to train up here as well, and then wonder why he hasn't tried to get in touch again. I expect Jenny has warned him off.

I toy with ideas for my next move. The scenarios variously involve me bursting in on combinations of Tom/Jenny/Ricardo and announcing either that it's over between Tom and I, and/or that I have been sleeping with Ricardo. But in the end, I do nothing. I don't seem to have the clarity of mind to decide, or the balls to go through with it. Skirting around each other though, is becoming problematic. Tom feels it too, and I'm sitting at the dining table surfing on the laptop, when he plonks down two cups of tea and takes a seat opposite me. I ignore him and continue to stare at the screen even though I'm no longer able to concentrate on it.

"Can we stop this?" Tom says, suddenly, urgently. "I don't think I can stand it."

I click on a random link on the screen and murmur, "Uh?" as if I'm too busy to have heard him. But I instantly relent and close the laptop and look up at him. "Sorry," I say. "That was…" I roll my eyes.

Tom nods. "Thanks," he says. "Can we? Stop this? New Year's Eve is tomorrow and I just don't think I can stand to spend it like this."

I shrug. "I don't know how," I say sadly. "I'm not sure if I can."

"Do you want me to go?" Tom asks. "Because, you know, that's OK. But I need to know. And I need to know if I should just go for a while, or if, I mean... well if it's all over, then tell me, and, I'll sort things out."

I shake my head then shrug. "I don't know," I say. "I haven't even started to work it out."

"If there was something I could say," Tom says.

I nod. "*Sorry* would be a start," I say coldly.

Tom coughs, seemingly at the mere thought of uttering that dreaded word. "I actually *did* say sorry," he says.

"You remember *how* you said it?" I say.

Tom frowns at me.

"Look Tom," I say. "You dumped a load of shit on my doorstep, and still managed to have a go at me. It's not on and I'm still pretty angry."

Tom nods. "Yeah," he says. "Look. I *am* sorry. That I needed to go elsewhere." That he defines it as a need doesn't go unnoticed. Of course honouring needs is so much more respectable than mere wants. "And I'm sorry if I was an arsehole about it," he continues.

I nod. "OK," I say.

"Do you?" Tom says. "Want me to go that is? Because really, if..."

"I'm sorry Tom. Don't ask me, because I don't know."

Tom runs a single finger across his forehead. "OK," he says.

"Do *you* want to go?" I ask.

Tom shakes his head vaguely. "No," he says. "I don't think so."

"OK," I say with a sigh. "Well, let's give it a couple of days, eh? See how we feel once the dust has settled."

"OK," Tom says, starting slowly to stand again. "That's a plan."

"Oh, Tom," I say. "I know it's stupid. But could you..." I nod at the plate.

He blinks slowly at me and pulls the plate towards the edge of the table ready to pick it up. "Sure," he says. As he turns to leave, he pauses. "Oh, by the way. Jenny wants to go for a picnic tomorrow lunchtime – if it's sunny – to Cap D'Ail. Says she has some news, and she's spending the evening with Ricky so we thought we could sort of celebrate New Year at lunchtime too. If you want to come..."

I smile weakly at him. "Thanks," I say. "Maybe. Who's going?"

Tom lifts one shoulder. "Us," he says. "Me, Jenny, Sarah. And you if you come."

I nod slowly. "OK, thanks," I say, then, "News?"

Tom shrugs. "Something to celebrate she says. At least someone's got some good news eh?"

I nod. "Yeah," I say pensively.

Tom nods. "Jenny would like it if you came," Tom says. "So would I actually."

I nod. "OK," I say. "Probably. If I can calm myself down."

Tom starts to leave again, and then jerks back and shooting a tiny, nervous smile at me, he picks up the plate. "Almost forgot!" he says, grimacing and flashing his teeth at me.

Reasons For Champagne

Tom creeps around me all evening, cringing like a battered dog trying to avoid being seen and beaten anew by his master. He's doing his best not to annoy me and I can see why, and even appreciate the effort, but there's something cloying in his tone, something desperate and begging when I catch his eye, and in truth it only makes me *want* to beat him like a dog.

That night, however, he returns to the matrimonial bed. He doesn't ask me if it's OK, which to be honest is a relief. Instead, he waits until I'm asleep and sneaks in without waking me. At some point during the night I become aware that he's there, but, not awake enough to analyse it, I simply feel comforted by the physical presence. It's as if in sleep I have forgotten that we're at war.

In the morning though, when I awaken to find him curled against my back, one arm draped somewhat proprietarily over me, it's too much too soon. Feeling a pang of physical revulsion, I lift his arm away and get up. Tom makes a sort of snoring groan to show he's still asleep and therefore not responsible for his actions. I'm unconvinced.

He gets up shortly afterwards and after muttering a neutral, "Morning," busies himself putting the picnic together, running up and down to organise with Jenny who is taking what.

I drink coffee and read the papers online, and when Tom finally asks if I am joining them, I surprise myself by saying, "Yes." I didn't know myself that I had decided.

Just as we're leaving, at the exact moment Tom goes upstairs to help Jenny with her stuff, my mobile rings. Seeing that it's Ricardo who is calling and anxious to check he's not joining us, I scoot through to the far end of the bedroom and answer it. "You're not going are you?" I say.

"Hello?" Ricardo says.

"Sorry," I whisper. "Hello. Are you going on this picnic?"

"No. I thought we could have lunch. I want to see you."

"I can't," I tell him. "I'm going on the picnic."

"Don't," he says. "It's perfect time."

"I can't," I say. "It's too late."

"You ready?" Tom asks, peeping around the doorframe. "Oh, sorry. We can hang on if..."

"It's fine," I tell him, then into the phone I say, "No, I can't. It's too late. I've just got an iPhone, so I'm not interested in changing my handset at all. Thanks. Bye."

I click the *End Call* icon and roll my eyes at Tom. "They're so tenacious," I say.

"Bouygues?" he says.

I nod.

"In English?"

I swallow and nod again. "Yeah," I say, winging it. "I used to get rid of them by not speaking French, but they're on to me now. Amazing huh?"

With the radio on I can't really talk to Tom and Jenny during the drive along the coast, so Sarah and I play I-Spy instead. She demonstrates a stunning range of vocabulary in both English and French, but little concept of which objects might, or might not be present, in or around a car. "Cheese, Cabbage, Caca, Chambre, Crumble, Camembert," she spouts.

"Where can you see any caca?" I ask her.

"Out of your bum," she declares, collapsing into giggles.

The drive takes nearly an hour and by the time we have parked the car and clambered down a few hundred steps to the bay – a process made considerably slower by Sarah's requests for piggybacks and shoulder carries, alternating with sudden stretches when she wants to walk – it's nearly two p.m. The sky is deepest blue and the air has warmed enough for me to want to take my t-shirt off. The sun reflects blindingly from the waves in the bay, doubling its intensity, and a nearly full moon is hanging low in the sky to the west. I point it out to Sarah, saying, "Look! The Moon!" But she is unconvinced.

"It's day, *stupid,*" she says. "Not night!"

"You rude little girl," I laugh, jiggling her up and down and making her chuckle.

We open the blanket in the middle of the beach. The restaurants are closed for the winter and we're sharing the entire bay with fewer than twenty people. I can hear from here that the couple at the farthest end of the beach is American and I wonder why tourists so often feel the need to shout at each other – the volume seemingly proportional to the nasal twang of the accent.

We start to delve into the cool-bags and spread out the picnic: a salad bowl with cling-film on top, two baguettes, a plate of cheese... Jenny produces proper wine glasses and knives and forks. But when I peer inside the bag I have been carrying and see Champagne, I start to wonder; I start to *worry*. Finally, having mastered my voice, I say cheerily, "Champagne? How come?"

Jenny positions herself cross-legged opposite. "Yes," she says. "Champagne!"

"Can I paddle?" Sarah asks.

Jenny turns to her, frowns, and then smiles. "Of course," she says, then, turning back to me, "It's a celebration. Didn't Tom tell you?"

I nod. "Yes," I say. "But not the reason."

Tom beside me shrugs. "Hey, I don't know either. She don't tell me nothin'!"

"Well," Jenny says, taking the bottle from me and then handing it back. "Actually, could you? I hate it when it pops. Yes. It's a surprise."

I start to unwrap the foil from the top of the bottle and fiddle with the wire cage. I'm fumbling in my nervousness to get it done, to find out why we're here. I force myself to slow down.

By the time I get to the point where the cork might pop, Jenny is in mid sentence about how beautiful the place is and I have to hold the cork in place to stop it popping of its own accord.

"... it's so *warm* as well," she is saying, "because of the sun, and the way the rocks keep the wind out. And the sea is so sparkly! How did you *find* this place?"

Tom nods at me. "Mark brought me here," he says. "It's your favourite beach, isn't it?"

I nod and smile. "It is," I say. "Hey, this cork's going to blow."

"Oh, wait!" Jenny snaps. "I want to tell you my news. It's bad luck to pop it first."

Tom and I speak in unison. "Is it?" we say.

Jenny nods. "Yes," she says. "Plus, Sarah likes the popping bit. I hate it myself. Makes me jump. Sarah? Sarah! Yes, come here a... that's right darling. Mark's going to open the bottle. So!" She pauses dramatically. "The good news is..."

"Jenny come on, the cork's moving, I can feel it," I say.

"OK. I got a job!" she declares.

"A job?" I say incredulously.

"Yeah," Jenny says, nodding at the bottle and raising her glass. "Don't sound so surprised."

The cork plops out unspectacularly. "Oh," Jenny says. "That wasn't very good was it?"

"Sorry," I say, filling her glass.

"You're suppose to make it pop," she says. "Isn't he darling?"

Sarah looks at Jenny and nods, and then glances at me – a deadly expression of disappointment. Then she shakes her head gravely, and runs back down to the water.

"She's turning into a proper little madam," Tom says. He looks at me and laughs. "The look she gave you!"

"I know!" Jenny says. "So anyway, back to me. I have a job as an English teacher. Twenty-five hours a week, so it fits perfectly around Sarah's nursery hours. And fifteen Euros an hour after, you know, *cotisations.*"

"That's excellent," I say.

"You sound relieved," Jenny laughs. "Did you think I was unemployable?"

I finish pouring my own glass of Champagne and put the bottle down. "No," I say. "I thought you were going to say you were pregnant!" I laugh. "So yeah, relieved is the word."

"How though?" Tom asks. "You don't even speak French!"

Jenny nods and grins. "I know!" she says. "I'm doing conversation practice with foreign students."

"So you're basically paid to yak?" Tom says.

"Exactly," Jenny agrees. "Brilliant huh?"

"You're certainly qualified," I laugh, a wave of relief washing over me.

We toast to Jenny's new job, and then Tom says, "Actually, I'm a bit disappointed. I thought you were gonna marry Ricky boy."

"Marry him? Huh!" Jenny says.

Tom frowns. "No?" he says. "Shame. I love a wedding. Dressing up and everything."

"No!" Jenny says, very definitely. "If you want a wedding it'll have to be you two."

I raise an eyebrow and shoot Tom a scowl that leaves both him and Jenny in no doubt that this won't be happening any time soon.

"There is some news about Ricardo too," Jenny says. "But that's not it. That's really not it."

I frown at her use of his full name. I have never heard her say it once.

"I think Mark already knows," she adds.

I shrug. "No," I say. "I don't think so. Know what?"

Sarah reappears, yanking on her mother's shoulder. "Can I have some?" she says.

"You don't like it," Jenny tells her. "It's Champagne."

Sarah pulls a tantrum face, so Jenny laughs and shrugs and hands her the glass. She takes the tiniest of sips, declares, "Yuck," and runs away again.

"She's terrible isn't she?" Jenny says. "Do you think I'm bringing her up badly?"

"No," I say. "You're doing brilliantly. Now what is it? About Ricardo?"

"Oh," Jenny says. "Yeah. He's, erm, going home, actually," she says, glancing around at the picnic and reaching for a baguette. "Back to Colombia."

Tom widens his eyes in a caricature of surprise. "What, you mean, not for a holiday?"

Jenny shrugs. "No," she says. "For a few years. So he says."

"And are you going with him?" Tom asks.

Jenny pulls a face. "Don't be daft," she laughs. "What would I do in Colombia? Anyway, he hasn't asked me."

"But if you..."

"Tom!" Jenny says. "He *hasn't* asked me."

Tom nods. "Oh," he says. "Sure. Sorry."

"I thought he was waiting for his passport," I comment.

"Yeah," Jenny says. "He told you that much then. Well, he got it yesterday unfortunately. Unfortunately for me that is."

"What passport?" Tom says.

"He applied for French nationality," I explain. "He's been waiting for years."

"Why does he need a French passport to go home?" Tom asks.

"Ironic, isn't it?" Jenny says. "No, it's more that he didn't want to leave till he got the passport. It means he can come and go as he wishes – he can go anywhere in Europe without all those visa hassles. Apparently it's a nightmare if you're from outside the EC."

"So he's coming back then?" Tom says.

"I don't know," Jenny says. "Not soon anyway."

"And when's he going?" I ask. My voice sounds a bit panicky. I need to get a hold on that.

"In a couple of months I think," Jenny says. "Just enough to organise everything."

Tom shuffles across to Jenny's side and lays an arm across her shoulders. "Babe," he says. "That's horrible."

She shrugs him off. "Don't," she says. "You'll just make me all maudlin."

"But..."

"Look. I'm not over the moon about it. It's not... you know... very flattering. I feel a bit... sort of... put in my place. But I'm fine."

"Yeah," Tom says. "It makes you seem a bit superfluous."

"Tom!" I say. "Don't..."

"Sorry, but... sorry," he mumbles.

"Anyway, today we're here to celebrate, not talk about him, eh?"

"Right," I say.

"And anyway," Jenny says. "Who needs sex when you have Champagne, and beaches, and wonderful friends?"

"Indeed!" Tom says.

"So happy New Year!" Jenny says, raising her glass. "To new jobs and new years and wonderful friends."

I steel myself and raise my own. "To new jobs and new years and wonderful friends!" I repeat.

***

Back home, our own New Year's Eve celebration ends up a little lacklustre. Though we do spend a little more on the bottle of wine, and choose baked fish over pizza, the meal feels more like an end of week splurge than an end of year one.

Jenny and Sarah disappear to Ricardo's for the night. I'm a little surprised that she hasn't blown him out in advance of his departure and I assume that this somehow makes her a better, more balanced person than I am. I would have kicked his arse.

Tom has cooked and is earnestly trying to make conversation by giving me a blow-by-blow account of a documentary he saw on the French economy. The interest payments on the state debt alone amount to two thousand Euros a year for each working person, he tells me. And I watch his mouth move, and think that he's right, that it is shocking, and that I should care. And I imagine Jenny and Ricardo eating Pot Noodle with the harbour twinkling behind them and feel hopelessly jealous.

Just as we finish dessert – double helpings of molten chocolate pudding – some yelping in the street below announces midnight, and to my horror Tom gets up, walks to my side, crouches before me and wheedlingly attempts a kiss. "I thought it might help," he explains.

"I think it might take more than that," I say quietly.

"Not fix things necessarily," Tom says. "I just thought it might help us work out how we feel."

I don't want to kiss Tom. I don't really want Tom standing this close to me. But he's here, now, crouched before me, and whatever is happening, I can't inflict a metaphorical slap around the face – not at midnight on New Year's Eve. I don't hate him that much; or at least some part of me – the part that controls kissing – doesn't. I sigh just enough to let him know that I'm not overjoyed at the prospect and lean forward and peck him on the lips.

"Happy New Year," he says. There's a slight vibration to his voice, and when I look, sure enough, his eyes are shining on wine and emotion.

I shake my head almost unnoticeably and let out a tiny nasal sigh. "Happy New Year," I say.

He leans forward for another kiss, and thinking, *"A mercy kiss,"* I close my eyes and lean forward and kiss him again. I think, *"Here's where I get up and say something breezy like, 'let's get this tidied away shall we?'"* But I don't. For entirely selfish reasons, I don't do that. For the kiss feels good. It feels almost like a homecoming.

Tom links his arm around my back and I stiffen – he's trying too hard – but he realises and drops it and stands. He nods towards the bedroom and winks at me.

I shake my head but smile all the same.

"Oh go on," he says.

"I'm not ready," I answer.

"It's just a shag," he says. "It's not a contract. You can still dump me tomorrow. If you want."

Despite my best efforts not to, I smile again. Tom nods his head towards the bedroom again, beckoning anew. "Oh go on," he says. "You can fuck me from behind and pretend it's someone else."

I grimace. "Tom!" I protest.

He shrugs. "I need a shag," he says. "I'm willing to negotiate about how, when and what you get in return."

"Tom!" I say again.

"Come on, you're killing me," he says. "I really need a shag. I'll pay you. I'll do cleaning duties for a week."

He's trying to be cute and succeeding - my dick is stiffening. "Why not?" I think. "It would hardly be the first time my dick took me somewhere against my will." And then, "A mercy shag – just to see."

It feels fine in fact. Tom and I have always had two kinds of sex: the gentle eye-to-eye lovemaking, and the rough and ready release kind, as emotional as a game of squash. This is clearly the second kind.

There's something in his eyes that keeps putting me off. It might be love actually. On second thoughts, that's definitely what it is. So I turn him around and take him, as suggested, from behind. Where usually I'm guided towards any movement that produces an "Ah yes," and away from anything that generates, "Ow! Ah!" today it's the other way around. In fact I slam into him so hard he yelps like a dog. I'm not sure if I'm having sex or exorcising my anger. On second thoughts, I *am* sure – it's the latter. This is clearly sex as punishment. The irony of course is that it's clearly what Tom wants and, I realise, rarely gets.

Encouraged, I slip into role-play. "God you like that don't you, you cheating little slut," I pant, gripping his thighs so my fingers ache and slamming into him so hard it hurts my balls, and thinking how paradoxical it is that I mean every word I'm saying, and that Tom is loving it all the more for that.

"God!" Tom says. "Ohouh... oh I love... huh... it. Uh, uh, ohh, God ye, ye, yes. That's – Ahh, ahh... amazing!"

Good Enough

Over the next few days, Ricardo phones me only once, but I genuinely miss the call. When he doesn't leave a message and he doesn't try again I feel both relieved and jilted. I would have at least expected him to tell me in person about his decision to leave.

For her part, Jenny mopes surprisingly little over his announced departure – every time I bump into her she is smiling and happy. It seems that after so much inactivity, going out to work is doing her good.

But the modified structure of Jenny's day changes mine too, as now, when she showers at six a.m., the water rushing down the pipe just outside my window invariably wakes me. If that doesn't get me then her newfound penchant for clompy high-heels certainly does. And then, once awake, my torment about the future takes hold and sleep is lost for good. For though the New Year's Eve mercy shag does lead to a slightly more relaxed atmosphere between Tom and I, it doesn't lead to a repeat performance and in my own mind, nothing has changed – nothing is resolved. Tom doesn't seem unduly troubled by this though, at least not enough to lose any sleep over it, so I get two hours alone in the silent flat before he gets up; time to sit and wonder if anything were possible what I would want, and where and with whom.

My only option seems to be to let things slide and to wait for some major tremor to realign my life into a comprehensible pattern. I watch and wait.

***

A tremor comes surely enough, on the third Monday of the New Year. But it's not of a nature to clarify anything – it simply adds a stressful time-line to the decision process. I'm eating a croissant and sipping thick black coffee when the phone call comes. Tom answers it initially but quickly gives in and hands it over to me. "Sorry," he says. "But it's too complicated for my French."

When I finally hang up, Tom, who has been watching me and biting his nails, says, "Bad news?"

I honestly don't know how to reply. I feel a bit light headed. Not with joy or fear, but just at the added pressure.

"What did he say?" he asks. "Has it fallen through?"

I shake my head. "No," I say spacily. "No... he said it's all OK."

Tom goggle-eyes me. "Wow!" he says. "Really?"

"Yeah," I say. "Whatsisname is gonna be declared missing at the end of the month, and then we can sign mid February. He wanted to fix the date, but I said we'd get back to him."

Tom grins at me. It's a sweet, genuine smile I'm unable to match. "That's brilliant," he says.

"Yes," I say again. "I suppose it is."

Tom twists his mouth. "You do still want to don't you?" he asks.

I sigh deeply. "I don't know Tom," I say. "I'm sorry but I really don't know anymore." And it's true that I don't know. I couldn't categorically say that I *don't* want to do it anymore. But I realise that I truly *have* been hoping that the project will fall through. I'm feeling a sense of near-panic here. It feels like the walls are closing in around me.

"I see," Tom says. "And can we? Pull out, I mean."

I shrug. "We'd lose the deposit," I say.

"All twenty grand?"

"All twenty grand."

"Shit," Tom says. "Well we can't then, can we?"

"No," I say. "I guess not."

"I got an answer you know," Tom says. "To one of the messages I posted on that hill-walking site."

"Yeah," I say. "The one from Egypt?"

"Egypt?" Tom says.

And I remember that I'm not supposed to know. And I realise that I don't give a damn. "Yeah," I say. "I traced the IP address. It was posted from Egypt."

Tom frowns.

"I checked your email," I say. "I read it."

"You checked my mail?" Tom repeats incredulously.

I nod.

"OK," he says, evenly, then, "Why?"

"Doh!" I say.

Tom feigns confusion, so I explain. "I didn't trust you," I say. I wonder if I should have said *don't*.

"Right," Tom says. "I don't suppose I have the right to feel outraged about that."

I shake my head. "I don't think you do, no," I say.

"How did you get the password?" Tom says.

I roll my eyes. "Well, it was gonna be *woofter* or *Brighton*, wasn't it?" I say. "You always use the same two. Anyway, what's woofter? Like *woolly-woofter* for *poofter?*"

"No," Tom says quietly, clearly still taking this in. "Woofter – our dog. When I was a kid. Those are so going to be changed. So, what's this about Egypt anyway?"

"The message was posted by someone in Egypt," I say.

"The one saying the place was sold and..."

"Yeah," I say.

"I thought that was probably posted by Chantal," Tom says.

I nod. "Yeah, me too. Couldn't work out why she didn't say, 'I've sold the place,' though."

"No," Tom agrees. "I suppose she might have told someone else."

"Someone in Egypt," I say.

"Yeah," Tom says. "Anyway, does this mean he's really dead now?"

I shake my head. "No, just officially gone. It means she can sell the house."

Tom nods. "If we want it," he says.

"If we want it," I repeat.

"I can't believe you checked my mail," Tom says.

"I can't believe you cruised the net to find a dick to suck," I say.

"It was the other... Anyway. Quite," Tom says. "I really didn't think it would be this important though; I honestly didn't think it would jeopardise anything."

I let out a gasp. "You *so* did," I say.

Tom scratches his chin. "I guess," he says. "I *hoped* it wouldn't then... I still can't really understand why it should."

I shrug. "It's mainly the dishonesty," I tell him, feeling a sharp pang at my own hypocrisy. "Plus, why risk a lifelong relationship for a blow-job? I don't really get it. Why fuck everything up for so little?"

"I didn't think it would," Tom says. "Fuck everything up."

I snort sourly. "Yeah, because I wasn't supposed to know."

"Yeah," Tom says vaguely. "Plus, you know me and lifelong relationships. Scares the willies out of me."

"I forgot," I say. "You're a non-believer."

Tom chews his lip. "No, I do believe," he says. "But I think maybe *I'm* not capable."

"Yet you expect me to want to buy a gîte with you," I point out.

"Well, I'm not saying I'll run off in six months' time or anything," Tom says. "I *am* capable of committing to a project for a few years."

I cough. "That's good of you," I say.

"Sorry. That sounded..."

"Honest," I say. "For once."

"I think monogamy scares me," Tom says, apparently emboldened. "A whole lifetime of..."

"Of what?"

"Never mind. It'll sound worse."

"What?" I insist. "A whole lifetime of sex with me?"

Tom tuts. "No! But it always gets boring *after a while*... everyone knows that. I just want to enjoy all the options."

I nod. "So in a nutshell," I say. "You're prepared to commit for a couple of years. But the cheating and lies will continue?"

Tom looks outraged.

"No, seriously Tom, it's fine; these things have to be said."

"Yeah, but it's *how* you say them," Tom says. "It doesn't have to involve cheating or lying."

I roll my eyes at him. "So how does that work then?"

Tom shrugs. "If we agreed that this sort of thing is bound to happen, then it wouldn't involve lying."

I laugh in disbelief. "An open relationship?" I say. "Is that what you're offering?"

Tom shrugs. "I'm not *offering* anything," he says.

It strikes me as a profound truth and I sit in silence for a moment absorbing it. "No," I say eventually.

"I'm just discussing," Tom continues. "It seems to me that things might last a bit longer. If we allow a bit of freedom, a bit of leeway."

"I don't believe that at all," I say. "That's the trouble. It's like going shopping to save money."

"You what?"

"If you spend time in shops you spend money. If you spend time cruising in bars or checking out the web then you'll meet someone else. Someone who seems better. At first glance they will anyway. If you want it to last, you have to stop shopping. That's my point."

Tom nods. "I see what you mean," he says. "But if you don't think your relationship can bear comparison – well, it doesn't say a lot about it does it?" His mobile rings at that instant, and he spins it towards him to look at the screen. "Jenny," he says. I shake my head and he nods and presses the cancel button.

"You were saying," I prompt.

Tom rolls his eyes to the ceiling, and then looks back at me. "What does it say about a relationship if it implies never looking elsewhere just in *case* you're tempted," he says. "That's *my* point."

I shrug. "It's an act of belief," I say. "It's a decision. That there *isn't* anything better. That something can be *good enough.*" I have a sudden feeling of déjà-vu and wonder if I haven't already had exactly this conversation with Tom once before.

Tom nods. "Yeah," he says. "I see. But I don't think I'm built that way."

"No," I agree. "Maybe not."

"I could try though," he says.

I blow though my lips. "Maybe that's not enough," I say.

"I *would* try," Tom says. "I promise."

"It's the *trying* I'm having trouble with," I say. "It just isn't very convincing."

"No," Tom says. "Well," he adds, cleverly, "maybe that requires an act of belief on *your* part."

I bang my hand on the table and stand. "Well, that's quite enough of that," I say, realising that we have somehow slipped into dialectic – point-scoring tactics for winning arguments rather than anything deep or useful. "I'm going for a walk. My brain's saturated."

Tom smiles at me. "Yeah," he says. "I could do with a breath of fresh air too."

I smile tightly at him. "Good," I say. "Go for it." Then just to make sure that it's clear we aren't doing this together, I add, "See you later then."

Expert Advice

Initially unsure of my destination, I walk briskly through the old town. I'm trying my hardest – for now – not to think about Tom or the gîte. There just doesn't seem to be anywhere sane for those thought processes to go.

It's three p.m. and the winter sun is already low enough in the sky to leave the streets in deep, cold shadow and my denim jacket is, I realise, insufficient. When I notice that I'm heading for Cours Saleya, I take a sharp left and start to wind my way up towards the Parc Du Château. Pausing after the first eleven steps (of hundreds) are two women – a fit looking wiry one in walking shorts and her very red faced friend. As I stride past them, the fat one, who looks like she's been eating Morgan Spurlock's McDonald's diet not for thirty days but thirty *years*, speaks to me in English. "Hey Mister," she says. "Can you tell us if the chateau is this way?"

When it comes to foreigners in France assuming everyone can speak English I have a similar reaction to most French people: I consider it arrogant enough to want to ignore them, or worse still feed them duff information. But knowing the number of steps to go, looking at the woman's face and seeing that she won't make it alive, and noticing something about the pair that I can't put my finger on, I do my good deed for the day and tell them that a) there is no chateau in the Parc du Château, and b) it's a *very* long way to the top.

"You see," the fat woman says, wheezily addressing her friend. "You made me walk all that way for nothin'."

The sporty woman catches my eye and almost imperceptibly raises an eyebrow, and I smile and wonder if I have just sabotaged her attempt at getting her fit, or perhaps her hopes of inducing a heart attack. I give them a little wave and charge on up the hill, only now realising that the vibe I picked up is because they are, in fact, a couple; they are family.

After a hundred or so steps and a sharply inclined alleyway, I pass the gates at the base of the park. I zigzag on and up through little archways and up more steps past the waterfall, and by the time I get to the top, to the balcony overlooking the bay, stunningly lit by the beginning of a red sunset, my heart is pounding and I'm sweating freely and my brain has slipped into a restful silence.

I watch another couple of tourists taking portraits into the setting sun and wonder if they will be able to see anything except the red sky behind, and then I take a few deep breaths and head down the other side of the hill towards the port.

A guy in his fifties dressed in beige Crimpelene trousers – *where do they get these things?* – is lurking in the shadows on one of the bends. As I glance at him he offers what I guess must be his most winning smile, in fact a fairly nerve-wracking grimace; so I jerk my head back to the fore and walk even faster, and wonder how many days he has to lurk in the shadows of the park before he gets a result.

At the bottom of the hill I pass out through the gates – always a relief when closing time at the park is so random – and walk on down to the port. I wish I had put my running shoes on – I would happily have jogged the rest of the way. I continue past the restaurants and down past the boarding area for the Corsica ferry, then climb an alleyway of steps back up to street level. As I round the corner, I nearly bump into someone coming the other way, and as I dodge around him, I see that it's Ricardo. "Oh!" I say breathlessly. "You!"

"Ah!" Ricardo echoes. "Hello!"

I'm already one step past him and I hesitate between lingering and speeding on.

He smiles at me. "You are late for somewhere?"

I consider lying but he gives me his face-cracking grin and I weaken. "No," I say. "Just walking, burning calories, getting rid of stress."

Ricardo looks around like a cornered animal and glances at his watch. "I only have a little time," he says, nodding at a bar/pizzeria over the road. "But perhaps we can have a quick coffee?"

I shrug. "Sure," I say. "Why not."

The woman in the pizzeria is as welcoming as Guantanamo Bay. "We're not open yet," she tells us as we push in the door.

Ricardo turns his grin on her and says, "Ce n'est pas grave. Nous allons simplement boire un coup." – *"It doesn't matter. We are just going to have a quick drink."*

Incredibly, as if hypnotised, the woman shrugs and picks up her order pad.

"I was sure she was going to say no," I say, once we have our drinks – two beers in fact – and the woman has disappeared out back.

"You just have to tell them how it is," Ricardo says. "If you're forceful enough people just agree."

I wonder if it isn't how Ricardo gets *everything* he wants.

"I'm so happy to see you," he says. "A good surprise."

His smile is such that I can't help but grin back at him, and I realise that I haven't used these muscles properly for days. "Yes," I agree.

"I called you," he says. "But you say no, and then you don't answer..."

I nod. "I know," I say. "I'm sorry. But, well, it's all a bit complicated really. It's bad enough just between Tom and me without you and Jenny in the equation."

Ricardo nods. "I understand," he says, seriously. "But you – *tu m'as manqué."*

I smile dumbly and maybe even blush a little and think that he probably can't see this because I'll be red from the walk anyway. "Thanks," I reply. "I missed you too."

"I needed to see you," Ricardo continues. "I will go back to Colombia now."

I nod. "Jenny told me. In February she said."

"I wanted to tell you," Ricardo says. "To explain."

I laugh lightly. "There's nothing *to* explain Ricardo," I reply. "Anyway, you already said that once you got your passport... I didn't think you'd go quite so quickly though."

Ricardo sighs. "I know," he says. "But my mother – she's not so good. Plus I think this is all a bit complicated for me too. You see, I say complicat*ed* now."

I nod gently.

"I don't want to carry on with Jenny now, but, you know, I don't want to... *Je ne veux pas la blesser."*

"You don't want to hurt her," I translate.

"Exactly," he says. "So I will wait now. I see her not so often. And then I will go. It will be kind of natural death."

"Beautifully put!" I say. "You *could* ask her to go with you," I point out.

Ricardo nods. "Yes, I know," he says matter-of-factly. "But she has other plans. And anyway, I want something different now. I think I am changed. So a fresh start is good."

I sip my beer and suck the froth from my lip. "I envy you," I say.

"Envy?"

"I'm jealous," I paraphrase. "A fresh start. Just walk away and start afresh. It's very appealing."

Ricardo shrugs. "It depends I suppose," he says, "how happy you are."

I swallow and nod meaningfully. "Yeah," I say. "Quite. I was actually hoping that the gîte wouldn't happen. That we wouldn't be able to buy it."

"But it's OK?" Ricardo says, crinkling his brow deeply. "You will buy?"

I nod and shake my head and shrug all at the same time. "It looks that way," I say.

"But you don't want," he says, glancing at his watch again.

"If you have to go..." I say.

He pouts and shakes his head. "Soon," he says. "But is OK. You don't want?" he asks again. "The gîte?"

I shrug. "If I have to decide, I'll probably say, 'yes'," I tell him.

Ricardo frowns. "Why?"

I shrug. "You have to say, 'yes' to things. You have to take chances. You can't spend all your time backing out of things. Plus we'd lose twenty thousand Euros if we pull out."

"Then you are happy with the decision," Ricardo says. "It's OK."

I blow a sigh through my lips. "If it had fallen through, that would have been OK too," I say smiling vaguely. "It wouldn't have been my decision, so..."

Ricardo nods. "Yes," he says. "I think it's not such a good idea."

"What?"

"To buy with Tom," Ricardo says. "He doesn't know what he wants."

I laugh. "That's good coming from you," I say.

Ricardo laughs. "Yes," he says. "You're right. But Tom... he loves you – but not enough to commit. This is what I think."

I grin and bite my bottom lip. "Again," I say. "You're not exactly a *master* of commitment."

Ricardo laughs and looks me in the eye meaningfully. "This is why I understand Tom," he says. "This is why *I* am not buying a gîte with Jenny."

I clear my throat. "Yes," I say. "Point taken."

Ricardo glances at his watch again. "I'm sorry," he says. "But now I must go."

I nod. "It's fine," I say.

"I want to see you again though," Ricardo says. "I want to talk more. This is not enough time. We can have dinner?"

I wrinkle my nose. "My life is so complicated, Ricardo," I protest.

"Please?" he says, standing. "It is important to me."

I frown.

Ricardo nods then says, "Tomorrow? Or Wednesday?"

I shake my head lightly in dismay at my own lack of willpower. "Fine," I say. "Wednesday."

"At my place? I can order pizzas. No Pot Noodle."

I nod. "OK, fine. But no Pot Noodle. And no funny..."

"No funny business," Ricardo interrupts, glancing at his watch again and reaching for his wallet. "I know."

"I'll get these," I say. "Just go."

Ricardo grins. "Now I am late!" he says, turning towards the door with a wink. *"À mercredi!"*

I blink slowly in confirmation and watch the door swing closed behind him.

I become aware of the pizzeria woman standing beside me. "Il est mignon," she murmurs. – *"He's cute!"*

"He is," I agree. "He is indeed."

Lies, Damn Lies, And Politics

That evening, Tom is particularly sullen. As we prepare dinner together and then eat it in near-silence, I first notice the change, then start to worry about him. This fact – this *act* of worrying about him – reopens some lost pathway through my confused synapses and I start to see Tom as a human being again. A complex, fallible, lovable, suffering human being rather than just an irritation. I feel a little ashamed at myself for the lapse.

After dinner I follow him to the lounge and sit opposite watching him skin up. "Are you OK, Tom?" I ask after a moment. "You seem overly quiet tonight."

Tom licks the edge of his cigarette paper and glances up at me with a weak smile. "I'm OK," he says unconvincingly. "I'm just irritated with myself for saying the wrong thing again."

I nod. "You mean earlier on?" I say.

"Yeah," he says, tapping the joint on the coffee table.

"What, you don't feel you expressed yourself properly?" I say.

Tom shrugs. "I just always say the wrong thing," he says. I sigh and wait for him to elucidate.

He lights the end of the joint, takes a few puffs, and then, speaking in smoke, he says, "It's like politics. I mean, it's easy enough to know what you're *supposed* to say."

"What do you mean it's like politics?"

"Yeah," Tom says. "Politicians are all the same aren't they? But you vote for the one who promises the most. The one who lies the best; the one who says the right things."

I nod. "I see what you mean," I say. "But I'm not sure *this* is about saying the right thing. I'm not sure there *is* a right thing. It's about being honest surely, and then trying to work out if there's a way forward."

Tom nods. "Yes," he says. "That's how it should be. But the truth is different. Everyone's the same; everyone cheats and does things they're not proud of. But some are better at lying about it. They're the ones people marry. And they're the ones people vote for."

I frown. "That's very cynical," I say.

Tom shrugs. "You'll end up with some guy who promises you the Earth," he says. "Someone who promises you undying fidelity and love till the end of days... You'll end up with a good liar, that's all."

I frown. "I don't think that's true," I say. "I think honesty is far more important than anything else."

Tom nods and proffers me the joint, which, as a goodwill gesture more than out of any real desire, I accept. "You say that," Tom says. "But the truth – that I don't think I'm capable of being faithful, doesn't suit you. So I should have just lied. I should have just said the opposite."

I nod and sigh. "I see your point," I say. "But I think there are people who believe in long term relationships. And fidelity. And..."

"Oh everyone, *believes* in it," Tom says. "Everyone *dreams* of it. But wanting and doing are different things. Wanting and being *capable of* are different things."

"Maybe," I say. "I still think there *are* people who do."

"Some people even believe their own crap – so I suppose that's called honesty," Tom says, pointedly. "But it isn't the truth."

I nod and pass the joint back to Tom.

"I wish you'd just tell me," he says. "I wish *you'd* just tell me the truth."

I hold my breath for a moment, then say, "Tell you what?"

"Well, you've already decided really, haven't you," he says. "You're going to call the whole project off." He swallows with apparent difficulty and then stares at the ceiling in an attempt at steadying his voice. "You *can* just tell me," he says.

I tut, and move across the room to his side. "That's not true at all babe," I say. "I honestly don't know what to do right now, I really can't work it out. And it's not for or against you, not really. It's about trying to calculate if it can work. Because I really don't see things the same as you. I'm not attracted by the idea of an open relationship. I really do believe that one relationship can last a lifetime."

Tom snorts. "It's ironic," he says. "The guy who doesn't believe in long term relationships is trying to stay in one. And the guy who *does* believe is thinking about ending it."

I sigh and stroke his back. "You're right," I say. "That *is* fucked up."

"So you are," Tom says. "You are thinking of ending it."

I shrug. "I don't know what I'm thinking Tom," I say.

"Do you love me at all?" Tom asks, his voice cracking. "Even a little bit?"

"Of course I do," I say. And in this instant, it's true again. His distress has opened a pathway across the gap. "Otherwise I wouldn't be here would I?" I say.

Tom nods and reaches for the TV remote. I think for a second – I *hope* – that he's just going to fiddle with it like a stress ball. But he points it at the TV and starts to zap through the channels. And the pathway to empathy closes as fast as it opened. "Well," he says, his attention already sliding into dope and TV. "That's something, at least."

I sit and watch him staring at the TV, just in case he's coming back any time soon; just in case he's going to click the off button and snap back into the room. But he doesn't. And it strikes me that human beings are so irritating; human relationships so *hard*, coupledom so terribly, terribly taxing – it's a wonder anyone ever manages to stay together for a week, let alone a lifetime.

Keeping Everyone Happy

The next morning, I bump into Jenny on the stairs. She's standing on the bottom step distributing a pile of mail between the different letterboxes. She's looking all smooth and bouncy haired again, and I assume she's on her way to meet Ricardo.

"Oh, hello," she says brightly. "Bloody postman couldn't be bothered to put the letters in the boxes again. It's so lazy!"

I laugh. "Yeah," I say. "I know. I found a recorded delivery letter on the pavement yesterday."

"So where are you going?" she asks.

"Shopping," I reply. "Jeans shopping."

Jenny glances from the pile to me and smiles. "Good, we can go together," she says. "I've seen so little of you lately."

"I... I'm just going to men's shops," I tell her. It seems that the only way not to lie to Jenny is not to spend time with her at all. She frowns at me, and I realise that Ricardo's existence is driving a real wedge between us.

"I've got to buy something for Ricky anyway," she says. "He bought Sarah a Wii so we need to find a little something to give back. You can help me. *If that's OK.*"

"Sure," I say. "That'll be nice."

As we head down Jean-Jaures, Jenny tells me how expensive the Wii game was. "I can't afford anything that expensive," she says. "But I was thinking maybe a nice jumper. He doesn't seem to have many jumpers."

As she chats aimlessly about Ricky this and Ricky that, about his great omelettes and how busy he is lately, about how much Sarah likes him and how sweet and attentive he is, I realise the other reason I've been avoiding Jenny. Her relationship with Ricardo is real, and that's a fact I have been doing my best to overlook.

"You'll miss him, won't you?" I say as we turn into Place Massena.

"You bet," Jenny replies. "He's a real catch. But I always... I... I suppose I never really expected it to last. I can't say why. But, yeah, he's great. Other than the fact that he's going away I can't find a single fault."

"I'm sure he has some," I say. "Everyone has. Isabelle once told me that until you can name someone's biggest fault you don't know them at all."

"Yeah," Jenny says. "Very true. Ricardo just covers them up better than most I expect."

We turn into the pedestrian zone. I point to Springfield. "Let's try there," I say. Then I launch into Tom's theory about love and politics.

"I think he's right," Jenny says when I finish. "To an extent at least; I mean if Nick opened his relationships with, 'Hi, I'm Nick and I am a violent alcoholic,' well, he wouldn't have many girlfriends would he. I expect it's the same with Ricardo. I'm sure there are things he doesn't tell me, but, you know, as long as they aren't slapping you in the face, well, it probably is better *not* to know."

As I wonder which is the most dangerous path – asking what suspicions she has, or suspiciously failing to ask – I play for time by jokingly picking up an over-embroidered pair of fashion jeans. "What about these?" I say.

Jenny pulls a face. "No surface was spared," she laughs, then looking around, "Are you sure this is a men's shop?"

I nod. "It is," I say.

Jenny nods thoughtfully then continues her previous thought. "Yeah, I'm sure Ricardo has a dark side."

"Really?" I say, turning away to hang the jeans back up.

"Yeah," Jenny says. "No one can be that clean. Of course, I have no idea really. But, for instance, all this going home to look after the mama – it wouldn't surprise me at all if he has a wife and kids over there."

"Jesus!" I say. "Shades of Hugo."

"Exactly," Jenny says.

I pick up a pink and blue striped jumper. "What about this?" I say. "For Ricardo?"

Jenny wrinkles her nose. "It's very bright," she says.

"It's the same colour as his shirt though," I point out.

She nods. "Yeah," she says, taking the jumper from me and laying it across her arm. "You're right. Yeah. That'll do. If he doesn't like it he can change it anyway."

"Do you *really* think he has a wife?" I ask.

Jenny laughs. "Course not," she says. "But I'm sure he has secrets. And it's probably better that way. So in that much, I agree with Tom."

"You think I should buy the gîte, don't you?" I say, rifling through a rack of jeans in an attempt at finding a pair that might reach higher up than the crack of my arse.

"Yes," she says. "Tom loves you to bits."

I nod. "He says he doesn't think he can be faithful though," I say. "He says he doesn't think he's capable. God these bloody low-waist jeans!" I say. "I can't stand them."

Jenny frowns. "Why not?"

I shrug. "Unless you have big girly hips they just fall down all the time."

"Don't you have big girly hips?" she giggles appraising me with half-closed eyes.

"No," I say. "I do not."

"Shame they don't have an M&S," she laughs. "I'm sure they'd have some good sensible jeans that would reach up to your nipples. As for Tom - if he can't be faithful, then you should just tell him to keep it to himself. If it upsets you, I mean. Just tell him to be a better liar."

I laugh. "That's what... a friend said," I say.

Jenny frowns, searching for a name, then says, "Tony?"

I nod. "Yeah," I say. "Actually, I think I'm done here."

"OK, I'll just pay for this," she says. Turning towards the counter, she pauses, and adds, "You know, we all have secrets, even me. I bet even you do..." She looks at me and twists her mouth thoughtfully. "Nah, you probably don't. Bloody Mother Teresa, you are."

I laugh. "I think you overestimate me," I say.

"Maybe," she says, "maybe not. Actually, I think honesty is probably *the* most over-rated human quality."

I pull a face and scratch my head. "Funny," I say. "I keep hearing this lately."

"And being a good liar is probably the most underrated," she says. "Keeping everyone happy is a gift. No matter how you do it."

Two Bit Farce

On Wednesday night when Ricardo opens the door, I can't help but laugh at the dimly lit interior. He shoots me an amused frown. "Why are you laughing?" he asks.

I nod at the room behind him. "The candles," I say. "You're such a Romeo!"

Ricardo shrugs this off and steps aside so that I can enter. "I like candles," he says. "You don't?"

I grin at him and pull off my soggy coat. "I do," I say. "But I don't exactly light them every night."

"Neither do I," he says.

"Exactly my point," I say under my breath.

"It's raining?" Ricardo asks, peering over at the window.

"Yes," I reply. "Quite hard. It just started." I follow him through to the kitchen where he pours two gin and tonics. "So, tell me about your mother," I say, thinking about Jenny's suspicions.

"My mother?" Ricardo says, shocked. "You are my psychiatrist now?"

I laugh. "Yes," I say. "I see what you mean... but, no, I just meant, how is she? You said she was ill."

Ricardo nods and gives me a little push towards the lounge. I frown at the gesture. "Sorry," he says. "It's cultural. Even after seventeen years."

"Pushing people?"

Ricardo laughs and nods. "Yes," he says. "Colombians do a lot of pushing. It upsets Europeans."

I nod. "Yeah," I say crossing to the window. "Don't try it in England."

"Anyway, my mother," he says, joining me at my side. "She's not good. She has Alzheimer's. My sister says she is getting bad very quickly now. She has whole days when she doesn't recognise anyone." I note that he replies without hesitation.

A gust of wind blows the rain against the window making the

interior feel somehow even cosier. "Can't your sister look after her?" I ask. "I mean, if she's already there?"

Ricardo laughs. "Maria Clara? She can hardly look after herself! Anyway, mother hates her. She was saying this morning that her bad days are the only good days, the only days she can get near her."

"Because she doesn't recognise her?"

"Exactly," Ricardo says.

"Will you live with her then? Your mother?"

"Yes," Ricardo says. "To start with anyway. Maybe later if she is really bad she will go to a hospice. But to start with, yes, that is the idea. And houses are very expensive in Bogotá. Her apartment is very big, so..."

I sip my drink. "They're expensive?" I say. "I'm surprised at that."

"Very," Ricardo says.

"I would have thought they'd be cheaper, its being a... developing country." I nearly said third-world. I realise I have made a lucky escape.

Ricardo laughs. "It's more expensive than Nice," he says. "Colombia is not like people think. Colombia is not Africa you know. Bogotá is like Paris or Madrid, only maybe a bit more dangerous. And more fun."

"I never went to Latin America," I say. "Well, except for a really awful holiday to Cuba."

"You went to Cuba?" Ricardo says, apparently impressed.

I nod. "It was terrible. I broke up with a boyfriend there. Plus it was Club Med," I admit shamefully.

"Mon dieu!" Ricardo exclaims. "Quelle horreur ! Varadero?"

I nod. "Yes, Varadero."

"You don't go to Havana?" Ricardo says. He pronounces it, *Habana*.

"Yes, I did," I say. "It was beautiful. But falling apart. Very poor. Soldiers with machine guns everywhere. I can't say I found any of it particularly relaxing."

Ricardo wrinkles his nose. "Yes," he says. "Not such a good regime in Cuba. In Colombia we have a democracy since, well, since independence really. Well, almost. Except for Bolivar and Rojas Pinilla."

And so, as we sip our drinks and look out at the boats bobbing in the port, Ricardo tells me more about Colombia. He's not jingoistic,

206

but he does love his country, and his face is a pleasure to look at as he wistfully describes the mountains around Bogotá and the *tierra caliente* (the hot lands) below.

When I finish my drink, he puts his own down and phones downstairs to a restaurant. As he orders two vegetarian pizzas I watch the circling beam from the lighthouse as it sweeps round and around. "The view here really is extraordinarily beautiful," I say. "Will you keep the place? You own it, right?"

Ricardo places the phone back in the charger and returns to my side. "Yes," he says. "I will rent it out. I have contact in agency. They will do everything. And it will continue to pay the... *prêt immobilier.*"

"The mortgage," I say.

Ricardo cocks an ear at me, so I repeat it more slowly. "A mortgage," I say again. "It's just for houses. For a car or anything else it's a loan. For a house it's a mortgage."

He nods. "OK, mortgage," he says, then with a frown. "Strange word."

"I think it's because you're in gage with it until you die," I explain. "A *mort* gage. Anyway, it's a good investment. I think you're right to keep the place."

Ricardo nods. "Yes, and when my mother is dead, maybe I'll come back a bit."

I grimace. "You sound very matter of fact about it. About your mother."

Ricardo nods. "Well it is life. And I am a doctor, so... She will probably be gone in less than two years. Her sister went very quickly."

"Alzheimer's as well?" I ask.

Ricardo nods. "She died two years ago. They have to tie her to bed in the end."

"They tied her to the bed?"

Ricardo laughs, genuinely it seems, at the memory. "Yes," he says. "In the hospice. She was biting everyone..." he raps his head. "Nothing left up there at all; my sister said she was like a mobile without the sim card."

I smirk despite myself. "Ouch," I say. "But she's not the only reason is she? You seem happy to go home anyway."

Ricardo exhales through his nose and grins at me. "Oh yes," he says. "It is a wonderful country. And it changes so fast. Not like Europe.

Much faster. I like this. New buildings, new bars, new laws. We even have gay marriage now," he says. "Not bad for a Catholic country."

I nod. "Not bad indeed," I say.

Once the pizzas arrive we put the open boxes on the coffee table and sit facing each other, lifting the greasy slices with our fingers.

"You must come one day," Ricardo says. "An amazing country."

I finish my mouthful. "Sure," I say. "But there are lots of amazing countries I have to visit. If it didn't cost so much I would visit them all."

"I know," Ricardo says. "But Colombia is special. Everyone who go there says so."

"And I don't speak Spanish," I say.

Ricardo laughs. "No one in Colombia speaks any other language," he says. "So you must learn Spanish."

I nod. "You see," I say. "Not so easy."

Ricardo nods. "If things were different," he says. "I would say come with me."

I smile at him. "That's sweet," I say. "But with the gîte and everything – well, I don't think there will be any holidays for years."

"No," Ricardo agrees, lifting a slice of the droopy pizza to his mouth. "That's why I say, *if* things were different. No gîte, no Tom, no Jenny. It would make me happy that you would come."

I look up from the pizza and catch him staring at me intensely, and in those deep dark eyes, I catch a glimpse of something sad, something meaningful. I wonder if I haven't missed something here.

"Well, I'm very jealous," I say, trying to lighten the tone. "A whole new life!"

Ricardo nods. "In a way it is also my old life. But things have changed so much."

I nod and tear off another mouthful of pizza, and Ricardo stares at me as I eat it. Something passes between us in that moment, and I realise that we are going to sleep together again. It's obvious and unavoidable. For some reason, it's *natural*.

"You will stay tonight?" Ricardo asks, apparently on the same wavelength.

I shake my head sadly. "I can't," I say. "I'm supposed to be visiting a friend. A friend who doesn't exist."

Ricardo nods. "When I wake ... waked?"

"When I wake up," I say. "Or when I woke up – if it's the past."

"When I woke up with you," Ricardo says uncertainly. "It make me very happy."

I grin broadly and feel my cheeks tingle. "That's very sweet," I say. "But I can't."

Ricardo nods. "But you will stay for a while," he says.

I smile. "What can I say? You lit candles!"

Ricardo laughs at this and pats the sofa beside him. "Come here," he says. "If we don't have long, then come here."

The patting gesture unnerves me a little. It's the same one I make when I want Paloma to join me. But as obediently as Paloma, in fact, considerably more obediently than Paloma, I stand and move around the table and take a seat beside him. He slips an arm behind my back and it feels perfectly normal, perfectly natural, as if I have not a double-life, but two lives – two entirely independent lives which are in no contradiction whatsoever.

Ricardo's interphone buzzes again. It sounds like a wasp in a biscuit tin and it's loud enough to make me start. Ricardo glances around the room and stands.

"Maybe the pizza boy again," he says. "He forget something perhaps?"

But when he returns to the room his face looks slightly crazed. "C'est Jenny," he says, quietly.

"Jenny?" I repeat.

"Elle monte," he says. – "She's on her way up."

Squashed against the wall, the gently falling rain wets only my legs – the overhang of the roof is protecting my head and upper body. My heart is racing and it seems to me, in this instant, on Ricardo's tiny balcony, that in the last thirty confused seconds, we have – perhaps influenced by too many dodgy sitcoms – made a *bad* decision.

The window beside me thuds as Ricardo's front-door opens and then closes again. I listen to the vague sound of voices from the room beyond, and wonder about the alternatives – telling Jenny that my friend Tony wasn't in; that I bumped into Ricardo... that would have been the best bet. It might have seemed suspicious, but that suspicion fades into insignificance when compared with what will happen if

Jenny leans against the window and sees me hiding here.

Suddenly, Jenny's voice is mere inches from my right shoulder. "Well that's what I thought," she says. Her voice is clear enough that she might as well be talking to me. "That's why I..." she continues. As she turns back into the room her voice becomes indistinct again.

I force myself to breathe.

One floor down to my left, someone else's windows open with a thud. A woman reaches out and pulls her shutters closed, making me aware of the hundreds of windows around the port overlooking this spot. I wonder if someone, somewhere is watching, laughing even at this two-bit farce.

I hear Ricardo's voice, and then the window vibrates again twice in short succession, and then there is silence.

I turn my head to the right and compose my features into a crazed expression of stunned relief and wait for Ricardo to appear and laugh at me. But nothing happens, no one comes.

The rain lessens, then abruptly intensifies. I watch the minute hand on the church clock move astoundingly slowly around the dial. I wonder if it's safe to go back in. Have they both left? Or are they having sex on the couch? I lean forward just enough to see that the lights are out. I twist and peer into the darkened room. I can make out the sofa, the dark doorway to the kitchen... As I imagine Jenny's face appearing mere millimetres from my own on the other side of the pane my heart starts to race again.

And then with the thought, *"Oh, this is ridiculous!"* – in a moment of fuzzy, crazy, risqué logic I'm ready to take whatever the consequences are. I push on the window and step boldly back into the lounge. I stand dripping for a moment, unsure what to do. There is only one way in or out of the building, so if I try to leave and they are standing outside the front door chatting – that would be a catastrophe. Then again, perhaps Ricardo has invented an excuse – something they must nip out to get. Perhaps he's counting on me slipping away quickly. If I stay and they come back I could always go back to the balcony. I look at the puddle of water on the floor, and realise that that isn't going to wash.

Just as I cross to the front door and press my ear against it, my phone rings making me jump out of my skin. It crosses my mind that in a real sitcom it would have rung while I was out on the balcony, forcing me to lob it into the sea. I pull it from my pocket and answer.

"I'll be back in one minute," Ricardo says breathlessly. "Don't move."

When I hear Ricardo's steps *and* voice approaching I start to panic anew. But then it's too late to do anything – his key is in the door, and it's opening and then he's standing before me winking and talking into his phone, doctor talk apparently – *"Tout à fait, dix milligrammes."* I gasp in relief and Ricardo frowns at me and then ends his conversation. *"À vendredi,"* he says. *"Oui, vendredi matin."* He clicks his phone off and crosses the room smiling. "You got very wet huh?" he says, pulling his own glistening coat off.

I shake my head. "Crazy!" I say. "I was out there ages. I didn't know if you had gone or if you were still here."

Ricardo shakes his head. "I'm sorry," he says. "I switched the lights... I say to Jenny very loudly I will walk her home. You could not hear?"

I shake my head. "The only thing I heard was Jenny when she came to the window."

"I know," Ricardo says. "Very close... I was shaking."

"What the fuck was she doing here?" I ask.

"She saw someone at the window," he says. "So she thinks I'm in. Only I tell her I am working, so..."

"Shit!" I say. "What did you say?"

Ricardo shrugs. "That yes, I am working. I'm allowed home for pizza, you know? And then I say I have a home visit on Place Garibaldi. So I walk her home."

"Did she notice the two pizza boxes?" I ask.

Ricardo shrugs. "I don't care," he says. "If she say something I tell her it's buy one get one free."

"And that you were very hungry."

Ricardo shrugs again. "Come here," he says opening his arms. "I'm sorry. That was horrible."

I step towards him and blow through my lips. "Yeah," I say. "That was pretty bad."

He wraps his arms around me. "You are soaked," he says, leaning back far enough to focus. "You must get these off."

"I think I should go home," I say.

"No," he says. "You must take them off. It's OK..."

"Don't say it," I laugh. "Please don't say that."

"What?" Ricardo asks, frowning.

"Please don't say, 'it's OK, I'm a doctor.'"

He leans back and frowns at me as if I am being particularly strange. "Why would I say that?" he asks.

I roll my eyes. "Never mind," I say. "Lost in translation."

"A very good film," he says. "But take these off please. We can put them to dry on the radiator."

I pull off my shoes, socks and jeans, and we distribute them on the three small radiators, then Ricardo hugs me again.

"That was terrible," I say again. "I mean, that was really bad."

"Yes," he agrees.

"I shouldn't have come," I say.

"No," he agrees again.

"I can't do this shit - I'm just not made that way."

He turns and pulls the cushions from the sofa. "No," he says. "I agree."

"What are you doing?" I ask.

"Preparing the bed," he says, throwing a cushion at me. "Here, help me."

Three Letters

As the days go by I start to wonder – perhaps a little melodramatically – if I'm not having some kind of breakdown. My thoughts about Ricardo swing violently from the desire to see (and sleep) with him again – to make the most of him before he vanishes – and wanting to close the whole crazy episode once and for all. It's almost as if my doubts about Tom, about the gîte are somehow merely Ricardo's fault; as if once he vanishes everything will be simple again; a simple ad break beyond which the film will resume as if it had never been interrupted.

Ricardo appears to be suffering from a similar syndrome – his attempts to see me are few and far between – but when they happen, they are desperate and pleading. "Please," he says. "In a few weeks I am gone. In a few weeks you never see me again." Occasionally, too, when his pleas coincide with my own phase of wanting, they are convincing as well, so over the next three weeks I see him precisely three times; we have sex, or perhaps I should say, make love, precisely three times too. I say *make love* because as we orgasm together I can see something deep and warm and longing in his eyes, and I know what that thing is because I can feel it behind my own. And because, afterwards, tearing myself away from him is like pulling a tooth.

Tom hangs around the apartment, nervously waiting for me to announce a decision on the gîte; too nervous to ask or in fact mention the project in any way. I don't bring it up either because I don't have an answer. When I'm missing Ricardo, when I'm hoping he'll phone, or scheming when I might get away to see him again, the gîte is clearly a stupid futile fantasy – in fact the most absurd fantasy I have ever indulged in, and at these times I wonder how I ever got this close to doing it; but when I'm yearning for Ricardo to leave, waiting for that blip on the radar of my life to finally start fading, it feels obvious, inevitable – Tom and the gîte feel like destiny.

There's a tiny detached part of my brain which seems able to oversee the two thought processes, seemingly so distinct that I wonder if each doesn't come from a separate hemisphere. The overseer analyses the whole thing with calm logic and announces that the end result will depend not on choice, but on timing, chance, call it what you will. It says that if I'm forced to decide before Ricardo leaves then I will be too doubtful to say, 'yes,' that I won't be *able* to do anything except say, 'no.' But if Ricardo leaves first there will be a life to be resumed and a void to be filled; a void that might only be filled with a 'yes.'

In the meantime the decision tortures my existence, disturbing my dreams with sweaty unremembered nightmares and shortening my sleep with bursts of five a.m. insomnia. The dilemma obsesses my brain to the point that I'm unable to follow a film on TV or read a newspaper, let alone read a book. Hell, I can't even seem to remember that there is cheese on toast under the grill, or a tea bag stewing in a cup.

These lapses of sanity provoke worried glances from Tom and a gentle, almost parental taking over of the daily tasks. But he never comments, as if he somehow understands why I'm like this, and at times I wonder if he hasn't in fact understood everything. I wonder if he doesn't secretly know that time is on his side, that all he has to do is sit it out.

And then it happens, and like all truly good things, and all truly bad things, it is unpredictable and sudden.

Tom, returning from babysitting for Jenny, tells me that he thinks she's depressed. "Now Ricardo's fixed a date I think it has really hit her," he tells me.

I look up from the previous weekend's *Sunday Times,* which I'm still trying (and failing) to read. "Sorry?" I say. "He's fixed a date?"

Tom throws himself onto the sofa. "Yeah," he says, apparently to the ceiling. "The thirteenth. I think the sooner the better to be honest."

"February?" I say. *"February* the thirteenth?"

"Yeah," Tom says, rolling to one side so that he faces me and propping his head up on one hand.

"Why, 'the sooner the better?'" I ask, adding to cover my tracks, "I bet Jenny doesn't think that."

"Well, that way Jenny can move on," he answers. "That way, we can *all* move on."

I stare at him and lick the corner of my mouth as I analyse the phrase and try to work out what it might mean – could there be another interpretation other than that *he knows*? And then the phone rings. I hunt around the flat for the missing handset, and locating it in beneath a cushion, with the words, *we can all move on*, still bouncing around inside my head, I hit the button, and a woman's voice greets me, French, Chantal.

"Sorry, I've been away," she says. "I needed a break." The lawyer, she explains, wants to set the date for the final signature; "So would the fourteenth of February, eleven a.m. be OK?"

My skin prickles. I listen to my heart beating, to the sound of my own breath. I can almost hear the creaking cogs as this particular set of points on the train-tracks of life hesitate between one direction and another.

Tom is frowning at me, wondering – suspecting, even – who is on the phone. I think, *"The fourteenth – the day after Ricardo leaves."* I hear the words, as if they are still echoing, *"We can all move on."* And I hear myself say, "OK, the fourteenth then. Eleven a.m.," then, "oh, and, um, can we meet? Just a couple of hours, but, I've got this vast list of questions for you before you vanish."

"Oui, pourquoi pas..." Chantal replies. – "Sure, why not? How about the afternoon – after the meeting with the notary?"

By the time I hang up, Tom has moved to my side. He's staring at me, aware that something has happened, something major – perhaps he heard the squealing of the points too.

His face is taut, his eyes are glassy, as if he has understood everything, but daren't quite believe. "Was that...?" he asks.

I nod.

"The lawyer?"

I shake my head, and momentarily he looks devastated.

"Chantal," I say. "We're signing on the fourteenth."

"Feb?" Tom asks.

I nod.

"Wow!" he says, frowning seriously and nodding. "The day after Ricardo leaves," he says, poignantly. "That's perfect."

I clear my throat. "Why?" I say.

Tom shrugs. "Well, to start with it will give poor Jenny something to think about."

I nod vaguely. "Yes," I say. "Of course." In my self-centred drama, I had forgotten that Jenny and Sarah were even moving up there with us.

Tom runs his tongue across his front teeth, now visibly fighting a smile. "Are we really doing it?" he says. "I can hardly believe it."

I stare into his eyes, and eye contact makes *I* contact, and I can't help it, I start to grin with him. "If it's what you want," I say. "If you're sure."

Tom's cheekbones start to protrude, his eyes start to sparkle. "I am," he says. "Are *you?*"

I nod. "I am," I say, and as I say it the whole sorry mountain of stress slips from my shoulders and slides into the muddy past with an unspectacular plop.

Tom screws his face up in a weird fashion, then through gritted teeth, he lets out a little yelp and jumps up and down twice. He looks about ready for infant school with Sarah. "Fuck!" he says. "Fuck *fuck!* I'm so happy."

He grasps my head with both hands and plants a big wet kiss on my lips. "You're sure you're sure?" he asks.

I nod. "I am," I say. "I told you." And in that crazy space of my seesaw mind, it is, at that second, entirely true.

Tom repeats the grasping, kissing gesture, and says again. "Fuck. I'm so happy," then, "shit, that's in two weeks. Shit we have a lot to do. We have to confirm the bridging loan, get this place on the market, organise a moving van... Can I tell Jenny? I'm gonna tell Jenny."

With that, he bounds from the room, and I stand in shock and joy, all mixed up, and think how easy it was in the end to say, 'yes,' and I think I realise for the first time in my life the power of words. For I have said, 'Yes,' or, *'Oui,'* – three letters in either language; and everything has changed, the future is born anew, and it feels right, and good, and true. I think of the Coldplay song that Jenny quoted and I think, *"That's how it happens then."* A life, a destiny, a future, all created from thin air, woven so naturally from the words we choose to say, not woven from those we keep inside. It's that simple.

Tom returns a minute later with Jenny and Sarah in tow. "This calls for a celebration," he says excitedly.

"Picnic?" Sarah says, her face hopeful as she picks up on Tom's excitement.

Jenny sweeps her up into her arms. "No darling," she explains. "We can't have a picnic every time." She rolls her eyes and looks at me. "So it's happening," she says. "How exciting." I notice but ignore something in her tone, something restrained, something complex. "You'll be able to build snowmen in Mark and Tom's garden," she adds.

"Snowmen?" Sarah says.

"Yeah, you haven't seen them yet," Jenny replies. "Actually, yes you have. In the book."

"In the blue book?" Sarah says. "Le bonhomme de neige?"

Jenny nods. "Indeed," she says, then, her accent not a patch on Sarah's, "Le bonhomme de neige."

"There's no reason why we *can't* have a picnic," Tom says.

Jenny glances at the window. "Weather's OK. I could probably rustle up some stuff. And Ricky's off this afternoon, so he could join us."

"I'd rather do it tomorrow," I say. "I need to do some things today – phone the bank and stuff."

Jenny shrugs. "Fine, tomorrow then. To be honest, I'm not sure I want him to come anyway. This is our celebration isn't it?" She jiggles Sarah, who remains cross looking, up and down. "We're going on a picnic," she enthuses. "Tomorrow!"

"We could go to that lake you mentioned," Tom suggests.

"It's better in summer, but, yeah, I'm sure it'll be fine. As long as the weather is OK," I say.

"That's settled then," Jenny says, swivelling to leave. "See you tomorrow."

Once she has left, I comment, "She seemed funny."

Tom frowns at me. "You think?" he says, apparently oblivious. "Well, I suppose she's going to be. Probably more and more... what with Mister Wonderful leaving and everything."

Phasing Out

We leave the house the next morning at ten a.m. The weather looks unsettled with dotted clouds moving quickly through a pale blue sky. There is still a distinct February chill to the air, which prompts a last minute dash by Jenny back up to her flat for extra pullovers. The round trip seems to take far longer than it should, and by the time she returns – wearing entirely different clothes, I notice – a policeman is approaching.

"Sorry," she says. "Ricardo phoned just as I was..."

"Can we actually go now?" Tom asks, nervously watching the policeman.

Jenny squeezes into the back seat and Tom takes off even before I have my door closed. "They're bastards here. Look, he already has his pad out," he spits.

As we head north to the motorway, the sky darkens, and I think we all independently wonder if this was such a good idea, but then as we circle around Nice and drive west, we leave the unsettled weather behind us and head into pure blue sky. The journey is unusually quiet, even Sarah remains virtually silent. The atmosphere inside the car isn't uncomfortable in any way, but rarely have I been on a car journey when everyone seemed so quiet, so thoughtful. I assume everyone is simply mulling over the newly confirmed future and everything it implies.

At the lake, we park the car beneath some parasol pines near the only café still open, and, heavily laden with blankets and cool-boxes, we tramp down to the shingle beach. It's packed solid here in summer but entirely empty today.

The water, a deep emerald green, reaches all the way to the horizon. "Wow it's huge," Jenny says. "And beautiful. It's artificial you say?"

"Yeah, it's an electricity reservoir isn't it?" Tom says.

Jenny frowns, so I explain. "Hydro electric. There's a dam over that way. The lake belongs to EDF."

"Nice to see man make something pretty for a change," she says.

By the time the blanket is spread, glasses distributed, Champagne poured and tubs of ready-made pasta salad from Monoprix prised open (this is a Tom-food picnic and it shows) it's warm enough to sunbathe.

Tom pulls his top off and declares, "Better make the most of it. It might be a while before you see this temperature again."

"Do you think there is still snow up there?" Jenny asks.

I nod. "A bit," I say. "But not much. I'm going up there next Thursday to talk to Chantal about how she runs the place. You can come if you want."

Jenny shakes her head. "I can't on Thursday," she says. "I'm working. And Sarah's at nursery."

And that's the moment that it dawns on me. "Your job," I say, furrowing my brow. "How are you going to...?"

Jenny licks her lips, glances at Tom, and coughs, waiting, it seems, to see how the phrase will end.

"What are you going to do?" I continue. I have been so wrapped up in my own stuff, I haven't even thought about it before. *"Jenny?"* I prompt.

Jenny grimaces. "Shit," she says. "I was going to tell you, but, well, I didn't want to spoil the celebration."

Tom swivels and stares at her gravely. "Jenny!" he says sharply. His voice is strained, making it sound more like a rebuke than anything else.

I frown at him, but then turn back to Jenny as she shoots Tom an equally complex look and continues, pleadingly, "I can't. I just can't. Not full time. It was all so on-and-off, I had to make other arrangements. And I need the money from the job, and Sarah's in nursery school now. But we'll come at weekends. *Every* weekend. *And* school holidays. I'll still be there to help out."

Tom turns to me and gives me a sort of, *what are you gonna do?* shrug.

I shrug back. "I should have thought about it," I say, thinking, *"You should have told me earlier."*

"Crap," Tom says.

"I'm sorry," Jenny says. "Really I am."

"I suppose the weekends and holidays *will* be the busiest period,"

Tom volunteers.

I nod vaguely. It's just dawning on me that Jenny had been going to contribute rent as well. Without that money, things will be *really* tight.

"Is it the money?" Jenny asks, as if aware of my thoughts. "Because I could still pay half-rent or something."

"Crap, yeah, the rent!" Tom says. There is something strange about his voice again, something unconvincing. Plus Tom never says, *"Crap."* I can't put my finger on what's going on. I wonder if maybe he's *glad* that Jenny won't be living with us full time. "We'll be OK without that, won't we?" he says, his intonation stuck halfway between statement and question.

I sigh sharply before saying, mainly to ease Jenny's manifest guilt, "I expect so. It's not a few hundred Euros that are going to make or break the bank."

"And we'll come up on Friday afternoons and back down on Monday mornings," Jenny says. "And of course if you two need a weekend in town, well, you can use the flat, and I'll cover for you up there."

Tom nods. "Actually, that will be good," he says. "It could get a bit much up there. You'll have to get a car though."

Jenny smiles. "Yeah, I thought you could help me find an old banger," she says. "You're kind of the car guy around here."

"Hey," I complain. "I'm good with cars as well."

"Not as good as me though," Tom says cheekily.

"I'm quite excited about that. I won't need a four-wheel drive or anything will I?" Jenny asks. "I mean, with the snow and stuff."

"You might, actually," Tom says.

I laugh.

"What?" he asks.

"You might know about cars Tom, but you know fuck all about the weather down here." I turn to Jenny. "You'll be fine," I say. "Obviously a four wheel drive is best, but really any old banger will do as long as you have snow-chains in the boot."

"You see," Jenny says beaming at us both. "The perfect combination."

In a way, of course, the new arrangement – were it not for the financial aspect – would be the perfect combination as well. Tom and

I get some time alone to run the gîte. We get visits and help during school holidays and weekends. And a place to stay in Nice for a night on the town once my flat is sold. But the financial implications are, in truth, pretty dire: four hundred Euros a month could well break us.

"I am sorry," Jenny says, "about the money thing. My mum's still helping me out so it's hard, but you know, I'm sure I will be able to pay *some* rent."

"It'll be fine," Tom says, shooting me a glance. "If you're paying rent here, we can hardly ask for rent up there, can we? We don't really need it anyway," he continues. "If you are gonna help us out then that's more than enough, isn't it Mark?"

What he says is honourable and generous and entirely untrue. "Yeah, of course," I say, trying in my head to rehash the figures and feeling a little sick.

"And maybe next year everything will be different," Tom says. "By next year we'll probably be making *loadsadosh* and we can pay you to work for *us.*"

"Yeah," Jenny says, vaguely. At that moment, I realise that not only is she no longer renting the flat from us, but that she has in fact lost her enthusiasm for the project as well. "Maybe. We'll see what happens, Tom, yeah?" she adds.

Tom shrugs and smiles at me. "It'll be fine," he says.

Because the gîte has been off-limits conversation wise, I had forgotten how scary his blind optimism can be. "We're not going to be making loads of dosh, Tom," I point out. "It's gonna be *really* tough, I hope you realise that. Especially now."

Jenny looks concerned and starts to open her mouth, but I raise a hand to silence her. "It's fine Jenny; don't worry. Everything you say is normal and fine. I'm just worried Tom here doesn't realise how hard it's going to be."

"Of course I do," Tom says. "I did the spreadsheets, remember?"

"The very *optimistic* spreadsheets," I say.

"Only the first one," he says. "Anyway, what's the worst that can happen?"

I laugh. "Um... we don't get enough customers, we run out of money, we can't buy food or heat the place, we starve, can't pay the loan, and they repossess. How does that sound?"

Tom rolls his eyes. "If it gets that bad, I can always get some temp work," he says. "You know I earned two thousand pounds for Christmas. That would pay the loan off for nearly five months."

"Four months," I say. "And that was before tax."

"OK, four," he concedes. "But I don't think I'll have to pay tax on... anyway, whatever."

I stare at him as a short film plays in my mind. In it I'm alone at the top of the mountain, surrounded by snow – a sort of Chantal left behind, only with Paloma instead of a baby. "I hope you're joking," I say. "Because I am *so* not going to be left up there on my own whilst you swan off to Brighton. Anyway, you won't have a flat there anymore."

"No," Tom says. "Of course."

Jenny glances at Tom, then catches my eye and raises an eyebrow in what I take to be shared concern.

Tom sees it and tuts. "God!" he says. "I only meant if things get desperate... rather than starve."

"I'd *rather* starve," I say, pointedly.

"Talking of which," Jenny says, ruffling Sarah's hair, and forcibly changing the subject, *"I'm* starving. Shall we?"

After lunch, Tom heads off exploring with Sarah, leaving Jenny and me sunbathing. To avoid talking about Tom and the gîte, or Jenny's missing rent, or indeed Ricardo's imminent departure, all of which make me feel panicky, I trawl the *Sunday Times* for fresh conversation matter. "That Colombian woman is still being held hostage," I say, flashing the newspaper at her. "They've just released these pictures of her. She looks rough, huh?"

"Yeah," Jenny says. "Well, you'd look rough after six years prisoner in the middle of nowhere." She pulls a little grimace. "I didn't mean... I meant, in the middle of the forest... In the middle of the *rain*forest," she says.

I laugh. "No," I say. "Quite. Did you read about this one? The life insurance scam?"

Jenny nods. "Is that the woman who was claiming for her husband, only they found him alive and well and living down the road?"

I nod and point the newspaper briefly at her. "Yeah," I say. "Anne Darwin. The husband says he can't remember who he is. They're trying to decide if he's truly amnesiac or not."

Jenny shakes her head. "Outrageous! Of course he isn't. She got a half a million pound life insurance payout. *And* they were up to their eyes in debt."

"Maybe that's what Ch..." I say, pausing as something catches the corner of my eye. I turn as, at the edge of my vision, two bushes part. Ricardo appears between them. "What the fuck's he doing here?" I say.

Jenny frowns and turns. "Oh good," she says.

"You said he wasn't coming," I say.

"Yeah, he phoned, when I nipped back, didn't I say?"

"No," I answer. "Well, yes. But you didn't say he was *coming*."

Jenny knits her brow. "What's wrong?" she says. "Is that a problem for some reason?"

I run a hand across my forehead and at the sound of gravel beneath Ricardo's boots, I look up. "Sorry," I say to Jenny. "I just have a headache coming, that's all." I turn to Ricardo and smile. "Hello!" I say. "This is a nice surprise."

Jenny glances at me and frowns, then stands to greet Ricardo, simultaneously reaching down for her handbag, which she lobs at me. "There's some Paracetamol in there," she says.

Ricardo, is of course, Ricardo. *Toujours, égale à lui même*, as the French say: smiling, funny, relaxed, sexy. Quite how he manages to sit between his girlfriend (the one he's leaving in a few days) and her best friend (his secret lover) and still have those serene gestures, still flash that cracker of a grin at everyone; quite how he can even now be funny and seductive, really is beyond me. And not for the first time, I can't work out if I want him or if I want to be *like* him; for if I could only learn ten percent of Ricardo's ease, my own life would, it strikes me, be *ninety* percent easier. His presence should, by rights, *add* to the stress of the day, but as ever he knows how to make people laugh, he knows how to make people smile, and thus despite almost insurmountable odds, it is Ricardo who makes a success of the trip.

The only inkling of tension comes when Jenny, recovering from a fit of laughter at Ricardo's sick impression of Ingrid Betancourt chained to a tree, grabs his head and tries to kiss him. He catches my eye, and, I think, in deference to my feelings, turns away, making it a peck on the cheek rather than a snog. He then scoops a shrieking Sarah onto his shoulders and jogs off along the beach.

"Did you see that?" Jenny says. "Honest to God, I feel like I'm being phased out. Gradually."

"You are," I think. *"We all are."* I lie, "No, what happened?"

"Nothing," Jenny says. "It doesn't matter. At the point we're at, it *really* doesn't matter."

But as soon as he returns – with a now beaming Sarah on his shoulders – she softens, apparently unable, like myself, to ever resist him for long. Even when she's in the process of being phased out.

He provides smiles and jokes and kiddie entertainment, and, after disappearing for a few minutes to the restaurant at the top of the hill, even supplies us with plastic cups of coffee and a key for the padlocked pedalos. This latter treat is designed to seduce Sarah, but although she almost accepts, actually taking both our hands at one point to leap aboard, a simple, unfortunate, "Don't let her fall in! She can't swim yet," from Jenny puts an end to the possibility. Sarah's grin slips to a frown, and within three seconds she has wrenched her hands free and is running, wailing, back to her mother's side.

So it is that Ricardo and I end up pedalling out onto the lake together in our very dirty yellow pedalo. The water is glassy smooth, yet as we reach the centre a chilling breeze hits us, so we head back to the edges.

Only the cries of the cormorants and the steady chugging of the paddles disturbs the silence. It's relaxing and heavenly, and we pedal without speaking for at least ten minutes, using simple pointing gestures to negotiate where to head for next. At one point as we follow the mini coastline I realise that a hillock is hiding us entirely from the beach and I lean in and give Ricardo a peck on the cheek. He looks surprised so I say, "I missed you!"

He laughs. "You were *hiding* from me."

I nod. "That too," I admit.

He shrugs and shakes his head. "But here is too dangerous." He nods over at Jenny as she, then Sarah and Tom slip back into view. We pedal on for a while before he says, "Jenny told me. About the gîte. You will buy it then."

"Yeah," I say. "I can't quite believe it myself. We're signing the day after you leave."

"Yes," Ricardo says. "The fourteenth."

"You still think I shouldn't do it," I say.

"Jenny thinks it is OK," he says. "So maybe. I think it is brave."

"Crazy more like."

"Yes," Ricardo says. "Maybe crazy too."

"It's weird," I say. "I honestly think it's a mistake. But it's as if I'm on a train, and it's going that way, and I can't seem to stop it. I think we weigh everything too heavily as we get older. When I was younger I just used to say, 'yes,' to everything, and things seemed easier. More fun maybe. So I think, *why not?*"

Ricardo says nothing, so I continue, "At some point, you just have to decide to build something, you know? It's like buying a house and..." I realise I'm rambling. I realise that I sound like I'm trying to convince myself.

"I suppose," I finally conclude, "that at some point you have to grow up and decide that *here* is where you will live, and *this* is the person, and just get on and make the most of it. Does that make any sense at all?"

"Yes," Ricardo says. "I understand that. But when you buy a house, even then you must ch... I don't know. Never mind."

"No go on," I say. "When you buy a house?"

Ricardo smiles at me and grins. "No, really," he says. "It's not for me to say."

I stare at the opposite bank for a moment before completing the phrase for him, "You have to choose one that isn't going to fall down. Is that what you were going to say?"

Ricardo pulls an embarrassed expression and shrugs.

"You're right," I say. "But the whole situation has led to a point where something has to give. I can't explain it, but some big decision has to be made. Tom gave up his job, I gave up mine. We cut ourselves free for this, we organised a bridging loan to buy the place, we signed the compromise, and now, well, we have to do something new or go back to where we were. It just has... I don't know, *momentum.*"

"You could do something different," Ricardo says.

"Like?"

"You could change your mind and go travelling. You could go to Africa. You could go to Australia. You could come to Colombia."

I laugh. "Yeah," I say. "Right. We'll tell them when we get back to shore. You can make the announcement. No, seriously, I've done the whole travelling thing. The next stage isn't about moving. It's about

226

putting down roots." Ricardo has stopped pedalling, so I add, "Hey, lazy boy, what is this?"

Ricardo shrugs. "Here is pretty," he says, nodding at the nearby bank. I stop pedalling too and the boat soon ceases to move forwards and starts to spin slowly towards the sun instead.

"So what about Jenny?" I ask. "You have absolutely no desire to put down roots with her?"

"No," Ricardo says. "In the beginning, maybe, I thought. But now? No. I think maybe I want to have relationship with... you know... a man. I never do this. Never a proper man-friend like you and Tom."

"Crazy guy," I say. "Men are the worst."

Ricardo shrugs. "I never tried. And my relationships with women haven't worked out so well. So..."

I snort. "You know, I never really believed in bisexuals. Not before I met you."

"You didn't believe," Ricardo repeats, uncomprehendingly.

I drape one hand in the icy water and try to keep it there. "No," I say. "I thought they were all secretly straight – just trying to be chic and kind of metrosexual like Bowie or Lou Reed. Or secretly gay, but too ashamed to admit it."

Ricardo nods. "In a way, I agree," he says.

Grimacing at the pain, I pull my hand from the water. I turn to him. "Shit that's cold," I mutter. "You agree, you say?"

He shrugs. "I think maybe no one is ever really both. Maybe one and then another, but never really both. And as you say, I think there are many who never meet the right person, so they just carry on."

"I don't understand," I say.

"Moi, je pense," Ricardo, explains in French. – "Me, I think I prefer men really. But I never fell in love with a man before. It was just sex."

I swallow and look across the lake. "Shall we go over there?" I say, pedalling already. As we head back out into the centre of the lake, I shoot Ricardo a sideways glance, just in case he's looking at me with meaning, with an expression that might explain what the past tense, what the *before* was all about. But he's looking over towards the shore, over towards Jenny and Sarah. Over towards Jenny and Sarah and Tom.

The Key

For the journey home, we split into two cars, Jenny and Sarah travelling with Ricardo, myself being driven by Tom. I stare from the side window as we drive around the lake and wonder how on Earth we are going to make ends meet. I must let out a sigh at some point, because Tom says, "You're really disappointed about Jenny, huh?"

I pull my eyes from the mirror finish of the lake, and smile weakly at him. "I'm surprised she didn't tell us straight away," I say. "I am a bit shocked about that."

"I think she only decided a week ago," Tom says. "For a while she didn't think it was happening at all, so it's not really her fault."

"No," I agree. "Mainly I'm just worried about the financial side of things."

"It's only four hundred Euros," Tom says.

"Yeah," I say. "That's probably ten people staying the night every month," I point out. "So if we needed an average of forty beds a month over the year just to survive, now we need fifty. And I'm not that sure that fifty is going to be possible. I was never that sure that forty was possible to be honest, but if I had known this, well, I might not have signed in the first place."

"That's what I thought," Tom says quietly, then, "You worry too much. It'll be fine."

"You keep saying that, but just saying it doesn't make it so. We need a plan, and I don't have one yet, and that is stressing me out."

"Maybe we can rent the flat to someone else," he says doubtfully.

"If the place was just about anywhere else, we could. But I doubt there's exactly a waiting list of people who want to live up there full-time. The only option will be to do holiday lets on the flat. And that will only be a goer in summer. And even *that* means redecorating the whole place as well, and quite when we'll find the time to do that..."

"Jenny will help," Tom says. "She promised."

"Yeah," I say. "Jenny *said* she was moving up there with us."

"Yeah," Tom says. "Well, even without her, we will be fine. Tonight we can redo the spreadsheet."

"You can redo the spreadsheet till the cows come home," I say. "But until we think of something new to put in the *plus* column, it ain't gonna balance."

"No," Tom says with a sigh. "OK then."

I check his features for clues. He has one eyebrow raised. "What?" I say.

"Well, there's no point discussing it really, is there," he says. "Not when you're in your doom and gloom mood."

I let out a heavy sigh and turn back to the countryside spinning past the windows. "You're probably right," I say.

Tom places one hand on my knee. "It'll be *fine*," he says again. "You'll see."

He drops me off with the picnic gear at the entrance to Place St Francois and heads off to find a free parking space – very probably a half-hour task. The second he drives away, before I have even arranged everything so that I can carry it, Ricardo has appeared from an alleyway. "Mark!" he says, super-spy style. "Over here."

I frown and carry the cool box, the blankets and the picnic basket over to him. "What on Earth?" I say.

"Come," he says, beckoning with his head. "We have to talk."

I frown at him. He looks a bit crazed. "I've got to get all this up to the flat," I say. "You can help me."

"No," he says. "Jenny thinks I have gone home. I wait here and then you come."

"Why?" I ask. "What's this all about?"

"I have something to tell you," he says. "Many things in fact."

"You always say that," I laugh. "But usually..."

"Today, I will tell you something," he says. "Now go, and come back quickly."

"Yes sir!" I mock, scooping the stuff up again and heading off across the square.

When I return, he bundles me on up the alleyway. "If we're heading for the park, it closes at sundown," I say.

Ricardo shrugs. "It's OK," he says. "I have keys."

"You have keys to the *park?*"

He nods. "Yes," he says. "The *pompiers* have keys. We train up there. And when people are locked in we have to let them out."

"Fair enough," I say, following him up the steps.

He lets us in through the iron gates and locks them behind him. "Are you allowed to do this?" I say, looking around at the long shadows cast by the setting sun. "It's a bit spooky."

"At least you know there is no one else," he says. "Or maybe another *pompier*."

I laugh. "Right," I say, jogging to catch up with his stride. "What's this about anyway?"

"When we get to the bench," he says. "Just around here..."

As we round the corner – a path I have never taken before – the bench comes into view. Ricardo sits and pats the space beside him. Once again feeling like an obedient doggy, I sit. "What's this about?" I say, shivering. "It's all very cloak and dagger."

"Cloakan?" Ricardo repeats.

"Never mind," I say.

"You're cold?" Ricardo says.

"Yeah," I say. "I should have brought a jacket. Now the sun's gone."

He starts to take his own jacket off, but I shake my head. "I'm fine," I say. "Now come on. Spill the beans."

"The beans?" he says.

I shake my head. "Sorry. It just means *tell me.*"

"OK, first a hug," he says. "Because after... I don't know."

I pull a face and hug him briefly, but my sense of intrigue is too strong, my heart isn't in it. "Anyway why couldn't you just tell me two hours ago?" I ask him. "God knows what I'm going to say to Tom when I get back."

Ricardo nods solemnly. "I do not know what you will say to Tom when you get back," he says.

"So come on," I prompt.

"There are many things... peut être c'est plus facile en français," he says. – *"Maybe it's easier in French."*

"Ça me va," I say. – *"That's OK with me."*

He continues in French. "Je veux..." – "I want you to come to Colombia with me."

"What?" I say, slipping into a frown of confusion.

"I want you to come to Bogotá with me," he says again.

I shake my head. "I... It's a lovely offer Ricardo," I say. "But do you have any idea how much stuff Tom and I have to do?"

Ricardo nods and sighs. I notice his hands are trembling. "You don't understand me," he says. "It's my fault. I haven't been clear. It's because I didn't want to tell... Anyway, I haven't been clear. I want you to come to Colombia *with me.*"

I shake my head slowly and look at him sideways. "*Why* exactly?" I say.

Ricardo rolls his eyes. "I told you I want to..." he coughs. "I said I want to have a boyfriend next time. But it's not true," he says.

"It's not?" I say shaking my head slowly.

"No," Ricardo says. "I want you. I want *you* to come with me."

My brow furrows and my mouth drops. "I..." I say, but words fail me. Eventually I manage, "That's crazy. I don't know what's got into you."

"It *is* crazy," Ricardo says. "Yes, but it's wonderful too. I haven't felt like this since... I don't know. Maybe never. We fit together."

"We *fit* together?" I say. "You are completely off your..."

"You don't see what has happened here do you?"

I stare into his eyes, and see that I know what he's going to say, and that it's true. I open my mouth to speak, but I'm lost for words. And I realise that I'm desperate to hear him say it, *because* it is true, and because I have maybe never quite been able to believe anyone who has said it to me before. There are no sexual thoughts in my mind, but my stirring dick forces me to take note of the fact that I'm feeling aroused. "Don't say it," I say.

"But don't you think it too?" he asks.

I shake my head. "Ricardo," I say. "I really like you. I *really* like you. You're brilliant, amazing... But..."

"You don't feel the same," Ricardo says.

"No," I say. "Yes, I mean... I don't know. This has never been an option. You were, you *are* with Jenny. I *am* with Tom. This was never destined to be anything other than..."

"It is," Ricardo says. "It is now."

"It is what?"

"An option."

"It's not!" I exclaim. "How can you possibly imagine that I'm going to run off with you to Colombia. I've never even *been* to Colombia. I don't think I've ever seen Colombia on the fucking TV." I frown. "OK, that's a lie, I have. But you get my drift."

"You can discover a new place," Ricardo says. "I can show you. You will love it."

I gasp at his absurd self-confidence. "What would happen to Tom? I couldn't do that to Tom. And Jenny? What do you think it would do to my friendship with Jenny? I have known her for twenty years," I say. "*Twenty years,* Ricardo. How do you think she would feel if she thought her relationship with you ended because you wanted me instead?"

"Jenny always knew the relationship would end. And she decided, not me."

I shake my head. "How does that work? That makes no sense at all, and you know it," I say.

"Jenny is going back to England," Ricardo says.

I wrinkle my face to express complete and utter confusion. "She *what?*"

"That's why she won't move with you. She wants Sarah to grow up in England. By September she is gone."

A crow sweeps, screeching, overhead – silhouetted against the last vestiges of light in the darkening sky.

I wrinkle my nose. "Nah," I say. "That's not possible. She would have said."

Ricardo shrugs. "I'm sorry," he says. "But she told me at Christmas. You remember, I went home early – I wasn't so happy."

"But that was ages ago," I say.

Ricardo nods. "I know," he says.

"It makes no sense. She would have told me," I say again.

Ricardo shakes his head. "Tom asked her not to. They agreed to keep it secret."

"Tom?" I say. "What's Tom got to do with this? Why would he? This is completely mad."

"If you had known," Ricardo says. "Would you have still bought the gîte?"

I shrug. "Maybe, maybe not," I say. "Probably not."

"They *knew,*" Ricardo says nodding. "Jenny told Tom before. She told me at Christmas. Your house isn't so well built. Jenny will go home in the summer. And Tom, said himself that he doesn't think it will last."

"No," I say. "I don't believe you. That's crazy. I don't know what you're trying to do, but this is bullshit." I stand to leave. "This is utter... *wank*."

Ricardo shakes his head. "Mark, I'm sorry," he says. "I didn't want to tell you these things. I couldn't decide which was best. But you have to know. They are lying to you. Your house is built of playing cards."

"No," I say. "You're lying. And I'm going home."

I turn and start to walk away, but Ricardo coughs. "You need the key to get out," he says.

I gasp. "What? You're keeping me prisoner now?"

He pouts his lips, shakes his head and laughs, apparently in real amusement. "No," he says. "I'm just saying, wait for me. I have the key. You can't get out without me. Calm down."

As we walk down, Ricardo, following one step behind my furious stomp, continues calmly to try to convince me. It makes me so furious I could punch him. "Ask Jenny if Sarah wouldn't be happier in an English school," he says. "She will tell you the truth. She wanted to tell you all along. She feels really bad. It's Tom who persuaded her. And then you will see that there is nothing. Jenny will leave. And eventually Tom will leave as well. He already told you this. You are better off with me. It's obvious."

"Jesus!" I mutter looking up at the darkening sky beyond the gate.

"Mark!" Ricardo says. "I'm happy when I'm with you. And if we can be together, then why not? And France or Colombia, what's the difference? You really have no idea how much I like you, do you?"

"And *you* have no idea how much I want to *punch* you right now," I spit. "Now open the fucking gate!"

Ricardo reaches into his pocket and clunks the lock open. "Even angry I like you," he says, still managing to sound calm. "That's a good sign, no?"

I push the gate open and unable to stop shaking my head at the utter madness, at the sheer *audacity* of the guy, I march homewards. *"He really is crazy,"* I think, then, *"Another one!"*

Bad Acting

Back at the flat, Tom and Jenny are sitting cross-legged either side of Sarah on the sofa. Their presence makes me feel cramped-out and I realise that in my urgency to escape Ricardo I have gone to the wrong place. I should have gone to the beach until I got my thoughts clear.

I must look flushed or pale or something because when he looks up at me Tom's smile fades. "What's up?" he says. "You look really..." He frowns but doesn't finish the phrase.

I look from Tom to Jenny and back again, and think, *"No way! I know these people."*

"I bumped into Ricky boy," I say, sick of the lies and jumping in at the deep end. "He wanted to talk to me. We had a bit of an argument."

Jenny glances at Tom. Tom glances at Jenny. Then they both turn back to face me. Something about those two swivelling heads disturbs me. "I need to piss," I say, playing for time.

"But what did he say?" Tom says.

"One second," I reply, my back already turned. "I'm busting."

From the toilet, I can just hear Tom and Jenny talking in hushed tones. When I return, they cease and turn to face me expectantly. Sarah, who is sitting between them, for some reason bursts into tears.

Tom and Jenny both say, "What did..." simultaneously, then it's Jenny who finishes, "What did Ricky have to say? I thought he had gone home."

I frown at them both. Something vague, something non-specific isn't right, the way a bad play fails to convince. I study their faces. Tom is smiling somehow inappropriately. Jenny's face looks glassy and bland, and for the first time ever, she seems impervious to her daughter's tears.

"Ricky?" I say.

"Yes," Tom says.

"I don't... I was with Tony," I say. "Did I say *Ricky?*"

They both nod solemnly. "You did," Jenny says.

"Sorry, must be because we spent the day with him. No, I was with

Tony," I say, at which both Tom and Jenny exhale slowly, discreetly.

"What were you arguing about?" Tom says, suspicion still in his voice.

So I invent a complex, embroidered tale, made more difficult because I'm not sure how much I said last time – I can't even remember if I gave the supposed boyfriend and lover names. I tell them that Tony has decided he's in love. That he's going to run off with his friend's partner. And that I argued that this really wasn't OK.

Tom, clearly impressed by my – even if I do say so myself – *stunning* performance, says, disinterestedly, "Well, if they're in love, I think he's right. Love is rare enough, without chucking it away when it does crop up."

"Absolutely," Jenny says.

"Yeah," I say. "Right. Anyway..." I brush a hand through the air as if a fly is bothering me. "I'm sick to death of their shit to be honest. There's just too much deception going on. I'm gonna go work out what's for tea before the shops shut. Are you staying Jenny?"

Jenny who has now noticed that her daughter is crying, shakes her head and stands. "No," she says. "I'm going home. This one's tired, aren't you? I need to get her back to our house."

"House," I think, heading through to the kitchen and opening a random cupboard. I suppose that's what they call a Freudian slip. I stare blankly at the contents and try to think about what's going on. Could it really be that Tom and Jenny have been lying to me? It's not a vast issue; waiting a few months to tell me that Jenny is bailing out isn't exactly *Earth shattering*. But it would be a deception. Another one. Why is it that no one tells the truth anymore? And how come everyone has secrets, except me? I remember Jenny actually telling me she had secrets. Maybe she *wanted* me to ask what they were. Ricardo said she felt bad about it. And then I realise that of course I'm being a complete hypocrite again. I have the biggest secret of all.

Before I even begin to think about dinner, Tom is at my side, handing me the phone. If he had asked, I would have said, *"later,"* but, the phone is in my hand and Tom is now outside the flat talking to the departing Jenny.

"Allo?" I answer.

"Bonsoir Mark," Chantal says. "Sorry to trouble you, but I was wondering if we could meet before instead of after the sale. I'm going back... away, the day before... unexpected reasons."

"The day *before* the sale?"

"Yes. But it's all OK, don't worry. The notary will have all the paperwork, but I can't be there. I'm sorry, it's unavoidable."

"Sure," I say, frowning. "Fine." The truth is that my brain is so full of junk that I'm unable to even consider if this is fine or not. If there was a French word for, *whatever*, that's probably what I would have said, but French doesn't do modern concepts like sardonically exaggerated disinterest.

But it sounds dodgy for some reason. I will have to phone the notary and check he thinks it's all still legitimate.

"Could we do it on Monday or Tuesday?" she asks.

"Well... OK, I suppose," I say.

"Monday or Tuesday?" she asks again, her tone slightly irritated.

"OK, Tuesday," I say. "Same time? One p.m.?"

"That's perfect," Chantal says. "That way I can get on and make all my arrangements. Ever so sorry, but it'll be fine. Thanks."

I realise that I have sounded a little short with her, so in an attempt at being more chatty, I say, "You off back to Egypt?" The silence that follows is so long, I wonder if the connection hasn't died. "Hello?" I prompt.

"Oui..." Chantal says, hesitantly. "Egypt... Pourquoi j'irai en Egypt?" – *"Egypt. Why would I be going to Egypt?"*

In the heat of the moment I can't remember why I *thought* she was going to Egypt. "I'm sorry," I say. "I don't know... I thought... I don't *know* why."

"I have *never* been to Egypt," Chantal says. She sounds like someone in front of the McCarthy commission denying they have been to the Soviet Union. She sounds like going to Egypt might be a war crime.

I think that maybe she's racist; enough French people are. Maybe Egypt is just a bit too *Arab* for her. "I'm sorry," I say, not quite sure why I'm apologising. "I must have got it mixed up." But as I say it, it comes back to me: the forum, the message. So it wasn't her after all. Or it was her, and she doesn't want me to know.

"OK," Chantal says, a certain hesitancy still in her voice. "So, Tuesday, one p.m.?"

"Fine," I say. "Perfect."

"OK then," she says. "Bye."

I tap the end-call button and frown at the phone. I think, *"What's wrong with everyone today? Why do they all sound like bad actors in a dodgy sitcom?"* I suppose it could be me. Usually when *everyone* else seems this way or that, it's not their fault at all. Maybe I have a paranoid filter installed today.

Tom appears in the doorway. He holds onto the top of the doorframe and hangs there looking at me. Even that gesture looks somehow contrived – it *must* be me. "Everything OK?" he says.

"Yep," I say, glancing at my watch. "Except that we have fuck-all to eat. I'm gonna nip out to Monoprix before it closes."

I'm already closing the front door behind me when I hear Tom, who has opened the fridge door say, "What are you on about? There's *a mass* of stuff here."

I pretend I haven't heard him. I need the space.

What You're Good At

By the time I return with ingredients that are suitably unusual not to be in the refrigerator already, I have decided that a clear-cut confrontation with the facts is the only way forward. I don't particularly want to drop Ricardo in it, but then, I reason, he will be far away from all of this in a few days. It hardly seems to matter anymore.

"Hi," Tom says cheerily meeting me at the front door. He follows me through to the kitchen and peers into the carrier bag I put down on the counter-top. "So what are these mystery ingredients missing from our nearly full refrigerator?" he asks, picking up a packet. "Humm, more scallops," he says. "Peas, mint,..."

"It's a recipe I saw in the Sunday Times," I say, quietly, my mind already on the next conversation. "Seared scallops, pureed peas with mint, and potato."

"What, like, mushy peas?" Tom laughs.

"Yeah," I say. "That's the one."

"You OK?" Tom asks, running a hand down my back and peering in at me with a concerned expression.

I shrug his hand away and turn to face him. "Tell me," I say. "I can read you like a book and you've been lying to me. You've both been lying to me."

His eyes dart around, searching my face for clues. "About what?" he says.

I laugh sourly. "Not exactly a denial, is it? *About what?* You might as well say, *'which lie?'*"

Tom shakes his head gently. "No, yes..." he says. "I don't know what you're on about."

"OK," I say. "Here's a clue. Jenny's not moving to Chateauneuf D'Entraunes."

"Yeah," Tom says vaguely. "And?"

"And you knew about that when exactly?"

"I don't understand," Tom says.

"Tom!" I shriek, actually starting to doubt whether he has lied at all. "I know! Now don't make me angrier by..."

Tom's face falls. He slumps back against the kitchen wall and shakes his head sadly. "Jesus!" he says.

I wait silently for him to continue.

"I can't keep anything from you, can I?" he says eventually. It's a vague attempt at being cute, but I look at him in stony silence, letting him know that I'm having none of it.

"I'm *sorry*," he says. "God, I keep having to say that at the moment. I mean, why do I seem to spend my life apol..."

"Don't even go there, Tom," I say.

"No," he replies. "Look, I thought it was for the best. I thought otherwise you'd drop out."

I shake my head. "I'm so angry with you both, I could... I don't know."

Tom swallows and shakes his head. "It's not Jenny's fault," he says, then dropping his head to stare at his feet, he continues, "she wanted to tell you, all the way through. I wouldn't let her."

I shake my head. "It's just..." I gasp in exasperation. "It's just so fucking childish," I say. "Because we could finish up Shit Creek without a paddle because of this. Nothing good can come of hiding that kind of thing. And it's just another lie. It's just another reason for me not to trust you."

"I know," Tom says. "There's really no point is there. You always find out. It's like living with fucking Miss Marple."

I wrinkle my nose at him to let him know that again, the joke won't wash, and then I head through to the lounge. After a couple of minutes he follows me through. "I fixed it though," he says, standing in the doorway. "I wasn't going to tell you, but..."

"Well there's a fucking surprise!" I exclaim. "What weren't you going to tell me *this time?*"

Tom sighs. "I arranged a loan. In case we need more money. I arranged a loan."

I gasp. "A *loan*? How the fuck is that going to help? We're up to our tits in debt as it is! Honestly. Sometimes you beggar belief!"

Tom shakes his head and crosses the room, taking a seat beside me on the sofa. He turns to face me, his expression earnest. "No, this is different," he says. "Listen, let me explain."

I roll my eyes and shake my head, and then with a little jerk of my head I indicate that he may continue.

"I asked my uncle. You know he's loaded. And if we run out of cash he'll lend us fifteen thousand Euros." I open my mouth to speak, but Tom continues, "It's interest free, it's only if we need it, he says I can pay it back whenever I want, and it's in my name, nothing to do with you. So if the cash from Jenny's rental cripples us, I've covered it. Fifteen thousand covers what Jenny would pay for like, four years."

"Three," I correct.

"OK," Tom says. "Three." He rubs his forehead. "*Is it* three? Anyway, you see, I fixed it."

"That doesn't excuse lying to me all the time," I say.

"No," Tom says. "But I was scared you'd drop out, and then I thought, what with all the rest, well, that that would be the end of us. And I really didn't want that." The quiver in his voice makes my anger start to wane.

"And admit," he continues. "I didn't *create* the Jenny problem. The actual problem, that she wants to go home, isn't *my* fault. I was just trying to fix it. And now I have."

I sigh and nod. "OK," I say. "But all these lies... Jesus! They just have to stop. It's... I don't know... it's just... it's just not possible, Tom."

Tom nods. "I know," he says. "I'm crap at it anyway."

"You're the worst liar I ever met," I say, a lie of my own – he's actually too good for comfort.

"Well, that's something at least," Tom says.

"I'm sorry?" I say.

He laughs weakly. "Well, you wouldn't want to be dating a *good* liar, would you?"

I stare at him sourly.

"Mark, I love you. And I want to do this thing with you. That's not such a crime is it?"

I blink slowly and nod. "OK," I say. "OK. Anything else you'd like to share at this point? Anything else you've decided not to tell me?"

Tom frowns. "About what?" he says again.

I shrug. "Who knows?" I say. "With you, really... who knows?"

Tom shakes his head. "No," he says thoughtfully. "That's pretty much it."

"Right," I say, only at that instant, I can't help but suspect that there *is* more. And I can't help but wonder what that would be.

"Oh, there is one thing," Tom says, coyly.

I wrinkle one side of my nose in a caricature of discontent. "Yeah?" I say.

"I'm starving," he says. "And I don't think my cooking skills are up to seared scallops and mushy peas."

I nod my head slowly and chew the inside of my mouth. "OK then," I say, in a caving-in tone of voice, "I'll get it going."

"You want help?" he asks.

I raise a hand to stop him getting up. "I really don't," I say.

He forces a smile, nods, and then reaches for the TV remote. "OK then," he says. "I'll just stick to what I do best, shall I?"

Cooking has always calmed me more than just about any other activity – OK, except for sex. By the time I have served up the scallops, minted peas and potato (I even manage to pile it up like in the photo) I'm feeling calm, reassured even, to learn that not only was Ricardo telling me the truth, but that what, perfectly reasonably, struck him as shabby and dishonest, had a perfectly reasonable explanation. That Tom wants this project so much he is prepared to personally cover the loss of rent from the studio strikes me as deeply reassuring.

The food turns out perfectly and is delicious – true restaurant cooking and a good restaurant at that. Tom is appreciative and my mood towards him flip-flops back to one of warmth and excitement about the project. I can't help but think that there is something fundamentally unstable, something a little insane even, in my ability to see an entire situation one way – and be furious – and then, with a pepper-sprinkling of new data, to see the complete opposite. I wonder again if the various conflicts of my life aren't pushing me to the edge of actual madness.

But for tonight at least, all is well. We cuddle up on the sofa to watch the first of the films from the box set – Tom's birthday gift from Jenny. The film Tom chooses, *In Which We Serve,* is a military number set during the Second World War, hardly my favourite genre, but the film turns out to be particularly good. The incredibly young Noël Coward is amazing.

Afterwards, Tom clicks the TV off and we kiss and cuddle and undress each other. And then, slowly, gently, we start to make love.

Tom spreads his legs in just such a way, and I reach for a condom and gel.

"We should get tested," Tom says, "dispose with these."

And as I roll on the condom, as I slowly, luxuriantly start to fuck him, I think, *"Yes, that would be good,"* and I think, *"Yes, if he could be trusted, that would be great."*

"Especially up there," Tom murmurs.

I wonder if he means because there is nothing else to do up there, or because the lack of opportunity will leave no option *but* to be faithful. And then I realise that my erection is fading, so I force myself to remember the scene from the Paris darkroom and it returns, only I realise that in this particular re-run Lucky Strike has been replaced by Ricardo in his fireman's uniform.

A second before he orgasms, Tom says, "I love you, you know?" and then with those words in my ears and Ricardo's face in my mind's eye, I too come. And despite the fact that the crime was purely imaginary, I feel even more conflicted, even more *sinful* than I did after Paris.

Casting Error

The Tuesday of the meeting I'm up before nine, eating a hearty breakfast and checking the weather reports for snow on the roads to Chateauneuf D'Entraunes. Tom is a slow starter today, so I leave him to snooze as I shower and dress in my thermals. Then over three cups of coffee I re-read the list of questions we have prepared. At the point where I realise that Tom will have to get up *now* if he is to come at all, I also instinctively realise that he *isn't* going to come. Sure enough, when I bounce on the bed and challenge him he says, "Sorry, I feel a bit woozy this morning. Does it really matter if I don't?"

"Woozy?" I say. In a way, *of course* it matters; it matters a great deal. This is the last chance to meet Chantal, to ask questions about anything before the gîte becomes *ours*. In a way, too, I would have thought that sheer excitement about our impending new venture should cure *any* ill. I point all of this out as gently as I can, but as I'm feeling quite loving towards Tom this morning, I avoid making an issue out of it.

He wakes up a little more and points out that he needs to call the bank and the estate agent this morning, and adds rather cutely that he would rather see the place on Thursday, "...just you and me, once it's ours," so I relent and head off leaving him to sleep.

As I head out the door, he shouts, "If there's snow up there then take the car. It's parked on..."

"It's fine," I shout back. "Eight degrees, but no snow. I checked."

"OK, be careful though," he says.

Out in the street, at the second I start to remove the chains, locks and alarms that have kept my seven-fifty *mine* all these years, my phone starts to ring, and thinking that it's Tom, that he's changed his mind, and that I'm now going to be late, I fish it from my pocket. But the name on the screen is, *Ricardo*.

I sigh and hit the answer-call icon. "Hi Ricardo. I'm just leaving," I say. "On the bike... I can't really talk."

"Did you talk to Jenny?" he asks, and I realise that I owe him an apology.

"No. But Tom told me," I tell him. "You were right. So, I'm sorry."

"Does he know I told you?" Ricardo asks.

"No," I tell him. "He didn't ask."

"Perfect," Ricardo says. "Not to make waves in a fish pond."

I'm not quite sure what that particular proverb was supposed to mean – it too has been lost in translation, and I don't really have time to care.

"Can we meet?" Ricardo says. "Because tomorrow I go."

"I'm on my way up to the gîte," I tell him. "I'm really sorry."

"You have to go *now?*" Ricardo says. "This second?"

"Right now," I reply. "I'm late."

"You still buy the gîte?" he asks in an amazed, irritated tone.

"I still buy the gîte," I confirm.

"OK, forget it," he says, sharply.

And then the phone is dead.

I sigh and stare at it for an instant. I'll fix it later, I think. I'll send him an email or something once he's far away on another continent. *Another continent!* A pang of some unrecognised emotion sweeps through my body. I sigh again and freeze the thought by swinging a leg over the bike and starting the engine.

Because I'm not working, and because I'm riding up into the mountains – almost exclusively my Sunday pastime for the last few years – I'm initially surprised at the density of traffic. But then a brief bumper-to-bumper queue of sad looking people trying to get into the hypermarket reminds me that it is in fact a weekday, not a Sunday. An advertising hoarding tells me that the temperature here on the coast is a reasonable nineteen degrees, (in all the gear I'm actually overheating a little) but I know it will soon get colder, I look forward to that crisp mountain air.

Sure enough, as I leave town and the altitude increases, the temperature drops significantly, not gradually but in steps, dropping five degrees half way around a bend, and then another five for no apparent reason in the middle of a bridge. My ears pop and the road starts to wind more sharply as it hugs the contours of the Alpine foothills. I drop the bike into the first bend, and then into the second, and my nose tingles at something in the air – the smell of snow perhaps – and then the bike rolls, seemingly of its own accord into the next bend and I'm away: I'm in the flow. I have no idea why, but there is no activity on Earth – and I mean not *even* sex – that absorbs me so entirely, that silences internal dialogue so completely. The destination is forgotten, it's just, as a corny advert used to say, *man and machine in perfect harmony,* now braking, now tilting, rolling, and now straightening up and accelerating up and out and into the straight with an adrenaline rush.

In what feels like a couple of minutes, I'm slowing down to cross Guillaumes – a ghost town today. In fact, Guillaumes looks like some nuclear plant may have leaked nearby causing the whole town to be evacuated, though of course French nuclear plants *never* leak, and when they do there is *never* any danger, never any need for evacuation... I think, *"Humm, so this is the nearest town, huh?"* and then as I reach the other side and power away up the next hill, I shrug and think, *"Who cares? I just get to ride the bike even further."*

At the junction to the narrow road that climbs to Chateauneuf D'Entraunes, I remember the loose gravel and slow to walking pace. It's just as well that I do because, as I take the blind bend, I come upon a parked car blocking two thirds of the narrow tarmac. I slowly squeeze through the gap, and wondering who would be stupid enough to park here, I pause and steal a glance at the driver. Shamefully, I'm assuming it will be a woman, an *old* woman. I physically jolt in surprise when I see Ricardo's face looking back at me.

I slam on the brakes and the bike slews to a halt on the gravel. Ricardo winds down the window.

"What are you doing here?" I say, then, *"That's* not your car."

Ricardo smiles weakly at me and shrugs. "I hire it," he says. "I sold mine already."

"How did you get here before me?"

"I was half way," he says. "I take some thing to the storage place on the 202. So I was halfway already."

I nod and frown. "OK... *why* are you here?" I ask him. I realise that the smoke drifting from his window is dope scented. Though I knew he smoked, I have never actually seen him with a joint before.

He shrugs. "If the mountain won't go to Mohammed," he says obtusely.

I nod. "Right," I say, glancing up the hill and then at my watch.

"Actually, look, I'm sorry. I'm late as it is."

Ricardo nods and waves his joint around as he says, "I can wait."

I sigh and shake my head. "I'm sorry Ricardo," I say. "I'm not... it's just, I really don't know how long I will be."

Ricardo shrugs. "So I come with you," he says, matter-of-factly.

I'm sure Ricardo shouldn't be coming to the gîte with me, but the truth is that other than the fact that the gîte has nothing whatsoever to do with him – a reply so rude I can't say it to his smiley, stoned face – I can't think of a single reason. "I'll meet you at the top," I say with a sigh, already pulling away.

The gîte looks alive, *perky* even if such a thing can be said of a building. At any rate, with the shutters open revealing sparkling windows; with swept flagstones and with bistro tables and chairs dotted around the courtyard, it certainly looks different from when I last visited.

Chantal is still in the process of sweeping the yard. She looks up, waves and smiles as I pull into view. By the time I have parked the bike she has propped the broom against a wall and crossed the forecourt to greet me.

"En moto!" she says. "Trés courageux!"

I laugh and pull off my crash helmet. "Cold," I tell her, gesticulating at the snow capped mountains to the north, "But beautiful!"

As the Clio pulls into view, Chantal frowns. "Tom?" she asks, nodding towards the car.

I shake my head. "A friend," I tell her. "He's come to see our new house."

Of course there is, I now realise, a very *good* reason that Ricardo shouldn't come to this meeting with me: he's the *wrong* person. It's a casting error. Tom should be here instead. Ricardo's presence is weird, unnerving even.

Chantal gives us a tour of the house and then the outbuildings, showing us what furniture she is leaving (thankfully most of it) explaining little idiosyncrasies of the place – how to lift the door to the attic as you close it, just so, where to put rat traps in the springtime, the best place to sit if you want to shoot at the dormice that scale the walls in summer!

And then we sit in the public dining room in front of a smouldering log fire and I run through my vast list of questions on occupancy and advertising, on tourist offices and food shopping, and I note as many key points as my cold hands can manage from her voluminous, rambling replies. Ricardo sits silently, smiling vaguely, an expression I know only too well as *stoned*. Every now and then he catches my eye and manages to send me a discreet wink.

His presence here feels truly bizarre, not least because it feels so entirely natural. And when I reach the end of my batch of questions and Ricardo, as if newly switched on, launches into his own list, things get seem even stranger. For Ricardo's questions are just as logical, just as essential as the list Tom and I put together: where is the fuse box (hidden behind a secret panel below the stairs); where does the sewage go (to a septic tank which needs emptying once a year); on and on it goes.

As I listen to the answers to these essential questions I entirely failed to ask, I have to remind myself that I am not buying the place with Ricardo but with Tom, and there is something surreal about that thought, as if my brain has now confused the two of them entirely.

Yet despite Ricardo's stoned cool, and in spite of his natural reassuring manner, where Chantal answered my own questions charmingly, her replies to Ricardo slip through thinned, suspicious lips, as if she can't quite believe he has the nerve to ask her such a question. Or perhaps, as if she is as confused about his presence as I am.

One question in particular really seems to fluster her – Ricardo's, "So, where are you moving to after the sale?"

Chantal blushes, then stumbles, then pales, before muttering, "My mother's place... in Limoges." At this point she cocks an ear and stands, saying, "Excusez-moi, le petit pleure..." – *"Sorry, the little one is crying."*

We watch her bustle from the room, and then Ricardo turns and stares at me; stares *through* me.

"Did you hear a baby?" I ask.

Ricardo shakes his head. "No," he says.

"No," I say. "Nor me. They were good questions though, so thanks. Without you I wouldn't even have known about the septic tank."

"No," he says again, a puzzled expression on his face.

"Something wrong?" I ask.

He shrugs. "She's lying," he murmurs.

I nod slowly. "Yeah," I say. "I saw that. I thought it was just me being paranoid."

He shakes his head slightly. "No," he says. *"Intriguing."*

Chantal bursts back through the door with her little girl in her arms, and it is immediately clear that the interview is now over. She jiggles the girl, who appears to me to be asleep, but who, upon being so energetically jiggled starts to cry. "Désolé," she says. "Les enfants hein!" – *"Sorry. Kids huh?"*

"Yes," I say.

"Is that all then?" she asks.

I shrug and stand. "I suppose," I say. I nod at Ricardo.

"I guess so," he agrees. "Anyway. He can call you afterwards if he has any questions, I suppose. If you're only in Limoges..."

Chantal chews the inside of her mouth and shoots Ricardo the beginning of a glare, which quickly vanishes only to be replaced by a sugary smile. "Of course," she says, then to me, "I'll give you the number on Thursday."

I have just picked up my pad and pen, so I flip the cover over and say, "Oh, I might as well write it down now."

"I don't have it," Chantal says. "But I'll bring it Thursday."

Ricardo narrows his eyes and smiles broadly at her. "You don't know your mother's number!" he says. "Shame on you."

Chantal shrugs and moves to the front door. "She changed it. I can't remember. On Thursday... You can have it on Thursday."

And then we're back on the flagstones and the front door is locked, and loudly *bolted*, behind us.

Stepping from the interior out onto the forecourt is stunning, as if, when inside, you forget the snow-capped peaks surrounding the place.

Ricardo notices it too. "Wow!" he says.

"Yes," I say. "Wow."

We walk over to our vehicles, and Ricardo opens his door and then hesitates. "She's not going to Limoges," he says.

I glance back at the gîte. Chantal is lurking in the shadows behind one of the windows watching us leave. "Not here," I say.

"I'll meet you at the bottom," Ricardo says, sliding into his car.

"No," I say. "In Guillaumes. At La Provençal."

Ricardo nods seriously. "OK," he says. He slams his door, and then unintentionally showering me with gravel, he accelerates off down the hill.

If Things Were Different

When I first enter La Provençal the bar is perfectly empty. A single, illuminated "33" beer sign reveals that the place *might* be open. I step back outside and walk to the other end of the square before doubling back.

Everywhere else is closed, probably for the entire winter, and Ricardo's rented Clio is parked outside. I re-enter the bar. This time, not only has a waiter appeared – a spotty adolescent in a ski jumper – but Ricardo is seated at a table.

I shoot him a double-take kind of a glance. "So were you here ten seconds ago when I last looked?" I ask.

He smiles weakly and points to the rear of the bar. "Toilet," he says simply. "I ordered you coffee, is that OK?"

I nod, pull out a chair and sit. "Yeah," I say. "Thanks. Coffee's great."

"Your friend is a strange one," Ricardo says. He seems deflated, as though his *ordinary* batteries are finally expiring.

"My fr... Oh! *Chantal!* Yes. I'm just noticing that."

"As long as you don't expect too much – how do you say, *service après vente en anglais?*"

"After sales service," I say.

"Of course," Ricardo says, his voice unusually monotone. "I don't think you will get so much."

"No," I say. "I wonder where she's going."

"Not to Limoges," Ricardo says.

"Maybe she doesn't want to give me the number. Maybe there's some terrible structural fault with the place and she doesn't want us to be able to hunt her down."

"If there is, you can cancel the sale," Ricardo says. "Even afterwards. It's called *Vice Caché.*"

"Hidden faults," I say. "Right... Well, yes. There's always that."

"But I don't think it's that," Ricardo says. "I think is something more sinister. Maybe her husband is dead. Maybe she push him in the shit tank."

"God, *don't!*" I say. "Hey, I just realised... she isn't coming on Thursday, so all that stuff about giving me the number on Thursday was bullshit too."

The ski-jumper kid brings our coffee, so there is a brief interruption whilst he hands us the cups and the bill. When he's gone, Ricardo sips his coffee and mutters, "One hundred percent Robusta. Yuck."

I laugh lightly. "I suppose Colombians know their coffee," I say.

"Oh yes," he says, putting down the cup. "Like the English and their tea."

I shrug. "Actually though the English drink a lot of tea, it's mainly just basic cheap stuff. We're rarely snobby about it."

"So you don't think she kill him?" Ricardo says.

I laugh. "Nah," I say. "Maybe he's still alive though. Maybe it's a life insurance fraud and she's going off to meet the husband. Like that Anne Darwin character." It's the first time I have clearly formulated the thought, but as I say it, I think, *"Yes, that's it. That's exactly what she's doing."*

Ricardo frowns, so I explain the story of Anne Darwin and her husband who "died" in a canoeing accident, only he was really living in the house next door; I tell him about Egypt and Chantal's strange over-reaction.

"If the husband is living next door, or in Egypt, is the sale still legal?" he asks.

I frown. "How do you mean?"

"If she can only sell because he is dead," Ricardo says. "Then what happens if he is alive?"

I shrug. "I would think once it's sold, it's sold," I say.

Ricardo shakes his head. "Not if the person who sells it doesn't own it," he says. "If the husband comes back, the sale will be... *caduc.*"

I shrug again. "Who knows," I say. "I can't see it myself, but who knows. Anything is possible."

Ricardo nods. "You are very determined," he says.

"I think you're very determined to talk me out of it," I say, smiling thinly.

He pushes out his lips and shakes his head. "Not so," he says. "I think is a mistake. But, no, you must make your choices. They surprise me. But maybe I am wrong. But, no... I would never... As long as *you* are sure... that it is not mistake."

I stare out of the window and snort. "Actually, I think you're probably right," I say. "But it's happening. Amazingly."

"And with Tom, you are OK still?"

I turn back to him and nod. "Yeah," I say. "He explained everything. He borrowed money to cover Jenny's missing rent if we need it. He's making an effort."

Ricardo nods. "I underestimate you," he says.

"I'm sorry," I say, looking into his eyes. "If things had been different... well... you know."

"If things had been different... what?" Ricardo says.

"Well, I would have loved to come with you," I say. "You're a gorgeous guy, and, well, it would be an amazing adventure."

"It would be," he says. "Amazing."

"But they aren't," I say. Ricardo furrows his brow, so I expound, "Things – they *aren't* different."

"Which things?" Ricardo says.

I shrug. "Oh everything really. It would need to be a different life," I say. "One where you aren't dating my best friend, and..."

"But that is over. It was *always* over, from the beginning. Well, from Christmas anyway – when Jenny told me she was leaving."

"Yeah," I say. "But the past doesn't just disappear because something new happens. You'll always be Jenny's boyfriend. Or Jenny's ex. I suppose, maybe if I had met you before we signed for this place... but even then..." I shrug. "Who knows?"

Ricardo nods. "It's my fault. I was not clear enough," he says. "I should have left Jenny. Then maybe."

I shake my head. "That wouldn't have done anyone any good," I say.

"She loves you very much," Ricardo says.

"Yes," I say quietly. "I know."

"But in August she is gone," he says.

"I know," I say.

"I don't understand," Ricardo says. "These reasons... they don't..."

"The main reason is that I love Tom, Ricardo," I say. "I'm sorry, but I'm not sure you realise that."

"Tom, *yes*," Ricardo says.

"Yes, *Tom,*" I say, a note of annoyance entering my voice.

"Tom who does not believe in *fidelité* or *la vie à deux.*"

"That's a bit the pot calling the kettle black," I point out.

Ricardo frowns, so I try a biblical reference instead. "Let he who is without sin cast the first stone," I say.

Ricardo nods. "Yes," he says. "Of course. I fall in love with you, so I am the same."

I pause and have to swallow at the use of the 'L' word. I force a cocky shrug, but my voice still falters as I say, "No one is perfect, Ricardo. That's all I mean."

"And where is your Tom?" Ricardo asks, glancing around the room. "Where is he today?"

I exhale sharply. "Yes," I say. "He should be here."

"*I* am here," Ricardo says.

I shrug. "I know," I say.

"Like Christmas," Ricardo says. "I was there."

I nod. "I know," I say.

"And when Jenny make your flat wet," he says.

I nod. "OK Ricardo," I say. "I get it."

"Do you?" he says. *"Do you get it?"*

I cover my mouth with my hand, and then speaking through my fingers, I say, "Don't... it's not fair. You'll have forgotten me by the end of the week."

Ricardo's nostrils flare. "Don't you..." he says. "Don't you tell me what I think. It's not such an easy thing to say to someone, you know?"

I swallow and nod. "I'm sorry," I say. "The thing is... I don't know what to say. I mean, there's only one of me." It strikes me that I have never been so much in demand.

"And you love Tom?" Ricardo asks, sadly.

"I do," I say.

"And me, not at all?" he says.

I sigh. "No, I do," I say. "I'm fighting it. I think you're amazing. Everything about you is... well, perfect."

"You think," he says.

I nod.

"Say it," he says. "Tomorrow I am gone, so say it today."

"Say what?" I ask.

Ricardo turns to the window and sighs heavily.

I frown. "Anyway," I say. "You never said that to me either."

"I didn't?"

I shake my head. "Not directly."

Ricardo stares at me and licks his lips, then swallows. I see his Adam's apple bob. "Probably true," he says. "These are hard words for me, always."

I nod. "I understand," I say.

"I... I do though," he coughs.

"Please don't," I say.

He nods. "But I do," he says. "I love you."

I close my eyes and exhale deeply. I could end up in tears here if I don't watch it.

"Ricardo love Mark," he says. "And Mark love Tom. Tough, huh?"

I rub the bridge of my nose. "I do," I say, quickly, snappily. It's an attempt at removing the emotion from the phrase.

He turns back to face me. "But," he says.

I shake my head. "No buts. Well... yes, one but: I can't come with you. The way it has all happened. The timing, the people, it's all wrong. I can't."

"So I wait for you," Ricardo says.

"No," I say. "That's not what I'm saying."

"No," Ricardo says. "It's me."

I wrinkle my nose. "I think you're losing me," I say.

Ricardo smiles for the first time. "No," he says. "Not at all. *I* am saying this. I will wait. And when Jenny has gone to... Slurry?"

I smirk. *"Surrey,"* I correct him.

"Yes, so when Jenny has gone to Slurry, and Tom has gone to Brighton, then you will see. It's OK. I can wait."

"Tom won't be going to Brighton, Ricardo. We're both selling our flats. We're both committed to this project."

"Tom... Never mind."

I lean in towards him. "I'm sorry?" I say. "Tom what?"

"Never mind," he says. "It's OK. You will wake up one day and you will see. I think it won't be so long."

I sip my coffee and shake my head in wonder. "You're crazy," I say.

He laughs. "Oh yes," he says. "But in a good way."

I look at him and think how easy it would be, in fact, to say, 'yes.' It would leave everything else in turmoil, my relationship with Jenny, with Tom, the purchase of the gîte, Paloma, my bike, tax bills, bank accounts, everything would be a post hurricane disaster site. But I would be far away. The thought is as tempting as ever. But I can't carry on living my life that way. It never made me happy in the past. "When I was younger I would have, Ricardo," I say. "When I was young I would have run off with you and damn the consequences."

"So? What change?"

I shrug. "I spent my whole life just chopping and changing, Ricardo," I say. "You don't know me that well. That's why you don't understand."

He laughs. "And now you want to build a house. You see I understand."

I nod. "Yeah," I say. "We can't behave like kids our whole lives."

Ricardo gives me a Gallic shrug. "Kids have fun," he says. "They run and climb and swim in the sea even if it's danger. I think is a good model, a good way to live, non?"

I laugh. "And then you grow up and you have to live by the rules."

Ricardo sighs.

"I know. You don't believe in rules," I say.

"I think some things are too big," he says. "Some things are too important for rules."

I chew a knuckle and stare at him. The desire to just say, *"fuck it,"* to leap from one train to another with a new unknown destination is almost overpowering. "I wish I could," I say. "I would love to be able to make you happy, to make everyone happy, but... I'm sorry."

He pulls something from his wallet, and then as if he is playing cards, as if this is in fact his trump card, he places it on the table, stares at it, then spins it and pushes it across the table. "Maybe you should just make *you* happy," he says.

I look at the photo and frown. It shows a big, weathered, wooden house on a beach. Around it are huge palm trees, in front of it – the photo is taken from the sea – rolling whitecap waves. "What is this?" I ask.

"A house," he says. "My cousin holiday house. He lend it to me."

"I thought you were going to Bogotá to your mother's," I say.

"After, yes. But now I go here first," he taps the photo. "For holiday. And then maybe half the time I will live there. There is a new health project in this area. Uribe got the FARC out of this region now – it used to be dangerous, but now it is OK – and we will set up a medical centre for the people near this house. For poor people. They need doctors now."

"It's beautiful," I say. "Stunning."

"I will take you there," he says. "When you are finished here."

"Huh!" I say, pushing the photo back. "Imagine!"

He takes the photo and strokes it lovingly before sliding it back into his wallet, then he puts the wallet in his back pocket and claps his hands. "OK," he says, brightly. "So now, I must go. I have Jenny for goodbye dinner tonight."

I frown at the sudden shift of energy. "Are you OK?" I ask him.

He smiles at me, and then the smile broadens and becomes the Ricardo beam. "Yes," he says. "I realise all is OK."

"It is?" I say.

"Yes," he says. "I will give you my email. We keep in touch. There is no hurry."

"I..." I shake my head. "I'm touched. Really," I say. "But..."

Ricardo nods. "No but," he says.

"Will I see you again before you go?"

He shakes his head. "No," he says. "Or maybe you can take me to the airport tomorrow? Jenny is working, and I have – J'ai une grosse valise." – *"I have a big suitcase."*

It's True Though, Isn't It?

As I head back to the coast I see that the weather has changed. The sky is a deep purple and the sun, somewhere behind the band of cloud, setting. It's hard to tell how much of the gloom is storm, and how much night time.

As I ride slowly down, the bike fails for once to silence my mind. I think about Ricardo. Poor Ricardo, with the crazed idea that I am going to somehow drop everything, dump Tom, and run off to Colombia with him. I think of the house on the beach, and imagine getting up there, waking up in that house on that beach, next to Ricardo. The idea maybe isn't so much crazy as crazily attractive. And absurd. But in the end it's all somehow... disproportionate, and it seems to have more to do with Ricardo's life than my own. Maybe I'm just the first guy he has felt that way about: first loves have a tendency to be unreasonable. Maybe he's sad to leave, and the idea of a link from Colombia back to this life – me – is reassuring for him.

But in a way, I can't help but feel that I have let him down. He's a beautiful man with seemingly limitless qualities and he deserves to be happy, and though I'm unsure how I got from there to here, it seems I'm now going to be responsible for making him unhappy. That guilt is an emotion I never expected to feel. I knew I would feel, *do* feel, guilt towards Tom for the lying, the cheating, but it never crossed my mind that affairs could lead to the double whammy of also feeling guilty towards the partner in crime.

By the time I lock up the bike, the first sparse drops of rain are plopping from the sky, the sheer volume of each droplet foretelling the downpour to come.

Inside the flat, I find Tom, Jenny and Sarah snugly installed on the sofa. They are watching another black and white film, a moody number set in a train station.

"The train for Ketchworth, is about to leave from platform..."

Jenny is holding a glass of wine and Tom a joint, and the flat feels cosy and safe against the coming storm. There is something about the muffled soundtrack of the film too, something about the terribly middle class accents, and the rolling Beethoven soundtrack that oozes a reassuring, *Sunday* sort of ambiance.

"Hi," I say. "I was just in time. It's about to tip down out there." As I say this a clap of thunder rattles the windows.

"I love a good storm," Tom says. "How did it go?"

"Shhhhh!" Jenny mutters, nodding at the TV screen. On it a couple are now sitting in a cinema, apparently discussing the film.

"It's the big picture now, no more laughter, prepare for tears..."

Tom pulls a face and grins at me. I frown – a little irritated that Jenny thinks the film is more important than our future livelihood. I shrug. "I'll make dinner," I whisper, then directed at Jenny, I add, "If that's OK?"

Tom winks at me. "We're starving," he says. "We ran out of munchies."

"We can pause it if you want," Jenny says, her tone of voice clearly demonstrating that this isn't an option.

"Nah," I say. "It's fine."

I change out of my bike leathers into jogging bottoms and, in the hope of warming up, a thick fleecy hoody, then I head through to the kitchen and peer into the refrigerator. "Pasta and tomato splodge by the looks of it," I mumble.

The storm cracks again, momentarily dimming the lights, and then, as if triggered by the clap, rain starts to plummet from the sky. I hear it lashing against the windows in the lounge, and Tom says, "Wow!" and turns the volume on the TV up.

"Oh Fred, it really was a lovely afternoon..."

I think, *Celia Johnson*, and then wonder how it is that I know that fact. The random items the brain collects! I switch off the kitchen light and stand in front of the window watching the rain spinning past the streetlights.

"You need help?" Tom says, the proximity of his voice making me jump.

I turn to face him. "Just looking at the rain," I say, then, "No, you're fine. Finish your film."

"Everything go OK though?" he asks.

I nod. "Yeah," I say. "It was fine. I'll tell you after, go back to your film."

Tom nods. "Sorry," he says, wiggling an eyebrow, and turning away, "but you know Jenny and her films."

I smile after him and then look back out of the window. A man scurries past with a cardboard box over his head.

"He thought we were raving mad, perhaps he was right."

I open the window – the sound of whooshing water is stunning – and I lean out to wet one hand before closing it again. *"No need to jet-wash the bike,"* I think.

I open the fridge again and take out two onions, an aubergine, garlic, a tin of tomatoes; then I put a frying pan on to heat and reach for the chopping board. Then my mind registers the open bottle of white that was in the fridge, and I pull it out and pour myself a glass.

I chop the onion, slosh some cooking oil into the pan, and wait for it to start to fry.

"Alec rowed off at a great rate, and I trailed my hand in the water. It was very cold but a lovely feeling..."

I sigh and think how sad it is that I can't make Ricardo happy. And then I think how sad it is for myself that I have to choose. Instantly I realise what a capricious, childish sentiment this is. Maybe *I am* childish and capricious, because the truth is that I don't want to choose, I *do* want both. And in that moment, the linear nature of a life lived strikes me as profoundly unfair. I don't want to be the one to disappoint Ricardo. I don't want to destroy Tom's dreams either. But more than anything, it's selfish. More than anything, I don't want, myself, to have to choose from this life or that. I want both.

"We had such fun, Fred. I felt gay and happy and somehow relieved;

that's what's so shameful about it all, that's what would hurt you so much if you knew..."

Why is it so hard to be... well, to be, just, *satisfied*, I wonder. What is it that makes happiness so God damned hard to keep hold of?

The sound of sizzling onion catches my attention, and I reach for a wooden spatula and stir it making it pop and sizzle loud enough to obscure the sound of the television. When the onions are browned, I pull the pan from the heat and start to chop the aubergine. I hear the distant voice of Trevor Howard – *how do I know this stuff?* – declaring his love.

"You know what's happened, don't you?"

I walk silently back to the lounge and lean in the doorway, taking in the dimly lit room, the flickering screen, the backs of Tom and Jenny's heads and the muffled sound of the film. I think of Saturday morning cinema when I was a kid.

"Yes, I do."
"I've fallen in love with you."
"Yes, I know."
"Tell me honestly. Please, tell me honestly that what I believe is true."
"What do you believe?"
"That it's the same for you. That you've fallen in love too."

Tom somehow senses my presence – *did I sigh?* – and turns. He beckons me over with a sideways nod of the head.

"No," I whisper, already turning away. "I'm cooking." But my voice is croaky, and I'm not sure if he heard me or not.

Back in the kitchen I lean against the worktop listening to the sound of the rain and the TV.

"I know you so little."
"It is true though, isn't it?"
"Yes, it's true."

My eyes are watering, maybe the onions, maybe tears. I swallow with difficulty. Tears then.

Through watery vision, and with a lump in my throat and a sick feeling in my stomach, I dice the aubergine and add it to the pan, which I slide back onto the ring.

As it starts to sizzle again, words from the TV are lost, which is a good thing, and yet, I strain to hear them all the same.

"How often did you decide you were never going to see me again?"
"..."
"... love your... eyes... smile..."
"...spoils everything... still time... my love."

I spin around and throw open the kitchen window again. Icy air blasts in but at least the sound of the falling rain drowns out everything else. I turn back to face the cooker. I wipe my eyes with the back of my hand.

"Jesus!" I mutter. I clap my hands and say, "Dinner!"

***

When the food is ready, I close the window and steel myself and return to the lounge where I crouch beside Tom. He pulls a face and nods over at Jenny, who I see is weeping profusely.

"Today was our very last day together, our very last in all our lives. I met him outside the hospital as I had promised at twelve-thirty..."

Jenny wipes her eyes and looks over at me. "I'm allowed to cry," she says. "I'm a single girl tomorrow." Then she sits bolt upright – as if someone has just applied an electric shock to her temples. She pulls her mobile from her pocket. "Shit," she says. "Is that the... Shit! I'm supposed to be at Rick's. Shit, shit, shit!" She jumps up, sweeps Sarah into her arms and clumsily stumbles towards the front door. "...leg's gone to sleep... fuck. Sorry!" she says. "Bye!"

"I cooked..." I protest, but the front door is already closing behind her.

I shake my head. "Crazy lady," I say.

"Sorry. Actually *I* should have remembered," Tom says. "She did tell me."

"I should have remembered," I think. "Ricardo told me."

"Those last few hours went by so quickly."

"How can *she* forget though?" I say.

"As we walked through the station, I remember thinking: this is the last time with Alec. I shall see all this again but without Alec."

Tom shrugs. "She drank the best part of a bottle. And we smoked. She has extenuating circumstances."

"Yeah," I say, my voice strange, strained. "I expect she's pretty upset."

"She's doing OK really, considering."

"Yeah," I say.

"Do you think we shall see each other again?"
"I don't know. Not for years anyway."

I cough. "Anyway, I hope you're hungry."

"I could eat a 'orse," Tom says. "The film's only got five minutes to go. Shall I stop it?"

I shake my head and stand. "Nah," I say. "You're fine. Is that Celia Johnson?"

"Yeah," Tom says. "And Trevor Howard. Great film, but she irritates the shit out of me really."

"Yeah?" I say, looking at the screen. She looks quite magnificent to me.

"I love you with all my heart and soul."
"I want to die. If only I could die."

"Well," Tom says. "You just want her to stop complaining and run off with him really, don't you? That's what any *normal* person would do."

"Yeah," I say. "I... I'll go serve dinner..." I add, turning away.

A Tiny Goodbye

Getting up before sunrise has never really been my thing. Sure, there is something magical about seeing that great ball of fire burst over the horizon, something far more optimistic than its poignant daily disappearance; but the sick feeling I get in my stomach, the seemingly endless hunger for food, the tendency to feel fragile and emotional – it's just not worth it.

But Ricardo's flight is at nine, and he wants – he insists – to be there for seven, so at five thirty I'm staring wretchedly at a coffee cup, trying desperately to keep my mind blank, trying hard not to think of anything that my fragile, emotional, sleep-deprived state might blow out of proportion. And of course, today of all days, there is plenty of ammunition.

At six I creep from the house leaving Tom sleeping soundly. This isn't about deception for once, it's just that my final goodbye to Ricardo is emotionally complicated enough without running the unlikely risk that Tom will decide he wants to come.

By six thirty, I'm helping Ricardo lift his suitcase, a vast wheeled affair, into the back of Tom's Mini. He smiles at me vaguely. "Thanks for this," he says. He manages somehow to look pale, early-morning puffy *and* pink, presumably from the exertion of carrying the case down the stairs.

"It's too early for you," he says, as he climbs in beside me.

"Yeah," I reply.

"It shows," he says. "You are very white."

I laugh weakly and slap my cheeks. "My blood doesn't circulate before ten a.m.," I say, pulling my seatbelt on, checking the mirror, and pulling away. "And I slept really badly. I always do if I have to get up early. As though the alarm clock might not work."

"I set two," Ricardo says. "My phone and a clock."

"Me too," I say. "But it doesn't help. Anyway, I've seen *you* on better days."

"Yes," Ricardo says. "I don't sleep too good either."

I don't ask why, and thankfully he doesn't expound.

As I drive along the morning-quiet *Promenade des Anglais*, even though it is still dark the streetlamps start, one by one, to flicker and extinguish. Ricardo stares silently from his side window beside me. For this I am grateful. I had been expecting some last minute plea and I'm glad not to have to muster the emotional strength to deal with it.

To fill the void and dissuade any need for talk, I turn on the stereo. Tom has been listening to my Holcombe Waller album – the reason I couldn't find it in the flat. I ask him every time to make his own copies for the car but he never listens and my CDs always end up scratched. The CD picks up where apparently it left off, in the middle of "My Little Wrecking Ball."

I glance over at Ricardo to see if the music meets with his approval but he's still stolidly facing the other way.

Halfway along the prom, workmen are putting out bollards to protect them whilst they mow the central isle, and the traffic suddenly becomes more dense. Ricardo glances at his watch, and I say, "You're *fine!* You have two hours."

"I know," he says. "Mais ça m'angoisse toujours. Je pense toujours que je vais être en retard." – *"It always stresses me out – I always think I'm going to be late."*

A moped weaving through the traffic clips my wing mirror and Ricardo has to open his window and readjust it with all the usual, *"No, a bit lower, higher, a bit more, left,"* palaver that this always seems to imply.

As he winds the window back up I notice that Holcombe has moved on to the next track, one of my favourites.

Because you love me, you love me; ooh you really love me;
yes you love me, you love me, nothing comes above me...

A favourite, yes, but I'm really not in the mood for it right now. I reach out to change tracks but Ricardo raises his hand blocking my path. "I like," he says. "This is an English singer?"

"American," I say. "Holcombe Waller. Weird name, huh?"

I glance at the car clock. Two hours! In exactly two hours time my life becomes simpler. And yet the thought of that simplicity leaves me feeling anxious. God knows Tom and I have enough adventures before us, but it feels like my life is just about to go back to black and white after a brief stint in colour. I put the thought down to sleep-deprived emotional poppycock. Tom and I were fine before Ricardo appeared; we'll be fine once he's gone, won't we?

Because you love me, you love me; ooh you really love me;
yes you love me, you love me, nothing comes above me...

I glance sideways at Ricardo and quickly reach out and hit the skip button and suddenly I can breathe again. Ricardo clears his throat in reproach or emotion, I'm not sure which, so I unnecessarily adjust my rear-view mirror, as if this feigned involvement in the art of driving will disguise my failure to react.

I swing around the airport's one-way system, and as we arrive at terminal two I resist the urge to go to the drop-off point, cutely signposted as: *Kiss And Fly*. Kissing and flying, would, I decide, be a cowardly act. Instead, bracing myself for the full, tearful goodbye drama, I point the Mini into the multi-storey car park. It is – I think a little coldly – no more than the situation requires.

We check Ricardo's mammoth suitcase – he has to pay a whopping eighty-Euro surcharge – and then cross the marble floor to a coffee bar.

"How come they only booked it as far as Paris?" I ask. "I thought you could book them all the way through these days."

"I'm only going to Paris," Ricardo says. "For one week – to my cousin's. Then next Wednesday I fly Paris – Bogotá."

"Oh!" I say, surprised and a little put out that his departure isn't quite as definitive – or at any rate, his destination not as distant as I had imagined. "I didn't know... anyway, I thought your cousin had a house on the beach."

Ricardo laughs. "I have big family. You will see. Anyway, this way, when you change your mind, it's not so far."

I laugh, falsely. "I won't," I say. "Change my mind, that is. At least, not in a week." I instantly regret the second sentence.

"We'll see," he says.

I blow through my lips and shake my head. Ricardo grins at me.

"Incredible," I say. "I can't work out if you're cute or arrogant."

"Both," he says, "probably."

"Well, whatever... you don't listen. Because I'm still saying the same thing here."

Ricardo shrugs. "I just think..." he says.

I wait for him to continue, then prompt, "You just think what?"

"Sorry," he says. "Not think. I mean, I just *believe.*"

A waitress appears before us so we order two espressos.

Ricardo shrugs. "I think what you believe happens. And I believe this... I don't know why."

I frown. "That's, like, a tautology, or... no, not a tautology. But if you believe something will happen because you think that things you believe will happen, happen..." I shrug. "Well, it's circular or something."

Ricardo frowns at me.

"Sorry," I say. "It's too early for philosophy."

He shrugs and reaches for his coffee.

"Anyway," I say. "How would that work? I mean, if Tom and I believe something else. Whose beliefs win out?"

Ricardo grins. "Maybe it depends how *much* you believe," he says. "You. Maybe, you do. But Tom, he doesn't."

I sigh. "You underestimate Tom," I say.

"Maybe," Ricardo says.

My coffee arrives too and I stir in sugar in silence. "Actually, you don't like him much, do you?"

Ricardo frowns at me. "Not true," he says. "I make no... *jugement.*" He says it French-style.

"Judgement," I say. "It's the same word."

"Everyone is different. Everyone is crazy," Ricardo says. "But everyone is different. I think some people build houses. And some knock them down. You don't call a plumber to fix the electricity."

I frown at him.

"Tom is not a bad person. But he's not the right person for building houses."

"Oh, like, horses for courses," I say.

Now it's Ricardo's turn to frown.

"It's an English thing..." I say. "Means the same as the business about the plumber and the electricity."

"But maybe I am wrong. Maybe it happens. For Tom, I hope."

I laugh. "Not for me then?"

"No," Ricardo says. "You I think will be happy. You are a builder."

"I spent most of my life knocking things down," I say. "Actually, I think I'm a demolition *expert*."

Ricardo looks at his watch. "I have to go," he says.

"But..."

"I know," he says. "Unreasonable. Airports do this to me."

"OK," I say, downing my coffee and dropping some coins on the counter.

"You should come to Paris," Ricardo says. "You could buy a ticket..." he nods over at the Air France ticket machine. "Just for a few days. It would be fun."

I smile at him and shake my head. "Optimistic to the last," I say.

He opens his arms to hug me, mafia style. He smiles deeply, making the skin around his eyes wrinkle, and then he opens his mouth into the big white Ricardo grin, and I step towards him and he wraps me in a back-slapping bear-hug.

"I will see you," he says. "In Paris or Colombia. But I will see you."

"You're a crazy guy," I say. "You know that though."

He holds me far enough away to look at me. "And you, not at all!" he laughs.

"Yeah," I say. "I suppose."

"So," he says, glancing at the security gate where a small queue is forming. "Oh!" he exclaims, fiddling with a pocket and then producing a crumpled envelope. "I wrote this before... I didn't know you bring me today. Is nothing, but... it has my email address."

I nod and take the envelope from his grasp. "OK," I say. "Thanks." I smooth the envelope between finger and thumb, and then use it to tap him on the shoulder. "OK, then, go!" I say.

He nods slowly, winks at me, and then spins away across the hall. I sigh and follow on more slowly, waiting for the emotion to hit me. By the time I reach the end of the queue, he is already on the other side putting his belt back on and picking his jacket up from the conveyor belt. And then he gives me the tiniest of goodbye waves and is gone.

I stand there for a moment, an obstacle in the middle of the milling crowd, with airport announcements ringing out around me and electric cars whizzing past and wonder at the fact that I'm not crying, that I'm not even tearful. Nothing. No detectable emotion. I sigh and spin on the shiny floor pointing myself towards the exit and start to walk.

Inside the painfully slow, motorised, revolving door contraption – *what is the point?* – I can see that outside the sun is shining and that it's going to be a beautiful day. Through the transparent plastic partition, beyond the idiotic rotating plastic pot-plant, I can see a woman struggling to negotiate the revolving doors with both a toddler and a heavy suitcase. She looks like... *Oh!* I wave but she doesn't see me. I think, *"Now what are the chances of that?"*

I stand outside in hesitation for a few seconds and then I turn and head back into the terminal building.

Vaporising Hope

By the time I get back through the doors Chantal is nowhere to be seen. I scan the check-in counters, and then move far enough into the hall to see the seating area of the coffee bar. I turn and peer at the queue for the security checks, but she isn't there. For a split second I think that I see not Chantal but Ricardo – in uniform – a momentary lapse of reason. It isn't, of course, Ricardo; in fact it's not even a *pompier* but a security guard. I cast around for Chantal again and am just starting to wonder if I'm imagining things when I glimpse her again, this time a hundred meters away coming out of the toilets and speeding off towards the other section of the building.

I start to walk briskly, but she's moving so fast that without jogging I am merely keeping up with her. I almost start to run, and then realise that I don't really know why I'm chasing her anyway. She pauses, hikes her daughter up a little higher, stares at a notice board, and then spins ninety degrees and crosses briskly to an empty check-in desk.

As the gap starts to narrow – I can see her now lugging her case onto the conveyer belt, placing her passport on the counter – I wonder what, other than, *"Hi,"* I am going to say to her. And then I realise I can ask her for her mother's phone number. Slightly breathless, I reach her side, but busy with the check-in girl and her view to the right blocked by her daughter, she doesn't see me.

"Un seul bagage?" the girl asks her... – "A single bag? Do you have any of these prohibited items? Did you pack your bag yourself? Has anyone asked you to carry anything?" And then she notices me and frowns over Chantal's shoulder. "Vous êtes ensemble?" she asks. – "Are you together?"

For a moment, Chantal thinks the girl means her daughter, and replies aggressively, "Of course we're together!" but then she realises and turns to face me.

I smile at her. "Bonjour!" I say.

She frowns, and opens her mouth and then closes it again. Then she turns back to the check-in counter and says, "Non."

The girl frowns at me, shrugs, and returns her attention to the computer screen.

Chantal half turns again. "Why are you here?" she casts over her shoulder.

I shrug. Something in her tone makes my smile fade. "I was here," I explain. "I brought a friend – the guy you met yesterday actually. Ricardo. He's flying to Paris."

Chantal frowns at me. She doesn't look happy to see me at all and I wonder why this should be. She turns back to the check in girl who slides her passport back across the counter.

Chantal reaches for her passport and closes it so quickly that she actually makes a slapping noise on the counter, and that gesture makes me suspicious – it makes me look at the document. I'm too late to see the inside, but just quick enough to see the Arabic writing on the cover before it vanishes into her pocket.

Chantal glances sideways at me as the girl slides her boarding card to her and launches, in a bored tone of voice, into the home-run of her check-in spiel. *"L'embarkement est à dix heure dix..."* she says, ringing *10:10* with a flourish of her biro, then *Gate A24*. I step forward and glance at the boarding card. I read the word, *Shenouda,* and wonder where that is. I glance up at the display board above our heads and see that it says, "AF340 CAIRO." I look back at the boarding card a second before Chantal swipes it away, and see that *Shenouda* is the surname. *Shenouda*, is *her* surname.

"Wh..." I say vaguely.

"Merci," Chantal thanks the girl. Then to me, as she sweeps away, she throws, "I'm sorry, I'm late."

The girl calls her back. "Vous avez oublié..." she says. – *"You forgot..."*

Chantal leans back, snatches her daughter's boarding card from the counter and then struts off towards the security gate.

I frown at the check in girl.

"Are you travelling sir?" she asks me.

I shake my head slowly.

"Then please step aside," she says, nodding to indicate the people behind me.

I nod. "Yes," I say. "Sorry." I turn to see Chantal already thirty meters away joining the short queue for security. I glance back at the sign again, checking that it really does say CAIRO, and then, still not quite sure what I'm doing, I start to follow her. When I reach the queue, she is fumbling in her flight bag. She sees me in her peripheral vision but turns her back to me. I pull a face and tap her on the shoulder. "Chantal!" I say. "What's wrong with you?"

She half turns her head; just enough to *almost* look at me. "Va t'en," she says. – *"Go away!"*

I frown in surprise. "Oh," I say. "Why are you being like this?"

She looks at me now and I realise that she looks scared. "I'm sorry," she says. "I... I don't have time."

I glance at the clock. "No..." I say, working out that she has plenty of time. "So, Egypt..." I add thoughtfully.

"Pourquoi vous ne vous occupez pas de vos propres oignons?" she asks. – *"Why don't you mind your own onions?"*

It's not the welcome I expect from someone to whom I'm about to give two hundred thousand Euros.

"OK..." I say, thoughtfully. "You have an Egyptian passport..." I'm still working this out here. I feel like my brain is stuck in first gear. "Your boarding pass says *Shenouda*..." I say, wrinkling my nose. *"Why* does your boarding pass say *Shenouda?"*

"Excusez-moi," she says sharply addressing the people in front. *"Je suis en retard... je peux?"* They nod their acquiescence and she moves two places forward in the queue.

Muttering a, "Sorry – I'm not travelling," to the same couple, I queue jump with her.

"Excuse me," she says again. "Could I?"

I glance to the front of the queue. In three more hops she will be at the metal detector. In three more moves they will ask me for my own boarding card and turn me away. And any opportunity will be lost – but any opportunity for *what* exactly? I don't know what I'm doing yet, but I do it anyway. I shout, quite loudly, *"Chantal!"*

She glances at me in a ratty, rodenty kind of way, and then she scurries forward another place in the queue.

I cast around, and see a security guard twenty meters away. I stride over to him. "Excusez moi," I say loudly. I glance at Chantal and see that she is watching me.

"Oui?" the guard asks.

"Cette femme. Avec l'enfant," I say loudly, pointing at her

theatrically. – *"That woman with the child."*

I see her break out of the queue and walk briskly, then run towards me.

"Is she in the right place for boarding?" I ask just as Chantal reaches my side. She grabs my elbow, and starts to drag me away.

"Tout va bien?" the guard asks me, now frowning. – *"Is everything OK?"*

I smile at him broadly. "Yes, sorry," I say, as I am led away. Chantal's fingers are digging into my arm. I prise them off.

"What are you doing?" she hisses.

The truth is that I have absolutely no idea. "What are *you* doing?" I retort.

"It's none of your business," she says. "Please... this is none of your business."

"Tomorrow I'm supposed to be handing over a cheque for the gîte. I'd say it *is* my business."

"Please," she says, indicating that I should lower my voice. Her daughter, who has been staring wide-eyed at me, starts at this point to cry. Chantal jiggles her and scans the hall nervously. "I don't know what you're talking about," she says, hopefully.

I frown at her. "A flight to Egypt, a false passport, a false name..." I say, checking it through as I say it. "A missing husband too."

"And?" she says.

"Reminds me of Anne Darwin," I say. I think that she will have no idea what I'm talking about, and am about to explain, but those final two words make her freeze. The colour drains from her cheeks. In fact, I have never before seen quite such a sudden and marked shift of a human complexion from pink to grey-green. I think, *"Bingo."*

She stares at me, silently chewing the inside of her mouth. She has a cold glassy expression – a look, I realise, of hatred. "I don't have to stand here and listen to this," she says, unconvincingly making as if she is going to walk away.

"You can talk to me, or you can talk to security," I say, nodding at another guard, this one carrying a gun.

"What do you want from me?" she whispers.

And I have no idea what to answer. What *do* I want from her?

"Well?" she prompts.

I stare at her. *"I don't like her."* That's my first thought. I think that I have, up until now, got her completely wrong. Then I think that no matter what I'm supposed to be buying from her, I don't want to give her my money. I don't want to give her any of it.

"Tell me what you want," she says again, her tone more friendly this time.

But I don't know what I'm doing here. I don't know why I'm holding her up, other than that something is wrong. *"What's wrong with this picture?"* as the Americans say. I don't even know quite what I *don't* want. Except that maybe I don't want to pay two hundred thousand Euros to a dodgy woman with a false identity who looks like she's in the process of fleeing the country. That strikes me as a clever thought, a useful thought. I hang onto it.

"I can't buy it..." I say, more to myself than to her. "I *can't* buy your gîte."

"What do you mean?" she asks. "Why not? You *have* bought it."

"No," I say. "I can't."

"It's too late," she says. "You signed the agreement."

I nod and think about this. "With who though? With Chantal Ancey or with Mrs Shenouda?"

She glances nervously around the hall again and then looks back at me with narrowed eyes. Hatred again: she looks like she would happily eradicate me like the rats she shoots with her shotgun. "You want a discount?" she asks, her tone somehow sly. "Is that it? How much?"

I shake my head slowly. "No," I say. "I want... No... I don't want it." And as I say this I feel a weight slip from my shoulders. Just saying that sentence for some reason feels good, and I realise where this is heading, and it feels like escape.

"I don't understand," she says. "Why now?"

"Because I can't," I say. "Because I don't trust you. I have no idea who you *are,* even."

She wrinkles one side of her nose at me and then, amazingly, she smiles icily. "I see. That's what you want then? You want me to pull out of the sale?"

I frown at her and nod. "Yes," I say flatly.

"You want the twenty thousand?" she says. "The cancellation fee? Is that it?"

I push out my lips. "No," I say. "Not really. That's not the point."

"But if I cancel..."

I nod. "Yes," I say. "I know."

"I can't," she says. "I can't afford it."

"No," I say vaguely. "I suppose you must decide what's best for you."

She gasps and stares at the ceiling. She rubs one hand over her mouth. When she looks back at me her eyes are still filled with loathing, but they are glistening with tears too. "OK," she says. "But you let me go. When I get to... when I get there, I will phone the notary. And you don't contact anyone about this."

I smile thinly and pull my phone from my pocket. "Yes," I say. "But you had better phone him now."

"I don't have time," she says. "My flight..."

"Ten past ten," I say quietly as I find the number for the notary and hit the call button. "It *boards* at ten past ten. You have ages." I hand her my iPhone.

"I don't have time," she says again.

"Oh give it a rest..." I say, my patience wearing thin. "If I have a word with security you'll have loads of time. Is that what you want?"

"But..." she says, shaking her head, then shaking the iPhone at me. "I don't know how to use this anyway."

"It's easy," I tell her. "You talk into it and the person on the other end talks back."

"There won't be anyone there yet, it's too early," she says.

We both hear the voice of the notary's secretary answering. Chantal raises the phone to her ear. "Maître Damiano s'il vous plaît," she says. "What do I say?" she asks me. "He doesn't know... he doesn't know anything."

I shrug. "Tell him you changed your mind," I say.

She gasps at me and shakes her head in disgust, then speaks (actually, for some reason shouts) into the phone. Her voice trembles as she says, piercingly, "Oui, Maitre Damiano, oui... Chantal Ancey de Chateauneuf d'Entr... Oui, voila... Je me retire de la vente." – "I'm pulling out of the sale... yes... I know... yes... I'm sure... yes... the paperwork? OK you can send it by email... yes... I can't, I'm going away... Unusual, yes, I know... I'm sure... Disappointed, yes, I'm sure. Yes. Yes please do. Your fees, yes, I know. It's not a problem... Of course. Thank you. Yes, I'm sure. Thank you."

As I listen to all of this, I wonder if I'm doing the right thing and I wonder if I have any choice. It feels somehow like destiny, only I don't believe in destiny. Bumping into her today surely isn't *nothing* though. Perhaps through this chance meeting, I am to be saved from something, fraud maybe; maybe from a life with Tom in the gîte – maybe it would have been that bad.

The conversation over, Chantal thrusts the phone back and snarls, "Happy?"

I pout at her. "Not exactly *happy*," I say.

"Anyway, it's done," she says.

"You need to sign the documents," I say.

"Yes, well, of course," she says. "As soon as they arrive. He's sending them to me by email."

I frown at something sly in her voice and realise that she isn't going to sign the documents, and that there's no way... unless... "If you don't sign them I will call the police," I tell her. "You do realise that?"

She stares into my eyes, clearly calculating the odds, working out the consequences like a chess player computing future moves.

"I will give them your name, *and* your false name. I'll tell them where you flew to," I say, racking my brain for more. *"This isn't enough,"* I think. *"This isn't going to work. I'm gonna have to call security after all."* An image of myself being questioned all day by police comes to mind. And I really don't have the energy. "I will tell them about Egyptour..." I continue.

At the word, *Egyptour*, her face shifts into a grotesque mask of pure, unadulterated disgust. And at that moment, I know that I have got her.

"How?" she asks. "How could you know that?"

I shrug cockily. "Just do the paperwork."

She shakes her head and turns to leave. And then she turns back and she spits at me. She actually spits at me. The dollop of gob lands on my sweatshirt. I look down at it, and I think, *"Gotcha."*

"You really are a *very* unpleasant woman," I say with surprising calm.

"I hope you die," she says. "I hope you die of ..." And though she doesn't finish the phrase, I somehow know that the missing word is AIDS. That alone seems reason enough not to buy her gîte.

I watch her jump the queue, and then I watch her place her bag on the conveyor belt, and I consider calling security anyway, just to punish her, but then before I have managed to decide she too is gone.

I stand and think, *"What the fuck happens now?"* And I suppose the answer is: *nothing at all*.

For there is no more Ricardo and no more gîte. Soon enough Jenny will be leaving, and very possibly Tom will fuck off too. It seems pretty likely that in the midst of this maelstrom, I have made the biggest mistake of my life, perhaps the biggest *mistakes* of my life, plural. And yet, which they were, I'm not quite clever enough to work out. Was it buying the gîte or *not* buying the gîte? Sleeping with Ricardo or taking Tom back?

But one thing is certain – there is no joy in this chess move; it leaves only emptiness. I feel very sleepy. I feel overwhelmed with a sudden sensation of exhaustion, dizzy almost, as if I have taken a sleeping pill. I just want to go home and sleep. I wonder if I'm going to faint. I need to get home and eat and sleep. But of course Tom is at home, and I don't want to see Tom; I don't want to see him at all. I don't want to explain to Tom that the dream is over, that there will be no rhubarb and no dog. I'm not strong enough to deal with his emotions on top of my own. I realise that Ricardo is probably still in the airport – a stone's throw away behind the barriers but out of touch. I think that I could call him; that he would maybe even come back, miss his flight. In fact, in the hope of scraping me off the ground at the last minute, I'm almost certain that he would. But the truth is that I don't want to see Ricardo either. I don't want to see anyone. I don't want to talk about it or think about it or *do anything* with it. I just want to curl up and die. OK, that's over-dramatic: I don't want to *die*. But I really would like to curl up in a ball for the next few months. I really would like to wake up in springtime and have someone else tell me what happened next.

Better Than Easy

I open the car door and slip into the driver's seat. I stare in an unfocussed manner through the windscreen and wonder, in more ways than one, where to go now. I fumble with the keys and slide them into the lock but I don't start the engine yet. I think logically that I might cry, but the feeling's not there. I just feel empty.

I sigh and wind down the window and watch a couple get into a car opposite and then drive slowly away, their tyres squealing on the painted floor.

As I reach for the seatbelt my arm rubs against Ricardo's letter, and I gently release the belt and pull the envelope from my top pocket. The envelope is grey and unmarked. I tap it against my left hand, wondering if I have the energy to read it and then I shrug and rip it open. As I pull out the letter – two handwritten sheets on photocopy paper – a photo falls to the floor. I see, as it falls, that it is the photo of the beach house. I leave it where it lands and shake open the letter.

Ricardo's handwriting is spidery and challenging to decipher. Plus the letter is written in French. I frown at the first two words for an instant before realising that they alone, are in Spanish.

Mi Amor.

I have failed to express myself. How do I know this? Because you are not here with me. I expect that will sound arrogant, but it is not that I am such an amazing "catch" simply that if you knew how deeply I feel about you – I think that you are someone who would appreciate that. I don't think it's something anyone reasonable would turn down lightly.

But yes, that sounds arrogant, and that is my problem, for I'm not so good with words, not when it comes to this emotional stuff anyway. Whether I say it or write it, it always looks theatrical or corny to me. I'm sure that will be the case here as well, but at least I don't have to face the embarrassment of saying this stuff to your face.

Of course what I want to say is that I love you – yuck, those words: so dramatic, so overused, so meaningless. So I won't say that. Instead I'll say that the days we spent together made me happier than I remember ever being. This is the closest thing to whatever I want that I have found. It's so close I didn't quite think it was possible.

I have to tell you as well that I don't want to spend a holiday with you in Federico's house, but that I want to spend <u>all</u> my holidays with you. I don't have some rose-tinted picture of what our lives would be: we would argue and fight like everyone else, but I can't think of anyone I would rather do that with. I would love to look at you one day and realise that we made it; that we got old and wrinkled together, that we spent a whole life of sex and arguments, of holidays and good times and bad times, and that through it all, we had been together.

Why you? I don't know. For some reason I believe. For some reason, maybe the way I feel when we have sex, maybe the way we laugh when we talk... I can't explain it, but it just seems to me that if I can manage a whole life with anyone it will be with you. Of course I may have got this all wrong. Maybe Tom <u>is</u> the one you need. He is cute and he is clever – despite what you think I like him a lot. So maybe he just needs time to change, time to commit, time to be able to feel secure enough to burn his bridges. And if this is so, then you can see something I can't and what can I say except good luck to both of you?

But if it doesn't work out then I hope you will let me know. In fact, even if it never happens I hope you will keep in touch. I would always be proud to have you in my life even if it's just as a friend.

But of course that's not what I want. You only get one life and it's supposed to be lived madly, excessively. I think the reason I want you is because you are crazy enough to know that; I think maybe you're as mad as me, maybe even crazy enough to suddenly still change your mind and come with me.

I think that you are tempted and that now you are thinking about it and worrying about cats and bills and plane tickets and money and visas and commitments to gîtes and sale contracts and letting down friends and it will all seem insurmountable, but it isn't – it's just a series of steps, a series of things to be dealt with and I will be there and we will do it all together, we will fix it all together.

And I know too that you think that running away with me is an easy option and that staying with Tom and making that work is somehow "better", but I have to tell you, I think you have it the wrong way around.

real person, a real person with real faults: he's obsessively tidy and irritatingly dogmatic that everyone else should be the same (which clearly, for me, is always going to be problematic); when he first gets home from work he's grumpy and irritable, so I have to steer clear of him for the first hour every evening; he won't tell his mother he's gay (in fact he still won't *admit* that he's gay – a constant source of spicy debate) so I visit Bogotá's single gay bookstore every time he visits her – my own personal protest. When he's ill – a thankfully rare occurrence – he's unbearably dramatic. I assume that this is a doctor thing, but I still struggle to remember that he didn't die when he had the migraine, and so, by deduction, he'll probably survive the bout of 'killer' flu as well. Worst of all, his technique of *shouting* every mispronounced word back at me makes him *the* worst Spanish teacher imaginable.

I'm still not quite sure what I did that February morning, still not quite sure if I stayed true to form or suddenly grew up. Was running away to join Ricardo in reality simply Mark making the same mistake all over again – dumping the old for new, *one more time?* Or was this one different? Maybe Ricardo was always the one for me and I thankfully saw that fact just in time. It feels that way. It feels right. Once the new course was set, it didn't feel like a mistake, not once. It all felt wonderful and shiny and new and exciting. But then didn't it always? Maybe that's just me. Maybe I need to learn to live with that.

The sun has risen a little further. I need my sunglasses now, which means that it's time for breakfast. I glance back towards the house. Paloma, who with the help of a massive dose of tranquillisers survived the transatlantic flight, but who I fear, may be too old to ever make it back again, is standing on the decking watching me. She's seen more boyfriends come and go than she's had birthdays: my constant companion, my witness. She sees me looking at her now and meows plaintively at me to return. She likes Ricardo, though that may just be because he feeds her tuna. And I think she prefers the beach house to the flat, though with a cat, it's hard to know. As she stubbornly refuses to ever put a paw on the apparently *terrifying* sand, this is, it seems, as far as her experience of Colombia will ever go.

Paloma meows again and then Ricardo appears beside her. He gives her a stroke, and then waves at me and shouts, "Mark! Desayuno!" – *"Breakfast!"*

Ricardo says that human happiness is difficult because we are built like cats – preprogrammed for survival to notice only that which may be dangerous, only that which may threaten us. So just as a cat in a garden won't see the sunshine or the grass, just as a cat will only notice the rustling in the bushes or the bird of prey overhead (or the imagined dangers lurking in the sand) we ourselves only notice the imperfections of our own lives, the faults of those around us, the things which might one day spoil things if we don't, like cats, kill them first or run away quickly. He believes that the route to happiness is simply to look around and make yourself notice everything that is just fine, to force yourself to overcome the basic human instinct to spot only the negatives. It certainly seems to work for him. I look at Ricardo and Paloma and the house and do that now.

I wave back and as I start to cross the sand, I feel, as I do every morning, a wave of warmth for him, a wave of love, which some mornings, like today, can actually bring tears of happiness to my eyes.

Because of course Ricardo doesn't only have faults – he has some astounding qualities. He is clever, funny, and always charming. He's *never* depressed and he's *always* up for sex.

I stare at the house and think about the photo, and how it turned out to be real – how the place turned out to be exactly as it looked. Ricardo said we would live on this beach, and here we are. Ricardo said he would be inside making breakfast, and there he is. And this is his most amazing quality – so simple, so obvious that one could easily overlook it. For Ricardo always does exactly what Ricardo says he will do. Every time. The product does, as they say, exactly what it says on the packet.

As time goes by, as experience *amazingly* demonstrates this fact to me time and time again – that when Ricardo says he'll cook he cooks, that when he says he'll phone he phones, that when he says he'll be late he's late, that when he says he'll buy candles he buys candles... and as Ricardo continues to *say* the same things to me over and over: that we'll be together our whole lives, that he wants to see me get old and wrinkly, that he loves me even when I'm angry, that he loves me even when *he's* angry... well, after a while, I start to believe him; after a while, I can't help *but* believe him.

And finally finding that after all these years – finding someone I can believe in, someone with whom my belief in the future is carried not by my own blind faith but by the empirical evidence that every day we spend together brings... well, it feels good. It feels brilliant.

THE END

Also Available

Sleight Of Hand

A Novel
by Nick Alexander

Sleight Of Hand - the fifth volume in the Fifty Reasons series - finds Mark living in Colombia with Ricardo.

But there is more to Colombia than paradisiacal beaches and salsa music, and though Mark believes Ricardo to be his perfect soul mate he is torn between the security of home and the rich tapestry of his Colombian lifestyle.

When a friend's mother dies, Mark hopes that attending the funeral will enable him to decide where his future lies but no sooner does Mark set foot in England than bonds of love and obligation from the past begin to envelop him with such force that he wonders not only if his relationship with Ricardo will survive, but if he will ever be able be break free again.

In Sleight of Hand, Nick Alexander weaves universal themes of honesty and happiness, desire and obligation into a rich narrative we can all identify with – a narrative that prompts laughter and tears, frequently on the same page.

"Sleight of Hand is novelist Nick Alexander's latest volume following the life of the now beloved character Mark. It is a tender, deeply moving portrait of what it means to be gay in the twenty-first century. Alexander has looked beyond stereotypical representations of sexuality, both gay and straight, to show us the infinite possibilities of what love, family and belonging truly mean. It re-imagines the boundaries of gay fiction and inspires us to re-evaluate our lives. A subtle, deeply moving examination of the ways we can re-imagine our lives." – Alex Hopkins, Out There magazine

Also Available

The Case Of The Missing boyfriend

A Novel
by Nick Alexander

C.C. is nearly forty and other than her name (which she hates so much she can't bring herself to use it) everything about her life appears to be wonderful: she has a high powered job in advertising, a great flat in Primrose Hill, and a wild bunch of friends to spend her weekends with. And yet she feels like the Titanic – slowly, inexorably, and against all expectation, sinking.

For despite her indisputable success, C.C. would rather be shovelling shit on a farm than selling it to the masses – would rather be snuggling on the sofa with The Missing Boyfriend than playing star fag-hag in London's latest coke-spots.

But opportunities to find The Missing Boyfriend are rarer than an original metaphor, and CC's body-clock is ticking so loudly that at times she can barely hear her mother wittering on about her own Moroccan boyfriend.

Could her best friend be right? Could her past really be preventing her from moving on? And if she unlocks that particular box, will the horrors within simply drift away and leave her free? Or will they sink her?

If she can shake off the past and learn to trust again, will she stop attracting freaks and find The Missing Boyfriend? Or will she just end up tethered and gagged at the bottom of the stairs?

"A bittersweet, bang-up-to-date take on the eternal quest for love."
– Rupert Smith (author of Man's World).

CPSIA information can be obtained at www.ICGtesting.com
Printed in the USA
BVOW09s0959011014

369081BV00020B/415/P